THETA

SASHA FOX

The Draconyma Cycle

Book One

A Snowfox Press book

THETA

Published by Snowfox Press

First printing, August, 2013
Second printing, January, 2026
ISBN: 978-0-9894414-0-7

Library of Congress Control Number: 2013946304

Cover art by Hilary Esdaile, Adam Burn, and Sasha Fox
Cover and Interior design © 2013, 2026 Snowfox Press

To you, my reader, in whose mind worlds are fostered great and small, and without whom this story would remain but a dream unshared.

———————— The Draconyma Cycle ————————

– **Theta** –

Dreams of Refugium

Ephemeris

Of Dragons and Starships

Wrath

——————————————— *foxprints.org* —

Acknowledgements

I owe too much to too many to list all and everyone who had a hand in helping me along the way, but there are some to whom I would do a great disservice if I failed to name them.

To **Chris**, **Adam**, **Tom**, **Aaron**, **Michael**, **Jesse**, **Bryan**, **Bryan** (and **Brian!**), **Zach**, **Kale** and **Clint**—You were with me every step of the way; without your collective enthusiasm and support, my momentum would surely have faltered.

Jason—Thanks to your analytical eye and careful shepherding of fact, many a detail was saved from going astray.

Tim—Thank you. Again. For everything.

And of course—**Maggie & Mike**, my beloved parents, and my most original source of inspiration.

Thank you.

THETA

1

Memory

JALE BERCAMMON PUSHED her finely-polished service cart down one side of the broad, opulent central gallery of the 'premier' deck on the OCS *Freeta,* steadfastly working her way through her evening rounds.

She'd pushed the exact same cart along the exact same route on the exact same ship four times each day for nearly twenty years, always precisely punctual. Though delivering meal service to the passengers had ceased to be among her official duties long before she had been promoted to Chief Steward, she enjoyed it and refused to delegate the task. She held that it kept her connected with the job, her people, and her schedule. As she commanded the largest department on the biggest of OCS Shipping's luxury liners, running it with nearly perfect efficiency numbers—not to mention the highest morale scores in the fleet—nobody challenged her.

Being a spacer hadn't turned out to be the exotic, adventuresome life she'd had in mind when she'd signed on as a lanky, wide-eyed young ferret of sixteen standard years, but she'd found herself comfortable as soon as she'd discovered her niche: people. Every passenger, every crewmember, everyone she met had a unique story; she found pleasure in listening to their tales, and took pride on her ability to engage even the most difficult in conversation. In her time, she'd helped couples with their relationships, heard the most incredible war stories, shaken her head at tragic losses and newfound treasures, and learned what she felt must be a tremendous amount about the world outside *Freeta*'s hull.

She'd realized long ago that she didn't need any of it for herself. She no longer felt the pull of exotic ports of call, nor did she wish for adventure beyond the stars; living vicariously through her passengers, she'd learned that adventure was rarely much fun, and seldom ended well for those involved. From her first year aboard, she'd come to embrace routine; advancing at a steady pace through her department, she'd reaped modest pay raises and merit bonuses, all of which had gone into her savings for no particular purpose. She didn't even bother to maintain a downside domicile, as it wasn't required. Her life had been steady and calm for as long as she could recall, and she cultivated it like a very simple, perfect garden, nary a leaf out of place.

Tonight, however, something had happened that had never happened before—Jale was almost twenty minutes late.

Something had sparked a vicious war between two of Brynton's major houses, and many Brynti citizens were clamoring to find passage off the toxic planet, driving up ticket prices and scrounging for what they could find. *Freeta*'s quarters were packed with refugees at double occupancy, and Jale's carefully-built supply tables were rendered useless. Worse still, the ratio of obligate carnivores was off, and so she had been forced to rework the menus to come up with alternative protein sources for the omnivorous.

Jale was displeased by the whole affair. She hated being late, and didn't care one whit about the fate of the houses of Brynton. Faceless and infinitely corrupt, the Brynti elite obeyed no standards of decency shared by the known universe. People were bought, extorted, manipulated and sold, and the only protection you had on Brynton was the that of your house, which was as capricious as its Lord's whim.

Jale sighed, steering the cart by muscle memory as she ran the numbers in her head. So lost was she in her thoughts that she almost missed the empty pair of blue eyes staring at her from behind one of the decorative pillars, but a glint of silver in passing caught her attention.

Jale sucked in a breath, eyes widening. "Oh!"

She pushed her cart against the corridor wall, then hurried over to take the lissome little robe-clad fox gently by the shoulders.

"Now now, Miss Theta. You're not supposed to be up and about, dearie. We have very specific instructions that you must remain in your quarters, yes we do."

She spoke out of habitual courtesy. Patient Theta, the sole occupant of the finest stateroom on the ship, couldn't understand a word. What intelligence might have once lurked somewhere behind those crystal eyes was buried beneath the terror and confusion of what the ship's doctor had described as massive brain damage. Theta sometimes responded to sounds with garbled mumbling, but mostly just wept and sobbed brokenly whenever spoken to.

"Such a shame," Jale murmured to herself, whiskers atwich. "So pretty, but so very lost. Well, at least someone cares about you enough to put you up in here. Now, in you go, dear."

With a tiny push, Jale directed the stumbling Theta back through the open door of the D14 stateroom, which slid shut a moment later. She reached up to enable the panel's exterior lock, but paused as she found it still engaged.

Jale recycled the lock to be on the safe side. She'd have to have a talk with Arvinne. With a little sigh, she returned to her cart and pushed away. Evening meal would be due soon, and she was even further behind than before.

As she continued her rounds, she couldn't stop her thoughts from returning often to the little denizen of D14. One of the largest disruptions to her routine, Theta had come with a strange set of very specific care-and-feeding instructions that required Jale to keep two of her staff on rotation. She had been enjoined by an unusually serious Captain Erin to ensure they were followed to the letter, under the threat of very serious consequences if there should be any trouble.

Why there was so much concern over the fox, Jale couldn't even guess. It seemed wasteful; the sickbay would have offered better care, and Theta certainly would never have known the difference.

She chuffed and shook her head. The fox's condition *did* seem to be improving, so perhaps it wasn't such a waste. In any event, she reminded herself, her job was to simply do her job, and she had plenty else to worry about.

Busy with the preparation and serving of the evening meal—and swamped afterward marshaling the after dinner entertainment—Jale completely forgot to speak with Arvinne about leaving the door to Theta's quarters ajar. When she checked her notes the next morning and cornered the stocky junior steward on the issue, he seemed genuinely surprised.

"Ma'am? No ma'am...I sure don't think so, anyway. Those doors do close themselves, y'know."

"Arvinne," Jale drew herself up to look down at Arvinne and put on her 'motherly' voice, "It's most perfectly fine to make errors, dear, as long as you admit them. Now you know as well as I do that she didn't open the door herself."

"Ah, she?"

Jale frowned impatiently. "Patient Theta."

"Patient Theta," Arvinne stated matter-of-factly, "is not a she. I've had to take care of him for a while now. He's...a he. Mostly."

Jale was very surprised. She looked around, making sure there were no passengers within earshot, then leaned close.

"You're *sure*, dear? Ah, what do you mean by 'Mostly'?"

Arvinne looked a little uncomfortable. "He...uh...you know how the instructions say to keep him clean and dignified, and all..."

"Actually," Jale corrected automatically, "to be precise, they say: KEEP PATIENT THETA CLEAN AND DO NOT SACRIFICE THETA'S DIGNITY; THETA IS TO BE TREATED WITH THE UTMOST RESPECT AT ALL TIMES."

"Er, yes, sure, that, but...when washing him...uh..."

Arvinne, Jale noticed, was blushing—the snow leopard's nose had changed colors, and his ears were downturned. She arched an eyebrow, gesturing for him to continue.

"I...Look, he's...definitely male, but physically...he's castrated or something."

Jale rocked back on her heels.

"Well, now. Well, that's something! I've never heard of anything like that. What does...no, nevermind. It's Brynton, I won't even begin to speculate." She shuddered softly. "You've been keeping up with his injections?"

"Oh yes ma'am," Arvinne jumped at the chance to change the subject. "Every four hours, and feeding and cleaning every two. Penny is doing it this shift, though."

"Mm," Jale tilted her head, looking at him with one eye. "Well, just be sure the door is closed when you are done, dearie. The captain has charged me specifically with taking care of this and not failing under any circumstances, oh yes. She made it crystal clear. So and so, I make it clear to you, dear. You understand?"

"Yes, but..." Arvinne frowned. "I swear I've always closed it."

"Well, if you say so." Jale shook her head. The junior steward was a bit absent at times, and she wasn't sure she trusted his memory as much as his intentions. Still, there was little more she could say, and browbeating him further would serve no purpose—he tried very hard and had a big heart, and that was all she could ask.

She dismissed him with a wave and a nod, then turned back to her notes. There was far too much chaos, this run, and she felt a growing frustration as she ran down the list. Half the duty items were out of order, and there were several obvious conflicts. With a sigh of annoyed patience, she set her mind to addressing the dietary restriction map for the passengers who had changed quarters since the beginning of the voyage. There was much more to keeping her department running than minding the affairs of one addle-brained passenger, however important.

Two days later, when Theta stumbled into engineering clad only in a thin robe during Penny's shift, Jale was forced to admit that perhaps the little fox was indeed overriding the lock somehow. It wasn't the most secure lock, but try though she might, Jale couldn't manage to open it from the inside when she returned him to his quarters the next day. Back in the well-appointed stateroom, the little white fox sat glumly on his chair and looked at the floor, rocking back and forth.

Jale rubbed her chin. Just before the ship had left port, a courier had arrived with a carefully wrapped gift, hand-addressed in gold leaf to 'Theta, care of the crew of OCS Freeta'; Arvinne had unwrapped it for him to reveal a soft stuffed animal. After a brief search, she found it and brought it to him. He snatched it from her and hugged it crushingly to his chest, burying his nose against its black fur.

Jale peered at him. How old was he? He looked barely past adolescence, but she knew that his species tended to be very small. After a while, as if sensing her attention, he raised his head and looked back, gaze steady.

Do NOT attempt to engage Theta in conversation.

That instruction had been very clear, nestled right below
DO NOT NEGLECT THETA'S INJECTIONS.

Jale looked away. There was something about his stare
that she found equally unsettling and compelling, as if he
was trying to pull her into his broken mind. Trying to avoid
meeting his searching stare again but not quite ready to
leave, she found herself gazing down into the portable cryo-
genic case. It contained exactly 116 syringes—exactly one
for every four hours of the journey. They were in sequence,
and the first tier was nearly expended; Jale was surprised to
notice that there were multiple types.

"I really oughtn't," she murmured aloud. It didn't help.
Her paw crept to the case and slid the first tray out, removing one of the empties for inspection. Disappointingly, it
read simply '30cc. Theta n-X'.

The next course, however, on which Theta was scheduled to remain for the rest of the voyage, actually had a
name. *Banerethin*. Jale tapped it into her datapad, feeling
vaguely guilty.

"I oughtn't've done that," she murmured.

"Mnram?" Theta asked. Definitely interrogatory.

Jale frowned and regarded the things spread out before
her. Suddenly, chagrin and guilt washed over her. Chief
Stewards did not go snooping through passengers' belongings, however incapacitated those passengers might be!
No, especially not the belongings of incapacitated passengers. She began gathering things back up and sliding
them back into their containers with shaking paws. In her
guilty haste she nearly deleted the name of the drug from
her datapad, but hesitated. For a moment she stared at
the little tablet, then slid it back into its case and stood,
looking down at her handiwork. It appeared as though
nobody had been there.

"Mnrarm? Meer!" Theta rose gracefully to his feet and
took a step towards Jale, tone wistful.

"I'm sorry, dearie," Jale murmured. *Do not engage...*

Theta tilted his head and blinked, black ears perking, almost as if he'd understood.

"I'm just looking after your things," Jale soothed, backing towards the door and away from perilous ground.

"Mnr gr!" Imperative. Paw raised beseechingly.

Further alarmed, Jale opened the door and slipped back through, with only the smallest "Sorry, dear!" She taptap-tapped the lock button and glanced away from his hungry, haunted gaze, then stood on the other side, trembling softly.

Her personal responsibility, the captain had reminded her. Why had she snooped? She shouldn't even have lingered! How could she have abandoned all her careful-ly-cultivated professionalism for a moment of idle curiosity?

Something about the look in those blue eyes both fascinated and terrified her.

"A tragedy happened to that one," she whispered to herself, slow to achieve calm. Regaining control at last, she double-checked the lock on the door, then went straight to sickbay.

"Banerethin? Banerethin...that could be a trade name." Doctor Jrmnia clucked his tongue.

Jale, watching him do his research, held off an instinctu-al little shudder. Jrmnia was the only one of his kind she'd ever met, and, while she respected his professional abilities, she rather hoped not to meet another. A pangolin, he'd said. Large and strange and covered in scales, he'd been her shipmate for a decade and still she found him terrifying.

Personally, she was convinced that the very existence of Jrmnia was proof that the ancients had been crazy.

His eyeridges rose as he finished tapping it into his system.

"Banerethin! Where did you come across that name? Do please tell me that we haven't taken any of that aboard, Miss Bercammon!"

Jale shifted her weight. "Why is that, Doctor?"

"This says that Banerethin is a class B restricted drug. I'm surprised you've heard of it, and that leads me to believe that you've seen it somewhere. And that, Miss Bercammon, under my authority as ship's doctor, is something that terrifies me. I could lose my license just for allowing it to be brought aboard under my watch."

"Ah, hum," Jale fidgeted. "Well, forget where I've seen it...what does it do?"

Jrmnia fixed her with a hard stare, puffing up. Black soulless eyes delved deep, and she looked away.

"Where, Miss—"

Flustered, Jale dropped her pad on the table and glared. "From a passenger with a level three diplomatic immunity on record," she improvised. "I didn't want to say because of privacy issues, and I don't wish to say more."

Jrmnia considered this, then deflated a bit. "Well, if your passenger has a level three immunity, it won't be my problem, at least. Banerethin...and I don't know why your passenger would need this...is the single most potent drug for inducing a psychogenic form of retrograde amnesia in a patient, with the timeframe of removal commensurate with the length and quantity of application."

Jale squinted at Jrmnia. "I am a Steward, Dr. Germ. I can't even accurately reproduce those words you just used, much less understand them."

Jrmnia actually smiled slightly at this, shaking his head. "Are they still calling me that?"

"There are quite a few species who can't come near close to saying your name. You'll have to adjust, dear."

"Oh, I did...Long ago. Doesn't bother me. At any rate, yes, well...Your passenger apparently wishes to remove long segments of his memory."

Jale frowned. "How much...ah...memory would 20ccs of Banerethin every four hours for the next nine days erase?"

"Are you joking?" Jrmnia looked exceedingly uncomfortable once again.

"No, Doctor."

Jrmnia shook his head, tapping at a terminal. After a while he gestured at the screen and looked up with an unreadable expression on his unreadable features. "It depends on many factors. Body mass, acidity, species...some are barely affected. Can you be more specific?"

"Ah," Jale hemmed. "Arctic fox, thirty-eight kilograms."

"Patient Theta."

Jale slumped. "Yes, Theta."

"Patient Theta does not, as near as I know, have a level three diplomatic immunity."

"Look, I shouldn't have said anything...I'm sorry."

The doctor smacked his bescaled palm down on the console. "Well, you did. You must always, *always* check with me before bringing drugs on board." He thumped the console again, swatting his broad tail on the deck for emphasis. "I'm going to take this straight to the captain. This chart indicates that someone is trying to erase somewhere in the neighborhood of two years of memories from patient Theta. I don't know why, considering that she barely has enough brain left for vital functions, from what I saw."

"He, actually. Theta's male—didn't you examine him?" Jale was slightly perplexed.

Jrmnia stared at her, looking more vexed and annoyed than Jale could ever recall seeing him. He turned away and began poking at his terminal, the tip of his tongue flicking in agitation.

"Wait, wait." Jale realized that he intended to carry out his threat right then. "Don't actually call the captain. This is her rest shift, and I really shouldn't have—"

Another wave cut her off, and the captain's rather tired face appeared on the display, clearly worried.

"What's wrong, Doctor?"

"Captain, did you know that one of your passengers, a certain Theta, is carrying on board a class B restricted drug?"

Captain Erin visibly stiffened, expression quickly changing to guarded alertness; the wolf's features became fixed. She leaned forward, eyes directly on the terminal.

"Who told you this, Doctor?"

"Nevermind that," Jrmnia didn't seem to notice or heed the captain's change in demeanor. He awarded Jale, standing safely out of view, a little arch of his eyeridge. "Captain, I must recommend that we eject the drug into space before we're arrested for smuggling contraband by Ramesan customs."

"Doctor Jrmnia," Captain Erin's lupine features contorted slightly, very awake. "Under no circumstances are you to do anything of the sort. Do not touch Theta, Theta's drugs, Theta's cargo, or interfere in any way with anything else whatsoever involving Theta." Her voice had risen with repetition of 'Theta'. "Theta is not your concern. In fact, delete any and all records you have of Theta, forget that we've had this conversation, and tell whoever told you about this that I will have their head if they talk about this with anyone else. Have I made myself plain?"

Jrmnia's eyes were wide.

"Captain, I've—"

"Doctor!" The captain bellowed, standing up from her chair to glare down at the viewport. "That was not a request. Not even remotely."

"Ah, I...ah... ...Yes, Captain."

"Jrmnia?"

"Yes, Captain?"

"I will have you confined if you disobey. Or worse. This is life or death."

The doctor nodded, wide-eyed, and Erin cut the comm. Jale stared at Jrmnia, and he stared back.

"Wow."

"I asked you not to call."

Jrmnia sat back, stunned. "I've worked with Captain Erin for fifteen years. She's a close personal friend."

"I'd listen to her," Jale said,

"Just...get out of here. You didn't come here, you've never heard of...that drug that does that thing that you forget. Maybe you should take some, yourself." Jrmnia shot her a nervous grin. "No, really, please don't. By Dia, I've never seen..." he trailed off.

Jale nodded. Her internal chronometer was warning her that it would very soon be lunchtime, and she hadn't even seen to the menu for the day.

Nineteen years, three months.

"Jale?" the doctor murmured pensively.

"Good-bye for now, Doctor."

"Be...be cautious with Theta, Jale."

The ferret nodded once to doctor Jrmnia, then left. She would be late to the galley to coordinate a meal service for the second time in a week, and that displeased her greatly. She had the distinct sensation that the world was collapsing around her.

"Jale!"

Jale awoke with a gasp, grasping for the clock. It was the middle of the night watch.

Why had she woken?

"Jale! Answer, dammit."

The comm! She stumbled out of bed, nearly tripping over her little rock garden. She went down on all fours briefly to avoid destroying the carefully arranged stones, then pulled herself up to the flashing console. Chaos!

She tapped 'receive', blinking blurry eyes into focus and frowning down at the screen.

It was Jrmnia.

"Jale, by Dia, you better get down here. Right now."

"What? Where? I was sleeping."

"Cargo hold eight. I'll meet you at the forward entrance. Come quickly!" He turned to glare over his shoulder. "Lock it out. Cut the damned power if you have to."

He cut the comm without even turning back.

Alarmed, Jale dressed as fast as she could. Things went on backwards, and she stumbled around in her haste.

Chaos.

When she arrived, out of breath, the doctor took her by the hand and all but dragged her over to the main airlock.

Inside sat Theta, banging his hand desperately on the large exterior release control, tears coursing down his cheeks.

Jale stared in horror.

"Mari caught the alarm at his station in Engineering, bless his heart, and cut the power to the exterior doors. Your little monster has already disabled the safety controls. According to Mari, the damned thing is one jumper short of cycling open, and the interior doors won't release because they're no longer safe."

"Oh my heavens." It wasn't nearly enough, but it was all she could think to say. She felt faint.

"Look, let me explain something to you. When we brought Theta on board, I insisted on giving him a cursory scan for cerebral activity as he was barely even alive. The two brain scans that I was allowed to take, which I've subsequently examined in greater detail, made it obvious that there was very little chance of spontaneous recovery. This level of consciousness is...ridiculous. I wouldn't believe it if I didn't see it with my own eyes. The way the safety interlocks are rigged is nothing short of genius, according to Mari. What. Is. Going. On?"

Jale swayed. Jrmnia gripped her arm.

"I—I don't know. He..."

The aft door hissed open and Mari swung through, the collie raising a paw and jogging up to them.

"Guys, If we don't...get this resolved soon...alarms...are going to go off on the bridge," Mari panted.

"How do we get in?" Jrmnia asked. "Let's just get him out and go, before the captain finds out."

Mari regarded Theta skeptically. "If he wants to cycle the airlock that badly, I say we let him. The way he's buggered it, it'd be infinitely easier to open that side. I don't have any idea how he's went an' done it."

Jale and Jrmnia both gaped at the engineer.

"Mari. Mari, if he cycles that airlock, I have a pretty good idea that the three of us will follow as soon as the captain finds out, and no joke."

Mari snapped his jaw shut in bewilderment, looking between the two. "Really?"

The pounding had stopped, and the pounder now lay curled up on the floor, looking defeated; Jale rested her paws on either side of the airlock window, staring in. A naked Theta still clutched his stuffed animal tightly to him.

"Can't we just pry open this door?"

Mari snorted. "Jelly, you know I've always respected you. I think you're the best chief steward ever...so it's with respect an' all that I say this: Don't ever become an engineer. This door is held shut by a crazy strong magnetic field. The only way to open it is to induce a state change, and flip the poles. That circuitry is electrically deadlocked at...deadlocked at...huh. You know..."

Mari tapped the door, muttering under his breath. "If... mm...I'll be right back."

He jogged over and climbed up into the loading crane operating station.

"Engineers," Jrmnia muttered in disgust.

Moments later, the airlock light cycled from flashing yellow to green and the door hissed open.

Jale and the doctor jumped quickly through to Theta's side. The doctor grabbed his arm and lifted him roughly to his feet. He didn't resist, standing and hanging his head.

"Doctor!" Jale was appalled. "Please, be gentle."

"Gentle? After what this freak almost did?" The doctor shook his head, big claws tightening around the fox's bicep. "No—I'm going to take him back and run some tests, and then I'm going to sedate him for the rest of the trip."

Jale stood straight, looming over the doctor. "Doctor Jrmnia, you will do nothing of the kind. I am sorry that you have been inconvenienced, but Theta will be neither examined nor sedated. If you don't mind, you will kindly back off."

The doctor released Theta's arm and literally took a step back, staring at Jale in surprise.

Mari leaned around the entranceway.

"Hey, would you guys mind getting out of the airlock chamber, please? We're not supposed to ever stay in this part, and I want to get it closed up. Gotta fix the system, too."

Jale nodded, gently leading Theta out of the bay. Theta's walk and motor control had improved amazingly, and his balance and stride were fluid even with his head hung and shoulders drooped. Guiding him gently away from Jrmnia, she began to notice other things—his glances, his winces, his silent desperation.

He's aware now.

Mari closed the hatch. "So, he overrode the power amplification circuit on the hatch doors. Convinced the ship that there was pressure outside the hatch. Bloody clever little bugger. Please, by Dia's foul fetid breath, keep him out of this part of the ship. Sit on him if you have to. He could blow the ship up next time and take us all with him."

"Wouldn't do that. Mm done."

Jale nearly dropped Theta's paw. She spun around and held him at arm's length while doctor glowered on in surprise.

"Theta? You can talk?"

"Mhr. Not.. Is.. Hrd."

Do NOT attempt to engage Theta in conversation.

Jale made a little noise. Such simple instructions.

"We should get you on back to your quarters."

"Please keep him there." Mari shook his head and sighed, glancing up to the panel he had disassembled. "I'm going to put this system back together."

"I shall take Theta back to his quarters," Jale announced, daring Jrmnia to contradict her. She reached down to retrieve Theta's paw and tugged him toward the exit without looking back. The doctor trailed after for a few meters, but did not follow.

After returning the defeated fox once more, Jale settled him onto the soft settee, handing his soft stuffed animal back to him. He took it quickly and squeezed it as if clinging for dear life.

She frowned, brushing his purple hair back from his eyes and tucking it behind his ears.

"Theta?"

"Ss my name? Th...th..."

"The-ta. You cannot remember your name?"

"Remmbr a few thing...Nrt mch."

Do NOT attempt to engage Theta in conversation.

Jale sighed. She simply *couldn't* leave Theta unattended in this state.

"Wnn...Whhn..."

Theta dropped his head against the big black stuffed animal and started crying.

Jale rested her paw on his head, stroking through his long purple hair. His face, clear of its confusion, was surprisingly young and thin. His hair had remnants of glitter in it; it hung across the symmetrical curves of his cheekfur. Jale traced her fingers over them softly, then slid her paw below his chin and lifted it to look into his eyes. Black fur around his eyes accentuated their depth and she found herself again captivated, mesmerized.

"Why are you so sad?" she asked gently, almost in a whisper.

"Ir...Ir drn't knowr really...Missing srm.. Something. Mishing someone. Mish...Mish..." He seemed to be rolling the sound around in his mouth as if tasting it, considering it.

Behind Jale, the door slid open; she flinched, and Theta hid behind her.

Captain Erin stormed in, flanked by the second mate and Doctor Jrmnia.

"Chief Steward," her voice was icy. "I gave you one simple but very important task in addition to your normal duties. You can't mind one semi-vegetative patient?"

Jale shrank back. This didn't feel fair, but it wasn't an allegation she could deny. She'd never done anything to get on the captain's bad side—this was very new to her.

"I'm...sorry that I have failed you, Captain."

Erin scowled, resting her paws on her hips. "You should be. This is a disgrace. I—"

"Shtopit." Theta slid around Jale and glowered angrily up at Erin.

Glowering at a captain on her own ship rarely has any positive effect, but Erin was arrested mid-berating. She stared down at Theta.

"Ss mry fault. Iss all mry fault...Thwar...Thr war..."

Confusion crept back in to his features, and his ears drooped.

Erin looked nonplussed.

"Captain," the doctor stepped forward, eyes fixed on Theta. "I would like to take our patient to sick bay."

"NRr!" Theta showed his teeth, spinning away from Jrmnia's outstretched hand. The Doctor chased after him, but the fox showed remarkable agility in avoiding his grasp.

"Ok, ok, let's just stop for a second," Erin raised her voice slightly and spread her hands out. "Doctor, leave him alone.

Thank you for alerting me to this situation; please go back to bed." She turned away from a frustrated-looking doctor to nod to the second mate. "I think I'll take it from here."

The second mate nodded and grinned, then turned to the doctor, taking him by the shoulder and escorting him through the door.

Once it had closed behind the pair, Erin shook her head.

"I render apology, Chief Steward. I didn't realize...this. Theta..." She paused.

Jale was trying to soothe Theta—he had started sobbing again, in big, racking sobs, one black paw over his belly, the other over his muzzle.

Erin moved closer, settling onto the settee and leaning across the table. She peered curiously at the distraught fox.

"What is wrong with him, Jale?"

Jale frowned at the sobbing ball of fluff, taking his paw to help him up and guide him onto the settee beside the captain.

"Theta? What's wrong, dearie?"

"I remrbmr," Theta whispered, his ears flat. "I'm...shtarting to rmmembr," he murmured, and then swallowed a sob.

The door hissed open again and both Erin and Jale glanced up in annoyance.

Arvinne stepped in with a big, kind smile on his face. "Theta, sir? It's time for your—" He froze, realizing that Theta wasn't alone, and the smile slipped from his face. "Oh! Am...I late, ma'am? Is...is Theta ok?" He stole a sidelong glance at the captain.

"It's ok, Arvinne. Theta's fine, and you can go," Jale said warmly. He seemed so very concerned that she was moved.

"But he needs..."

Theta looked up and wiped his muzzle, sniffling. "Thnk you, Hrrvn. Mm sorry you hrd tr do arrl thrr. Rrrgh! Hate thrt Ir canr speak."

"That's talking! What did he say?"

"I believe," Erin grinned. "That he just thanked you and apologized. He's having trouble speaking."

Arvinne grinned, looking relieved. "Oh, I'm so glad he's getting better. He seems so nice. Does this mean I won't have to change his..." He trailed off at Jale's acid glare and Erin's wince.

Theta looked away.

"Yrs...I should br able tr mrnage," the fox mumbled.

Arvinne looked stricken and asked to be excused. Jale glanced to the captain, who dismissed the youngster herself, all the while seemingly trying to fight off a creeping grin.

"What do we do, Captain?" Jale turned to her after Arvinne had left. "The instructions we received..."

"No longer apply now that he's awoken. The agent was clear on that. But Theta," Erin turned to address him directly, "I can't have you wandering the ship and trying to blow yourself out of our airlocks. Air is expensive, you know."

To Jale's surprise, Theta cracked a slight grin at her humor. "I'm done," he articulated carefully. "Prroms I won't try t-to...kill mysrrf on this shrrp. Can I be alone?"

His speech had improved substantially in fairly short order, Jale noticed with some surprise. She frowned. "Captain, I suggest that we let him rest as he requests."

Erin nodded. "As he's given his word. Before we go, Theta, I do have a special instruction for you, left should you wake up enroute. There are two messages on your console that you must read, and a trunk was left for you in cargo."

Theta lowered his head, closing his eyes and nodding in acknowledgement.

Jale stood with Erin, and they walked to the door together. Before she stepped out, she glanced one last time at Theta, who had curled up on the settee, clutching the stuffed animal to his chest and weeping softly into it.

She meandered back to her quarters, very tired. Settling once more onto her bed, she who so loved the stories of others was faced with the realization that she had very few of her own. Certainly nothing like what story that fox must have—a story that would leave one in such a state of despair and confusion, clutching a black stuffed coyote to ones chest and sobbing unabatedly.

Despite the turmoil of her thoughts, as soon as she'd settled her long form into her bed she felt exhaustion overtake her.

She quickly fell to sleep, and did not dream.

II

Askew

FOR TWO DAYS, Theta did little but sit on his bed and cry. He had infrequent visitors; Arvinne came regularly with food, and occasionally with little treats he'd scrounged from the kitchen. Jale stopped by a few times. Even the captain herself dropped in once to check up on him.

The little kindnesses took the edge off the crushing despair that had come with the slow return of memories, but the future was a gaping void that echoed the black emptiness inside his soul—he'd lost everything that he knew. The thought would send him into another round of sobbing, and he would clutch the soft stuffed animal to his chest once more, burying his face against it.

Sometimes, after a while, he would even sleep. When he awoke, the pattern would invariably repeat.

Four days after his adventure with the airlock, he woke from a long, restless slumber and looked himself over. He was a mess, unkempt and unshowered. He still felt a dull ache inside himself, but he found that, though he tried, he could no longer collapse back within.

He sighed and rolled to his feet, glancing immediately at the console. It terrified him. There was a message there, just for Theta.

It would be from *him*.

He took a bottle of water from the dispenser.

"Theta," he said.

"Theta." It rolled off the tongue nicely, and his speech had become clearer each day. He barely felt the stiffness in his muscles or tongue anymore, and in fact had begun to feel better than he had in recent memory.

"Thay-ta. Thee-ta." He played with the word for a while, experimenting with various pronunciations and stresses, trying to see which felt more right.

It wasn't his name, of course.

My old name died with me.

Tears began to wet his eyes once more, and he rested a paw on the bridge of his muzzle.

I would give my life to see him one more time. I would give my life again to see him one more time.

His memory was spotty, but he remembered enough.

More than enough.

He slid over to the terminal and swiped his paw across. It read his keychip and prompted him for his key. He tapped it in, reluctantly, and saw that there were two messages.

One was double-encrypted, but he knew exactly what the extra key would be.

He vacillated for a moment, paws trembling, then closed his session with another swipe of his paw and sat there shaking.

I can't deal with this yet. Not yet.

He stared at his paws for a long while before the tremors subsided and the world around him began to filter back in. He straightened, wrinkling his nose at a scent that was familiar but far too strong.

He stank.

With a little sigh, he pushed himself back from the console and made his way to the bathroom, nosing around for the various cleaning paraphernalia then stepping into the water shower. It was the first shower he'd given himself since he could remember, and it took him some time to figure out how to use the various brushes, scrubs and lathers that he'd become accustomed to having other slaves use on him. Still, he managed to get himself cleaned up and rinsed off without much trouble, then activated the dryer.

Warm, dry air coursed through his fur, and he closed his eyes in pure animal pleasure, dabbing his head hair with an absorbent towel. After a few moments, his fur was rustling with static, and the cycle was winding down.

He opened his eyes reluctantly, loth to leave the warm innocence of the dryer, a little momentary haven where nothing needed to exist outside of sensation. The cool quickly began to seep in, however, and the spell was broken; he stepped out of the dryer and began rubbing himself down with a conditioning towel.

His paws and feet were black from the elbows and knees down, and the rest of him almost completely white, and that was as it should be, at least...he rubbed his temples as if hoping to invoke the memories held within his skull. Something had altered his fur pattern—rather than his species' customary fluff, his was short and tapered in most places, lending him an incredibly lithe, very effeminate appearance. The black around his eyes and the tapering of his fur were genetic alterations, he knew, but he couldn't remember how he knew that.

A small box beside the wash basin caught his eye. He opened it to find myriad silver components carefully set out in a little tray at the top. These, he recognized; without even thinking, his paws went through the instinctive motions of setting the jewelry in place. Two studs went through his tongue, and a half dozen highly polished tiny silver studs along the outer rim of his left ear. He lifted the tray and nearly fell to his knees, leaning on the counter for support.

"My collar," he whispered to himself. "He sent my collar."

He snatched the polished black silver band with fumbling paws, turning it around to examine. It had been cut; the back portion had been seamlessly re-welded with a small, neat latch, turning it into a simple choker. There wasn't even a hole for a lock. He dropped it onto the solid countertop and brought his fists down hard on either side, his black-furred ears flat back, teeth bared in frustrated anguish. After a full minute of watching the tears drip from his nose to land within its circle, he picked it up and slid it around his neck anyway, defying the symbolism.

It will stay on as if it were still welded. Even if he'll no longer have me, I am still his.

He straightened from the counter, a bit dazed, and made his way to the closet. He had vague memories of going through it before, but they were fragmented and dark, and full of more raw emotion than memory. When he opened it this time, however, he sat back on his haunches with a small gasp.

"Inari's breath," he murmured.

His paws reached up, almost of their own volition, brushing aside things less-remembered to retrieve an intricate silver and black garment of platinum wire and black latigo.

He sniffed it.

It had been completely cleaned; the smell of death did not linger. He slid the rings around his fingers and, operating on instinct, had the whole thing on almost before he realized he intended to. A gauzy shawl went over the top.

He spun out into the center of the room. The motions were automatic, but this time he watched himself flow from one to the next in the mirror.

This is who I am?

He rolled across the floor, feather light, rising on one leg and sweeping a graceful arc with his shawl.

This is who I was. For him.

Perhaps I still am his...why else would he send this?

The door slid open and Arvinne stepped through.

Theta whirled on him, and the steward's eyes widened. In half a breath the fox was to Arvinne's side, supporting the precariously tilting tray of food that the white feline was in the process of dropping and resting a soft paw on his shoulder.

"Oh, I'm so sorry, sir." Arvinne handed the tray over without thinking, blue eyes fixed on Theta. "I didn't realize you'd...My gosh."

"Welcome, Arvinne," Theta murmured in his greeting voice; high pitched and soft, it was a trained voice, unaffected by emotion or worry. An able voice, warm and un-slurred. He was pleased to notice that Arvinne immediately stepped in, rather than away. Theta set the tray on the table to the side, smiling warmly.

Perhaps I'm no longer a monster.

Arvinne took off his hat and crushed it in his fluffy paws. "Master Theta, I'm real sorry for intruding. I shoulda knocked first, but I've gotten used to just coming in."

Theta gaped at Arvinne for a full second, then tried to cover his shock by spinning away and sliding into the bathroom once more. "Excuse me for just one moment," he muttered, voice slightly husky.

Master Theta? He racked his brain for the meaning. In his world, the word only had one and it did not apply to him. It could not apply to him. Could it be a subtle insult? A poke at his past?

How dare he! Anger flared up within Theta, but he closed his eyes and calmed his breathing. No, not logical. Perhaps Arvinne didn't know. The liner crew were clearly not Brynti, after all.

Theta swallowed, awash in conflicting emotions and mental confusion.

Master...what else could he have meant? He rummaged through the grooming brushes to make it seem like he was actively doing something to excuse his precipitous departure. Social etiquette...he closed his eyes to think.

Master...as a polite form of address?

Some little association fired off, and he some fragmented memory surfaced. Something from a children's book. Yes...an adult had referred to a child as...perhaps that was it.

He took a deep breath, trying to slow his heart down.

The moment had long since grown long, and the silence decidedly uncomfortable.

"Please," he managed, still working to calm himself out of view of the poor steward, "Just...just call me just Theta. It's hard to explain, but I..."

Don't deserve?

Cannot abide?

He slid back around the corner and leaned against the frame, smiling hesitantly. "I'm just Theta. I'm sorry if I seem..."

Annihilated?

Insane?

"A little crazy?" Arvinne hinted quietly with a cautious grin.

Theta smirked back wanly. He nodded.

"Yeah, I...a lot crazy. Arvinne..." he met the steward's gaze straight on, and took a step forward. "Arvinne, I died. I was k-killed by the one I love most."

Theta felt his head spin and swallowed what almost emerged as a hysterical giggle. He knew he shouldn't be talking about this. He ripped his gaze away from the shocked steward and stared at the floor.

"It w-was his right to do it, and l-law...the law r-required it." Arvinne's mouth was hanging open, but Theta couldn't stop. "I was a slave, you see. I was his slave, but he loved me. I was his dancer, his lover...I was HIS. I d-don't know how long...b-but I—"

Tears began flowing once more, and again Theta sat on the floor, wrapping paws around his knees. After a moment, he raised his head, blinking blurry, unseeing eyes.

"Do you know what it's l-like to lose y-your destiny?"

Arvinne knelt and rested a big paw on Theta's arm comfortingly, taking his little black paw in his other. Theta was dumbfounded—by now Arvinne should have run screaming; Theta felt like running away screaming from himself.

"I...gosh. You...what do you mean by died?" Arvinne asked, his voice gentle.

Theta pulled away and hid his muzzle between his paws. He looked up at Arvinne between digits, tears soaking his facefur and dripping from the tip of his nose. "I died," he grated quietly, shaking. "Hanging from a rope, lights go out, down the drain d-died in his arms. I d-don't know why I'm alive. I don't know how I'm alive. I don't even d-d-deserve to live, I don't want to l-live, I don't..."

"Now then, Theta," Arvinne said, grabbing him by the shoulders and giving him a gentle shake. "Of course you do deserve to live. And it's clear he wanted you to. Just look where he put you up. And we'd instructions to keep you all dignified, and...Now look, I don't want to pry or nothing, but if you were a slave, why are you so sad to be gone from there?"

Theta stared at him. He struggled with the question—some things should be self-evident. "You...it's...I mean...it's like breathing." Frustration welled up within him, and he bared his teeth. "It's...you could never understand."

Suddenly, Theta hated Arvinne and everyone like him; everyone who knew life without this pain he felt between his eyes, deep in his core. He writhed back to the wall and clutched himself tight. "Get...get AWAY FROM ME! Just...just...leave..."

The steward stood and backed off quickly, palms up, a hurt expression on his face which bit Theta far more deeply.

Theta clutched his head and laid back against the wall, face and ears burning hot beneath his fur with a melange of rage, shame and fear.

Arvinne hovered uncertainly, glancing back towards the door.

Maybe I am a monster, after all.

"Wait...I'm sorry," Theta mumbled. "I'm...so very sorry, Arvinne. You've been so kind to me. Please...don't..."

He wanted to say 'Don't go', but it wouldn't form. "... Don't feel bad. I'm v-very n-not right. I'm not sure I'm supposed to be alive, or even if I am. I mean, I know, logically, but I don't...Can't—"

"Look, it's ok." Arvinne broke in, but kept his distance. "Gosh, you really should talk to Jale. She's the most wonderful to talk to about things, and she's heard about all sorts of stuff. I doubt you could shock ol' Jelly. Not that I'm shocked, mind you, I mean, but for me, well...I don't have no reason to pry further, an' I'm sorry if I hurt you. I'm real happy to see you awake and walking and speaking, though. I felt real bad for you, when you came on board." Arvinne looked embarrassed, and paused for a moment. When no response was forthcoming, he half bowed to Theta, holding his hat to his chest. "See, I'm going away now, but I'll always come around if you're needing someone to talk to, ok?"

Theta's eye caught the black stuffed coyote on the bed; he leaned over and grabbed it to him, curling around it once more.

"T-thank you," he murmured, looking away. He was grateful, but he felt as though he was losing control of an increasing agitation within, some abscess of emotion festering at his core. Little whispers spoke incomprehensible insults just outside his hearing, but he knew that he was being mocked, and he couldn't keep them out. He wished Arvinne would leave, but still he hovered.

"Listen, Theta...I'm gonna ask Jale to come down here, so eat up, alright? She sent this steak special, just for you. Best of the lot, and all the other omnis are getting synthesized protein. But you need feeding, if you don't mind me saying. You don't weigh nothin'."

Theta's breath caught. The expression of care was so moving that it broke into his growing bitterness. He raised his head and opened his mouth, trying to find any set of right words, but was cut off by a strange and very loud wail. He snapped his jaw shut, flowing to his feet and peering around for its source.

"Passengers, stay where you are. Crew to stations NOW." The voice—Captain Erin's voice—was harsh and shrill and rang throughout the quarters and corridor outside.

A strange grinding noise began, as if in reply; Theta looked up to Arvinne but found him equally perplexed.

Arvinne met his gaze; after a moment of uncertainty, he tossed a quick nod to Theta then turned to leave.

Two steps into the corridor, he froze and dropped his hat.

"Get back inside kid," a loud voice growled. It was thick not with caution but with menace, and had an accent that was very strange to Theta's ear; Theta flattened himself against the bulkhead, silent and still, watching in the mirror as Arvinne slowly retreated back in with his paws spread.

The air outside was hazy with smoke, and even as the steward stood in the doorway and looked out, Theta could see heavily armed and armored figures moving rapidly through the corridor. Their armor had little regularity, and the species varied wildly. One stopped at the door to shove Arvinne back in, then closed it.

Theta heard the outside lock snap shut. He spun away from the wall to Arvinne's side, finding the snow leopard visibly shaken.

"What's going on?" Theta asked, voice hushed.

"Oh Dia. Theta...Pirates. It's pirates, I think. I've heard...I think...We've gotta hide."

Theta just shook his head, casting about for anything that might improve their odds while Arvinne tucked himself into the closet.

He rolled his eyes, then lifted the elegant little eating dagger from the food tray and slid it into the band that ran around his waist. After a moment, he shook his head at his own foolishness.

No better weapon against power armor. I'm just as much of a fool, I guess.

Theta smiled to himself, then blinked at a stray thought, his eyes widening.

The console.

The message.

This could be his last chance, and he must know. He leapt across to the terminal, sliding into the chair beside it. Pawswipe, passkey entered, as fast as he'd ever authenticated himself.

His paw hovered over the first message. The unencrypted message.

Not that one.

He tapped the second instead, and entered the sixteen character passkey. His personal access code to Master's quarters.

The message opened. It was from him.

> *My dearest Mishy,*
> *Kotoraski morota gera.*

Theta drew back. The words sounded very strange, but hauntingly familiar; alas, their meaning eluded him. He murmured them under his breath several times, but could not discern their intent; shaking his head, he read on.

> *If you're reading this, then Dr. Chevan or the ship's crew has failed and thus, by extension, I have failed.*
> *I sincerely hope that you're reading the other message instead. I have attempted to give you back the one thing you deserve, whether you want—*

The terminal went black.

"NO!" Theta screamed. He tapped the control area, but it did not respond. In a blind rage, he brought his fist down onto the face of the display, cracking the durable surface. It felt very good, so he did it again, snarling his fury at the shattered console. He rose, brushing his benumbed paw over the little dagger.

He drew it, but resisted the urge to snap it off in the ruined screen.

"Anything is better than nothing," a high-pitched, icy voice whispered in his ear. He spun and snapped, driven by instinct, but his teeth closed only on air—there was nobody there. He didn't quite recognize the voice, but it felt familiar.

"Anything is better than nothing?" he repeated under his breath. It made no sense. Where had he heard it before?

"Passengers and...remaining...crew of the ship, listen carefully," a clear voice came through the shipwide public address system, louder than Erin's had been. "We have control. Stay in your quarters and do not leave them. We have activated the door locks, and anyone caught in the hall will be shot. Your cargo and valuables are forfeit; your lives will remain in your possession, however, if you offer no resistance and if your ransom is met."

Theta growled softly under his breath. His first instinct was that Master would fix things, as he always did. As nobody else could. As he did when Alixa became jealous of him and...he shut the thought out. Not the best thing to think of at the moment.

None can protect me. HE sent me away.

"*That is correct—I cannot protect you, dancer.*"

His voice came from behind Theta; the fox whirled again, eyes wide, searching.

Nobody was there. Was Arvinne playing tricks on him? A hot rage ran from his nose to his tail, and he seethed momentarily before catching himself.

He shook his head, grinding his teeth and trying to organize his chaotic thoughts.

Arvinne was a friend. Aside from Jale, Arvinne was his only friend.

He didn't want to lose what remained of his sanity, and he felt it slipping away quickly.

He needed a real voice to talk to him.

"Arvinne?"

Coaxed from the closet, Arvinne sheepishly settled and joined Theta's scheming. Escape was proposed, but quickly dismissed. Arvinne made the point that even if Theta got them out of the stateroom, there was nothing they could accomplish aside from getting themselves killed and possibly others with them. Hiding, they agreed, was silly, and plotting an ambush would be futile against a trained force.

They would simply have to wait.

For the next four hours, the pair sat across the table from one another. Theta tried to use his own words to silence the voices in his head; Arvinne listened as he told him far more than he ever should while trying to stay in control of himself and his emotions. He certainly hadn't meant to spill his whole story, but once he started he couldn't stop. By the time he had finished, the steward looked both sick to his stomach and horrified.

Arvinne's obvious and increasing antipathy for Theta's master confused and distressed the fox. He'd tried to explain that despite all the horrible things his master had done that he was truly a great person, that evil itself could be a virtue, that there was in ways method to his madness...but he had difficulty articulating the whys and Arvinne wasn't buying any of it. Eventually, frustrated and confounded, Theta simply gave up trying to convince him.

Perhaps one just had to *know* Knoskali to understand.

Theta rested his paws on the table and leaned back, slightly exasperated and unsure of how to continue.

"So, here's something else I just don't get," Arvinne broke the silence that followed. "After all those years of abuse and..." the steward shuddered, frowning. "How come he kills you and then sends you away? Why wouldn't he just keep you locked all safe away until after the war was on?"

"*Because it was the end of us.*" Knoskali's voice echoed in Theta's head.

Not real. Not real!

Theta struggled to fight off his most basic instincts and keep his eyes and ears fixed convincingly on Arvinne.

"I haven't figured it out yet. I..." He dipped his muzzle, closing his eyes. "I don't know. Somehow I think I started the w-war on Brynton. I wasn't good enough. I must have failed. I—"

"Shh, ssh," Arvinne placed his paw on Theta's, arresting his descent into self-impugnment. "Look, it don't matter what you did or might've, but near's I can say, it wasn't your war to start...so don't blame yourself. Now you seem like a properly good sort who ended up in a terrible, terrible place, but it's not your fault. If we make it out of this alive, we'll find you some help, yes we will. You'll be amazed what they can do nowadays! Almost as good as the ancients, they say. We'll have you back to normal before you know it."

"*He doesn't know us, Mishy. He can't understand.*"

Knoskali's voice sounded as warm and loving as it had in the last moments, as it had just before taking Theta's life.

"Master," Theta breathed wistfully. Then tensed. Though the voice had seemed real, almost sounded real, some part of him knew it had been in his head. The presence lingered, like a shadow in the back of his mind. Like Knoskali. Theta felt a crawling sensation ascend his spine.

"No," he growled bitterly. "You're not him. You're not real. Go away!"

Arvinne looked surprised, Theta noticed.

"Oh, no, no! Not you. I didn't mean you."

The steward did not appear at all relieved. Theta closed his eyes, trying to think of a valid excuse that didn't involve explaining the voices in his head. The anger that had been slowly replacing his depression flashed to the surface, untargeted, and he found himself growling under his breath.

Arvinne sighed worriedly.

"Theta—?"

The door control beeped, unlocking with a soft snick.

Both sets of eyes turned to the entranceway.

It slid open, and a grim and disheveled-looking Jale stepped through, followed by five large, armored forms.

Theta rose.

III

Predation

THE PIRATE IN CHARGE of the little group that gathered all of Theta's belongings in the center of the little stateroom was a wolf nearly a meter taller than he. He wore power armor, and had black smudges in his white fur; his white hair was close-cropped to his head, and he had weapons strapped to every point of him. His helmet was off, and Theta could see a little network of furless scars across his face and muzzle. Every action and motion seemed intended to convey an aura of menace.

Of course, Theta reflected, Knoskali was also nearly a meter taller than him, and he had no doubt that the black coyote would have turned this little pirate into a greasy spot, power armor or not; dominant and imposingly large was something he'd met and been conquered by, and he found himself unbowed before it in lesser form.

He felt merely contempt for their bluster, instead of the fear they hoped to foment; the pirates were amateurs, by contrast, when it came to using terror as a tool.

Still, he knew, they could kill him just as dead, whether they did it professionally or not. He swallowed his burgeoning rage, trying to conjure up a more appropriate expression of cowed submission.

"This is all you brought with you?" The leader scowled, moving Theta's grooming case with a booted foot.

"I did not leave under the best circumstances."

The pirate snorted, staring down at the small pile. "Clearly. It's a pretty sorry collection, considering the room."

"*This is not good! He has no regard for prisoners and he'll kill us happily. He'll kill us! He'll kill us!*" the *other*'s voice squealed. The Not-Knoskali voice.

It had been rambling on in its nasal tone like an unscratchable itch, and it was becoming impossible for Theta to ignore the simpering monologue long enough to reply to questions.

"*He'll kill us! He'll kill us all! Help. Please!*"

"Shut up!" Theta snapped in frustration, not-quite-as-under-his-breath-as-he'd-hoped.

The pirate stared at him in disbelief; his soldiers gawked, and one laughed in surprise.

"What did you say?"

Theta locked his jaw, very agitated—suffused, in fact—with the rage that had been building within. The other cringed back and was silent. He raised his eyes to glare at the wolf, and the anger that had been swelling between his eyes began to blur his vision.

"I was NOT talking to you. It's—"

'A private conversation?'

'Personal'?

'Nothing'?

"—It's none of your business."

The pirate reacted quickly to the insubordinate reply, aiming a heavy blow at the fox's head; Theta dodged it easily and automatically, and spun around behind the armored form. His paw slipped to his belt, finding and drawing the eating dagger he'd stashed there. Ruthlessly he quashed an incredibly potent, incredibly stupid instinct to mount the wolf's armor and slash his exposed throat.

Restraint proved to be a good thing, as the other pirates had leveled their weapons at him; they seemed more amused than angry, however, murmuring amongst themselves appreciatively. Their leader himself showed little mirth once he'd turned around and found his quarry. He growled, leaning forward to menace the small fox.

Theta locked eyes with the wolf and bared his teeth in reply, flipping the dagger in his paw; out of the corner of his eye, he saw several of the pirates stiffen at the motion and take more careful aim.

"*Calm*," Knoskali's voice settled in his mind, like a soft murmur from a speaker just out of view.

"Yes, pirate," Theta said through clenched teeth. "This is all I have to my name, and it is very sorry. I'm equally sorry to disappoint you."

The tall one maintained eye contact for an interminable half minute, then straightened and turned to his cohorts with a shake of his head, a small grin dancing across his lips briefly.

"Ok, boys and girls, let's keep moving. Lots of ground to cover. Remember, it could be anything, of any size."

One of the pirates, a large white rat, slung his weapon and reached for the black stuffed animal carefully placed atop the pile.

Theta's heart skipped a beat.

If he tries to leave with that, I will kill him, whatever the consequences. My last gift from Him. *All I have left.*

Even the *other* was silent.

The leader lifted his chin, and Theta realized that the pirate was still watching him out of the corner of his eye. "Leave that, Yeri," he snapped with authority. "Leave it and let's go."

The rat set it back down with a small shrug, and shuffled out to join the others in the corridor.

After his soldiers had filed out, the white wolf turned back to stare at Theta, expression fixed in a strange sort of frown.

Theta's hackles rose and he took an involuntary step towards the pirate.

"*No, Mishy*," whispered Knoskali's voice.

Jale and Arvinne both rested paws on him, thinking they were holding him back, but only Knoskali's voice truly restrained him.

The wolf arched an eyebrow, then turned partially to the side, showing his paw resting firmly on his hip holster. He patted it, then winked.

"If you ever pull a weapon on me again, I will kill you," the pirate growled. "Until then?"

He threw Theta a not-entirely-mocking salute, then perfunctorily gestured for Jale to follow him out, all but snapping his fingers. As she was leaving, she shot Theta a wide-eyed glance over her shoulder.

When the door closed behind them, Arvinne collapsed back onto the settee with a huge groan. Theta frowned, sliding the dagger back into place and walking over to the snow leopard's side, peering at him concernedly. He'd taken a vicious kick in the ribs from one of the pirates during the search, and looked to be in some pain.

"Are you alright? Is it your side?"

"I'm thinking you're more than a lot crazy, Theta," he wheezed. "Do you have any ken how these sort live?"

Theta smirked. "No. Do you?"

"Well..." Arvinne paused. "Well, no, not to a certainty. I just heard stories and all. But...anyway, you're real quick! How did you dodge like that?"

"It was a very slow swing," Theta murmured, shaking his head ruefully. "Power armor can be very bad in confined spaces, especially if you have the helmet off. Bad choice. More for show, in this case."

Why do I know that?

"*Because*," Knoskali sounded puzzled, as though it couldn't be clearer, "*you're my dancer.*"

"*That doesn't make any sense.*" The other interjected. "*She never finished—*"

"*Enough of that. You can go away now.*" Knoskali's voice was disapproving.

Theta rubbed the side of his head and closed his eyes, hair spilling across his face. "Never finished what? But...I'm a he, anyway," he murmured, bemused.

Stupid other.

The other never seemed to hear his thoughts as Knoskali did.

Theta opened his eyes to find Arvinne staring at him quizzically; he flinched away from the snow leopard's questioning gaze, and sighed.

That's right, Arvinne. You're stuck in a stateroom with an insane, resurrected, turned-loose slave fox with a death wish and voices in his head that don't even know what gender he is. The corridor outside is crawling with pirates, who are probably going to kill everyone and blow up the what's left. Welcome to the real world—it's rather mad.

He giggled softly at his thoughts, then flopped on the cushioned surface and cocked his head at Arvinne, ears perked forward. "I bet...that you wish you were anywhere else, right now," he said. "I'm sorry you're stuck in here with crazyfox."

To his surprise, Arvinne laughed at that.

Then winced.

"I doubt I'd be finding better odds outside this stateroom. With you to keep 'em distracted, I might make it out of this yet," he chuckled, laying his head back down.

Theta shook his head, humor fading. "I have a bad feeling about this whole thing. They're looking for something in particular. I'm not convinced they'll want witnesses or hostages."

Arvinne gritted his teeth and stretched out again, closing his eyes. "We can hope. We shouldn't do nothin' drastic, I think."

Theta wasn't sure.

"*Patience*," Knoskali whispered.

They were both asleep when the door hissed open again, nearly a full standard day later.

Theta roused instantly, sliding silently to the floor and easing out of view, brushing the eating dagger with his paw to be sure it was still present.

Someone banged something loudly against the wall several times.

"Get up. Steward's Assistant Arvinne? Passenger... Theta? Come out here."

Arvinne stirred; Theta considered his options for a moment, then drew a nervous little breath and stepped out into the main part of the room.

The speaker was some sort of feline, of medium build. He wasn't wearing power armor, sporting only an energy pistol across the belly of his grey and green shipsuit; behind him, however, loomed two canids in light armor, each lethally armed.

Theta studied the trio briefly, then moved close to the clerk type, standing at a slight angle; this encounter felt far, far more dangerous than the last.

This was business, not show.

"I'm Theta. Steward Arvinne is laying down. He's in pain from the abuse of one of your cohorts."

The clerk nodded fractionally.

"Steward Arvinne, can you hear me?"

"Yeah?" Arvinne said.

"Congratulations. You made ransom. You'll stay in here until we leave."

Theta shifted, eyes narrow.

He made ransom.

They told him first.

I did not?

"Passenger Theta," the clerk fidgeted with his datapad. "I'm sorry to inform you that the shipping line did not wish to pay to guarantee your life."

Theta pulled his lips back in a small snarl, exposing his front teeth.

All these stupid little games.

"That's unfortunate, pirate. I suppose you're here to execute me yourself?"

The feline tapped at the pad in his paws, then raised his head to glance at Theta, whiskers twitching.

"Well, yes," he sounded only slightly reluctant. "It'll be quick and painless. It's either that or you go out the airlock, and we don't like doing that, as it's neither."

"*Run! Hide! Help!*" The other yelped. Theta flicked his ear irritably; he was slowly learning to somewhat suppress the unwanted voice.

"*Patience*," Knoskali's mellifluous tone settled in more smoothly. "*Read the situation.*"

"What's going on?" Arvinne growled, limping out of the sleeping chamber. He was hunched over, and he shambled toward the group as though in great pain.

Theta bared more teeth, taking a small step forward, drawing attention back to him.

"I've been dead before. I probably should have remained so." Despite his exterior cold calm, his pulse raced and he felt sick to his stomach. Anxiety warred with fury, but fury was surging forward like never before and keeping it under control was becoming very difficult.

The feline clearly didn't understand, but discarded the fox's words with a flick of his paw. "It's not personal. Just business."

Theta twitched.

One of the two in black stepped forward, rifle lowered. He looked a bit bored.

"On your knees, fox, and face the wall. This won't hurt," he said, tapping Theta with his barrel.

"Well, not much," his partner snickered.

Theta's paw slid down to the handle of the eating dagger; he had no intention of dying on his knees in front of Arvinne. Apparently, Arvinne had no intention, himself, of allowing it; he straightened and viciously slammed into the rifle bearer, knocking him heavily to the floor and quickly delivering several heavy blows to the canine's head, driving it back into the hard decking of the entranceway. After the second blow, the guard was limp beneath the heavyset steward. The other guard, recovering from his initial shock, took a quick step back and raised his rifle.

"*Dance.*"

Knoskali's single word was clear, but Theta was already in motion. Half a breath and his body knocked the guard's rifle off its aim just as he fired it. An instant later, his dagger was in the guard's throat, where it became lodged in the neck muscle before doing any significant damage.

The guard shrieked and dropped his rifle, clutching at Theta and trying to tear him away; Theta clenched his jaw in annoyed determination, snarling curses under his breath as he began to saw the guard's neck open with the fairly blunt utensil. Despite frantic flailing of his target, and the intervention of the clerk trying to remove him, Theta managed to free the knife from the muscle and slash both the guard's artery and his airway, then kick away from the collapsing form without much impairment.

He spun away to find the clerk's energy pistol resting between his eyes.

There was a moment of pause; Theta's eyes nearly crossed, staring down the underside of the weapon. Arvinne had stopped beating his guard, once he realized that the form under him was completely inert; he now just stared at the energy pistol, wide-eyed and too far away to be of use.

Theta couldn't figure out why the clerk hadn't fired or spoken, until he noticed the feline's finger frantically tugging on the trigger.

Safety.

Theta sneered mercilessly, raising his blood soaked dagger under the clerk's jaw.

"Doesn't work. Drop it or die," he growled. The clerk didn't seem to notice or care that Theta's voice trembled slightly, or that he was holding a mere eating dagger to his neck. He dropped the perfectly good energy pistol from shaking hands, raising them into the air.

"*Kill him*." Knoskali's voice resounded in his head.

He needed no further provocation; he drove the dagger into the clerk's carotid artery with an inarticulate shriek of pent aggression and rage, and then jerked it free. The clerk fell to his knees in shock, one paw clutching at his neck as the other blindly groped for his discarded energy pistol; Theta leg-wrestled him over onto his back and brought the dagger back down, and then again, stabbing repeatedly. The helpless, terrified look on the clerk's face burned into his mind as hacked and tore and stabbed until the feline was long dead and the dagger's blade broken off in his ruined trachea.

Blood spattered Theta's chest and face, and the deck, and the carpeting, and the front of the clerk's cute little shipsuit. He tasted it, he smelt it, and it soaked wetly into his fur.

He shook with fury.

"THAT is PERSONAL," Theta shrieked, standing to deliver a kick to the slack face of the corpse beneath him. His voice dropped to a purr. "It is, isn't it? Oh, there's nothing more personal than killing, is there?"

He reached to pick up the energy pistol, intending nothing more than to empty it into the corpses until they were slag.

"Enough, enough...Theta, stop! Someone will hear us!" Arvinne's voice was hoarse and scared.

"They must pay. I must kill them. Not personal. I'll show them just how not personal death can be," the fox frothed, tears of shame, rage and terror blurring his eyes.

"*Enough*," Knoskali's voice was gentle, persuasive. The other's voice was rambling on in the back of his head, mere background noise, a captive audience to the bloodbath before him.

Sobbing in an incoherent rage, Theta dropped to his knees, clutching the energy pistol against his chest and staring blankly at the carnage.

"Theta," Arvinne shook his shoulders urgently. "Theta, they're dead. They're already dead."

Theta's eyes widened, and he sprang to his feet—the guard Arvinne had beaten was twitching.

"Not dead enough," he hissed, flipping the safety catch off. He moved to each, firing two shots into each pirate's head.

Arvinne staggered to the corner and vomited.

"Dia's breath," Arvinne moaned, wiping his lips. "What have we done?"

"What have *you* done, is what you should be asking. You were going to go home safe and sound, Arvinne...you probably just traded your life to slightly prolong the life of an already dead ex-slave."

Arvinne shook his head, a little dazedly. "I couldn't just watch you executed. I might've lived longer, and all, but I would have been haunted by that for the rest of my days."

Rapidly approaching booted footsteps from the corridor outside brought the discussion to a quick halt. Theta pointed his energy pistol at the door, taking cover behind the clerk's body. Arvinne tapped the lights to low and picked up a rifle, but barely had it pointed in the right direction when the door opened once more.

The tall white wolf that had led the search of Theta's quarters stepped quickly inside.

"Stop—" he started, then froze so quickly that he nearly fell on top of the body of the second guard.

"Hands out. Stretch them out. Away from your body," Theta snarled.

Arvinne held him at gunpoint as Theta stepped up and relieved him of his weapons.

"Well, I see that *you* stopped them from killing you all by yourself," he murmured in a strange tone of voice, eyes glinting. "And with that stupid eating dagger, no less, from the looks of things. Well done." He snorted, looking down at the form he'd nearly stumbled over. "Poor dumb Molin."

"Why are you here?" Arvinne asked softly.

"Because we took over your ship." The pirate grinned rakishly, playing cool. "I thought you'd remember that. Would this have been my fate, fox, had my boys not had my back?"

"It still may be," Theta said somberly, fighting back the other's voice. It was, distractingly, going on about something unrelated, which further shortened Theta's temper. "What do we do now?"

"Well, that's a very good question." The pirate studied the pair, slowly kneeling down to their level. "I can make part of this go away. If you'll let me go, I'll make you only a slightly worse deal than I came down here to offer. Neither of you can go free, at this point. Bad PR, and bad for business. But if you'll agree to be...prisoners...we can spare your lives. That's the best deal I can give you."

"Why are you here?" Theta asked.

"As I just told your friend, here—"

"That's not the answer I'm looking for. What's your name?"

"Janesson." The pirate seemed nonplussed by Theta's directness; his voice wasn't quite as steady as before.

"Janesson," Theta repeated. "I know you're not here to do a general hit and run."

I do?

Janesson's ears perked ever-so-slightly higher.

"Why have you taken this ship? Do not lie to me, or I will shoot you and take my chances."

The pirate regarded at Theta for a long moment, then nodded slowly, eyes narrow. "I—we got a message from an ally that the head of one of Brynton's biggest houses was shipping 'something very special' on this run. We didn't know what it was, but the information that we have suggests that it's extremely valuable."

"But you never found it, and now you're cutting your losses. Ok," Theta nodded. Much more made sense. "Will the ship and crew be released?"

The wolf hesitated.

"Do NOT lie to me," Theta snarled through his teeth, ears flat. The other was now having a dialog with Knoskali in undertones which he couldn't quite make out. He was certain that they were talking about him, and his general level of anxiety was increasing sharply. His teeth were bared, shoulders rising and falling as his breathing rate increased.

Janesson, not privy to what was going on inside Theta's head, shrank a little, eyes widening, and raised his paws higher.

"I wasn't going to. I'm just worried about your reaction. The shipping line only paid ransom for its employees and basis rate...Ah, that means that they paid based on their maximum average occupancy...and the captain overloaded for this run." He spoke quickly, trying to rush by. "So basis rate means that a third of the passengers need to be either taken as sl-prisoners or executed. We don't have the space to take everyone, so we picked out the most...ah, able."

Theta blinked.

"*It's a good strategy,*" Knoskali whispered. "*Keeps costs down, recoups losses, and keeps people from failing to respect their demands.*"

"I figured that," Theta muttered; he wasn't entirely sure whether he was responding to Janesson or Knoskali. "So, are your pr-slaves sold at commercial auction?"

The pirate squirmed.

"I'll take that as a yes."

"Look," Janesson said, "When I saw that you'd been picked, I came to try to save your life...for no good reason." He seemed a little desperate. "I had an offer for you...it's not a great one, but it's what I've got. But if you don't take it you'd better be prepared to take this ship away from us, yourselves."

"Slavery?" Arvinne asked.

Janesson ground his teeth. "Look, it's the best I've got. I couldn't let you both go before, and I can't let either of you go now. I'm pretty sure I can make the slave thing work, but that's about as much as I can do."

Theta looked to Arvinne. Arvinne shrugged, holding a steady bead on Janesson.

"Arvinne, I need more than that. I can't agree for you."

"Can't say's I particularly want to be a slave, Theta. Now I know you—"

"NO," Theta growled. "—I don't. This is different."
Isn't it?

Silence prevailed. Even Theta's voices had nothing to add.
Great...just when I could actually use their advice.

He could easily have offered much more if he had no intent of giving it. Then again, he might have thought that too obvious. Then again, should I of all people be trying to make character judgements?

I wish Arvinne would decide.

"Ok, let me help you a little here with this process," Janesson's ears began to flatten a little, and he glanced over his shoulder. "Every section is under local lockdown. All hatches are closed, and there is no way to get anywhere other than the immediate corridor outside of this room. There is a finite and shrinking amount of time until my watch officer notices that there a bunch of unmoving tags and sends a squad to find out why. If they come in on this scene, they'll just blow the hell out of everything. So your choices are basically 'live' or 'die'. If you live, there's a good chance you'll end up free again at some point."

"Is there anyone who would pay your ransom with our freedom?" Arvinne asked.

The pirate shook his head and chuckled.

"Trying to beat me at my own game? It's possible, of course. You could try it."

"*That's the least likely deal to be honored*," Knoskali's voice was subtle. Hinting.

"No, I think not. But what about employment?" Theta slid the question in gently.

Janesson looked taken aback. "What? Employment?"

"Surely you need cooks. Arvinne is exceptional. I won't negotiate for my freedom, and I ask no concession, but he was just trying to protect me. All this blood is on my paws, not his. I know why you can't let him go free, but you can take me as your prisoner and give him a job."

"What would make you think I was empowered to offer such a thing?" Janesson's scowl deepened.

Theta beamed at him. "Well, it's obvious. Since when was a captain of any ship not empowered to hire?"

"Captain? What makes you think that I'm the captain?" Janesson lifted his chin minutely.

Arvinne was looking at Theta sidelong.

"You are."

"And if I am?"

"I understand why you can't just let us go. I understand why, but this is my proposal. Hire Arvinne, don't enslave him. You may take me as a slave and dispose of me at your discretion. Those are my final terms. Alternatively, I kill you and then as many of your men as I can when they come in here after you."

The wolf smirked. "Done...My word on it, if he accepts."

Arvinne shook his head, ears splayed.

"This doesn't seem right..."

"Take it, dammit," Theta muttered.

"Alright, sure," Arvinne muttered.

"Very well." Janesson straightened cautiously, lowering his paws. He grinned wanly. "So...if we're truly settled, would you please stop pointing guns at me?"

Theta lowered his aim, then stood, placing his weapon on the ground and sliding it towards Arvinne, who seemed confused by the action. He appeared baffled all the more when Theta knelt before him.

"I believe," the wolf murmured, "that he just surrendered to you. Are you sure you're ok with this? Do you work for me? Are you going to trust me?"

Arvinne looked at Theta, then Janesson. After a moment, he arrived a decision and dropped his rifle. Janesson reached out with his foot, sliding them out of reach.

"Remember when I said if you drew a weapon on me again, I'd kill you?" Janesson loomed over the pair.

Theta froze.

Arvinne sucked in a quick little breath and hunkered down.

"...I lied." The wolf grinned. "Let's take this very slowly, shall we?"

IV

Recompense

JALE STARED AT HER THIN PAWS. Tall and lean, she was long in the torso and short in the limbs, as ferrets were wont to be. Little paws. Very restrained, she worked with words and well-ordered systems. Why, she hadn't even engaged in much physical activity in years! Certainly not the sort to be fighting pirates. Not the sort who even *could* fight pirates.

Not even to save her junior steward, or Theta, or the friendly young family of pronghorns in C-3, all of whom had been taken as slaves, nor the old jackal in D-12 who had been executed, nor any of the brave engineers who had lost their lives attempting to rig a system to jettison the pirate ship that had lamprey-docked to the ventral hull.

No, had she tried anything herself, she would have merely failed and died. For that matter, it was miraculous that so many had survived; the pirates had left alive most of those they had promised to kill, and taken less than fifteen as slaves.

And yet Jale was utterly crushed. She-who-had-no-children had come to realize that her staff had become her family; the loss of the youngest, though, had shattered them into a group of hurting, isolated individuals. Crew cohesion was nonexistent—four days back enroute to Ramesan, and Arvinne's loss loomed like a black hole that threatened to consume the entire department.

But people must be fed. While they had remained on emergency rations for the first day after the pirates left—no small feat in and of itself, as there were no fewer than six types of emergency ration pack, to match differing dietary requirements—the meal service had resumed on the second. Like a life form recovering from an attack, the ship tended to its wounds, and its systems slowly began to resume their normal function.

Struck by the analogy, Jale wondered if cells were saddened by the loss of their compatriots. She smiled briefly, but amusement waned more quickly than it had arisen; her smile looked ugly in the wash station mirror, contrasting badly with her thoughts.

Earlier in the ship's day, she had visited the captain with a simple offer. She had requested, as department head, to assume the captain's traditional duty of informing Arvinne's family. When her offer was rejected, she'd flat-out insisted, refusing to leave until the ashen-faced Erin had finally given in. She had also, very cautiously, requested the captain allow her to contact Theta's benefactor, and received a small nod.

Jale turned away from her image, wiping moisture from her eyes. The captain was annihilated. She refused to come out of her quarters, and had turned command over to the first mate while she prepared pages upon pages of reports. The pirates had known exactly what they were doing—Captain Erin had been detained in her quarters through the entire raid, and allowed no outside contact. Indeed, they had expertly fragmented the command of the ship and ensured that any one of the crew knew only the very specific details they required. The captain, once the pirates had left and she'd been briefed, had taken the news very badly; as a captain should, she felt responsible for all under her watch.

For Erin, the event would almost certainly spell the end of her career, as well.

For her part, Jale wasn't sure that she wanted to remain, even if she was kept on. Arvinne's grinning face found her often in her quieter moments, and she'd taken to running to private places to cry after offering thin little excuses. She wasn't sure what to do, but she hoped that contacting Arvinne's parents and Theta's people would be at least some small expiation, and free her to consider her future.

She stepped into the shower, allowing the hot water to wash through her fur and take her away, at least momentarily, from her dark reflections.

When they dropped out of Rellin drive near the border of Ramesan's control zone, days overdue, a tender and five patrol vessels were there to meet them. A team of inspectors came aboard to do forensics and interview everyone even before the ship arrived in port; after, *Freeta* was quarantined for several days, with all aboard, to allow time to complete the investigations. When the initial reports had been written and cross-checked and all parties questioned, and everyone figured they would finally be allowed to go downside, the counselors showed up in a small army.

It took three more days for Jale to finally be allowed off the ship.

The company had assigned her a domicile downside while they investigated the case, and so for the first time in many years she found herself in one of the Ramesan transport pods on the way to a bed firmly anchored to the ground by real gravity.

Jale had always felt a bit agoraphobic when outdoors, and the bright light of day had always hurt her eyes; typically she wore dark goggles and set the transport pod to full blackout when on the surface—a habit that marked her immediately and irrevocably as a spacer to all who met her. This time, however, she left the pod transparent, almost defiantly—though she still couldn't manage without the goggles despite the dark grey summer sky.

Catti City splayed across a wide grassy plateau, draping itself over the network of rivers running through it and spreading for many miles, keeping itself low to the ground; the highest structure was the spaceport admin office, an arching, sculpted shape with a modest eighteen floors above a wide, spreading campus.

She leaned back in her padded seat as the transport pod slipped from under the outstretched arms of the building, down into the transport corridors and away from the busy offices, quickly picking up speed. Exhausted, 'counseled' into oblivion, and thoroughly warned against disclosing any details that weren't public, Jale simply wanted rest. She watched the world go by until the autonomous pod vanished into an underground tube.

With an airy sigh, she turned her attention to the pod's console, pulling it close and logging herself in. Several messages awaited her attention, but she passed them by to jump into her personnel records and look up Arvinne's family. It didn't take very long to find their home in the coastal grasslands on the outskirts of the province; she sent them a quick note requesting to meet. When she looked up, she found herself emerging into daylight once more; she was quickly ensorcelled by a view of the outside world flashing by as the pod sped across a long, high bridge.

She'd forgotten how little justice pictures did to the world downside.

Perhaps this time she'd stay a while.

Eventually, the pod shot back down into a long tunnel, and the view became simple corridors slipping by her windows at very high speed.

Peering at the trip indicator, she found that she had a quarter hour left before she'd arrive at her domicile, so she decided to pull up Theta's information as well.

The amount of data regarding the broken fox was surprisingly small. The captain had granted her access to the entire collection, but in the end, even the origin wasn't listed. The only thing she was able to find, aside from the care and feeding instructions, a few personal notes, and a dire warning not to fail, was the destination contact.

She pondered for a while, then searched up the contact and sent a communications request to the residence. Moments later, a sleepy-looking red fox answered, framed by a rather ornate glass window looking out across a river. He appeared to still be in bed.

"This is Carson. Orri is still asleep, if you're looking for her."

"Oh no, it's you I'm after, dear. I had a matter of some importance I was contacting you about. Do you know a Theta from Brynton?"

"Theta?" The fox frowned, reaching up to wipe the sleep from his eyes. "No, I don't think so. I only lived on Brynton briefly," his voice dropped, hints of bitterness creeping in, "but it's something I'd rather forget. I left nothing and nobody."

Jale paused, momentarily unsure how to continue. She tried a different tack.

"Sorry, let me start all over again. My name is Jale Bercammon, and I'm the chief steward of the OCS *Freeta*. On Brynton, we were given a passenger with instructions to deliver him to you; he's a white fox, purple hair—"

"Myshel," Carson whispered. His eyes had widened, and his face had become very slack. All hints of politesse were abruptly gone from his manner.

"So you do know this fox. Myshel?"

"Yes! No," he muttered, then leaned forward. "I don't want to have this conversation. I cannot have this conversation. Never, ever call me again," he hissed in an urgent undertone, ears flat in what appeared to her to be either rage or panic. He glanced back over his shoulder, bared his teeth, then cut the comm.

Jale sat back in surprise.

"My goodness."

Moments later, a message arrived on her console. It was simple.

> *That part of my life is over. Stay away, keep him away from me, and tell him never to call or show up.*
> *Ever.*
> *And that I'm sorry.*
> *Carson*

"My goodness," Jale said once more.

A while later, the transport pod zipped up out of the transit conduit into a little above-ground tube, slowing quickly as it entered an area dedicated to living space. Little, low dwellings nestled almost randomly in the shade of low, thick trees; people moved about on the grass, some lounging and sitting, others playing, still a precious few others moving as if in a hurry to get somewhere. After a moment of deceleration, the pod slowed to a stop at a marked spot in the tube and the ferret stood, stepping out onto grass. Grass! She hadn't felt grass beneath her feet for many years, nor, truth be told, had she wanted to. Now, however, it was an almost welcome softness beneath her bare paws.

The air smelled like grass, and leaves; it rustled her whiskers and brushed through her fur. Air on a spaceship generally didn't move, and smelled like nothing, and generally when it moved or didn't smell like nothing, it was cause for alarm. Jale didn't feel at all alarmed, and took a few minutes to simply stand by the personnel pod, savoring all those little planetary somethings that she'd been so happy to leave, a lifetime before. After a bit, she smiled softly to herself, then pulled out her portable datapad to read its simple directions to her abode.

Less than a quarter of a kilometer of walking on warm grass found her at her assigned domicile. It was a rather nice little house, if modest. Low and squat, hemispherical in shape, it looked able enough for the volatile weather conditions that defined Catti province. Its windows were wide, to capture the province's famous zephyrs, with broad, extended gables at the four corners to allow them to remain open in the rain, and screened with metal screen. The little building was shingled in simple organic wood, from the top down to the ground, and deciduous trees grew around it on all sides.

"Fancy fancy," Jale murmured, shaking her head. It seemed such a waste.

Her embedded ID chip unlocked the outer door when waved across the reader, and she went inside. The ferret tossed her bags on the floor of the single-room dwelling, kicking the door shut behind and turning back to look around.

Immediately, tired eyes found the big bag-bed beneath the window directly across from her. She'd often had trouble sleeping downside, and her usual instinct was to shut all the windows and shutter them tight to keep the world out. This time, she was unsure. The 'rightness' that she'd always felt about living aboard no longer felt so right, nor the 'wrongness' of downside so wrong.

Indeed, Jale's nicely-ordered worldview was in turmoil. She kicked off her trousers, and settled onto the expansive, softness-filled bag; after wriggling down until it shaped around her like a giant platelet, she tugged the covers atop and sighed, staring at the ceiling, thoughts returning to her lost junior steward.

Arvinne was a very kind-hearted sort; he didn't deserve a life of slavery. What could possibly have made the pirates decide to take him? He was supposed to be protected as a member of the crew!

What ever would she tell his family?

Hundreds of faces had looked to her for help as the pirates had raided their cabins. Many colleagues had lost their lives. Thirteen passengers had been taken as slaves.

But why *him*?

It simply didn't make sense to her. The more she thought about it the less sense it made; after a while, when exhaustion had pushed her to the point where she could no longer keep her thoughts from drifting, she abandoned analysis and gave herself up to slumber.

Eleven hours later, when Jale woke from a surprisingly deep sleep, the sun was down. Local time showed two hours to dawn.

Jale rose and shambled to the food preparation station, where she made herself a cup of tea. The night air through the windows was crisp and chill, and she pulled the blanket more tightly around her as she shuffled over to her terminal.

Nothing new awaited her, but she was quite awake.

She spent a few hours reading newsnet reports about the attack, but it didn't really hold her interest. She hadn't been quoted, and the newsnets always got things wrong anyway. Besides, she'd been there. Apparently it was big news, though.

She wandered around briefly, poking into cupboards and drawers to see what was there. After thoroughly exploring the place, she unpacked her few belongings and flopped back into a big comfy chair near the center of the domicile with her datapad. Without a schedule, she felt rather helpless; in any event, she had nothing whatsoever to do until Arvinne's family responded to her.

There was nothing more she could do for poor Theta, either. All her little queries to find anyone else to notify had turned up nothing. It was as if Theta came into existence when he stepped on board the transport, and ceased to exist as soon as the pirates removed him. It almost seemed worse for the poor fox, she thought, that nobody knew or cared about his plight. At least Arvinne had family and friends, and the company. They would always try to find him, but Theta? To her it felt as though the company was quietly happy to be free of the liability he'd represented.

Thoughts of his brave defiance before the pirates' leader almost brought her a new round of weeping. She had been certain that he would be killed by the big pirate in grey...but then they had listed him on their attestation as a slave.

She was lost in her own reflections for some time, reading through the last entries in her little daily diary on her datapad. After a while, she set it to the side with her second empty teacup and stretched her arms.

"It's good to see you well, Miss Bercammon."

She gasped and looked up, standing so quickly that she knocked over her chair. Leaned comfortably against the wall before her were two...thugs. Burly and imposing—but sharply dressed—they loomed silently against the doorframe. Before them stood a slim, sharp-looking mottled coyote in a military uniform. She didn't recognize the military.

"How did—nevermind." She shuddered. How long had they been there? She was disturbed.

"Mind if I have a cup of tea?" The coyote removed his hat and held it to his chest.

"Be my guest," Jale sighed. This was already much like dealing with the pirates again.

The coyote took his time in preparing two cups of tea, passing one to Jale and retaining one for himself. As he seemed content to just stand and stare out at the morning, sipping his tea, Jale opted to start the dialog.

"What...can I do for you?"

The coyote took a small sip from his mug, savoring it for a moment. "You were, I believe, in charge of some property that was to be delivered here." He looked down at his claws, then dusted them on his tunic and looked up, squarely in her eyes. "He did not make it."

"Theta?" Jale's eyes widened slightly. She hadn't found the pirates particularly intimidating, but this coyote had a very sharp look. "I tried to contact his destination contact, you know, but..."

"Yes. Carson is...out of the picture at this point. I work for a...very interested party. What happened, Miss Bercammon?"

"First," she drew herself up, "I'd have your name so as to know with whom I'm speaking."

The thugs shifted slightly, but the coyote merely nodded, an amiable expression warming his countenance.

"A fair request. My name is Gnosi, and I work for a certain interest who I will not name at this time."

Jale thought that sounded rather ominous, but pressed on.

"One more question...what is your interest in the child Theta?"

Gnosi set his hat on the counter and leaned back a bit; his goons took the hint and relaxed.

"Not exactly a child, even if a young adult in age. Theta is...very dear to my master, who was trying to get him to safety." He paused, as if considering his statements carefully. "My master hasn't quite decided where 'home' or 'safety' is for Theta; in this case, he guessed here... Apparently a mistake, from one who makes few. Now, Miss Bercammon...if you please?"

"Call me Jale." She shuddered slightly, having heard her last name much too often of late. Last names and the archaic honorifics that went with them were practically anachronistic in modern Ramesi society, and while she ofttimes appreciated the distinction it lent her, it was usually rather awkward.

"As for Theta...or is it Myshel...?" She caught a flicker of interest, a quick hard stare, from the coyote. She paused.

"Oh rash it," she sighed. "You can hardly do any worse to him now. "

Jale settled back into her now-righted chair, propping her elbow on its arm and resting her head on it. Leaving out no detail, she told the entire story, from *Freeta's* arrival on Brynton to being counseled mercilessly by mental-health staff. ("And thanks to this," she'd snorted, "I'll probably need even more.") As her story went on, Gnosi began to look more and more anxious, though he didn't interrupt.

When she had finished at last, the coyote looked as if he'd just swallowed a particularly awful-tasting bug.

"Jale, do you swear that your story is true and accurate?"

Jale frowned. "I do not lie."

Gnosi's ears flipped back, and he looked genuinely distressed; his cool composure had begun to flake a bit.

"These pirates...did they have any symbols or identifying marks?"

"None that I saw. Some few had patterns in their fur, but they all were different."

"But they split everyone off and kept them isolated, you say? And their leader was a large white wolf with some sort of facial scars." He made notes on his datapad. "Weaponry and armor were assorted, and they lamprey-docked. That's...at least something."

He tapped another button and slid his datapad back into its holster.

"Jale, I'm afraid I have a request-that's-not-a-request."

Jale stood slowly. "And what is the nature of your... non-request?"

"You must come with us. We're heading to visit Arvinne's family."

"What?" She was a bit blindsided; that wasn't quite what she had been expecting to hear. "Why?"

"Because you must come with us back to Brynton, and we'd like to allow you to discharge your duty first."

Jale leaned weakly on her chair. "To Brynton? But I... my job..."

"They'll see it our way. Don't worry about such trivial things."

Jale's struggled to think of any excuse to use, anything to say, but she could come up with little.

She did not want to go anywhere right now.

She especially did not want to go to Brynton, to presumably face house justice from the head of house of he-whose-Theta-she'd-lost.

Personally responsible, indeed.

"As I said, Jale— It's not a request. Arvinne's father and brother should be returning shortly from their fishing, and if we leave now, we won't have to interrupt them long from their work."

She allowed herself to be led outside, leaving her tea untouched; a large, sleek black ship lurked silently, looming across the front of the house, its landing pylons digging in to the soft earth. She was amazed that she hadn't heard its arrival. Gnosi politely assisted her up through the under-nose hatch and settled her with respect but authority into the cockpit jumpseat behind the pilot, who had remained on board. The coyote settled himself into the right seat, and immediately the pilot began a nearly silent vertical lift.

Amazing.

Expensive.

It took them only minutes to cross the grasslands and reach Arvinne's family's house, much less than the hour and a half it would have taken her by high-speed pod. They flew over the modest fishing hut with engines making significant power to announce their presence. As they circled to find a landing spot, two tall snow leopards moved out into the open and gestured them to a small, firm field. Jale's heart beat frantically, looking down on them. This was almost the most terrifying thing she'd ever done; she had a terrible desire to just beg the pilot to turn around and go home, but she held herself together.

At the bottom of the hatch, she paused for a moment to catch her breath as the two half-ran towards her. The family resemblance was unmistakable.

The younger reached them first, doffing his cap.

"Gooday, mum. How's can be of help, mmn?" The feline's lowland Catti brogue was much thicker than she'd ever heard Arvinne's, but his vocal timbre was similar enough to make Jale's throat close. He looked friendly, if slightly wary, and quite different from his brother. The father jogged up a second later, resting a paw on his shoulder and searching Jale's face.

"Arval and Rinnir?" They nodded in turn. Suddenly, the father turned half away and closed his eyes. Jale's breath caught, and she fought back tears.

"I'm afraid that I must come the bearer of terrible news." Her voice quavered, but she fought to keep it steady. "Arvinne has been captured by p—pirates, and he's been taken as a slave."

The young one's tail lashed once behind him and then fell still, and he reached up to push his long, shaggy black bangs from his face. Arvinne's father turned back to her, opening his eyes. "When we was hearing about the attack, we were knowing it was his ship, but thinking all was safe... and now here you showed up...but...you're saying he's alive?"

"Yes, sir, last we left him."

"Alive, though, as yet," he breathed. "That at least be something, by Dia. Is there...I mean, I know the way it falls, truly, and I do know a thing or two about how these sorts work, but isn't there anything as we can do?"

"No, sir," Gnosi cut in smoothly, as if he were there in official capacity. "We're putting all our resources into tracking down these pirates, and if we can find and free your son, we will."

Jale sucked in a little breath, wiping her eyes. For all she knew, that was true. Gnosi had been furiously dispatching messages during the entire flight.

Arval turned to his father and buried his face against his chest. His father rested an arm about him, slightly awkwardly.

Rinnir had a few questions, mostly about how his son was faring before the attack, and whether he'd been doing his job well; Arval just wept gently. After a few minutes they mutually ran out of things to say, and stood in silence for a few minutes more.

"Rinnir, I am at your service, should you find that you have any questions or concerns, dear."

"Please...try as like to bring him back alive. He's a dear lad," the older feline said, looking away once more.

Jale nodded, eyes moist.

Nothing in the universe could travel faster than a ship. Of all the various civilizations hanging in the void of the known universe, none had figured out how to make radio signals traverse distances more quickly than the stately speed of light. As the value of information is often inversely proportional to the time it takes to get it, very fast courier ships with massive Rellin drives and minimal payload had been conceived and built to meet economic demands, and now plied known space on scheduled—and unscheduled—runs.

They were built simply to ferry information and occasionally very valuable people.

Jale, not being very valuable, had never ridden in one, never thought she'd ever ride in one, and was shocked to find herself being loaded into one less than an hour after they'd left Arvinne's family homestead. They'd powered out over the ocean in the little black stealth vessel, then pulled into a near-vertical climb to break orbit and make rendezvous. Gnosi's thugs and pilot had returned to the surface with the ship, and the courier ship was outbound less than an hour thereafter.

Jale found the interior of the ship rather spartan, for a long-distance vessel. There were four little individual quarters and a communal head, plus a small corridor that led toward the aft end of the extremely long ship, presumably for maintenance access. While on in-system drive, Gnosi and Jale sat behind the cockpit, buckled into two bench seats with a table between. The ride out of the control zone had been surprisingly rough in the overpowered, underdamped ship.

"Me oh my," Jale chuckled wanly, as the ship began accelerating to enter Rellin drive. "Ladies and gentlemen, welcome to your Brynton gateway. Our normal time enroute is slightly less than twenty days. Your stewards will tend to all your needs; dispatch a message to the Steward's department if you have any special requests or dietary requirements." She intoned. "Back to work again. Would anyone like their meal prepared?"

Gnosi laughed a genuine little laugh. "Back to work again, indeed," he chuckled. "Now me, I'm always working. My job is my life, life's my job, and such. I'll have the steak and potatoes, if you please."

"Never had a steward before," one of the pilots called back, with a grin. A 'proper weasel', as her mother had always called them, he made an odd pair with his fellow pilot, a trim deer who seemed to presently be doing the actual flying.

Are all pilots small? Jale wondered, struck by the realization that she'd never seen a tall one.

The weasel turned back to his panel for a moment, then swung his chair around to face them, flipping his visor up and unbuckling his chinstrap. "Us, we'll eat later, though. Grabbed grub just 'fore we left. Ah, I forgot to brief you when you boarded, but your quarters are #2, port side. Head's back there, with the sign over," he pointed at each. "Galley's aft through that curtain, but it's not quite as nice as what you passenger liner types have on that big ol' L820. I think you'll find that we're a bit faster, though. You do it in twenty two days, we do it in six."

Jale nodded, wrestling down the knot of anxiety that had been living in her stomach all morning. Life was a fluid, and she was just along for the ride. Gnosi and the crew had, so far, been very nice to her, despite the ominous overtones of the journey.

Perversely, her sense of adventure was up.

For the first time, it occurred to her that maybe her life had become a little too boring, these past few years.

"Steak and potatoes, hm?" Jale stood, and stretched, then went aft and stuck her head back into the galley. She was shocked to find only color-coded pallets of insta-meals and a reconstitution unit. One box was labeled 'steak and potatoes', and she shook her head with a little musteline grin.

Maybe chaos had its points.

V

Anhedral

JALE'S SENSE OF ADVENTURE lasted right up to the last day of the journey back to Brynton, when she woke to overhear Gnosi quietly praying for fate to spare his life.

Shaken, she lay on her back in her little rack bed, trying to get a handle on her anxiety. After a while, she wrested herself from the grip of worry and slid to the floor, groping around until she found her slightly ripe clothes more by smell than by sight or feel. After pulling on her dingy brown trousers and top, she shambled the two meters between her quarters and the head, where she washed her face with trembling paws.

The little deer was waiting at the table with a plate of reconstituted food and a cheerful grin for her when she emerged.

"G'mornin, Steward! I made breakfast for," he nodded to it, far too happy for Jale's mood. "Seemed only fair. We should have you dirtside within the hour."

"Oh. Why thank you, Pilot Erra."

Jale sat and poked through the food. It would be terribly impolite not to eat, but she had trouble finding any appetite; even the smell made her nauseous. Gnosi, when he arrived, appeared to have a similar issue.

"It's been nice having the two of you aboard. Most of our unscheduled runs, we get a bunch of spoiled jerks," Erra said, seemingly oblivious to the dark mood his passengers shared. "Why are my quarters so small? Can I get bigger ones? Where's the bath? Why do I have to ride on this dumpy old barge?" He shook his head, grimacing. "Anyway...yeah. Thanks for being good company."

Gnosi laughed, though it seemed to Jale quite forced. "Your hospitality and services are appreciated, and you've a fine, fast ship. How much longer to the control zone?"

"Oh, we're really close. I'm going to head forward soon." Erra leaned back, peering up into the cockpit. He shuffled his plate forward with a little grimace, then stood. "In fact, looks like about five minutes out...I'd better get back to it."

Jale met Gnosi's gaze, and he leaned over to scoop his plate into hers. Discretely, she threw it away in the galley disposer and returned to her seat.

Shortly thereafter, they dropped back out of Rellin drive and things got bouncy once more. Courier ships had their own deceleration corridors, higher above the solar plane than the standard arrival corridors, and Jale was pressed into the seat as they rocketed towards the planet in a hard deceleration within. The comm equipment lit up the second they began to transition back into normal space, working at capacity to deliver all of the courier's accumulated messages to waiting relay stations.

"Well, welcome to Brynton," the weasel called back a few minutes later as they entered a standard pattern. "The universe's cesspool, I say. Looks like there's already a shuttle launching to pick you up, though."

Gnosi flinched.

The "shuttle" was the single most posh vessel Jale had ever been in. It was opulent. It was escorted by a wing of military craft in black and red, and it had a full contingent of -extremely- thorough security. Jale was manually scanned very carefully before she was even allowed to board; Gnosi mood deteriorating by the moment, was escorted into the back by a set of guards to be debriefed.

The only other occupant in the main cabin was the backup pilot, a gigantic black canid in flight gear sitting at attention in a jumpseat behind the main door.

So much for my theory about pilot size. He barely looks as if he'd fit into the cockpit.

Jale stretched out in the soft seat that seemed to mould to her back; like the situation, it threatened to suck her down and envelop her in its depths. She felt as though she were a tiny part in something so large that it would consume her and leave no trace.

She was afraid.

The backup pilot noticed her anxiety and grinned reassuringly to her.

"Shouldn't be more than a hour until we land, miss. You don't get space sick, do you?"

"Oh, no, dear," Jale was startled enough to laugh. "I've been in space most of my life."

"Oh," he said, seeming relieved. "Whew. You just seemed nervous."

"Well, I'm worried about what awaits me on the surface, not the trip down," she said quietly, surprising herself with her own candor.

The canid nodded, peering at her. "You mixed up in this Theta business?"

Jale dipped her head in reply. "I'm afraid so. I'm not entirely sure why I've been brought all the way back here, really, but at least I will be able to discharge my duty to notify his...ah..."

"Next of kin?" The pilot suggested, his velvety voice somber. "Is he dead?"

"Oh, dear, no," she breathed. "At least...I don't know. I certainly hope not."

The canid's green eyes glinted, and he leaned forward. "You know...it's not really my business, but I'm cleared to know...if you tell me what happened, I can probably tell you whether you should be afraid."

Jale hesitated. "Why...why do you want to know?"

The pilot leaned back and rested his paws behind his head. "I saw Theta once or twice...mostly it's just curiosity."

"Well," Jale said, "I suppose it wouldn't hurt to tell it once more."

And so she did.

When she got to the point about the airlock, she noticed that the pilot's paws were clutching the armrests of his jumpseat, though the rest of his demeanor came off as almost bored. When she mentioned that Theta spoke afterwards, however, the pilot lost most of his carefully cultivated composure.

"Talking? Theta was talking that soon?" While Gnosi had seemed distressed about that point, the canid appeared almost elated; in fact, when she reached the part about Theta confronting the pirate's leader, he removed his helmet and rested his big paws on it, grinning fit to split his head.

"That is exactly right...well done. What I would have given to see that," he laughed softly. "White wolf, silver armor, little scars on his face like he was pushed face-first into an overactive restraint net, right? Somewhere around my height?"

Jale bit her lip, feeling suddenly unsure. Perhaps she'd said too much; Gnosi had said to trust this crew and do what she was told, but she herself had no idea who they were. Even Gnosi, himself, was still mostly a mystery after a week on a tiny ship.

"I'm sorry, yes, I think so," she resumed, deciding to keep the rest brief. "Anyway, after that they took me around to all the rest of the cabins to verify the occupant manifest, then they locked me away in my quarters. After that, nothing interesting happened. On their attestation, it listed Arvinne and Theta as having been taken as slaves."

The pilot bared his perfect teeth in a predatory grin. "Ol' Jane has always had a soft spot for anyone who stood up to him. It'll be his death someday. "

Jale's fears solidified. "You know this pirate."

The aft hatch opened, and Gnosi strode through quickly. "Jale, I—" He sucked in his breath, splaying his toes and stopping instantly as he caught the pilot's little wave of greeting. His features went blank with what Jale registered as uncharacteristic fright.

"Hi, Nosy. Been a while," the large canid said cheerfully. He stood, then bent over to Jale, grinning conspiratorially. "Nosy and I go way back. Mind if we go talk shop?"

Mutely, Jale shook her head. Something was very wrong; she watched the two step into the back, thinking that Gnosi had the look of someone about to be spaced.

She lay back and closed her eyes. One day of freedom. She'd had one day of freedom on Ramesan; one day since she was sixteen. Now, she might not live beyond the next few hours.

If I survive, I'm going to take a year off, at least.

She didn't see the pilot or Gnosi again. The ride down was smooth and fast, and the landing gentle. Fifteen minutes after the shuttle had finally come to a stop, the main cabin hatch opened and a tall uncompromising looking... gentleman...of an albino skunk stepped through, clad in scarlet robes.

"Miss Jale Bercammon? You will please come with me," he murmured, accent rounded and smooth.

It took much of Jale's willpower to push herself out of the seat, but she did. It took even more to follow him down the ramp and out, finding herself in a large hangar with guards at every point. The skunk turned as he reached the bottom, taking exactly four precise steps back.

"Miss Jale Bercammon, I am the majordomo of House Selesz; on behalf of Lord Knoskali, I welcome you to both Brynton and his house."

"I, uh," Jale was certain there was a correct, formal response; what it was, she had no idea.

A smile brushed the lips of the majordomo. "I believe the phrase Miss Bercammon intends to use is, 'On behalf of myself, I accept your hospitality and bid you convey my arrival to your master.'"

"Dear me...Yes, I suppose that would seem about right," Jale was slightly flustered. This was not all what she'd been expecting. Then again, she wasn't entirely sure what she had been expecting.

"Normally I would offer you a tour of the grounds. At this time, however, we have just...mm, completed a war on an opposing house, and it is not yet considered safe. You will be escorted to suitable quarters while I report your arrival."

The majordomo made a small sweeping gesture with his paw, and two young huskies stepped forward; they looked like bookends, both wearing close-fitted light blue robes and black steel collars around their necks.

Slaves.

Jale barely kept herself from flinching back.

"You have no luggage, Miss?" one asked, looking up at her with bright eyes. He had a spot of pink on his nose that vaguely resembled a heart.

"I, no. I left in a hurry."

"Very well. Right this way, Miss," the other gestured.

Numbly, she followed along. This was the world Theta had lived in? Jale felt markedly less sympathetic for his plight by the minute. Son of a scion, perhaps? Sent away in disgrace after a prank had started a feud, an addled and broken aristocrat?

That didn't really feel right.

She decided to reserve judgement.

The huskies escorted her through a long hallway from the hangar, deep into a building built both from native stone and the most expensive alloys. Every door was tremendous; the main door, which she was told by one of the grinning slaves was actually the back door, had a smaller entrance inset, through which they passed. It was mostly for effect, she figured, but the effect was still somewhat awe-inspiring.

Form follows function follows form.

Jale had never thought that people would live like this. Even the lighting was stunning; the ceiling was aglow with semi-symmetrical moving prismatic arcs that lent a warm glow to the air but resulted in the feel of a natural, early dusk.

She was led into a transparent lift, which overlooked a great forest/garden at the center of what appeared to be a building of absurd scale. The floor and walls of the lift, though firm, were nearly transparent, as were its mechanisms; Jale peered, then tapped with her foot, unable to restrain her curiosity. It felt soft to the touch.

"You're actually standing on a cloud," one of the huskies confided with a little grin. "This entire lift is held together by fields. If the building lost power, we'd all fall right through the floor. It's made up of...of..."

"He'll never remember," the other quipped. "It's made up of polarized, reinforced water vapor."

Jale wasn't sure whether to take him seriously, but she edged closer to the door anyway. Fortunately, after rapidly ascending almost forty stories, the lift arrived safely at its destination without dissolving.

The pair led her to a door at the end of a wide hall, then through.

"Your room, ma'am."

Jale froze, aghast.

"This...this is where I'm staying?"

"Yes, Miss Bercammon." The pink-nosed husky frowned, brow creasing in worry. "It is not to your liking?"

"This is ridiculous," Jale muttered.

She stared across the open room. It was, by her account, one of the largest single rooms she'd ever seen. It was built into three levels, with a massive kitchen at the top, a den and eating area below, and an entertainment level that wrapped around. One side had a pool with water running into it from the wall; steam rose vigorously. There were five tiers, each a different color than the last, and each progressively cooler, judging by the rising steam. The bottom tier had ice floating in it. From that last pool, the water ran as a little creek encircling the room before vanishing out of sight around the corner, where the living space appeared to continue.

The room itself was built on a mezzanine, a little corner tier on the side of a great fortress high above Fenna City. The persistent lower cloud layer, an atmospheric phenomena Jale recalled as being specific to Brynton's northern continent, hung like a field of toxic mist just below the lip of the ledge, a thousand feet below the solid overcast above. She had an incredible view of the colors and textures outside the building, for the walls and the ceiling were composed of the same material as the lift, almost completely transparent. A polychromatic web of light, similar to the lighting in the entranceway, ran across the ceiling to illuminate every corner differently.

"I'm very sorry," the slave to her left seemed surprised and a bit down. He looked at his bare paws. "We...we thought you'd like it, but I just remembered that you were... are...you're a spacer." He dipped his muzzle and bowed, eyes downcast. "Would you prefer an interior room?"

"Oh, no no, no, dear...You misunderstand. It's beautiful. Beautiful but ridiculous."

She looked around, in awe of the opulence. The OCS *Freeta*, an Alaran-designed L820 MkIV proudly dubbed 'pride of the luxury liners', had maintained an elegant ballroom, a formal dining room, and had several fancy staterooms at bill rates that made Jale's head spin. This… was extravagance so far removed from that as to be almost of a different reality.

There was a long pause; the slaves fidgeted slightly, looked at each other, and then back at Jale.

"Ah, the majordomo suggested that you might be hungry after your long trip," the one without the splotch began cautiously. "And…if you're weary from your travels, or wish a bath or shower, you should find that the sleeping area around the corner has all the amenities you could wish."

"Why thank you. Ah," she paused. The silence continued; they were still looking at her expectantly.

It seemed illogical that they'd be waiting for a tip.

She sighed.

"Is there anything I can do for you?"

The pair glanced at one other again, baffled and slightly concerned.

"Look, see," Jale rubbed her neck and staring down at the slightly shorter-than-her canids, "I've never been here before, dearies, and you seem to be waiting on me, oh yes, so…I apologize if I'm being rude, but is there something that you need?"

Pink-nose blinked in honest surprise. "Oh! Well, I'm sorry Miss—"

"Jale, please, just Jale."

He winced at the correction, tucking his tail slightly and lowering his gaze.

"Miss Jale…I'm sorry. I—we didn't realize. Normally, I would be unpacking your luggage, and he would be starting dinner, but you don't have any luggage, and you haven't asked for dinner. I think you're the first outworlder we've been assigned to."

"You would make my dinner?"

"Uhhuh!" The other perked up. "Do you have any non-species-specific dietary requirements? Are you hungry?"

"I...well no, and...why, a bit, but...don't the two of you have other duties? It seems like a remarkable waste of your time."

Again they awarded her with slightly stupefied, almost hurt expressions.

"No, Miss Jale. I...do you find us wanting?"

Pink-nose perked his ears. "Wait. Miss Jale, we're assigned to you for the duration of your stay. Did you get that?"

Stupefied, herself, it took Jale a moment to reason that out. When she did, she took a half step back, reaching up to rub her neck.

When on Brynton...

"I suppose I do now," she sighed again softly. "I'm sorry if I caused offense. What are your names?"

The one with the pink splotch on his nose grinned to her, ears akimbo. "I'm Pinky; he's Jewel."

Jewel bowed.

"How...long am I going to be staying here?"

Again, the pair exchanged a look. Jewel turned back and shook his head. "We're not told that sort of thing. That's between you and Master."

"It's hard to guess, too, but I'd say at least a week," Pinky said, looking thoughtful. "Please, though...can we get dinner started? May I draw you a bath?"

Still Jale hesitated.

Slaves.

"Are you sure you wouldn't rather be off doing something else? I really don't need..." Jale found that she couldn't quite say the word 'slaves'. "I'm quite self sufficient."

"Please," Pinky whispered, leaning close. "We'll do anything you like, but please don't send us away. After...after last time, ah...well..." He flushed. "Anyway, you're our second chance. If you send us away, we'd be moved out of the hospitality section, and we like doing this. My br— Jewel is a great cook, but we wouldn't fare so well for other things."

Jale shuddered. She'd heard that slaves were sometimes even used as furniture on this planet; she could appreciate the desire to remain. Still, the thought of being waited on hand and foot rankled.

"You know, I'm a bit of a cook, myself," Jale murmured. "I'll be happy to let you cook dinner, as long as you let me help."

Jewel bowed his head. "Of course, ma'am; anything you wish."

Jewel, Jale discovered, did *not* need her help. When she insisted that he make food for all of them, not just her, his preparations increased in speed and content. Initially, she'd thought to step in and at least do the grunt work—as she sometimes did during a busy shift in the galley—but after a few moments she realized that she should merely step back and let an expert work. She watched him for some time, quite significantly impressed. He worked like a true master of the craft, but in her judgement he couldn't even be Arvinne's age! Eventually, seeing things too well in hand for her meddling, she wandered away from the food preparation area.

She caught a sly grin from Pinky as she descended to the lower tier.

"Does Miss Steward approve?" he inquired with a little grin.

"Does everyone know everything about me here?" Jale asked in slight annoyance; immediately she regretted her tone, as the husky looked crestfallen.

"Ah, no ma'am. At least, I don't know as to say, but we just had a basic briefing, and it included a few things like that."

"I'm sorry, Pinky dear. I think the stress is getting to me." She rubbed her temples. "I don't even know what I'm doing here. Gnosi had little to say, except that I was required to come back, and now, instead of being tortured for failing to keep his Theta or Myshel or whatever safe, I—what?"

Pinky's eyes had gone wide, and he'd slid up close.

"You knew Myshel? How? Keep him safe? I don't understand," he hissed, when she paused.

"He was sent off planet on my...my, oh my, I'm not sure I should be telling you this."

The husky's shoulders rose, and he blinked a few times, stepping back. "Oh, I'm...I'm very sorry for prying, Miss Jale. Please, please don't tell *him* that you told me." He looked almost desperate to ask more, but held himself back; they stared at each other for a while longer, each having information the other wanted, both terrified of sharing it inappropriately.

A chime rang.

Jale turned to find its source, but Pinky was already in motion to the door with a little restraining gesture her way. He stood in the vestibule to talk with the visitor; though Jale strained her ears, she couldn't make out the conversation. Moments later, he returned, placing a paw over his chest and performing a little bow, eyes closed.

"Miss Jale, Lord Knoskali bids you welcome, and invites you to relax and enjoy his hospitality. He has sent word that he will receive you tomorrow morning, for a light breakfast in his Lambda room." Pinky straightened, and looked up with a nervous twitch. "He says that you should, ah his words were 'spread out and make yourself at home', and expect to stay at least one standard week."

Jale pursed her lips, squinting as she considered this and tried to remember Brynton's rotation cycle. "What time is breakfast? Is a reply expected?"

"No ma'am. Ah, if you wish to adjust your schedule, your sleeping area should have a bottle of nightcaps, but breakfast will be in fourteen hours. We work on a standard day, so tomorrow will be a dark day."

Jale nodded. Long rotation cycle.

"I...you know, I haven't had a bath in years."

Pinky perked.

After cleaning herself thoroughly and soaking for a while in the warm water, Jale took a few minutes to catch up on her grooming. She stepped out of the sleeping area to a find the huskies putting the finishing touches on a decadent dinner service set for one. At her insistence, they joined her. She tried to draw them out of their tight-lipped servility, but had little luck—While they answered any question she asked them, she couldn't get them to expound on their history, or their lives before, except to tease out that they were brothers, and that they had only been slaves for about four years.

After the second course and the dessert had passed by with no real meaningful conversation, she opted to retire for the night; once the table was cleared, the slaves slipped off to their sleeping quarters through a barely discernible trapdoor in the wall, and Jale made her way back into her own.

Sitting on her bed, she reached for the bottle of two-hour nightcaps; for the first time in years, Jale measured herself out a nine-hour dose and swallowed the small capsules. Unsurprisingly, the caps provided were of a very high grade, and she nodded off almost immediately after sliding under the wide, thin blanket.

When she woke, it was dark outside, and a red glow rose from the clouds below. She rinsed the sleep from her face, and cast about for her clothes. The chair on which she'd lain them the night before had only a simple note to her attention stating that *appropriate* clothes were laid out upon the footlocker, and that the gold was recommended.

The clothes, she noted with slight amusement, fit her hard-to-fit form perfectly. They were fine. Very fine! She looked at herself in the mirror, surprised at how sharply she was arranged.

"Ma'am?"

She twisted around instantly, shocked, to find Pinky and Jewel standing before her, each holding a box. Their eyes widened and they shrank back.

But then, what's privacy to a personal slave? When on Brynton...

"Yes, dearies?"

They seemed nervous. Pinky stepped forward, lifted his box illustratively. "Your coiffure?"

Jale, quite amused, found herself guided to the wash room and expertly made up by Jewel, while her short brown hair was styled by Pinky. When they were done, she looked nothing like the drab, efficient Chief Steward that she knew herself as. She frowned as she regarded her image.

"Thank you, my friends," she murmured. "Now I suppose I can die pretty, at least."

The Lambda room had its own waiting area, a clean room of obsidian floor and walls, with a vaulted ivory ceiling. She and 'her' slaves had been led there by Knoskali's messenger, a doberman-type in an odd shiny outfit with a heavy robe over the top. He seated them and rapped twice on the door.

"Miss Jale Bercammon and her servants," he announced.

"Send them in!" replied a silky voice. Jale shivered...it sounded familiar, but she couldn't place it.

"This way."

They were led to the room; the slaves stopped at the door and knelt, looking down. Jale was escorted by the elbow towards a seat at a small, round table made of some black and blue marbled stone, inset with leather. The seat was pulled out for her, and she sank into the chair, looking up at Lord Knoskali, head of House Selesz.

He raised his head.

Jale gasped.

"Well good *morning*, Miss Bercammon," the black coyote who she'd met in the shuttle leaned forward, resting his paws on the table. Spread wide, they seemed to dominate its entire surface. This morning he wore not a flightsuit and helmet, but the heavy robes of the Brynti elite and an air of cool power.

"Perhaps all pilots are small, after all," she murmured obliquely. Knoskali raised an eyebrow, but Jale was left to wonder whether her meaning was taken.

He sat back, staring down at her with cool green eyes. "It is my sincerest hope that the hospitality of my house has not been diminished," he rumbled with a little scowl. "I trust you find your room and service adequate, and that you slept well?"

"I did," Jale murmured. "The service has been delightful."

Knoskali leaned forward dubiously, resting his elbows on the table, chin on his clasped paws. "Are you sure? There have been complaints about those two," he looked beyond her to Pinky and Jewel, who shivered in fear on the floor.

Jale felt for footing in the conversation. "Yes. I don't know what there could be to complain about. They've been amazing."

Knoskali's teeth showed in a little grin. "Indeed? Perhaps they've worked extra hard to please you. Perhaps the one who complained had no basis. Well," he grinned amiably. "Who's to say? And there you have it," he tapped the table. "The running theme of our little visit is second chances. Some are given, some are earned." He leaned back and sipped his beverage, his ears forward, as if inviting her to speak.

Jale sat stiffly in her seat.

What does he want from me?

The lord reclined silently in his chair, holding eye contact with Jale over the brim of his steaming mug.

Minutes passed.

"Well," Knoskali murmured, voice honey sweet, ultimately reasonable, "I just *know* we can arrive at some sort of arrangement, my dear. I think perhaps I should put this another way. Slavemaster," he raised his voice. "Breakfast."

There was motion in the corner; a door Jale hadn't noticed swung open and several slaves circled the table, laying out food, varied beverages, and utensils. When they were done, they swept away.

"Slave." Knoskali indicated one in particular, and the slave stopped and turned. "My dear Jale, does this slave look familiar to you?"

Jale nodded gravely. The slave in blue was Gnosi; the coyote seemed lost and out of sorts.

"Yes, he does," she said.

Yes, he does, you bastard.

"Doesn't he look lovely in his new uniform? I think it suits him well. This is my mercy, and his second chance," a hint of implacability swept feather-light through the coyote's otherwise warm tone. "He had one little job to do for me—to secure the transit channel and prevent anything from happening to your scheduled run and my precious cargo. Sadly," Knoskali said with a sigh, "he proved unable to accomplish this task, so I've found him another position within the organization that won't challenge his abilities. At least, it better not," the coyote's voice dropped flat, and he waved Gnosi off with a little scowl.

"Ok, so," he continued, voice dropping into very businesslike tones, "let's not belabor the point. My Mishy is very dear to me. The *Freeta* had one job, and that was to get him to his destination safely. That didn't happen. I'm holding you responsible, as I have it that you accepted his charge on your personal responsibility. Do you dispute that?

Jale's breathing had quickened, and her paws clenched at her sides.

"In the terms you put it," Jale said stiffly, voice clipped, "How could I?"

Knoskali grinned happily, as if she'd said something funny. "Well *put*, darling. Oh, and do let us eat before the food grows cold. I don't wish to wait forever for my breakfast, after all...and you *do* have a rather long day of work ahead of you."

Jale felt her heart skip a beat, and she froze.

The coyote, pretending ignorance of her discomfort, pulled out a black, jeweled eating dagger and gestured to the food.

"Eat. Drink. I insist. I can do that," he grinned his smooth grin.

Jale felt sick to her stomach, but she, too, began to slice small portions and ingest them. She swallowed more than chewed many of the pieces, eventually clearing her plate. The food was incredible. The beverages were incredible, fragrant and warm. All of it slid down like cardboard into the lump in her gut.

"There, that wasn't so bad now, was it? Now on to business," he tipped his glass to her, then took a small sip of the fragrant extract, swirling the rest around in his glass. "My Mishy...your Theta...was alive last you knew. That's good for you. Very good for you. That's good for OCS shipping, and pretty much everyone else on the *Freeta*. Speaking of which, you're officially retired from your company, at a first mate's full vested pension rate. Congratulations!"

Jale waited, staring at him levelly and keeping her mouth shut.

"Cool, they said. So it seems." The coyote twirled his eating dagger idly in a big paw. "Mishy is alive. I want him back. I—no," Knoskali's expression clouded slightly, and for the first time since Jale had met him, he seemed a little less than certain. "No, correction: I want him free," he said, and for the first time Jale believed his words. "My intent when I sent him off to Ramesan," the coyote sounded earnest, as if he'd suddenly switched off an act and wasn't playing any character but himself, "was to free him. I will see that done. I will not see my dancer as the slave of a pirate. Any pirate."

"Free?" Jale cleared her throat. "He was a slave?"

"He was my dancer, and my most special, most dear slave. This world was anathema to him, on my terms, and he could not exist within it any longer. He is also very special, though he doesn't know it and may not live to see his potential," Knoskali growled, driven and direct, totally different than the silver-tongued Brynti lord he'd been a moment before. "I made a mistake. I made several. This is my second chance," he said grimly. "And that's where you come in."

"So what does one Lord of house Selesz need of Jale Bercammon, chief steward?" Jale asked lightly, leaning forward.

"Retired chief steward," he murmured with a wry grin.

Jale just stared expectantly, refusing to meet his humor.

"Well, very well," Knoskali's voice swung back to sugar sweet. "Really, I need someone already responsible for Theta. I need someone I can trust with Theta's safety to find his captors and negotiate for his release as my proxy. Someone who needs a second chance," he frowned. "And if in the process you're able to help your junior steward as part of the bargain, you may consider that my thanks."

Jale steeled herself against the rush of excitement she felt. "What's the catch?"

"The catch is that it's not likely to be easy or simple. I have a ship being provisioned. You'll take Gnosi as your first officer, but you'll be in command. He's really pretty good at his job, but I'm having a bit of fun with him. Maybe not so much fun for him. So!" He grinned. "And if you fail, and Theta dies, my advice is just to keep flying outbound as fast as you can. You'll be caught and killed eventually, of course, but at least you'll prolong your life by some small amount."

Jale shuddered, baring her sharp little teeth in a grimace of distaste. "You play rough."

Knoskali stood, and she stood as well.

"My dear Jale," he smirked. "You have *absolutely* no idea. Pray that you never do." He let that hover in the air a moment. "At any rate, I have much work for you, assembling a crew and getting your little ship ready, but...let's just have that start tomorrow, shall we? Take the rest of today to relax and unwind! You seem a bit tense. We'll meet for refreshments after dinner this evening." He leaned forward, and the habitual smirk slipped away like an abandoned affectation. He dropped his voice so that only she could hear. "Another part of the reason I'm using you is that you will ensure Myshel is not brought back to me, no matter how much I may wish it. I couldn't ask that of any of my people. You'll be a friendly face; you'll be my envoy. If he doesn't want to have anything to do with my people or my House once rescued, you will see that nobody forces him."

Jale didn't understand completely. She nodded acknowledgement anyway, wondering what she'd gotten herself into.

The coyote seemed ready to dismiss her, but then turned back, wearing a strange expression. "I...sent two messages for him. Do you know if he read either of them, and if so, which?"

"Truly, I do not know. Last I visited him before the attack, he was still too distraught to even touch the console."

Knoskali scowled slightly. "So there's a possibility he doesn't know," he muttered to himself, almost gruff. He shook his head, looking off into space as if deep in thought. "Not good. I must consult my doctor at once."

With that, Knoskali met her eye, awarded her a tiny nod and then spun away, sweeping quickly through a private door.

"Ma'am?" the doberman politely gestured her out, and she followed his lead, Jewel and Pinky in tow.

When she arrived back to her room, she sent Jewel to make tea without even thinking twice.

VI

Polemic

ALONE IN THE SLAVEHOLD of the 'Free Fleet' ship *Varaunt*, Theta had quickly abandoned his tenuous hold on sanity. The voices in his head debated freely, unchecked and increasingly wild as he receded into the darkest depths of his own soul.

Janesson had honored exactly the terms of their bargain—once aboard the little overpowered, over-weaponed raiding vessel that had attacked their ship, Arvinne had gone forward with Janesson and the crew; Theta had been taken aft, under guard, with the other slaves. Less than a day later they had made rendezvous with *Varaunt*, and the slaves had been settled into their impermeable little cells in the much larger ship.

Occasionally, driven by some semiautonomous trigger, Theta would eat the food provided by the scheduled dispenser. Sometimes he'd stand up to stretch, or perform mild calisthenics, or circle his little two-meter by two-meter by two-meter cell before returning to the floor's built-in pad. He felt almost like an observer behind his own eyes.

There was no outside contact.

His dreams had become strange, and the waking world indistinguishable from them. Time ceased to hold meaning. He had frequent lapses into semi-somnolent delusions, always visions of flying, always in cold air above wet green, on wings of black. A frustrated, incoherent rage would build inside him until he wanted nothing more than to throw himself against the walls until they gave; a gentle word from his Knoskali voice would still him even as the other gibbered in the back of his mind.

"*Control.*" Knoskali's voice would slide into his thoughts, familiar and warm, "*Control is power. Restraint will set you free.*"

Days would pass where he would sit silently, then wake, drenched in cold sweat, mumbling unintelligibly under his breath; sometimes he would lie shivering on his back, wet and chilled to the core despite his thick fur, lost in some fantasy world of dark skies and green mountains below. As his days went on, the verdant land below began to wither and blacken as it was invaded by a foreign army. Great feelings of despair and confusion lent animus to his rage and doubt, and he'd often storm around the tiny space, springing from side to side in single strides, eyes open but unseeing, avoiding the structure of a different world inside his mind.

There was fire below, and its source personified.

Lightning split the heavens.

On the twentieth day, Theta woke. His head was crystal clear. Rage had retreated to the back of his consciousness, a mass connected to every part of his mind but waiting, coiled like some great spring of nerve. The voices in his head were silent. The world—this world—and everything in it stood out in stark relief; every particle that stirred, every rustle of fur in his periphery, every strand of hair that crossed his vision was sharp and in focus. Scent. His own. It was foul and terrible. Others. His ears swiveled; things moved around him. Tiny things. Things that before this moment he would have heard but never noticed.

Every piece of information collated and coalesced into a seamless mental map of the world around him; the sobbing slave in the cell above him, the breathing of the sleeping family of cervines to his left, the booted footfalls outside.

Approaching footfalls.

Eight pairs.

Theta's lips drew back into a little happy snarl of anticipation. It was time?

A slight confusion crept in, and his vision clouded. His beta state faded as a dream fades on waking, and suddenly he was just Theta.

The door to his cell opened and he was ordered out.

He counted eight pirates, all armor-clad.

"Time to go downside," the nearest soldier murmured to him, softer than he expected; Theta blinked, recognizing him as the rat who had searched his quarters. The pirate was casually holding something out to him; without thinking, he took it.

His breath caught as he recognized the stuffed coyote. The rat rested his paw briefly on Theta's shoulder before turning back to working with the others to roust the slaves.

The rough treatment Theta had expected did not materialize. The dozen slaves, once released from their cells, met only methodical indifference coupled with incredible efficiency; no effort was wasted on intimidation as they were individually restrained, then escorted in silence to a large processing area. Each was taken into a cell and submitted to a battery of computerized tests, ranging from the physical to the mental. Hours and hours of tests which, Theta reflected in mild amusement, was probably itself a test of endurance.

When finished, each slave was taken back into the main processing area and seated on the floor. One by one, they were led off once more, until only Theta remained.

"Theta? This is your name?"

Theta raised his head to find a large form leaning over him. Something about the speaker made him immediately and immensely uneasy, but he held himself firmly in place, resisting the instinct to roll away. His restraints wouldn't likely allow that sort of motion anyway—they tended to lock firmly together on any sudden or full movement.

"Yes? That's me," Theta murmured. He stared up at the doubtful canid, who was glowering at him with a dubious frown. The canid's jowls seemed permanently open at the corners, and he breathed through his mouth, exposing a set of foul, stained teeth as he chewed sloppily on some sort of malodorous black leaf. After a moment he shook his head.

"No way. Your name is–?"

"Theta," Theta answered patiently, nose wrinkling at the canid's breath.

"Gotta be a mistake," the canid grunted. He turned away without another word, pounding off.

Theta mentally dismissed him from his attention, returning his gaze to the floor and his thoughts to his prior state. He didn't care. Now if only he could recapture that beautiful transparency of purpose...he closed his eyes once more, trying to summon forth the crystalline clarity that had momentarily pierced the fog and malaise that he had only then realized dominated his senses.

Even still he couldn't concentrate. He glanced up, looking across the chamber to see the grey-suited canid who had accosted him arguing with a large, crisply uniformed hyena. Though he couldn't make out the conversation, he could read the tone of the interplay. The hyena clearly didn't like the canid, and after but a short discussion the canid was dismissed.

He returned to Theta, scowl deeper than before.

"Well, guess you's really coming with me, hey? Seems," his voice dripped with bitter sarcasm as he bent to release

Theta's restraints, "as if you's our latest conscript, yah. I'm Nefra. Now let's go, hey?"

Theta rose, only slightly stiff and sore. There had been no spontaneous comments from his internal peanut gallery since he had awoken.

Strangely, their absence made him feel very alone.

He followed the canid mutely.

Unrestrained, his possibilities for action were endless... and yet, of all of them, none seemed more appealing than simply following along to see what would happen.

A dizzying array of turns and G-tubes later, Nefra guided him into a room full of floor-to-ceiling bunks, most occupied, some not.

Theta turned back to Nefra, cocking his head.

"So I'm...what, now?"

Nefra, leaning against the hatchway he'd just escorted Theta through, wiped his paws on the hips of his greasy grey shipsuit and smirked sourly.

"You's a conscript, yah. You fight for them when they tells you. You're to come back here with us, yah. See?" He snorted, looking Theta over once more. "The quartermaster, he marked you to be held up for our little gang here."

"And I'm not going down with the rest?"

"Neh, 'down' is just one big, charted rock, yah. Charted for them bad guys, anyway." He laughed roughly. "Yet hey, they just sort and train slaves there. Then sells 'em, like a clearinghouse. I came through there, myself, long back, and I hear we're here to buy and sell. Hey, see, you were special or somethin', or...really pissed someone off, hey?" Nefra shook his head.

"Perhaps," Theta answered cautiously—Intuitively, he felt that Nefra was very much not his friend, and he had very little trust to spare. Hard knocks had piled up, and he'd found through trial and error that saying less had generally served him better of late.

"Well, guess they figured for you in the aptitudes. Really can't see why, though, for the physicals, hmm? I'd think you would have been up on the market for other things," he hinted with his brown-stained sneer.

Theta's eyes narrowed infinitesimally, but he ignored the bait. After his former life, he was mostly unconcerned with how he was treated or disparaged.

He had reserves for this, and they were miles deep.

"I guess it just didn't work out that way. So what sort of job am I in for, here?" He grinned softly, attempting to catch the relationship before it fell unrecoverably into enmity.

The canid reluctantly straightened from his slouch against the doorframe, then flopped into a deck chair behind a short metal desk. He still wore the same nasty sneer; Theta, despite how poor his initial impression had been, liked him less by the second.

"Hey, the usual brutal period of training, an op or two, yah, then a quick death more'n is likely. Most of your type don't last too long back here, no. Anyway, as I said before, I'm in charge. If you do what I tell ya, you might live a while. Don't go behind my back, or around me. Do what I say and what my buddies here say. In fact, everyone else. And for the record, I'm supposed to tell you that you're being evaluated as potential crew."

Nefra rummaged in the top drawer of the desk, then withdrew a small knife and began trimming his claws casually, leaning back in his chair. "Yah well, that's what they tell me to tell everyone, but I never seen it happen, and I know from the start that you're dead meat. Usually they only bring in volunteers, anyway, hey? You lot all die or get sold off quick like. Mostly die. Anyway, you's here for now, yah? So toss your...toy" he scowled at Theta's stuffed animal, "in the bottom rack, right there—" he gestured with his knife to the bottom bunk in a stack of four beside the door—"and get into the gear in that locker—you're the last of this batch, and combat training starts when Kolle gets back, few minutes from now."

Theta's ears perked at 'combat training', and he grinned. "Hey, whatever you say, hey?"

He regretted his playful jab before he'd even finished saying it; Nefra glowered blackly at him, knife paused in its trimming—the canid seemed to be trying to divine if his mockery was insult or incidental. Theta managed to maintain a cautiously blank, slightly puzzled expression, ears akimbo, and turned away. Stiffly, he tossed his little stuffed animal atop his bunk's single sheet, then flopped down into it to pull his gear from the sling above. The bedding...the frame, the gear...smelled of sweat and coyote—a variation of a scent he knew very well—but also of many other things. It was not very pleasant, and his lip curled.

Well, he'd smelled and slept in much worse.

He flicked a glance back to find Nefra's black eyes still fixed on him. He shuddered silently, looking around for a place to change from 'Slave green' into his new 'Conscript grey' shipsuit.

Most of the 'combat training' Theta found horrendously dull. Far removed from the basics of advanced weapons usage and small unit tactics that the name suggested, it instead focused chiefly on the simple basics of surviving on ships in a system of rank, of using shipboard services, of emergency drills and stations, of how to report to a superior, how to 'properly' follow orders, and so on. It was so basic, in fact, that he began to think most of the new conscripts taken on must have never been in space before; certainly they seemed to act it, as though every task was of monumental difficulty.

They were kept awake for long periods of time, and yelled at constantly; they were pushed and prodded and hounded, dunked in cold water, run around the ship, forced to perform menial tasks. Sometimes they were beaten mildly. The instructors never let up the pressure, and after a while conscripts began to crack, one and two at a time.

For Theta, it was nearly comical; the yelling had little intent behind it and the physical violence was mostly for shock value. He began to realize that he was unintimidated by threats to life or limb—he blamed death for that little gem.

He carefully guarded his thoughts and worked his way through, managing to elicit very little in the way of unwanted attention after the first few days; contrarily, after a few more he began to find the whole thing rather fun. He'd plowed through every task assigned to him, and by the last week he was one of the few who had received no negative marks. Indeed, his lack of fear began to gain him a grudging respect from the trainer, and the end drew near swiftly.

Five days before the end of the training schedule, however, a simple conversation nearly disrupted his equilibrium. While spending a rare meal break trying to help a conscript named Prell, sharing things he'd learned during his training as a slave, Prell had thrown him into momentary chaos with a simple question.

"Yes, but so much training? What could they possibly have needed to spend all that time training you for?"

Theta had promptly launched into the story of how he'd been trained to be an elite dancer, but had trailed off quickly. It wasn't right. He'd told the story several times before, but this time it wouldn't come. It felt wrong. Certainly he remembered being trained to dance—those memories were very clear. He'd had the steps beaten into him; he could readily recall the metallic taste in his mouth from every time he was shocked for a misstep. Four hours a day for five days a week.

He remembered every lesson, but for the first time he'd realized that all his dancing training had made up only a small part of his day. It had loomed large in his memory, taking on a larger-than-life perspective, but as it crumbled under examination awareness dawned that there had been much more to his time. A different sort of training. Training in something which left him sore. Training which he realized had taken up the bulk of every day, for over a year.

He did not remember anything about the *other* training, except going to a special room, every day, and that was all. It had a big blue door, and was numbered D8-180-C in small white letters. It had several locks. Innumerable little loose threads seemed willing to guide him to what was within... but they all pulled free and left nothing when tugged on.

Between one breath and the next, Theta had discovered something about himself that had left him questioning the very facts he'd considered the foundation of his life, and he found himself thrown into utter confusion.

After a long pause, he'd excused himself from a startled Prell and found some private space to sit and think, but nothing came. From that point forward, he limited his contact with others even more severely than before, racking his brain during every free moment to try to find a missing piece, any recollection that would give him more threads of memory.

The rest of the week passed by in a daze. Theta barely responded to prompting during the half-mocking, half-serious graduation ceremony that marked the end of training, though nobody really took note.

Nefra, once training was complete, awarded everyone their combat assignments and sent them off for more specialized instruction. Most, including Prell, were sent with Trainer Kolle to learn infantry unit tactics. A handful went with Trainer Kenaris, who was to instruct them in support roles. Trainer Lefa was given two to instruct in heavy weapons.

To Theta, Nefra gave no assignment; instead, he seemed to spend his days intent on finding every scut job he could assign to his least favorite conscript. Sometimes, when nothing sufficiently nasty actually needed to be done, Nefra made things up. Scrub the head. Clean the racks. Empty the reclamation chute! To the galley with the dirty dishes, then return with food. Any moment Theta found time to sit and rest, or try to eat, or sleep, Nefra sent him off on another job. He was never afforded the opportunity to bend his thoughts to the hole in his past. By the time he hit his rack each night, he was exhausted and fell immediately to sleep.

Waking brought more work.

The conscript barracks shone like it hadn't since it was constructed, and still Theta worked non-stop. A week after the end of training, he was so far ahead that Nefra began to make messes for him to clean. Before long, that too was abandoned, and he was relegated to galley runner.

It was during this duty that he ran into Arvinne.

The snow leopard was clad in a white shipsuit, idly joking and talking with two other members of the galley crew when Theta came to retrieve Nefra's evening meal. Though Theta's head was down as he trudged into the galley, laden beneath the crate of empties from lunch, his friend recognized him immediately.

"Theta!" Arvinne turned away from his surprised cohorts, raising a paw in greeting. "By Dia, what are you doing here? Aren't you down with the conscripts?"

Theta nodded wearily, trying to muster what enthusiasm he could. He slid the empty crates into the bin, then raised his paw in greeting, taking the pause as an opportunity to lean against a wall. Exhaustion caught up quickly as soon as he stopped moving; he reeled, then shook his head.

"Yeah, I'm just up here picking up my boss' dinner. How's it going?"

"Look here, you're a genius, Theta! This cook thing is working out beautiful and all, and I'm getting along splendidly up here. Gents?" Arvinne grinned up to his cohorts. "This is the fox I was talking about."

Theta nodded polite greetings.

The taller of the two, a black feline, leaned forward and touched Theta's proffered paw with an amiable grin. "Good to meet you, at last. We've heard some fairly...colorful stories. I'm Merrol," he inclined his head, then tossed it back toward his antlered companion, "and this is my deer friend Vaese. Why don't you two go get caught up, Arvy? We've got nothin' this shift until the next set comes in, anyway."

"Except his boss' dinner," Arvinne said, then sniffed, bringing up the food chart data with a brush of his paw. "Who is he, again, Theta?"

Vaese giggled, tapping on the bin beside Arvinne. "Oh Arvy, Nefra doesn't get the fresh dinners. He gets the slave trash. Speaking of which, Theta darling," Vaese's voice was pure liquid velveteen, to Theta's perked-ear surprise, "if you're ever hungry," He touched Theta's paw in much the same way the panther had done, but lingered longer, stroking across its surface, "We'll always have a little something for you down here."

Theta shifted uncertainly, feeling his face grow hot beneath his white fur. He resisted the desire to yank his paw away, trying for a polite smile instead.

"Vay? Knock it off," Merrol said, though he and Arvinne both seemed quite amused. "You're scaring the poor thing."

Theta conjured what he thought to be an appropriate smile as Vaese retreated with a little wink; Arvinne took him by the shoulder and steered him out of the galley.

They settled in the empty mess hall adjacent.

"Don't mind Vaese," Arvinne giggled. "He's a trip, really. Merrol an' him are both top-rate...really, everyone on this ship is great." The snow leopard was effusive. "They're incredibly nice to me...treat me great. It's...like family."

Theta rubbed the back of his neck wearily.

"They're pirates, Arvinne. They killed who-knows-how-many aboard your ship, they took slaves, and they probably do far worse all the time. They were going to kill me!"

Arvinne's face fell. "Ah, yes...well, guess that's true and all." He bit his lip and turned away. "But...It's not...not really what most people think. They're...they do this for good reasons, most of them."

Theta steepled his paws, drumming clawtips together and hiding a fleeting little smirk. "Trust me, I'm the last person to whom you must justify positive feelings for someone others perceive as evil."

He'd meant it to be ironic, but it just came across as bitter. Arvinne looked as though he was struggling within himself, caught on some angle he hadn't considered before. The fading happiness was painful, and Theta relented.

"Look, this is the real world. The only morality is that which we bring to it ourselves. There are no innocents, and there are few who are truly evil. I'm sorry; you're right—People can only be judged individually."

Arvinne met Theta's gaze, his glance sharper than Theta had expected. He nodded slowly.

"I take your point, in both ways. You're smart for your size, fox," Arvinne said with a sly grin.

Struck by reflex, Theta reached up and touched Arvinne's cheek in gentle affection.

"I'm sorry, but I must go. Nefra knows exactly how long it should take to get his food."

Arvinne nodded and stood, looking as if there was much more he wished to say; with a little shake of his head, Theta bid him a quick farewell, collected Nefra's box, then jogged back to the conscript quarters as quickly as he could manage.

When Theta returned, he found Nefra murderously angry. The canid's rage was for him alone.

"Well, well, looks as like you's have a friend somewhere a-high," the nasty mixed-breed snarled under his breath. He threw a datapad across the desk, rising as Theta slid his dinner box in front of him. Theta turned away quickly, wanting to put some distance between Nefra and himself, but was shocked to be yanked back by his hair. A meaty arm wrapped around his throat, cinching tight.

"New orders! Know about you, yah." Nefra fumed, hissing in his ear. His grasp tightened by the second. "Little *niiza*, I'mma wring your neck."

No, you're not.

Theta's vision blurred briefly; he raised his paws in a moment of directed instinct, uncertain of what he was doing but certain that it was correct. The grip on his neck slackened, and he twisted down and away. He broke free surprisingly easily, but as he started for the knife on Nefra's desk, pain shot between his ears and his vision doubled.

He fell to his knees, clutching his head. Suddenly he was knocked flat to his back. A heavy weight straddled his legs, and blows rained down on his stomach. He tensed it and grunted, raising paws to deflect the next few blows aimed squarely at his head. Some level of instinct made Nefra seem slow and ineffectual, his punches soft and easy to deflect. After a moment, Theta was surprised to see Nefra recede from his vision. He rolled to his feet in one fluid motion to find two of the trainers holding the canid back and pinioning his arms. Blood streamed down Nefra's face, soaking into the chest of his shipsuit. The flow increased alarmingly to drip and run from his fat chin, but the trainers didn't seem to be very sympathetic to his cause, bellow though he might.

What did I do?

What have I done?

The pain between Theta's eyes had quickly subsided to a severe headache. One of the trainers—Lefa, he recognized with blurry eyes—came over to him, awarding him a cursory once-over. After a moment she knelt and lifted his chin, peering at him from behind wide golden eyes.

"Well that was fascinating," the wolf muttered, turning-head slightly to eye him. "I don't think I've ever seen that before. Are you alright?"

"Yes," Theta whispered. "I'm sorry. I didn't meant to hurt him."

To his surprise, Lefa laughed loudly and sat back on her haunches.

"My ass!" she shook her head, thumping Theta on the shoulder. "He was trying to hurt you, and you most certainly meant to hurt him. Did a pretty good job at it, too. You fight dirty."

Theta dipped his muzzle and splayed his ears flat, looking away. He couldn't remember what dirty thing he'd done to so injure Nefra; reminded suddenly of the memory hole from his training, he found himself very afraid.

How can be I lose my mind more than I already have..? What caused that pain in my head?

A sick fear gripped his stomach.

"Oh don't feel bad about it." Lefa wiped a few spatters of blood from his fur with a cleaning rag. "Ain't nobody deserved it more, and we all saw what he was doing. Thing is, I just don't know why he got so angry about your new orders. He was raging as soon as he got 'em."

Theta shook his head mutely. "Orders?"

"You got your new orders finally," Lefa gestured towards the desk. "Courier left a few minutes before you arrived."

At that moment, ship's security arrived in a swarm. They took statements from the trainers, stared at Theta for a while, then dragged the increasingly groggy Nefra to sickbay.

Inari's breath...what did I do?

Theta's new orders brought him into the dark, red-lit tactics room early the next morning. Banks of computing power provided continual analyses of streams of data, graphed on two- and three-dimensional displays as the ship's tactical staff selected and analyzed potential targets in real-time. Several consoles were dedicated to the near space around the ship, and large display held one large image with strange symbols and colors. Theta stared at it momentarily, baffled by its odd shapes until he realized that it was a political map of known space. Strategic targets were highlighted.

He was amazed that he was even allowed to see this room, but this is where he had been ordered to come...and he'd been welcomed, albeit briskly, as soon as he'd arrived.

"So, combat support controller? What is that?" Theta glanced sidelong at the red fox to whom he'd been assigned. She was walking fast, and he'd been unable to get many questions in as she escorted him past a very busy quadrant toward a much quieter, partitioned section.

Irrai didn't immediately respond; she pulled the sound-proof partition closed and brushed her chip over an access panel. After a few taps, the displays came up, most of them showing inactive. One displayed an image on the screen, which she hastily cleared; belatedly, Theta recognized the layout as the decks of the Freeta.

"Listen well, snowflake, 'cause I don't like repeating myself. The combat support controller," Irrai said, gesturing to a blank console beside the one she'd cleared, "coordinates the conscript specialists during a ground assault or boarding battle. Basically, your job will involve monitoring the action of the squads and dispatching the close support personnel—cipher techs, reserves, special entry personnel, and so on—as soon as they're needed. To do that, you'll be sitting with me right here in tactics most of the time; for the rest, we need to provide segmented operations by comm. That's usually during special types of surface engagements, when you'll deploy with the unit, or as we say, 'forward'. I'll be giving tactical orders to the primaries, but you'll be dispatching support on my direction.

"You'll also help us with tactical analysis and learn the basics of small unit command tactics, so that you can back me up in a pinch."

"I...don't understand why I'd be the one to do that." Theta's soft, high-pitched voice dropped in concern. "I've never done anything like that. Are you sure...I mean, shouldn't someone with experience—"

"Raw aptitude, snowflake." Irrai cut in with a sharp grin and a glint in her eye. "Magnificent test results. Well, that, coupled with the fact that our last experienced support controller is no longer...ah, with us." She flashed him a somewhat predatory smile. "So...you get to show me you can think on your feet a bit. Get it right, and you'll find that this is a pretty good job for a conscript. Get it wrong, and you'll be with the front line troops on the next engagement...without armor."

He nodded pensively, raising a paw to brush his hair back and conceal his little shiver. This seemed like a terrible idea, but he couldn't think of any way out of it.

"Now this," she changed the subject, pointing to a small, padded case, "is a dispatch helm with your name on it. It's designed to be worn with or without body armor. Goes around your head, then clips in back...It should automatically adjust to fit your vision. There are manuals with it, but you don't need all the features right off. Study the core functions and spend most of your time working through the tactics sim built in." Irrai drew herself up, smirking a little challenging smirk down at him. "Got all that, snowflake?"

"Yes ma'am," he murmured, with another little nod.

"Oh yeah...Snowflake? One last thing." Irrai dropped her voice, slightly more serious. "I'm moving your bunk.

You're my report now, and frankly that Nefra's a creepy sort. You're going to be in rack four, bunk D, on deck 12, berth F. Got that? 12-F-4-D. It's a proper crew rack, but I've cleared it—If anyone bothers you about it, send them to me. I'd prefer you move right now, then report back."

"Ah...yes ma'am! Certainly." Despite his worry, the prospect of escaping from the conscript barracks improved his mood significantly. He was especially happy to get away from Nefra's domain—the canid had not returned the previous night.

Unexpectedly, Theta found that his new job had come with a dramatic increase in freedom; treated like a junior member of tactics rather than a slave, or even a conscript, he was even allowed to do what he chose in his off-duty hours. He took meals with Arvinne when he could, slept when he could, and even found time to practice his dances in an empty compartment. Frequently, he was called on to run messages and other errands, but most of his duty time involved working in the tactics department on rudimentary tactical analyses during his duty shifts.

He found tactics shockingly interesting, and voraciously devoured every problem set to him with a zeal and speed that left those around him reeling. Most often the full analyses he produced as practice exercises were rejected as too unconventional, but more than one staff tactician asked him to write up his approach for private review, and the tidbits he contributed to the serious analysis sessions found fertile ground in the battle and contingency plans.

Indeed, some intangible element of tactics and wargaming struck a chord, resonating somewhere deep within his soul. The clarity of mind he'd felt so briefly before he often found again when analyzing complicated situations, and his instinct was a powerful and often surprising element in an otherwise hyperanalytical process.

"Instinct," Irrai confided in him when he expressed his private concerns about his poor mathematical skills, "is what we call the subliminal analysis of data that even the conscious mind doesn't recognize or know how to count; some people've got bad instincts, and most have no instincts, or either don't listen to or second-guess the ones they have. For those sort, tactics is broken into a series of formal processes. Now you, on the other hand, shouldn't trouble yourself with the formal part. Not your strength; leave that to staff tacticians like Rofert. If I were in personnel, which I'm not, I'd have you trained in open space operations and fleet tactics, 'cause there the problem set is exponentially divergent. You're simply wasted on moving the ground-pounders."

Theta wasn't sure how to respond, so he said nothing, peering at his feet.

Irrai snorted in amusement, with a little shake of her head. "Still, and it's not that you're doing wrong," she murmured, leaning so close that her nose almost touched Theta's ear, "you should be careful about Rofert. He's really sensitive to rank and protocol, and I think he sees you as a threat. He's very...adequate...at what he does, but doesn't have that spark of genius. He's one more reason I'd like to see you out of assault tactics and into space-side. So just... for now, defer to him and show him every ounce of respect you can muster."

"Yes ma'am."

"Well, anyway, we're passing by a mining complex tomorrow and we need a comprehensive plan of attack to present facts and figures by third watch briefing. I'd like you to draw up the retreat plan."

Theta blinked, peering at Irrai. "You mean a plan segment?"

Irrai's ears perked forward, and she leaned close. "If I meant a plan segment, I'd have said it. No. I mean the whole thing. I'm gonna take a nap. I've given you the full dataset, so take care of that after lunch! Good boy."

Theta felt a cold chill run down his spine. His plan? Submitted as the validated plan of retreat to the staff meeting?

"Y—" he arrested himself mid-thought. "Yes ma'am."

"Good answer, snowflake." she smirked.

After turning in his folio of contingency scenarios and curling up in his rack, it took him forever to calm down enough to get to sleep. His imagination ran wild with thoughts of the scorn he'd face when his plan was discussed. Indeed, conjured images of Irrai's disappointed face, and the loss of all her misplaced trust, haunted him and would not leave him at peace, no matter how complete he felt his plans. Eventually all the faces began to blend together, and he slipped off to a restless doze.

A piercing buzz cut through Theta's slumber less than an hour after he'd achieved it.

Rubbing the sleep from his eyes, he tapped the little console built into his rack. It was a message from one Chief Fekel, ordering him to report to 3-W. The request wasn't unusual; as the lowest member of the tactics department, he was often sent on errands at odd hours.

He frowned, rubbing his head—he hadn't been to deck three before.

"Deck three..." he muttered to himself, shaking his sleep-fogged head and considering his route. After a bit, he realized that he'd almost fallen back asleep; a cold chill had him sitting up in his bunk with a little gasp.

Seconds later, he rolled into his shipsuit and dropped silently from his rack. After a brief pause to dim the night lighting which had come up with his motion, he made his way aft. He paused briefly to let an ordinance gang go by as they emerged from his destination G-tube. He received an amiable wave, returned it with a friendly nod, then swung into the zero-gravity shaft and kicked himself down towards the lower decks.

When he emerged back into normal gravity on deck three, he began to wonder why anyone working down here on third shift would need a runner to tactics. He shrugged away his misgivings, despite his hackles lifting. They did seem to want him to get to know the layout of the ship, and he'd been to much of it by now.

He frowned, looking around for a lighting panel; the lighting was very low, and the deckplates had the trace automatic lighting of a machine deck.

Strange.

He began make his way towards where the midships through-corridors should be. Machinery whirred and hummed around him as he began to wend his way back forward.

Halfway down the through-corridor, some animal sense kicked over and he froze.

Instinct. A subliminal correlation of data.

He was being stalked.

Slowly he began moving forward again; as he walked around a bend in the corridor, he took a quick step to put some distance between himself and the two large shapes he could feel behind him. His next random turn, however, brought him up short against a secure door.

He turned back, but two hulking forms were already blocking the way.

He did not know them, but there was a third who he did know by smell.

Nefra.

Big, strong paws held Theta's head back, pinning his skull against a big armored chest and viciously clamping his muzzle shut; little wheezing breaths were all he could steal as he struggled weakly beneath the armored caniform atop him.

"Suffer, little *niiza*," the pirate's voice was low and sincere, dripping with bitterness. "Suffer like as he suffered."

The other of his two assailants, a towering black-furred mass of muscled horseflesh, leaned forward and touched the bloody edge of his knife against Theta's throat, tracing its edge lightly under his jawline.

"Nah," the equine murmured with a glower. "Knife's too quick, too easy, and you've already felt its bite. Let's play a different game."

The equine dropped the knife to the deck, then reached down and unclasped his belt, snorting softly. He knelt before Theta, nose to nose, and stared into his eyes.

"You killed our friend, *niiza*," the canid—some sort of shepherd—whispered, squeezing Theta's muzzle until teeth cracked.

With a mirthless grin, the equine pulled his wide belt free. Theta sucked in a deep breath as strong hands wrapped it around his neck, meeting behind and drawing it tight; slowly, the pirate increased the pressure until Theta's throat was compressed and he couldn't breathe.

"We're going to kill you. Slow," the canid behind him whispered into his ear.

Theta struggled perfunctorily, but achieved no play; his heartbeat throbbed in his skull, filling his awareness with its familiar, desperate throb.

Gradually, it became all that he could hear, and his struggling felt feeble and very far away.

Not again.

He closed his eyes.

Theta's body fell slack and inert beneath the canid's weight, muzzle hanging open and lifeless above the equine's wide belt and huge, strangling hands.

He was not there.

Fire bloomed to the heavens, rising around him like a great cloud as he rocked his way through the violent updrafts; Something far below caught his attention, and black wings furled, providing only the smallest little inputs for guidance as he dove to meet the surface a thousand meters away. The smell of viscera and war rose to him, and his heart was glad for it, leaving his mourning for the once fallow land far behind as he prepared himself for battle.

He dove through his intended victim, through the charred soil, and down into a tunnel of blackness.

At the end, there was a glimmer of light.

It approached rapidly.

"I am."

The light exploded around him.

VII

Rebirth

"I AM."

With those words, every fiber of Theta's being reacted with one purpose, and for the first time in his life he exerted his full and absolute strength, effortlessly pulling free from the horse's lazily-slackened grasp and the canid's blood-slickened paws. In one fluid motion, he was back on his feet, the forgotten knife limber in his hand; his breath came easily, though his throat was sore from holding his neck muscles rigid. He drew several quick breaths—they hurt terribly. Numb and dizzy as he was, though, it was fading. Power coursed through him, filling every fiber, every nerve with a cold resolve. His mind raced, form shaking with energy.

It took barely a second for his assailants to recover from their initial shock and advance on him once more, seeming more angry than wary.

Unwise.

He backed up to the wall, grinning a blood-flecked grin.

The world was slow and clear. With two stab wounds beneath his ribs, blood running down his battered and broken body, and a tightening chest burning in pain with each breath, he knew how this would end.

This would not be a fair fight.

He didn't want it to be.

He slipped effortlessly past the equine's clumsy grab, taking a few long, prancing steps along the wall. Tucking one ankle behind the other, he awarded the two a mocking bow, then raised his head.

The pair had stopped advancing; the equine was staring down at the long, deep slash along his stomach, too surprised to bleed.

"Now, my friends," Theta murmured, and his little vulpine grin shifted to a predatory snarl, "we dance."

Minutes later, Theta staggered to a communications panel and sent a message requesting security. He was too badly injured to pursue the skulking Nefra, who had turned tail and run; in fact, his level of energy was falling rapidly, and the almost uncontrollable elation that had sustained him had faded to a sick uncertainty that lingered within.

Pain, too, had returned; nearly every part of him hurt tremendously, and stabs of pain radiated from his chest.

Yet even though his teeth were coated with his blood, they were bared in a grin. He remembered.

He remembered, and if he survived, as he'd survived before, he'd finally be something resembling a whole person once more. He remembered Knoskali. Every detail, every scarce irregularity that graced the lord's perfection. How much he'd loved the black coyote, and how much he'd cherished the littlest of pleasures he'd been awarded amidst the pain and abuse.

He remembered House Selesz, and he remembered his training. Almost all of it, now, rather than just dancing, his final night, and fleeting memories of pain and exertion.

This time, the memories didn't fade, nor become elusive when he tried to pin them down. They were there, immutable and sharp. He remembered the *other*, a slight figure in a black House Selesz uniform with garnet insignia, whose cold, spare voice had mutated to gibbering insanity within Theta's head. The real *other* would never gibber any more than Knoskali would have.

His reflections were interrupted by the sound of ambling footsteps on the decking of the corridor.

Not Nefra's.

"Hello? Anyone down here?" The young voice was uncertain.

"Security? Over here," Theta called out with some effort.

Perhaps in response to the pain in Theta's voice, the footsteps hastened.

Theta fought down dizzy nausea to grin up to the curious red-shipsuit-clad brown wolf who swung around the corner. The guard's greeting faltered as his eyes and nose told him that something was very wrong; after a moment of wide-eyed pause, he was calling in a strained voice over his own comms for the medics-and-quartermas-ter-RIGHT-NOW.

Theta slumped against the wall as he was approached, but kept his head high.

Quartermaster Jenks was the next to arrive. After quickly surveying the scene, he approached Theta and demanded an answer.

Theta gave him the best account that he could, leaving nothing out, though he quickly realized that the burly hyena wasn't finding his story compelling.

"You're not a slave anymore." Jenks' voice was quiet and low, a soft growl for Theta's ears only; he glanced up briefly as more security arrived and began checking the silent forms on the floor for signs of life, then leaned closer, lips drawn back in reproach. "Slaves. Slaves are chattel to be sold. Not responsible for their actions, nor accountable in our system of law. You'd be cleaned up and back to the slavehold."

Theta ground his teeth, wiping the blood from his lips and trying not to wrinkle his nose. Hyaenidae had a rather raucous component to their scent that made his eyes water, but at the moment, the odor was well masked by his own sweat and blood, and the visceral scents of the little blood-stained machine deck alcove. He swayed, then slumped; he would have fallen to the deck had the burly quartermaster not caught him firmly by the shoulders.

Jenks knelt, holding him at arms length and meeting his eyes.

"No. You're not a slave any longer, so you do not get an easy out. You've been given freedom and with that freedom comes our rule of law." The hyena shook his head, and shook Theta's shoulders slightly. "We trusted you, and tried to show our faith in you, wanted you to become part of our crew!" His disappointment and disgust made Theta cringe. "And you'd have me believe...well, whatever happened here, we have plenty of data to review. I can't understand why people still try things like this without knowing they'll be caught. For all his faults, I'm not sure I believe that Nefra would be that stupid."

"He ran, the coward!" Theta was momentarily distract-ed. "He ran from me. I could barely stand up when I was done with those two, but he still ran." He clenched his jaw in a little grimace; breathing was difficult, but speaking was worse. "I still don't understand something they said repeat-edly, though. What's a '*niiza*'?"

Jenks' eyes narrowed very slightly, and he caught his breath, fixing Theta with a thoughtful glare.

The sound of rapid bootfalls from the corridor behind Theta broke the moment. He started to turn and nearly blacked out.

"Easy there, easy there mister Theta," Jenks held Theta firmly in place. "You're not going anywhere. It may be as you say, but I still doubt your story." The large quartermaster turned to the newcomers. "Surgeon Resca? This one's alive, but in bad shape. Other two are very dead."

Theta's vision greyed as he attempted to look up at the doctor. His knees gave way fully, and he sagged in Jenks' grasp, head drooping at an angle; above, he could see the doctor's eyes widen slightly.

"Unrecoverably dead?" The doctor's tone implied a detached, professional interest, but he quickly set to work, pulling a scanner from his belt and passing it along Theta's form.

"Yes sir." The brown wolf affirmed from somewhere outside of Theta's vision. "Nothing under fifty. We checked."

Jenks' paws squeezed Theta's shoulders very hard as he held him up for the surgeon's scans. After a long few moments of dizzy pain, Resca gently separated him from the hyena's less-than-gentle grip and arranged him flat on a litter. Two well armed pirates frowned down at him from either side; another set bent to each end, lifted, and then they were off, leaving two crumpled forms on the floor behind for Jenks to prod at.

Theta looked, briefly, then looked away. In death, his assailant's faces lacked the malice and anger that they'd held before.

He felt no regret.

The ceiling of the corridor drifted by dizzyingly as the doctor circled around him, passing a different type of scanner across his torso. Everywhere it scanned felt prickly and numb. Turns, turns.

I will kill anyone who would kill me. It's as deep a moral code as I need.

He took a deep breath, then expelled it as a little inarticulate growl.

I am.

Theta closed his eyes, but found that it immediately led to severe vertigo and opened them wide once more. It was much more difficult to open them again than to close them in the first place.

"Urgh," he groaned.

Might be dying. Again.

Everything felt too right, too in the moment, too important for him to be addressing his end. He felt a frisson of fear run through his chest and stomach at the thought, but steeled himself against it with another little growl.

"Nonsense." His voice shook.

"Nonsense!" He reasserted, more firmly, though his voice was alarmingly weak and faint.

"Nonsense," he whispered. "I do not fear death."

A coolness spread within him, and a sense of calm followed.

Moments later, as they passed into a G-tube and began to ascend, he closed his eyes and whispered a very private prayer to Inari.

Couldn't hurt.

They passed through a doorway, and his litter was hoisted onto a large frame; suddenly there was silence and time ceased to exist.

He felt like he was suffocating.

Breathe. One breath follows the last.

His chest heaved as he strained to draw air.

More faces looked down at him. A horde of medical staff, staring impassively, as if waiting for him to die.

A week of misery and suffering later, Theta's perforated lungs still drew breath into his body, and his own diaphragm and intercostal muscles still powered them. The surgeons had spent many hours on him the first few days, but the formal surgeries had quickly given way to an incredible amount of poking, prodding and scanning amidst veiled astonishment as his recovery had proceeded at a remarkable rate; nine days after his attack he had come so far that he was even allowed to stand for short periods, though the guards wouldn't let him leave his medical bay.

On the last day of the week, part-way through first watch, he woke from restless dreams, fur matted and soaked with sweat. Blinking his vision clear, he found three of the ship's security complement looming over his little secured berth and staring down at him.

Though his hackles rose in distrust, he did not resist as he was lifted from his cushions and dressed in a garish green-and-orange striped shipsuit. His forepaws were loosely restrained, though a covert glance at the wristcuffs showed them to be the terribly vulnerable MagSmart series IV.

He bit back a smirk as he was led off.

Mere minutes later, he stood defiantly in the dead center of a large grey room. At his back stood two members of ship's security and a dozen pirates, most of them department heads, muttering to each other as they took their seats.

Official witnesses.

Theta stared straight ahead, over the central rostrum before him, blue eyes fixed in challenge on the dangerous set of stormy eyes behind it.

Captain Janesson steepled his digits, staring grimly back at him. The wolf looked very tired, and slightly unhappy; the amusement he'd shown Theta before had faded to an unenthusiastic flatness as he regarded the latest source of trouble aboard his ship. After a moment, the captain raised his eyes and stood to address the assembled.

"This will be a very short mast about a single matter, but a very serious one. Quartermaster Jenks has concluded the investigation, and I have arrived at a judgement.

"Crewmen Carenda and Orifin, who I don't doubt most of you knew well, were killed by the conscript Theta, standing here." Janesson leaned forward. "Now, it is generally regarded that conscripts haven't yet earned the status of crew and aren't considered protected under our charter.

Rebirth

Equally, being granted conscript status, they've lost the protections accorded prisoners and slaves. In short, conscripts have the responsibilities of crew but none of the rights.

"That's a relatively unstable situation, but in the two years our charter has stood in its current form, it's never been tested. This mast will set precedent on several issues, and discuss amendments to our laws; afterward, the changes will be put to a ratifying vote amongst the crew. First, however, justice must be done."

Theta shifted his weight and opened his mouth to speak, but Janesson briefly met his angry gaze and raised a digit for silence.

"There are many issues at play," the captain continued, holding up a datapad. "Many. But in lieu of guidance from our charter I have only the discretion of the quartermaster to guide me. The two of us have spent many hours going over all the articles that even peripherally relate to this situation. We've written up an entire addendum to the charter, which, again, will be put to ratifying vote." Janesson dipped his muzzle to Jenks, who nodded back.

"However," the captain turned to the crew once more, his voice darkening with discontent, "something more basic stands in this case. This wasn't a duel, but an unprovoked attack on this conscript by three members of the crew."

Theta's ears perked; several of the witnesses stirred uncomfortably.

"After reviewing the inexhaustible supply of clear evidence, we arrested Crewman Nefra, who has given us a full confession. He's admitted to conspiring to have Orifin and Carenda stab and strangle Theta on deck three. He offers no defense as he feels his actions were justified in the interest of simple revenge for deaths that took place aboard Theta's ship.

"This crew cannot abide revenge killing. We cannot abide mob rule in the corridors and machine decks, nor

115

conspiracies, nor any of this nonsense in the middle of a deep space run. This ship needs its personnel in place and working together, and this sort of..." Janesson closed his eyes, teeth barely parting as he snipped each word off. "This sort of petty stupidity is something we don't have time for. Economic and social doctrine demands that we work together to achieve our goals, and that we keep justice central and within the confines of our charter.

"With this in mind, I offer my final verdict: Theta stands completely absolved, and Orifin and Carenda have received their justice. That leaves Nefra to answer for his actions. I have offered him a simple choice: He may leave this ship as a slave at our next port of call, or he may leave this ship immediately out an unconnected airlock. He'll be given one week to decide."

The audience seemed surprised and not entirely happy; it murmured and susurrated. Theta, too, was surprised. He had not anticipated fair consideration in the matter of killing pirates on their own ship.

Janesson rose, fierce and cool, and the noise ceased.

"This is my final judgement. Does anyone in attendance wish to make public dissent?"

There was a long moment of silence.

"Very well. This mast is now complete; please return to your stations."

Theta wavered on his feet as the assembled filed out; standing so long was beginning to test his endurance, but swaying also masked the more subtle movements of his paws. Even before the room had emptied, he had defeated the tension field of his wrist restraints. Moments later, he was alone with Janesson and Jenks, bound in appearance only. He cocked his head at the two, maintaining a carefully neutral expression, and they both stared back.

"You," Janesson breathed through his teeth, "have now killed five of my men. I've seen the security video from your last round, and I'm confident in saying that you had no business surviving that encounter. Who and what are you?"

"Who am I?" Theta raised an eyebrow. What was this bait? "My name is Theta, and I am simply your slave."

"Our slave, are you? Simply our slave?" Janesson asked bitingly. "Just a simple slave."

He lifted a datapad from the rostrum and looked down at it. "Let's look at the medical reports for this simple slave, shall we? There are quite a few.

"Theta, also known as patient Theta. Age unknown. Home planet unknown. Affiliation unknown. Species... unknown, though physical examination indicates pure-blood arctic fox morphology. Gender...not quite male. Examination revealed that your claws have been removed and replaced with some hardened alloy, which the doctor did not attempt to examine *in situ*."

Janesson stared hard at him, grey-green eyes steady and alert. "So far, in our crazy little world, that only amounts to being a little queer. But then, here on page two, the report goes off the deep end. Your system is swarming with some very interesting nanites that seem to live in complete symbiosis with your body, slag themselves instantly when removed, and are deeply incorporated in every system you have. The doctors have never heard of anything like it outside of theory."

The captain tapped the pad, dropping it back onto his rostrum and looking down at Theta. "As near as they can tell, the nanites are repairing all damage to your body extremely rapidly, augmenting your senses, and perform-ing dozens of other functions that have yet to be identified. And if that was it, I might just shrug. Technology varies. However, this is the part I truly don't understand: Your genetics, so they say, are completely undecipherable. One of the doctors put down a note theorizing that your very genetic sequences are, in some way, encrypted. And even still, they insist that your body doesn't act like anything they've ever seen. The hormone balances, hyper-aggressive immune response...I have dozens of pages analysis, theory, and frantic scribbling by confounded medics, several of who have all but begged me to hand you over as a specimen to study. So, I repeat...who are you?"

Theta was surprised, and fascinated. He took a breath, paused, and then closed his mouth on what he had been about to say. What *had* Master Knoskali done to him...?

"I...really?"

The captain nodded, folding his arms across his chest. Jenks leaned forward, head cocked as if inviting an answer.

Theta bared his teeth, standing straight and defiant in spite of the pain.

"I was the dancer of House Selesz, and Knoskali's personal slave. Do you know what that means?"

Janesson and Jenks turned to stare at one another, both looking exasperated.

Slowly the captain sank into his seat, bewildered.

"You...I don't believe it."

Jenks, recovering his wits, began laughing softly. He leaned forward against his little table beside the rostrum. "Amazing. Simply amazing."

Janesson, unlike Jenks, seemed painfully unamused. He stood and hit a button on his console—Theta heard the lock on the door behind click as it engaged—then drew an energy pistol from his belt and stepped around the rostrum, leaving Jenks slightly startled.

"Captain?"

Theta watched Janesson's approach, simply lifting his chin. Four ways to damage the tall captain and defend himself sprang immediately to mind. He flexed his paws against the loose, inert wrist restraints, but chose to wait.

Jenks quickly lost all his amusement, stepping around the table, eyes fixed on Janesson.

"Captain..."

"You," the wolf muttered, stepping up to Theta. "Do you...no. You do know that we were looking for you aboard the *Freeta*. We thought we were trying to find a thing,"

Theta flattened his ears, growling slightly as Janesson jammed the tip of his energy pistol under his jaw.

"We paid a lot of money for that tip off, and it looks bad that we came away at break-even, with three dead crew, rock bottom ransom value, and very little slave value. Now that I know who you are, I have to justify the next action I take to a crew that's already displeased with me about my findings on your latest victims. Do you have any idea how much of a quandary you've put me in?"

Theta grinned a little grin, though his enervated legs betrayed him by wobbling slightly.

"Captain," Jenks cautioned, taking another step closer. His eyes were wide, paws out as if pleading for calm.

"I know, Jenks. He's incredibly dangerous, and he could probably kill me, trussed up though he is." Janesson growled, sliding the energy pistol back into its holster. "But he chooses not to, yes?"

"Yes," Theta agreed. "This is a time for diplomacy. Right now, unless I miss my mark, you're trying to figure out how you're going to deal with me. You know that I might be valuable to somebody who is the enemy of House Selesz."

"Oh I'm sure you would be," Janesson rumbled. "But I will never sell out a member of my crew. Not for profit, not for spite. Which brings me to a dangerous schism. I lead the crew only so long as they see fit; Jenks represents the entire revenue crew, and will not let me make a decision that isn't in their best interest."

"Got that straight," Jenks affirmed, though he looked bewildered.

"Forgive my lack of faith, but since when are pirates so honorable?" Theta asked softly. "It would seem to me that you were in a career where money by nature trumped kindness. And I'm your slave, not a member of your crew."

Janesson actually put his paw over his eyes at that, rubbing his temples. "*No*, not a slave. I thought that was clear; you, more than any of the other conscripts, are probationary crew."

"So...assuming I accept that," Theta tried a new tack, thrown from the line he'd planned to take, "you're saying that Jenks won't let you spare me?"

"I do not represent you," Jenks answered his question slowly and obliquely, as if considering each word with great care. "The captain does, but I only represent the revenue crew. Our system isn't exactly perfect."

"The other problem," Janesson broke in, still seemingly frustrated, "is that you're killing our crew. I don't know if I can keep you on board. Nefra wanted revenge for one of the three you killed on the transport ship, but I have no idea who's going to come after you for revenge for those three idiots. Which brings me to another question: Since when do dancers kill so effectively?"

"My recall is imperfect, but I remember most of it now. I was trained." Theta smirked, sliding his wrist restraints off and dropping them to the floor. "Trained at the highest level."

Jenks cringed, but the captain merely nodded as if this was nothing he hadn't expected.

"Theta—" Janesson began, but was interrupted by a buzz from the near terminal. The two officers reached the display simultaneously, but Jenks deferred to the captain. Curious, Theta perked his ears.

Janesson snorted, peering at the display. "Great timing. Jenks, do I still have your permission?"

"Aye. Want me to go?"

"Yes. Make sure Dela is on tactics, and be ready to go in a hurry, just in case."

"Aye, sir. Ah..." Jenks hesitated, glancing sidelong at Theta. "Sir, are you sure...? I can bring up a command station here."

Janesson shook his head. "Am I sure that it's safe to be alone with him?" the wolf grinned, tapping the door unlock code into his terminal. "Not completely, but go anyway. Theta and I have some things to discuss, including...that, and I want you on the bridge."

Jenks nodded acknowledgement, frowned down at Theta, then left. As the door shut behind the tall quartermaster, Theta wavered a little on his feet, turning back to Janesson. "Sir, if we're going to be here much longer, I'm either going to sit down or fall down."

"By all means, sit." Janesson gestured to a chair, pulling up his own. "We have a lot to talk about. Are you feeling well? Do you need a doctor?"

"I'm fine...tired and weak, but fine." Theta settled cautiously into the indicated chair.

"I met your predecessor once, you know." Janesson settled himself lightly into his seat. "He was nothing whatsoever like you. I also have had plenty of time to come to know Knoskali, and that you're his...product...doesn't surprise me much at all. Well, let's talk. Irrai seems to think you're a tactical genius, and all your tests showed extreme aptitude in almost every problem domain. So let me pose you an interesting tactical problem."

Theta found himself leaning forward, ears so stiff they almost hurt. His eyes were focused on Janesson's.

"After building you, shaping you...and I don't know what else, but I know his tastes, so I can fill in a lot of blanks...Knoskali, one of the most powerful of the Brynti lordship, bundles you up on an outbound freighter, bound for Ramesan. According to you, he then wipes your memory, and...here's the best part...somehow, his pet intelligence force, which is probably the single sharpest of any I've encountered, leaks information about your transit. Everything, in fact, except who or what you are." Janesson leaned back. "How does that story sound, to you?"

Theta shook his head, having considered the possibilities at length during his time abed. "I think I know what you're getting at, but the further you project a tactical position, the greater the inherent entropy. Without little 'booster steps' along the way, it's unlikely that this could be a predicted course of events, and the 'booster steps' I can imagine don't have the right feel."

Janesson arched an eyebrow at this. "Go on?"

"Well," Theta murmured, "First, assume I'm being truthful. I'm not interested in trying to prove you can trust me."

Janesson shrugged.

"The nearest branch that I can see," Theta continued, "results in you attacking the *Freeta* before I'm aware, questioning the crew about me, then removing me and selling me to his enemy, who I, out of a sense of loyalty, somehow manage to assassinate. But if he leaked that intel to you on purpose, why didn't he specify what you were looking for? Seems like a rather poor plan. And who's to say his enemy wouldn't just kill me? For that matter, your crew almost did that." Theta cleared his throat, voice dry and scratchy.

Janesson shook his head. "No. So you see no way you could be used as a weapon?"

"Oh, I didn't say that...it's very possible, but honestly, my read of the situation doesn't support me being used as a targeted weapon. I don't think, anyway. I would like to say that I knew what Knoskali wanted of me, but unfortunately your little attack disrupted my console before I could read his messages," Theta grumbled.

Janesson smirked. "Sorry about that. Well, that's...more than I'd thought about it, but really about the same point I ended up. Would you tell me if you knew more?"

Theta nodded quickly. "I will not compromise Knoskali, but I promise you that I have nothing to conceal in this."

"As I said, I know Knoskali, and we've...done business in the past. I've never come out ahead with him, and I've never known him to do anything without a plan. Every word he says, every look, motion...is always sculpted for the exact effect he wants." Janesson's tone was tinged with reluctant admiration, and Theta felt his lips curl back in pride/amusement/sympathy.

"Well, he's the single most amazing creature I've ever met," Theta murmured. "I will always love him."

Janesson seemed startled; he actually backed away. It was subtle, but Theta noticed.

"What? What? Why do I always have to justify myself? Yes, I was his slave. That's just how he lives. Yes, he did horrible things, and yes, he killed me, and yes, he may be trying to use me as a weapon...but I loved him, and he loved me. Knoskali is amazing, and graceful...he's as powerful as a storm, but as deep and calm as a glassy lake. He... he..." Theta trailed off, arrested by the expression on the captain's face.

"You're very broken. Knoskali is incredibly rich, incredibly powerful, and doesn't care for anyone except his empire. Certainly love is beyond him. He's the most evil entity that I've ever met."

Theta felt a shock course through him just as though he'd been slapped in the face. "You...cannot understand. Inari's breath...You're a pirate! You're evil yourself, by definition! Your—"

Janesson rose from his chair, angry. "Enough! You know, I intended to offer you a position on my crew, but you don't even seem to know what we're about. It's people like Knoskali who *made* us what we are. Our fleet was formed by merchant freighter crews working under contracts that turned them into wage slaves. Thirty years ago, they staged a mass revolt, and struck back at the companies who were enslaving them. Many of us are former slaves; I, myself, was sold into slavery as a child, when my parents couldn't pay their taxes, then trained to serve on a warship. Do you know who my malefactor was? It was a young Brynti lord. A certain black coyote, as a matter of fact. I witnessed some of the things he does to people. Don't fool yourself—his heart isn't capable of love."

Theta stood, himself, glaring malevolently up at Janesson with his ears flat back against his head. He could feel his pulse throbbing in his temples, and the air cooled his bared teeth. "That's it? That is your justification for what you do? What slaves did the *Freeta* have aboard? How does 'We all started as slaves' justify killing, taking slaves, selling slaves, and everything else you do as a matter of course? I won't judge you for that, by the gods—It's a tough universe, and we are entering a lawless, boundless age—but how dare you...how *dare* you judge and unilaterally declare him evil by comparison?"

There was a long moment of silence. To Theta's surprise, Janesson blinked first.

"Well..." The captain sighed, running a paw through his close-snipped hair. "Well, it's complex. My feelings run deep when it comes to that coyote. Clearly, yours do as well. If you say he loved you, I'll at least believe that you believe."

Theta was still trembling softly, paws clenched at his side. He closed his eyes, seeking calm; he was overreacting badly, and he knew it. His emotions, especially when they concerned Knoskali, were incredibly volatile and extremely hard to temper.

More moments passed in silence before Theta opened his eyes once more.

"Well? Are you going to kill me now, too?" Janesson mocked playfully.

Tumbling into amusement, Theta arched an eyebrow and bared his teeth. "That depends. Are you going to try to kill me?" Suddenly he fell back into his chair, laughing weakly. "Oh, this is so ridiculous."

Janesson shook his head, grinning lopsidedly down to him. "It is, and it isn't. You're right, in some ways, you know. We rationalize everything a bit too easily. I've thought about it before, but I got worked up when you compared me to...to him. We pirates, we are what we are, and you're right. It's just that...I think of him as my counterexample...the pinnacle of what I hope to never become." He settled onto the edge of his chair non-threateningly, elbows resting on his knees.

"And perhaps I'm too conditioned to being *his*. But... where does all this leave us?"

"Well, Mister Theta, everyone aboard this vessel works for their keep, and there's a job just for you. We evil pirates need some muscle in space-side tactics—Dela is good, but Dela's only apprentice...ah, her talents lie elsewhere. Your former boss recommended you very strongly, and I want you to train to fill that role. It's an important position on this ship, and a respectable one. It could be a new start for you, something you can settle into or grow from...and a way to escape your past. Are you willing? Can I trust you?"

Theta sighed softly, looking down at his paws. "What about the revenge problem?"

"Ah...could you perhaps try not to kill people who come after you?" Janesson hinted, a glint of amusement in his eye. "Perhaps just...beat them into submission? Maybe at most just a gentle maiming to warn off others?"

"I'm not trained to subdue, Captain. I'm trained to kill." Theta smirked. "But...I could try. I'll warn you, though: I will never betray or otherwise knowingly work against Knoskali. Otherwise...well, I suppose I'd be willing to help out for a while, though I don't know where my destiny lies and I don't intend to give up on finding it."

"I think," Janesson murmured, "that I can work with that. Welcome to our crew, mister Theta."

Theta took the captain's proffered paw softly. "Please... just call me Theta."

VIII

Outward

"MISS JALE?"

Jale's indistinct dream fell away, feather light, and she opened her eyes, blinking them into focus and raising her head.

"Why good morning, Pinky. Is it that time already?"

The husky bobbed his head, paws clutched together behind his back. "Yes ma'am. Jewel has a light breakfast ready as you requested."

"Very good. Thank you, Pinky. Also, please advise Knoskali that I will indeed join him for lunch if his offer is still open."

"Yes ma'am!" The husky half-bowed, then quickly straightened and jogged back out into the atrium, leaving her to her morning ablutions.

After rinsing her face and paws, she slid out of the thin nightgown that she'd taken to wearing to bed and began to assemble herself. Shipsuit, insignia, boots, overcoat—Captain Bercammon, Brynton's newest unlimited-ton master, was business and burnish. Such a difference three weeks had made that she barely recognized herself.

Three weeks, two days, and a great deal of training, paperwork, and effort stood between Captain Bercammon and the Jale who'd arrived on Brynton in fear for her life. Knoskali's stunningly efficient personnel and training department had drilled into her all the precepts that her job entailed, built expertly on her in-space experience and knowledge, prepared her to learn, and then pumped her full of an incredible wealth of training and knowledge, turning her into a legitimate—if inexperienced—captain. In many ways, a line had been crossed that she could never again retreat behind, and she felt it from toes to nose.

The ship Knoskali had allocated had been staffed, stocked and provisioned, its crew set, and its clearances filed with various authorities. Most of the work had been done on her orders, and she'd stood her qualifying examination three days before on the very same ship. Preparations had drawn to a close the night after, and they were scheduled to depart in two days' time. Despite the intensity and the rush, she felt ready and able—though her knowledge in some areas was lacking, she had been assured that her overall competence was proven.

After a quick check in the mirror and a little shake of her head, she strode into the atrium, drawn to the smell of breakfast and the pungent smell of megvha, a local stimulant beverage. Jale had developed a taste for the creamy, sharp hot drink and the long-lasting alertness it brought; of the items on the table it was the first to gain her attention, and the first to be refilled.

"Ma'am, Master Knoskali has you on his lunch schedule. He reminds you to bring the final voyage plans and duty roster to review."

"Thank you again, Pinky," Jale murmured, inclining her head slightly. "You know, dear, I'm truly going to miss the pair of you. I'd never thought I'd be the type to have anyone else in my personal space, oh no, but to my surprise I've found that I've come to enjoy your company much."

To her surprise, Pinky seemed slightly emotional, shifting his weight from one side to the other and lowering his head. He seemed unhappy. "We're going to miss you, too, Miss Jale, very much. Very much."

Jewel padded up and stood shoulder to shoulder with his brother, done with his cleaning. He nodded somberly in agreement, pressing his paws together nervously. "We really hope you find him, ma'am. For your sake, and for his too."

Jale nodded lightly and then turned away, hiding her expression in her mug of megvha. The odds of finding Theta were not favorable. Gnosi, restored to his rank and status and working as her executive officer, had indicated that every day departure was delayed created an exponential increase in the search tree. The day after she'd met Knoskali, she'd been dropped into the middle of a dizzily rushed project to crew and plan the search—everyone had been scrambling frantically and word had been that they would depart as soon as the ship was out of refit with her as the 'flag'.

And then, two days later, Knoskali's mood and attitude had suddenly changed significantly. He'd become less volatile, a little calmer. The furor had died off, and suddenly Jale had found herself in training to be a legitimate captain, with knowledge and licenses to match, rather than simply the 'responsible party'.

She chewed on a seared meatroll, but its delicate delectability was lost on her as she thought of the difficulties inherent in finding one lone fox slave in the vastness of the universe. From Gnosi's briefings, she'd come to realize that the slave markets didn't keep records of sales, and were very reluctant to talk about any clients or 'goods' that passed through. Worse still, the slave traders shifted bases often, noting their movements via encrypted instructions left on mapped communication nodes, often piggybacked on other data. Not only would they have to figure out which slaver base Theta had been sold to, but where that base was currently located, what broker at the base had purchased him, and who he'd been sold to—information that everyone would be loth to provide. And that was only the start!

Jale leaned back in her chair, cradling her drink in her paws and gazing up and out, over the building's mezzanine and across the heaving undercast. Today, monstrous electrical storms raged beneath the omnipresent high red clouds that raced, miles thick, across the upper limits of the troposphere. The flashes of lightning were almost hypnotic, arcing from cloud to cloud; mildly-toxic rain danced off the transparency surrounding her living quarters and cascaded in rivulets and streams along its surface, lending further entrancing distortion to the scene. She sighed softly, enjoying the show.

She'd never felt less agoraphobic.

The doorchime rang.

Pinky rose and scampered to the entryway, returning moments later with Gnosi in tow. Jale eyed him. Since arriving on the planet, Gnosi had shown little personality beyond grim and efficient, and this morning started no differently; he saluted, then settled in a seat across from her with the comfortable familiarity he'd begun to develop in her presence.

"Ma'am, I have the readiness reports." He settled a datapad on the table.

Jale nodded, straightening her seat and tearing her attention away from the storms. "Very good. Would you like some megvha?"

Gnosi eyed the carafe, ears perking—Jale could swear she almost saw a smile on his lips. "You know, this time I'd love some," he murmured.

Jewel sprang immediately to the task of pouring him a cup; Pinky had been working quickly to set up a serving of breakfast for the coyote, and pulled his paws out of the way just in time.

Jale shook her head in silent amusement. "Easy, boys. Can you summarize the reports for me, mister Gnosi?"

The coyote settled forward, resting on his elbows. He swung his datapad around for her review. "As you can see, crew has all reported in. Provisions are about eighty percent loaded, but munitions are full up. The handling and emergency simulations have been run for engineering, bridge crew, and tactics. I took the liberty of ordering a series of battle drill simulations that should be underway as we speak, and...well, there are a dozen pages to the report, but I think it's safe to say that we're about as ready to go as we can be, except for the last few tons of provisions. And us." Gnosi seemed rather pleased with himself, Jale was happy to note. The return of emotion to the coyote couldn't be anything but a good sign.

"Marvelous job, dear Gnosi. Did we get the tactician we were hoping for?"

"We did! He reported yesterday. Been at work nonstop, too, sorting out his department. I'm surprised at how good a crew we've got," he admitted. "I...have had doubts about this mission. But the more I go over the duty roster, the more convinced I am that the Master does mean to find his Theta. I've never seen him mobilize something like this that didn't involve fun for him, or profit for his house, or at least some strategic advantage."

Jale shrugged. "Well, I don't know what his angle is, but without anything else to go on I'll just take him at his word, if you don't mind, dear. Speaking of," Jale presented her own datapad. "I have lunch with him shortly, so we should probably review our plans of record."

Gnosi sipped his megvha and nodded, leaning over the tablet.

Lord Knoskali, all business, glanced perfunctorily over the same tablet a few hours later, then slid it back to Jale.

"Very well done, Captain, and two days ahead of schedule. Your alternate plan for departure tonight appeals to me."

The black coyote sat back and sipped his drink. Jale knew from his manner that he intended to continue, so she simply reclined and waited, sampling her own beverage. It was delightfully cool and minty.

"My dear," he began slowly, "I have committed some of my finest personnel and placed them under your command. I'd be lying if I didn't say part of it wasn't for the sake of amusement." His perfect white teeth flashed in a little grin, which quickly vanished back into the indistinctness of his black fur. "But that's not the only answer. I think you can find my dancer, and I think you, above all, will know how to handle him. I'll warn you that he may not be what you remember, and he may not have retained his sanity. In your databanks, there's a message from me to Theta. He absolutely must read it, and that's the most important part of your mission, right there. It has encoded words that will start a dramatic series of changes within him. I also have included a network of nodes and stations that *Varaunt* might...have stopped at, just for you, dear Captain.

"I would *suggest*," the Lord's tone dripped honey, "that you get my fox to read the message before trying to make contact, if you can. I'd also recommend that you avoid engaging the *Varaunt* should you come across her by some chance."

Jale's attention was riveted; he knew something that he wasn't letting on.

Knoskali leaned forward, eyes sparkling. "*Varaunt* outguns you significantly, and it's unlikely they'll react well to a friendly greeting. However, I gave you one of my best tacticians, so use him wisely. You know, I'd like him back, along with Gnosi and the rest...so do be careful with them."

Jale frowned into her cup, considering this. "I see," she murmured. "And will I get further intelligence, should you find it by some chance?"

"Your executive officer is one of my better intelligence personnel. He knows how, so listen to him." Knoskali burnished his obsidian claws on the folds of his onyx robe, as sinisterly nonchalant as Jale had seen him. Abruptly, he raised his head and locked eyes with her, for what purpose she could not say. The intensity behind his direct stare sent cold chills down her spine, and she drew back, paws clutching the arms of her chair.

"Listen to him, Jale, but remember always that you are in command, and you are responsible. Take his counsel, but never his orders. You alone are in command, and he reports to you. Forget that at the mission's peril."

The two sat in silence. After a long moment, the coyote peered back down at his claws, a little scowl darkening his features.

"One more thing, Captain, and listen well, for it is critical. You will be surrounded by a crew of people working for me. However, you are not working for me—you are at all times working for Theta, and Theta alone. Do you understand?"

Jale narrowed her eyes, then nodded slowly.

"Good. I knew you would. Well, that's most of the preamble. Now for the meat of the thing."

Knoskali tapped the surface of his desk, and it darkened into a large star map, showing all of known space. Quickly, he became more abrupt and straightforward than Jale had ever heard him, and she took careful notes as he outlined search priorities and things that she must not reveal or do. Once he had finished, he swept the map away and straightened.

"There are two other matters of importance. First, my intelligence has informed me that it is possible that an attempt will be made to stop your ship. It's a general action against my House, from what we can tell, rather than an attempt to sabotage this particular mission...but assume nothing. They can't narrow down the vector of attack, but suggest that it will either be a saboteur, an attack by light ships, or both. I can protect you against engagement by having my ships escort yours until you enter Rellin drive. Of course, a saboteur is the most likely. Intel has picked apart your crew records, but if someone is there, they're not likely to act overtly. So...watch out. The further I extend my hand, the harder it is to keep it safe."

Jale's stress level, which had died down and stayed low after her qualifying exams, began to elevate once more. She nodded, trying to evade the notion that she was acting as the hand of this tyrant. She chuffed softly, closing the notes on her datapad. "Understood. I notice that you've included sealed orders for me for a week enroute?"

Knoskali nodded, turning to the giant wrap-around window. "Correct. Now, one last order of business." He smirked, spinning his goblet in his paws and looking out across the dark, stormy skies. "This one is a bit whimsical, but...take your Pinky and Jewel. I don't want to move them back to pleasure, and two more mouths won't strain your stores. If they misbehave, you can sell them along the way and use the proceeds for your ship's operating fund."

The thought of those two coming along on such a dangerous mission made Jale's eyes widen; she shook her head, sitting up straight. "But that—"

"Ah, stop, stop...no buts," Knoskali admonished gently, still gazing out at the cloudscape. "I don't generally take requests, and if I want suggestions I'll ask first."

The coyote took another swig from his cup, leaning back in his chair; Jale could just see him gazing out into the turbulent skyline from beside its broad back. Clearly not dismissed, Jale summoned her patience to await his whim.

"So, Captain," he began after a few minutes had passed. "What do you think of my planet?"

Jale blinked and bared her teeth slightly, taken aback by this tangent. She'd seen images of the pre-schism Brynton, and the ecological devastation of the planet as it was still shocked her.

"It's..." she struggled for wording, holding back the harsh terms that threatened to slip into the pause. After another moment's thought, she snorted and stood, looking over his shoulder into the murk. "It's...every bit a testament to the achievements of your society."

To her surprise, Knoskali laughed softly and half-spun back to her, awarding a soft salute. "And I'm sure you mean that just as it sounds. It's funny, actually. Perhaps you simply haven't seen enough to fear me properly, but that's a quality I do appreciate...when it suits me. Well, I have some time to kill, so allow me to tell you the story of my beautiful Brynton, dear Captain Bercammon, and of her society's achievements."

The coyote turned again towards the window, gesturing for her to stand beside him and lifting his legs to rest his paws on its sill. Soundlessly and wordlessly, answering to no signal Jale had seen, a slave brought him a fresh drink. He traded his for it and sighed in apparent contentment, then began to speak in a soft, reflective tone of voice.

"My little planet was once young. Settled just before the onset of the period of isolation, in fact, although they didn't know that then of course. The planet was discovered as both habitable and comfortable, with plentiful natural and mineral resources. As soon as the second wave of settlers landed with tools and prefabs and began to lay the foundations for Settlement City, however, they found themselves face to face with a large, flying, aggressively-curious native species that they came to call the Elechen. Wearing only their natural teeth, claws and armor, and having no technology or construction, they were regarded by the settlers as a primitive intelligence. Hostilities were narrowly avoided, and they managed to demonstrate peaceful intent."

Jale had never heard any of this, and it certainly was more detailed than the glossed over history she'd learned as a youngster. Folding her arms across her chest, she arched an eyebrow but remained silent.

"Well, as it turned out," the coyote continued, with a shake of his head, "they were more intelligent than we gave them credit for. When we proved...mm, non-hostile they actually welcomed us. They were fascinated by our interactions with the planet itself, how we farmed it, mined it, raised livestock on it, constructed dwellings. We never found enough commonality in spoken language to communicate verbally, but we nonetheless built a symbiotic relationship and a symbolic language that endured for centuries. It's unlikely that we would have even survived without them during the isolation.

"Nearly four hundred years later, the first of the Alaran trade ships began to arrive, and with them great change. Other cultures, it seemed, had technology far more advanced than our own, and knowledge that we lacked. My dear Brynton was in grave danger of being left behind. What we lacked in technology, however, we more than made up for in resources and intelligence and cunning, and so we traded aggressively to narrow the gap. The Elechen became unhappy when they felt we were becoming destructive to the planet, and we had no way to communicate the concepts of profit, advancement, or technology. We couldn't explain that without the knowledge of the Alari, Bryton would forever stay a backwater."

"And what's wrong with that?" Jale interrupted. "Even Hope refused the first Alaran traders. They're neither a backwater nor..." She gestured to the window, words eluding her for a moment. "Nor this!"

"Oh certainly not a *backwater*, but we outgross them eight to one in every sector outside of tourism." The lord snorted, seeming amused. "And there are far, far fewer of us earning far more. But we have the benefit of looking back, my dear Captain. Surely you can see that it was equally probable that the more advanced worlds would dominate those who were resource-rich but technology poor. Our very survival and freedom would have been at stake."

"That was hardly a certainty."

"Little is." Knoskali turned back with a little smirk. "Strategy improves probability, and that's one of my lessons here, Captain."

"I see." Jale didn't, really. "Well, it's done now, at any rate. So about these Elechen of yours, then. You claim to have a symbiotic relationship, but I, for one, have never heard of them."

"You wouldn't have. As we grew stronger, we began to dominate the relationship...and yet they began to resist our will, even in their decline. They would have overpowered us, but into the impending fray stepped a great leader, a wolf named Jolar David. He soothed them, befriended them, and calmed their collective wrath by promising to end the trading. He lied most beautifully. In less than a decade he quietly rallied the Brynti from an agrarian society into a cohesive civilization under a common charter, and expanded the trade imbalance into a great force which left the aliens as our slaves. From a stagnant, socialist society, he laid the foundations of the greatest capitalism in known civilization in under a generation. Isn't it lovely?"

Jale rubbed her temples—her head hurt from seeking subtext in his words, and she felt ill just imagining the situation. "Lovely? No, I don't think so." She shook her head. "No, if that's the truth of it, and I sorely hope it isn't, it sounds like a terrible thing to do to a race who welcomed and trusted you with their planet."

"Our planet. Survival of the fittest, my dear. And speaking of the fittest, some fifteen standard years after David came to power, a mere three decades after the first trade ship arrived in orbit, the Elechen rebelled. Apparently, seeing our expansion growing exponentially, they decided to defend their home."

"I should hope they would!"

Knoskali lifted a paw, a single digit raised. He turned his head to smirk up at her. "Patience, my dear Captain. It will serve you better than it did them. In the end, and far too late, they decided to rise up actively...only to find us prepared to strike back with infinite force. We crushed them with the weapons we'd traded their planet for, and within a year we had wiped them from the face of this world, destroying them in battle and hunting down their holdouts in the mountains. Once they were eliminated and those who sympathized with them cleansed from our society, we paved over all record. There are none now alive to even whisper their memories. That, you see, is the epitome of Brynti politics—as you may yet come to understand."

Overwhelmed and speechless, Jale sank back against Knoskali's desk.

"Master?" A messenger spoke from the doorway.

Knoskali spun slightly in his chair, looking annoyed. "Yes?"

"I'm sorry to disturb you, Lord, but Brent is here."

Knoskali snorted, waving a paw dismissively. "Set him up with a pleasure slave, if he'll take one. I will be a while longer."

The messenger bowed and left.

Jale shuddered, not entirely sure if that meant what she thought but distinctly not wanting to find out.

"Where was I?" Knoskali seemed lost in thought. "Ah yes. My, my little story has grown a little long. Let me finish, and then I fear we must part, you and I, likely for the last time. For your sake, it had better be. The original houses have fallen long hence, but the current houses are stable and prosperous. We rarely war directly," and a hint of displeasure crept into the coyote's tone, verging on anger, "but we do at times contest through silly games of intrigue, which at times spill over. Still, even with our games, we're the most efficient industrial complex in the known universe. With every house relatively specialized across its manufacturing base, no restrictions to our use of the environment or resources, and with full economic collaboration, we're making money and turning out projects that no other planet can match. That our skies are a beautiful shade of red is but a small price to pay."

Knoskali stood, towering over Jale. Startled, she scrambled back to her feet, looking up into his expressionless face.

"Find my Theta."

"I must ask...Why the story?"

"Good hunting, Captain Bercammon," Knoskali said with a smirk. He turned his back to her once more and stared out the window, folding his paws behind him.

With that, she *was* clearly dismissed. Restraining her curiosity and frustration, she turned and allowed herself to be escorted out.

"Bring us abeam, please sir." Jale said softly to the shuttle pilot, who obliged by slowing his craft and matching orbits.

Jale looked over what she could see of her ship. Dubbed a 'pocket cruiser' by its original manufacturer, it had received an extensive refit to allow it to operate independently in deep space before it even saw service. Before releasing it for in-system space trials, Knoskali had brought it in for another round of upgrades, including advanced stealth systems which gave it a tiny electromagnetic footprint and highly advanced sensing and scanning arrays. It had also received a special absorptive coating to give it optical camouflage and protection against direct scans, so mostly Jale saw only the position and recognition lights that highlighted the curves of its sleek form.

Jale had once thought that love was beyond her.

"Quite the ship, isn't she?" Gnosi's soft voice startled her, coming from near her elbow. She peered down to find him standing in the companionway, just high enough up the cockpit ramp to stare out the windows. She smiled softly down to him.

"Quite. I wouldn't call myself an expert on ships, though at this point I'm certainly well-read...but I must say that it hardly seems fair for someone like me to command a ship like this as some sort of punishment."

The shuttle pilot shot her a strange look.

She smiled politely back.

"I'm not entirely sure it's punishment, but what do I know?" Gnosi sounded amused. "I've always found life in the Master's service to be anything but straightforward. Part of me thinks that he works as hard to keep from being understood as he does to actually make things happen."

Jale sat silently for a minute, leaning back in her seat and gazing at the ship before her. On one hand, she was struck by the absurdity of this whole affair, and yet on the other, as ridiculous as it seemed, it was also deadly serious. She forgot, now and again, that she wasn't really a captain. *He* was amazingly good at making people believe they were the actors he cast them as.

She shook her head and snorted.

"Alright, sir, that'll do. Take us in."

As they swept along under her ventral strakes, Gnosi slid back into the main cabin and Jale stood.

Moments later, they were docked.

Jale settled the huskies into her cabin and made her way to the bridge. She'd instructed Gnosi to spin the engines up and signal the escort, and she arrived on the bridge to find an orderly systems startup in progress as they made ready for deep space.

"Attention on deck!"

Jale didn't catch who said it, but suddenly everybody not actively engaged in a task stood to attention.

She grimaced. "Carry on. Status, Mister Gnosi?"

"Engine reaction is sixty-eight percent nominal. Escorts are on station, and our departure is cleared with a twenty minute void time. All departments report ready, and the board is green," Gnosi said. He leaned close. "I have briefing for department heads scheduled for zero eight hundred. Ship time is now standard coordinated, twenty-one thirty-one hours."

"Very good." Jale murmured back. She glanced down at her panel, pursing her lips. "Watch-on-watch until fourteen hundred tomorrow, then we'll move to our three watch rotation. Schedule an emergency battle-stations drill during midwatch."

"Aye, ma'am," the coyote acknowledged quietly. "Eighty percent nominal."

"Helm, douse position lights."

"Aye."

She brought up the orbital exit clearance on her panel, and began making alterations to the outbound route, plotting a semi-random zig-zagging course with irregular speed changes. After a moment she sent it to the helm.

"Helm, I've sent you a new course that's nothing akin to our departure clearance. Please configure for it."

"Aye, ma'am. Course revised." The skinny, dark-furred skunk at the helm showed no doubt or unwillingness to follow her non-cleared, non-briefed course. That was a good sign. Perhaps she *could* pull this off.

"Tactical," she turned to the operator at the near-space tactical station, "Monitor position and velocity on our escorts, and pick me out anything moving parallel or towards us within a hundred kilometers."

"Aye, ma'am."

"Ninety-six percent nominal."

"Good enough. Helm, engines ahead one half, flank when we hit nominal. After our first turn switch to program departure and engage full stealth mode."

"Ahead one half, aye."

The visuals that displayed the space outside shifted as the ship surged forward; Jale stepped back to settle into her chair, touching the interphone button.

"Crew, this is your captain speaking." Jale put on her most authoritative voice.

"We're embarking tonight on a dangerous mission of unknown duration, but we won't go into battle with a ship named HX-339A4. No, this ship, at the behest of her owner, has been given a name. It's a proud name, for a fine ship. This ship is to be known from this day forward as the HSS *Dancer*, and she and I are both proud to have you aboard." She let go of the interphone button.

"Let the log reflect the change."

"Aye, ma'am."

Leaving even her escorts searching for her, *Dancer* broke orbit and began her run up to Rellin drive, slipping silently off into the dark.

IX

Search

JALE SIGHED and leaned back to rest her head against her chair's headrest, tapping her claws on the glossy surface of her console.

"Lovely," she grumped. "Helm, secure from stealth mode. Tac, commence active scanning if you would, please."

The midwatch helmsman nodded, tapping two fingers on his panel. Around the bridge, a subtle ring of lights changed quickly from blue to red.

"Ship reports secured from stealth mode, ma'am."

"Well, at least this time there's actually something here," Gnosi said, leaning forward. His display was operating the main bridge projection, and everyone but Jale stared intently as he zoomed in on the little deep-space asteroid cluster, swinging around the composite graphic of a jumble of smooth, machine-scarred rocks twenty kilometers away. "I'll bet it certainly used to be a slave base."

"Yes, I'm sure it was...at some point in history." Jale muttered drily, looking at the augmented video display. Lots of debris. A few severely-pitted anchor points were machined into the biggest asteroid; their decay profile, when she selected them, indicated that they had been exposed to space for the better part of a year.

She sighed again, dismissing the target data from her console with the flick of a digit. She was done with this delaying game.

"Nav, update our charts, please. Slave base S6 is abandoned. When you're done, please change our coordinate system back to universal reference and plot me a course to Fonaci's heliopause."

"Aye, ma'am."

Gnosi turned to her, muzzle wrinkled into a small, confused scowl. "Hold on, now, Captain. Let's just follow our plan of record—we have three more bases to check in this area. For that matter, we're not even done scouting this one."

Jale caught a surprised glance from her weapons officer and grimaced. She tilted her head slightly in Gnosi's direction and dropped her voice. "The next two coordinates are even older than these, dear. I *know* these aren't the cream of the crop for the Selesz intelligence network. In fact—"

"Contact!" The tactics officer interrupted her aside, the young ocelot's voice controlled but tense. "Eighty kilometers. Large target, powering up..." she froze for a microsecond, then sat straight, eyes widening. "Warship!"

Jale's breath caught; everything else was forgotten in an instant as the target appeared on her subpanel, datafields filling in as the tactical computers began to arrive at conclusions about what they saw.

"Stealth! Quickly!" She flew through the sequences for pulling up the angular plot, then raised her head. "Helm, give me an evasive chop and drop to land me on the other side of that debris field, as quickly as you can please."

The helmsman nodded, quick on the controls. He swung the ship about with a burst of power that brought the engines right to their emergency limit, then cut the thrust.

"Full stealth mode, and set battle condition," Jale snapped, voice steady but thin with anxiety. She shook her head, biting her lower lip and considering her options.

Anything moving could be presumed hostile, and this was a rather large something. She glanced sidelong at Gnosi; he appeared quite calm at his station, in theory monitoring overall ship and department condition. She wondered if she shouldn't have him take over—there was no substitute for experience.

"Receiving an audio transmission, ma'am," the tactics officer said, interrupting her thoughts. "Passive arrays, wide band. Modulation is captured."

Jale's heart felt like it was aflutter in her chest, but she managed to retain her calm externally; she watched stealth display with veiled desperation, willing the lights to illuminate faster as the complex subsystems powered up.

If she gave up command now, she knew she'd never get it back.

She shook her head and stood. "Let's hear it Naane."

The bridge audio system crackled softly as the tactics officer switched it over, and the message was repeated. "Unidentified vessel, power down and hold position or you will be destroyed."

Jale strode to the tactics station, resting one paw on the console and peering over her officer's shoulder. She frowned, then turned to her helmsman.

"Helm, as soon as our thrust vectoring system is stealthed, please alter our course downward—or rather, negative Z, local coords. At least twenty degrees down, and I want you to put that big rock between us and them." She received a small nod, and peered back down at her tactics officer, who was staring intently at the display. "Have we a match on registry? Any idea who they are?"

The tactics officer shook her head and tapped her primary display, pointing at various symbols and acronyms that Jale didn't recognize. "We can't find out more without interrogating their system and blowing stealth," she rumbled, allocating Jale just enough attention to respond. "But her make is Alari. Newer design, probably better firepower and definitely heavier armor than us. Similar drive power, longer LOA. Um...building the full analysis for you now."

"Stealth is up, ma'am," the helmsman said. "Course adjustment complete."

Jale nodded without turning, watching in fascination as the nimble-fingered tactics officer ran through a rapid series of analyses and estimates, selecting the best of the computed data. She glanced at Gnosi, arching an eyebrow and lifting her chin. He caught her gaze and shook his head, teeth bared in a slight grimace.

"My best guess is that they're mercenaries, or a new alliance we have no data on." His ears drooped slightly as he turned back to his display. "Being here, they're probably not friendly. The Alari don't sell to just anybody, so it's unlikely they're in the trade."

"Ma'am?" her weapons officer spoke up calmly. "I'm maintaining a passive lock on the target, and active countermeasures are ready."

"Very good. I do hope it won't come to it, but stay ready on those countermeasures. This would be a terrible time to engage. Tac?"

"I've got the shake, ma'am. I think—yes! No, I'm sure of it. We can elude them. Escape without them marking our outbound vector inside five degrees of certainty. No way they're reading us right now, not even visible light."

Jale nodded, tensing her legs to keep them from shaking. The coldness she felt in her belly made it exceptionally difficult to concentrate; glancing around at the bridge stations, however, she noted that her crew all seemed alert but calm, and the seeds of panic refused to sprout.

"Unidentified vessel," the audio system rattled, "we have a firing solution. Power down and hold position, or we will destroy you."

"Bluffing," the tactics officer said, confidently tapping her display. "I wager my life on it."

Jale looked again to her executive officer, who shook his head doubtfully.

Hire good people...and trust them.

"Very well..." Jale spoke cheerily, summoning a calm that she in no way felt. "Then let us call his bluff. Helm, continue on this course. As soon as we're fully in the shadow of that rock, the biggest one, we're going to make our escape as quickly as possible. We'll enter Rellin drive for twelve minutes, on a course opposite his position from the rock. That should allow our entire run-up and entry to be hidden from detection, stealth or no stealth. Even if he catches our vector, he won't be able to extrapolate our destination. Once we come out on the other end, we'll go to our previously plotted course."

The helmsman nodded again, and Jale hoped he'd actually understood; she made her way back to her chair, settling woodenly and avoiding anyone's eye.

Gnosi left his station to stand beside her. "This is too risky," he growled, not speaking softly. "It's too slow, too dangerous. He may actually detect us—we can't be sure—but we can be sure that any distance we gain will attenuate his fire. We should go to Rellin drive, and do it now, directly away."

"No!" The tactics officer bounced up from her station and removed her headset, eyes wide. "Particles from the reactive drive at full power will still emit detectible EM! Even vectored and dispersed, it increases our detection risk by a factor of four! The computer says, and I—"

"Back to your station," Gnosi snapped at her, voice dropping to a growl.

What if I'm wrong...what business do I have giving these orders? What would Erin do...?

Jale ground her teeth, holding tight to her cool, competent exterior. She did not look in Gnosi's direction, keeping her eyes fixed on the main bridge view.

"Now, Jale!" Gnosi hissed. "Every second we lose is an exponential increase in the damage of their weapons." He raised his voice. "Helm—"

"No!" Jale chirped, spurred to action. "My previous orders stand, so please follow them. Thank you, XO, but please return to your station."

Gnosi ground his teeth briefly, then wordlessly flumped back into his own chair; Jale hardened herself against his displeasure and whatever was to come.

Moments stretched into minutes, into a quarter of an hour. Suddenly, the main display flashed a warning as the other ship fired.

Jale flinched. Everyone else tensed, looking over their systems, but no alarms sounded. Seven sets of eyes turned towards the tactics station.

The tactics officer sat back and exhaled a small sigh, drying her paws on the legs of her shipsuit. "They fired at an extrap of our previous trajectory, and they were firing for effect. We've got 'em." She turned to Jale with a predatory grin. "We could pick them apart, if we wanted."

"That was your only warning. Surrender or die." The transmission hissed and warbled, slightly distorted by the rocks off of which it reflected and refracted as *Dancer* passed into the protective shadow of the asteroid belt.

"Warning shot, eh? I'll have to remember that one." Jale shook her head with a rueful grin. She dipped her muzzle appreciatively to her tactics officer. "Excellent work. As for engaging, dearie...while I admire your style, this time I think we shall quit while we're ahead. Helm?"

"Rellin when you want it, ma'am."

"Without delay, if you please."

Jale switched the main bridge display to a tactical depiction of the escape course. All eyes were forward as *Dancer* slid away from the asteroid field, accelerating rapidly to the threshold velocity required to enter Rellin drive at the terminal point. Moments later, the drive system was engaged and the former slaver base left far behind, along with their assailant. Jale's panel watchdog indicated that their maneuver had gone undetected; despite her confidence in her systems, however, she didn't begin to breathe normally until *Dancer* had stopped, made her course change, and re-entered Rellin drive without any further contact with the hostile ship.

Safely underway to Fonaci, she once again felt the tug of exhaustion.

"All departments are to stand down from battle condition." She looked around her bridge, feeling a sudden surge of warmth for her crew. "Good work. I want each of you to please submit an after-action report and a system performance evaluation before you go off-shift. Also, I want an analysis of the probability that our little...encounter... was a coincidence. I have a hunch that the bases in our list are marked." She caught a sharp glance from Gnosi. "Once again, though, good work. Thank you all."

She stood and stretched, then left her crew for the cool sheets of her bed.

Gnosi accosted her as soon as she set foot on the bridge the next morning. She listened patiently to his exhortations that she turn and set course for another of the slaver bases for several minutes before finally cutting him off.

"Be completely honest with me, mister Gnosi. Why is it so urgently important to you that I turn back?"

"It's not necessarily back. We're only half a day from S4, right now...it's just a little sidestep. We don't need to come as close this time, unless there's a base, and we can remain stealthed—if there's nothing there we can get right back on course."

"That's still not a why," Jale flexed her paws and stretched her arms, still exhausted from the previous night. A lonely mug of megvha steamed fragrantly beside her chair, waiting unattended; she eyed it longingly, then frowned at the recalcitrant coyote who stood in her way. "I've not heard a real why. It doesn't matter who you may be—I'll need you to give me a bit more information if you want to steer me that way, yes I will."

Gnosi pinned her with a rather frustrated, confounded look; she merely continued to stare at him until his ears flattened slightly and he moved aside, allowing her to walk to her seat.

Jale tried to pay him no heed, cradling her drink and pulling up her messages. As much as she tried to focus on the after action reports, however, she could feel the eyes of her XO on her; he was clearly resistant to being commanded by her, and subordination seemed an increasingly uncomfortable fit. Still, Knoskali had been adamant—She alone was in full command, and would be held fully responsible. Gnosi was not privy to her secret orders, Knoskali had told her; his one and only duty, the Lord had said, was to obey and assist her. The consequences of his insubordination could be dire; in thirty-eight hours, sealed orders would open...but much could happen in that time to undermine her command.

She found her eyes moving across the same text she'd started trying to read minutes before and raised a paw to rub her temples, closing her eyes. It seemed certain that only when the sealed orders unlocked would she find out the realities of this mission. *Varaunt*, alone, stood out in her mind as the gaping hole in the data—the invisible mass that *Dancer*'s fate was orbiting, moving out in the dark beyond the fringes of vision.

Thirty eight hours and she'd know.

On the other paw, her course to Fonaci space was a hedge to her bet; if her orders failed to be as comprehensive as she expected, there was a good chance that her destination would help her plot a new course of action.

If there was anywhere that they could dredge up a lead that might take her to *Varaunt*, she mused, surely it was Fonaci Prime. In her past life, she'd spoken to plenty of less savory Fonaci passengers bound for Ramesan, and the one thing consistently mentioned was that almost any information could be obtained in the Fonaci system—for a price. Weapons and goods illegal on most planets were sold openly, and the market there ran on a central bank system that allowed anonymous transactions. In theory, it was the planet through which most pirates laundered ransoms and stolen goods.

Of course, slavery was technically illegal, even in the Fonaci system. Brynton was the only major planet where that particular perversion wasn't outlawed; indeed, on Brynton slaves were a currency all on their own. It took no great mental leap for Jale to arrive at the conclusion that Knoskali had given her such an outdated list of slaver bases as a clear sign that he had no intention of her chasing Theta through the commercial slave network.

She hoped.

She felt a shift in the air beside her, and tilted her head up to find Gnosi standing there. She ruthlessly suppressed an initial jolt of anxiety, and the wash of irritation that followed, managing to restrain all but an inquiring lift of her chin.

"Yes, XO?"

"Captain...please reconsider. It'll only take—"

"No, Gnosi."

"Jale—"

"For the final time, no! I'm absolutely not going to divert to your coordinates unless you tell me why, mister Gnosi." Jale turned her chair until it faced her executive officer fully, affixing him with her double-barrel black eyed stare.

He bared his teeth in reply, lips curling slightly in a moment of unfettered contempt. "Listen, *steward*, I'm telling you flat out—go to this next set of coordinates. I represent Lord Knoskali, by the twin gods! You should listen."

The bridge crew pretended obliviousness, but Jale caught covert glances and one raised eyebrow; she felt a heat fill her chest and face. Resting her paws on the arms of her seat, she lifted her weight off and half stood.

"Gnosi! That's quite enough, sir. I suspect our mission will lead us far deeper into unknown space before this is over, and you've been questioning my orders on this matter since yesterday. Give me your real reason, and I'll reevaluate your suggestion—otherwise I consider the matter closed! Have I not made myself clear?"

"You're—"

"Enough."

"But—"

"That is enough." Jale snapped. She stood fully at last, drawing herself up and awarding the coyote her most withering, displeased look, trying to hide the fact that she had no idea what she'd do if he didn't back down. "If you have no further information for me, I expect you to remain silent on this matter. Yes?"

Gnosi turned away, and for a long moment Jale expected him to swing back in active rebellion. She felt surprisingly calm, though she shook slightly with emotion; perhaps chaos was indeed beginning to alter her to its whim. Her composure went untested, however; with a grunt of displeasure, Gnosi simply logged out of his terminal and stormed off the bridge without looking back.

"Ma'am?" Her morning-watch tactics officer, a lanky young equine by the name of Geff, touched her shoulder.

"Yes?"

"May I speak with you in private?"

Jale blinked up at him and cocked her head. "Why of course."

Attached to the bridge was a small, private office reserved for her use; to this she directed him. He followed her in and closed the door as she slid around her desk.

"Ma'am, I wanted to answer one of your questions. Gnosi has a private map of nodes that he's getting his own intel updates from," Geff said, voice deep but soft. "He wants to stop at S4 to get the data from his net, and he's not happy at being unable to retrieve the data drop at the S6 location. He's told us not to tell you about it...said you're not cleared to know, so I'd prefer you didn't mention it directly."

"Oh lovely," Jale said, wilting into her chair. "Not unexpected, though I'm surprised to hear about it, that said. Why *do* I hear about it, if I may ask?"

Geff stiffened, expression growing fixed, as if she'd uttered some slight against his character. "Ma'am, we're your crew. Not the spook's."

"Spook?"

The young horse's stiffness slowly transitioned to stolid equine bafflement; there was a long moment of pause before his countenance cleared.

"Oh." He swayed, relaxing from the near attention he had snapped to. "Sorry, ma'am—I forgot your background. See, in our service, every larger vessel has several aboard who work directly for Knoskali's intel-ops. Some are known, like Gnosi, but there are usually a smatter at other posts as well. We call them spooks, because they're mostly there to watch us all. You, you're our captain, and he's our spook, or one of them anyway. They work for the Master, not the ship."

"I see." Jale, who had almost begun to feel anchored, was adrift once more. Her only confidant had an agenda he refused to share with her, and there was much more going on politically aboard her own ship than she'd suspected. Knoskali's games were opaque to her, and she had no idea who to trust anymore.

She blinked up at the open young face of her tactics officer. She'd picked him herself.

"Well, then. I actually had guessed that it might be something like that...Gnosi's reasoning, anyway, but well...I wanted him to give me the details, and I was hoping he'd trust me enough to tell me what he's looking for. I thought we were actually working together, but...Ah..."

She closed her mouth, realizing that she should probably be more circumspect. Dizzy with confusion, she rubbed her paws together and stared down at them. After a moment, she looked up to her officer, who was peering down at her with another slightly perplexed expression.

"Very well. That's...good to know. Thank you, Geff." She nodded her head and raised her paw, indicating that he could leave; he nodded in reply and slid back out, leaving her alone in her little office.

Jale leaned forward and rested her head in her paws, stress a knot in her stomach as she fought down the nearly overwhelming sensation that this was all beginning to unravel as quickly as it had been made.

"Get ahold of yourself, Jelly," she murmured softly. The sound of her voice was soothing; somehow it betrayed little of her emotion, warm and controlled, hinting at none the tangle of fears she held inside. "We'll simply take this one thing at a time. We'll fight until the bitter end, no matter what the shape of things, yes we will, and we'll give it a good shake, however it plays out."

She rested her paws on her terminal and organized her thoughts. She'd have to try to bring Gnosi under control. She desperately needed him, 'spook' or not; that must be the first order of business. She tapped out an invitation for him to join her for dinner the next evening, then sat back to consider her options.

The alarm woke her the next morning a mere six hours after her head hit the pillow. After a bleary-eyed check to make sure that she had no urgent messages, she rolled out of bed and stretched. The smell of breakfast reached her senses; as usual, Jewel had beaten her to the morning regardless of the setting on her alarm. Sometimes she wondered if the husky was sneaking in and checking it while she slept.

Stumbling about in a daze, she found a cup of megvha in one of her paws before she even realized Pinky had entered.

She raised it to her lips for a long sip, then smiled down at the remarkably convenient husky.

"Thank you, Pinky."

"Of course, Miss Jale. You look real tired."

"It was a long night, dearie." Jale shook her head, opening the door between her sleeping area and the rest of her quarters. "In truth, likely just the first of many to come."

Pinky nodded and followed her through.

When breakfast was finished, Jale worked up a sweat doing light calisthenics, then took a quick shower. She slid into her shipsuit and boots, then checked herself over. She did certainly look the part; she even had managed to develop some of the 'captainly' mannerisms that she'd stolen from Erin of the *Freeta*, and being a department head had served her well in dealing with staff.

She paused at the thought, suddenly feeling a wave of nostalgic longing that she could only imagine was homesickness. Briefly, she indulged it, sitting down on the edge of her bed and resting her chin in her paws. She reflected on her tidy little quarters with her little rock garden, her tidy little department with its smiling happy faces, her tidy little life with its calm certainty...and yet, despite the familiar calm of the images, it all seemed remarkably small and dull, almost fake, like artifacts of a particularly tidy, boring little dream.

A tidy, boring little dream that had somehow landed her here, playing captain to an expert crew on a grand stage...a crew that believed her to be who she seemed, and allowed her to lead them as if she was truly in command. A crew that followed her without question, even after they had watched her initial trials and seen her stumble around in ignorance while she learned her part. It was a strange concept, and she had trouble reconciling it internally. The only other who seemed to share her doubts was Gnosi; for a while, she'd taken comfort in his doubt and leaned on him to question her decisions—to provide a safety net—but yesterday's revelation had jarred her confidence. Her tidy little dream seemed to have given way to a wild, out of control nightmare, sweeping her along.

"We are who we pretend to be," she whispered to herself, then shook her head. She bore the ultimate responsibility for the ship, crew and mission—Knoskali had been vehement that she was in full and absolute command, and he had repeated it often as if he intended to beat the fact through her skull.

In sixteen hours, her sealed orders would unlock.

As for Gnosi's growing reluctance and insubordination...certainly he knew more than he confided in her, but how much? It seemed to Jale as if he itched to control the ship through her, but to what end she couldn't guess. She flattened her lips, displeased by the thought. Whatever his game was, she'd force the issue tonight.

She sighed softly.

"Pinky?"

The husky was by her side nearly instantaneously, ears perked. "Yes, Miss Jale?"

"Pinky...am I the captain?"

The husky blinked, blue eyes widening. "Ma'am?"

"I...need someone to talk to. Someone who knows me, who isn't Gnosi."

Pinky nodded, slowly squatting down and cocking his head up to her, looking slightly worried.

"Do you know what we're about, out here? What we're doing?"

"Yes...ah...anyway, I think so ma'am. We're trying to find Theta and save him, right?"

"Right. Do you think Gnosi is doing the exact same thing?"

A brief wariness crossed Pinky's expression, and he bit his thumbclaw, making no immediate reply.

"I trust the two of you. I hope you believe me when I say that I intend the best for the two of you, but more importantly do I just hope that you trust me, dearie. But I don't know if I trust Gnosi, and oh no, I certainly don't trust Knoskali, nor do I think he wants me to, and I need someone that I can trust. I need you to be absolutely honest and direct with me."

Pinky blinked and lowered his head slightly, not meeting her eye. "If I can trust you," he murmured quietly, moving closer, "you'll get what I mean when I tell you I'm afraid to trust anyone. Me and my brother...we can't go back to what he had us in before. Many don't survive, and I...we...can't take a risk of it."

"Dear, I have absolutely no intention of returning you to what it was that you were doing before. I've seen the both of you work together, and I think you're smarter than you let on, and I feel that your talents are wasted just being personal assistants and cooks."

To her surprise, Pinky actually growled softly and closed his eyes. He took a breath before looking back to her and speaking, his gaze frighteningly direct. "Miss Jale, I hope you can forgive me for saying this, but you're pretty naïve sometimes. We weren't personal assistants. We were slaves, and not the sort used for physical strength or manual dexterity. We were a pair of young, warm bodies, and used accordingly." He looked away, ears flat. "I'm sorry, Miss Jale, but...well, you don't want our honesty. We both are grateful to you, ma'am, so don't...don't take that wrong, but the last time we trusted someone who asked us to, we nearly died."

Jale was completely taken aback. As his words sank in, she felt a heat rising through her chest, and her throat tightened, suddenly struck by what should have been blazingly obvious.

The silence grew uncomfortable.

"You mean...you were...for that?" Jale wasn't sure what to say. "I'm sorry, Pinky. Why..."

"We don't need pity," Pinky murmured softly, biting his lip. "I'm sorry...oh, Miss Jale, please don't...be upset," he turned back to her, suddenly fearful. "I shouldn't have said anything, but you must understand why...why we're... we do both trust you, mostly, but I don't want to see my brother...not again..."

"Pinky, Knoskali specifically ordered me to set Theta free. When I do, you and your brother will go with him. For what little it may be worth, you have my word. I had no idea that it was so bad for you. Unless...Theta? He didn't do anything, did he...?"

Pinky made and held eye contact for a long few seconds, something he'd never done before that moment. Jale held his gaze, knowing how little there was to find in her eyes but trying to will as much sincerity into her face as she could.

"No," Pinky whispered. "Theta, he never did hurt us. Theta was a slave, same as us, but...he was for Lord Knoskali himself, and not shared around. Well, not as much. We didn't know him too well, but...see, there's rank among slaves, and he never used it. Never so much as claimed it. Aloof but very nice. Very quiet. Even when Alixa...well, anyway, Lord Knoskali...he's not at all nice, but he's...I don't know. But Gnosi," Pinky cringed and shook his head, looking away again.

"Yes?"

"Just...watch out for him. He's real dangerous. Mean dangerous."

Several hours later found Jale nosing into the cabinets and equipment lockers of the lowest deck, trying to push the unsettling conversation from her quarters to the back of her mind. As captain, it was her prerogative and duty to perform periodic stem to stern inspections, checking in with the department heads and looking for anything that might not have made its way up the chain of command. Occupied with more pressing functions, she hadn't managed a tour since before the crew came aboard—but after the previous day, she'd come to the conclusion that it was time to pound the deck and drop in on her staff.

Once finished poking around the E- and D-decks, chatting up the handful of crew stationed on the bottom two decks, she swung into the forward-most G-tube and bounced up to the far busier central deck. The widest and longest on the ship, C-deck housed the engineering and data systems departments, as well as the medical facilities, machine shop, and much of the ship's storage. It also held the massive Rellin Cavitation Drive—required by its function to form the centerline of the ship—and the gallery that surrounded it.

Dropping in on the various stations, she was surprised to find the crew excited to talk to her, eager for the opportunity to tell her everything about their jobs. Keeping her tone casual and conversational, she was rewarded by enthusiastic descriptions of ship systems at levels of detail that made her head spin. She found many of the gaps in her knowledge shrinking as she asked careful, pointed questions.

By the time she'd finished her visit with C-deck, the ship had already changed over to afternoon watch, and her feet hurt from being on them; a short break lounging in an auxiliary G-tube turned into an accidental zero-G nap. She grinned sheepishly when she shook herself awake half an hour later. Sleeping on duty! She hadn't done that since her first year in space. Shaking her head, she kicked off and headed for B-deck.

The upper decks had less bustle, consisting chiefly of crew support such as berthing, the mess and galley, and exercise and sanitary facilities—though they were also home to the bridge and electronic warfare operations. After managing polite attention to the warfare systems officer as he described the countermeasures capabilities of the ship for half an hour, then stumbling through fifteen minutes of awkward conversation with the ciphertechs—who generally preferred to speak to compute systems—she took her leave; her head was full of jargon, and her energy was waning.

Her final stop was the galley, which she'd deliberately chosen to fill that role. She looked over their service and organization in great detail as a matter of professional interest; try though she might, however, she could find no fault with the operation or efficiency. She sampled the food, inspected the stores, and talked shop for a long while before finally declaring that the nervous cooks could get back to work without her further interference. Though she hadn't expected to find anything grossly out of place, she'd hoped to be able to at least add her touch to their operation.

Yet the more she saw, the more detached from the department she felt. The galley of *Dancer* had never quite felt like home; she'd found the flow of life on a warship to be significantly different from that on a passenger liner, and even where her experience overlapped there were sharp contrasts. On a mission as open-ended as *Dancer*'s, every department remained prepared for crises of indefinite duration and scale, and kept itself one step away from full combat readiness at all times.

It was a different world, but she was enjoying the challenge and learning much more about her job and her ship every day. Still, her knowledge in many areas was significantly lacking—while she'd been very well trained in all aspects of command and operation, and had received a crash course in each department's basics, the details were largely glossed over for the sake of expediency. A real warship captain would have no such lack, something that niggled in the back of her mind.

"We are what we pretend to be," she murmured to herself, every so often. A simple reminder, a little token to adjust her reality and maintain her perspective.

On her way back to her quarters, she mentally ran through damage control procedures for each section she passed through. It had become habit, just one of the little exercises taught to her by the expert training staff of House Selesz—every day was a different set of mental drills, required reading and structured tactical games designed to expand her knowledge. It was tough, but it was her responsibility to know. In space, every ship maintained at least a basic standard of readiness at all times, but for a warship the need was greatly heightened—each department on *Dancer* held its own high level of expertise in dealing with ship-wide emergencies from their stations, in any of the several battle conditions that could be set... and as the captain, she was expected to understand and coordinate their actions during any situation that the ship might encounter.

There was redundancy in personnel as well as systems, to a level that Jale had initially thought quite excessive. All systems had backup systems, and all backup systems had backup systems; crew had counterparts at stations on different decks, cross-trained and ready to serve their alternate function from an alternate control point should the need arise.

The structure of order and organization was something she found great comfort in, as her knowledge grew—and yet, it wasn't the stagnant routine she'd settled into for her past decade, but some new thing entirely. It demonstrated to Jale a facet of herself that she hadn't ever recognized or acknowledged—a curious, adventurous side with a new-found lust for learning that left her with regret for how long her life had languished.

Her former life.

As she neared her quarters on A-deck, in close proximity to the bridge, her feet were all but dragging with her exhaustion. Naturally, that section had the most complex damage control procedures of all, and as she closed on her quarters she began to consider abandoning the exercise in favor of simply walking through her door and collapsing into bed. Her willpower held, however, and she stood by a dividing bulkhead, reciting the various tasks for firefighting, securing from decompression events, securing against boarders...by the time she'd finished, exhaustion had caught up firmly; she oozed through the door to her cabin with a weary sigh, landed face-down on the bed, and was quickly asleep.

When Gnosi arrived at her quarters for dinner a few hours later, he seemed positively cheerful.

"Why the luxuries of a captain have no bounds," he laughed, nodding to the ample service spread out on her table. "Even your own private chef!"

Jale contented herself with a polite nod and slightly frosty smile. As much as she wanted to indulge in and share his humor as a social being, business came first.

"Please, sit. And help yourself—I've sent the huskies away. The food is secondary this evening."

Gnosi nodded and slid into his chair, grin slipping from his face.

"Let me first be very clear. I do understand and accept that you have a great deal of knowledge that I do not possess. I also think it likely that you are under orders to which I am not privy." She held up a hand to forestall Gnosi's reply. "*My* orders are very clear: Find Theta, and ensure his freedom and safety. However, while I invite your dissent if you think I'm making a bad decision, I'd suggest you not test my authority."

Gnosi pushed back from the table slightly, looking angry. "Aren't you taking this a little too seriously, *steward*? Don't let command go to your head. I'm on your side, but I've been in space for much of the last fifteen years," he growled and began to rise.

Jale's eyes narrowed, and she rested her elbows on the table, meeting his glare. "Sit down! So have I."

The coyote snorted, tossing down his napkin but dropping back into his seat. "It's not the same thing. I've been on warships. Warships like this one, while you've been coddling upset passengers and having tea with the captain on a posh passenger liner."

Jale sat up straighter, inviting eye contact. Gnosi stared up at her, and his ears flattened back a bit as he was sucked into her black eyes once more. She leaned forward dominantly, baring her teeth slightly to mask the amusement that threatened to ruin the moment.

She had him.

"Perhaps it's not the same thing, no, but the system of command is something I do understand, dearie—and *mutiny* is no less dirty a word in commerce than it is in military."

The coyote's eyes widened, and he stammered for a moment, shocked wordless. After a while, he finally tore his gaze away from hers, then looked back up...at her chin.

Tally another point for ferret eyes.

"I wouldn't ever mutiny," he spat the word as if it had left a bad taste in his mouth, "but you have to be reasonable. I know the slavers and how they operate, and I know the parameters of our mission. I've captained ships before, you know."

Jale nodded. "Oh yes, I know; I expect, therefore, that you'll probably understand why I don't want insubordination from my executive officer, open or veiled."

Gnosi chewed his thumbclaw, glancing back up at her for a long moment. "What did he do to you? I barely recognize you."

Jale speared a bite of meat with her eating dagger, affecting a casual coolness. "What he did was make me captain, and give me a job to do. If you're thinking that I'm letting command 'go to my head', as you put it, you'd be right, dear. The lives of the crew, and this mission that we're all tied up in, I consider with the deadliest sincerity, make you no mistake. Now, am I the captain, or am I your puppet?"

He actually squirmed, pinned to his chair. "You're the captain, ma'am. I've only been trying to keep us within our search parameters." Another long moment passed, and he looked away. "I'm...I apologise for my comments."

"Gnosi, I truly don't wish to try this without you." Jale allowed herself to soften a bit. "And I don't want you to roll over and do whatever I say without comment, but I do expect you to respect the position."

Gnosi grinned up at her, looking slightly sheepish and a little sly; he lifted a filled dumpling from the tray. "Well, I'll admit that I was kinda wondering if you'd really stand up for yourself...And now I know. Consider it a test."

Completely unconvinced, Jale merely arched her eyebrow and moved along, gesturing for Gnosi to eat his fill.

If that was how he wanted to play it, it was fine by her.

"Now then, I do have a job for you. I am convinced that the key to this whole thing is the pirate ship *Varaunt*." She studied his features for any reaction. Finding none, she plowed forward undaunted. "When we arrive in Fonaci space, I want to dredge the news networks for pirate attacks, missing ships, ransom demands...anything whatsoever that we might be able to correlate. To do that, we need to be able to intercept the message dumps from inbound couriers, in addition to making a regular connection to the data network on the planet for cross-referencing...and we cannot allow it to be detected. Krella assures me that against a world like Fonaci Prime, both of the above will be trivial. What are your thoughts?"

Gnosi munched, retrieving a filled mug and inspecting the ceiling. "Well, that seems like a sound plan to me, but...a bit unnecessary when I have a whole region full of mapped data nodes of my own that covert couriers already deliver to bimonthly. But yeah, sure, if you want just skip the known and go for the unknown, we can use the Fonaci for that. I might even have a few...ah, inroads into their commercial data net already in place." He glanced at her, muzzle wrinkled into what she realized was a conspiratorial smirk. "They are our closest neighbor, after all, and behind most of the original planets technologically."

Jale nodded briskly, as if that made perfect sense. Resting her paws on the table, she fixed him with another direct glare. "For myself, I trust your mapped nodes to have very useful data on them, oh yes, but not the data that I'm looking for, and not at the immediacy I need. The more important thing, though, is that I also want you to barter for information that might lead us to the network of mapped communication nodes that *Varaunt* might themselves reap. If we can establish what region they're operating in, and we know the nodes in that area, we might be able to stalk them."

Gnosi sipped his drink, leaning back in his chair. For a long while he was silent, staring into his drink as if deep in thought.

"Gnosi?"

"Yes? It's...doable, yes. It's been done before. That said, It won't be easy, and it won't be cheap. Pirates tend to be very cautious in their operations, and if we're not careful we're as likely to buy bad information from someone who then tips off our quarry."

Jale had considered that; she shook her head. "I think that's an acceptable risk. More to the point, Knoska-li speaks highly of you as an intelligence officer and I expect you'll manage with due care, yes? Well, let's get it done, dearie. I leave the preparations and execution in your capable hands, and Krella will help you with the data analysis. You can have anybody else that you need from operations. If you could have a few ideas drawn up for my review by tomorrow evening, we'll go over all the details and get preparations underway."

Gnosi set his cup down, pushing away from the table and leaning back, staring at her unreadably. "You do realize that all our lives are on the line, right? One second late, one move behind, one little misstep and we all lose. Knoskali is quite serious that we won't live long, any of us, if Theta dies."

"Of this I am not unaware." More sprang to her lips, but she held it back. Treacherous ground. She pushed back from the table herself, taking a small tart and using it to occupy her outward attention.

After staring at her for a few moments, Gnosi turned away, looking conflicted.

"If you have anything else to tell me," Jale prodded lightly, "Please consider this the best—and the last—time to do so."

"Tell you, ma'am?" Gnosi's eyes widened. "No, nothing I can think of."

"So be it, then. Well, all that aside, we shouldn't allow my personal chef's efforts go to waste. That at least I'm sure we can find consensus on." She nodded to the desserts in their little box, then took a flaky pastry from the top.

The coyote nodded warily, but followed her lead.

As they demolished the spread of little deserts, what little conversation resumed shifted to more comfortable subjects, but Gnosi's tone maintained its strained, reluctant edge. When all was finished and the huskies returned, he promptly excused himself and left.

Dangerous? Oh I do believe you, Pinky.

She checked the chronometer on her terminal.

Four more hours.

X

Intransigence

"ZERO FIVE HUNDRED, SHIP TIME. Wake up, Theta."
Theta rolled over, clutching his pillow to his head and flattening his ears against the computer's soft, fluid voice.

"Fifteen more minutes, please."

"I'm sorry, Theta, but you said that fifteen minutes ago."

"It's fine, just fifteen more minutes," he groaned.

The person directly below him in the triple rack rolled over and growled pointedly.

"It is time to wake up." The computer sounded serious now, slightly stern.

Grumbling quiet curses under his breath, Theta sat up and jabbed at the terminal's mute button repeatedly with his pawpad, metallic silver claw rattling on the display. Even as he opened one bleary eye a mere crack, he was forced to clench his jaw against the throbbing pain of the dull headache he knew would be there. With a little sigh, he surrendered to inevitability and swung his legs out, forgoing the use of the bunk's handholds and dropping lightly to the floor.

Silently he made his way to the curtained-off wash basin by the ambient light of the room. Let the next person to rise turn it up; his eyes preferred the dark. He tucked the curtain shut, rinsing his face and paws, ignoring as best he could the pain that coursed through his body from all his healing injuries. After brushing his hair and cleaning his teeth, he put his supplies back into their little compartment and turned to the dispenser. A swipe of his paw across its chip reader was rewarded with a clear, thin strip; he placed it under his tongue, and within moments the pain in his body began to fade.

Squinting through the mental fog of his stubborn headache that responded to no analgesic, he shuffled over to his locker and exchanged sleepwear for his simple blue shipsuit and black gaiters. Once he'd achieved a reasonable state of dress and checked himself over, he glanced at the chronometer. Twenty minutes before he was expected at his station—just enough time for a detour to try and wrangle up something to help bring him to alertness, perhaps even a bite to eat.

Four decks up and five sections forward, he entered one of the ship's four mess halls. Rows of metal tables, clean and set, sat unoccupied, awaiting the first meal of the day and the horde of hungry pirates that would descend upon them. He worked his way between the empty aisles and past the deserted serving counters, poking his head into the galley to look for signs of life; to his surprise, he was instantly recognized and greeted by a large, familiar form.

"Theta!" The snow leopard removed his long heat-proof gloves, setting them on the nearest flat surface before padding over, work forgotten.

"Arvinne."

"Oh, it's lovely to see you!" Arvinne was effusive, grabbing Theta softly by both shoulders and beaming down at him. After a few seconds, his grin faded a bit. "I...now I'd heard that you got in some trouble," he murmured. "We've only had the rumors of it down here, but it sounded bad. Are you..."

Theta avoided his gaze and brushed his question off with a nonchalant wave, trying to synthesize a happy grin.

"Nah, things are ok. Things are fine. Footing's a little shaky, but if it works out I'll be part of the crew, just like you. Haven't you noticed that I'm not wearing conscript colors anymore?"

"Oh!" Arvinne's eyebrows rose in surprise and he looked over Theta's suit, blinking at his insignia. "Can't say as I even looked twice. Tactics, huh? On the bridge? Why...that's wonderful news! But I thought, ah..."

"That I didn't like pirates?" Theta chuckled ruefully, rubbing his neck. "I'm equal opportunity for villains these days, I suppose. In theory, they have some use for me, though the tactics department isn't actually on the bridge. Speaking of which, I can't really stay and chat, as I'm on shift in about fifteen minutes. Kinda needed a pickup, and I was rather hoping that you guys might have some megvha hot."

"Megvha, is it?" Arvinne shook his head slowly. "I'm not even sure what that is, I'm afraid."

Theta bit his lower lip. "It's a somewhat addictive stimulant beverage paste from Brynton...It's mildly psychoactive and illegal on some planets, but great for a quick boost."

"I don't think we have anything like that. Well, not so's I know of, anyway. We do have a few types of stim drinks, but they're mostly just from powder."

Theta closed his eyes for a moment, pinching the pressure points at the bridge of his muzzle. "That's a real shame, but I guess I'll have to make do. Do you have anything hot?"

"Well of course. Couldn't survive without it, you know." Arvinne leaned forward and rapped a claw against the large urn directly beside Theta. "This's verti, in here. 'Swhat most of the crew drinks all day long, so there's always some hot. Sometimes seems like my only job is making it up."

"Sounds exciting." Theta rubbed a temple, squinting up at the cook. "Is it sweetened?"

"A bit, aye, though most add more sweetening. Say, you sure you're alright? You look terrible, if you don't mind me saying."

"Yeah. I get really bad headaches. The medics think they'll go away, but I'm not so sure. I had them before, on Brynton. Stimulants tend to help as I recall, so I might as well try the verti, as long as it's ok."

Arvinne nodded. "It's listed as universally safe. Let's see what you think." He turned and retrieved a vacuum flask from a locker full of them, then filled it nearly to the brim, dumping a pinch of sweeting in before wiping the rim and sealing it.

Theta reached up and took the proffered container, flipping it open and taking a long whiff. He closed his eyes, feeling himself relax at the warmth and fragrant aroma; looking back up, he smiled softly, reaching way up with a paw to gently touch the steward's nose.

"It smells wonderful. I'm sure it will help. You're my hero, Arvinne."

Arvinne blinked, looking a bit startled; he turned away and retrieved his gloves, sliding them back on just as a timer began to beep. "Don't mention it," he tossed back over his shoulder, a little gruff. Theta cocked his head, pondering the awkward shift of mood as his friend began working the ovens, swapping pastries to cooling racks and quickly sliding meal packs into the empty bays. "Can't say's I'd mind seeing more of you, Thay. Wasn't even sure you were alive after, you know. They got real vague an' all."

"I'll...I'm sorry. I can at least try to swing by sometime." Theta sighed softly, leaning against a galley locker and crossing his arms. "I have about as much to study as I conceivably could learn in several lifetimes, and only a couple of weeks to do it...Just between us, my assignment is probationary. I want the job, but..." He shook his head and held back a sigh, watching Arvinne work.

The ten days since his final release from the medical bay had been particularly brutal. Dela herself had taken on his training and evaluation, demanding to check his qualifications and abilities herself before accepting his services. From the first instant, she'd been a vicious taskmaster. Keeping him perpetually off balance, never allowing him to rest, and berating him in front of the department loudly and frequently, she succeeded where the conscript trainers had failed.

Discovering and expertly exploiting his psychological vulnerabilities, she'd stripped him to the bone and left him reeling, grasping for any handholds he could find. She gave him all he needed to learn, but showed no tolerance for failure or error, and her sharp tongue was capable of reducing him to speechless obeisance. His strengths vanished in her presence as if she absorbed them; his weaknesses were amplified and reflected back to him as a gross caricature.

In many ways, she intimidated him as much as the *other* had, but kept him much further off-balance.

Worse still, the "simple, elementary" exercises she assigned him he found mind-bendingly hard, and despite trying his best to study what was given, his recall and application of process was proving imperfect. The ingenuity he'd relied on to gloss over his weaknesses and lack of knowledge, that intuition that Irrai had praised, was failing him nearly every time he leaned on it.

He sighed, stepping forward to rest a paw on the snow leopard's shoulder. "Sorry, but I need to go. I really would like to have some time to sit and catch up with you. You're my only real friend, you know," Theta murmured.

"Could just meet up off shift, and all." Arvinne finished his task at last and slid the doors shut once more, patting his face with a towel. He turned to Theta and knelt down, eye-to-eye. "Look, I won't bother you, but I think company might do you good, if you don't mind me saying."

Theta nodded slightly, looking away. "I...well, I think so too. Look, when I get off—should be twenty-one hundred—You might come by. Deck twelve, berth F, bunk 4D. I'll just be studying, but I can make some time... perhaps we could even grab third meal."

Arvinne brightened and nodded. "Would mean a lot. I'll hold off on eating, then. Vaese is on tonight, not me. He'll be happy to know you're well, too, you know."

Theta nodded, then glanced up at the chronometer with a little grimace. "I'll send you a message."

He raised a paw in farewell; Arvinne returned the gesture with a small grin.

Four hours later, Theta sat staring at his 'situation data' display, claws rattling asynchronously on the control console as he processed data and sent commands at a furious pace. His paws were shaking and moist, and his eartips trembled as he struggled, locked in a complex battle of maneuver. He muttered inarticulately under his breath, eyes flicking to the corner of his station to find that his firing commands had been rejected.

He snapped his jaw shut. Weapons station was reporting that the fire control datalink was down; once more, the solution would need to be recalculated. He balled up a fist, letting it fall with a 'thump' against the structure of his console. How many systems were failed? It seemed grossly unfair and unrealistic to simulate so many problems at once on an undamaged ship.

He froze, suddenly doubtful. Dragging a long breath through his teeth, he paused to consider the possibilities, eyes unfocused even as his paws started another turn under manual helm override.

"Related...how could they be related?" he muttered under his breath. One black paw quickly brushed sweaty purple hair back from his eyes in a rare moment of reprieve, then flew back to the thruster control; even as he started another wild jink, he ran through block diagrams in his head, eyes narrowed. The databus and processing nodes were distributed around the ship. The power was discrete, but this was a link failure and not a power failure, and all the datalinks in that area were failing.

His eyes widened and he snapped his jaw shut on a surprised expletive. Was he being jammed? Muttering a string of quiet curses, he diverted his attention from maneuvers to the systems console and dispatched a message to engineering. The power bus itself could be modulated for broadband emergency fire control data transmission, but it required a series of physical changes at the weapons station. Working as fast as he could, he set up a feedback loop to alert him if his weapons came back online. Sweat dripped from his nose as he switched back over to his situation display, returning to find his ship momentarily adrift. As he was issuing rapid commands to slide into his opponent's eddy baffles, Dela brought her plump fist down onto the panel with a meaty 'thwack', startling him from his concentration.

He'd done something wrong.

Again.

"Mister Theta."

He wilted, freezing on his controls.

"Mister Theta," Dela rolled each word around in her mouth, like a hunter savoring the helplessness of some trapped prey animal before moving in for the kill. "Mister Theta, I must know...please, tell me, just how do you expect to gain a firing solution from this angle? Once again the battle platform is maneuvering for a volley, and once again your own main weapons are shadowed. Ye should have taken your shot when ye had the chance. So many opportunities. Wake *up*, lad." Her deep voice was thick with irritation, and though he couldn't see her face, he could picture her expression as easily as he could feel her hot breath on the back of his neck.

He cringed down against his console, ears akimbo. Dela wouldn't be interested in excuses or his reasoning. He should have detected the jamming sooner, should not have given the other ship so much distance to maneuver.

He bit his lower lip, bearing down; his only chance to please her now was to win the whole engagement.

"Standby," he snapped softly, fighting to stay out of the battle platform's firing arc as it began to lazily deploy its munitions, sending volleys of high-energy weaponry a hundred meters off his port quarter. Twisting the simulated ship to the limits of its little electrons, he turned with the battle platform, managing to keep her from bringing her guns to bear. Nevertheless, he found the whole tactical situation beginning to turn against him, steadily unraveling before his eyes.

Before long he was fighting against a tide of conflicting data and missing sensor reports, frantically filling inexplicably large gaps in the dataset while the advantage of maneuver and position slowly slipped away from him. Mistakes began to pile up as he fought to save the engagement, fending off his own exhaustion; he became so caught up in survival that he nearly missed the flashing alert informing him that he had his weapons back. After a full second staring at the happy green blip, he bared his teeth in a relieved grin and began to fire, targeting the battle platform's heavily armored weapons control systems and watching in delight as they were knocked out one by one.

"Ah, lovely." Dela's voice cut into his reverie, angrily sarcastic. "Now you've decide to turn-to? Idiot! Look at your tracking delta! His is nearly at zero. Why have ye done this?"

Theta blinked, then growled at the screen, baffled and flustered. The target's locking systems should have been disrupted, and its weapons control destroyed...but his display indicated an active and persistent lock. "I...what? I thought I could transition through his eddy coma for sensor scatter. I thought I had taken out all his weapons!" He groaned aloud, frantically sending control and power commands to try and remove the ship from the edge of the battle platform's firing arc. "Dammit, it should have worked. Why wouldn't...how did he...rrgh!"

The display flashed a long stream of alerts in amber and yellow, indicating major hits across multiple areas of the hull and loss of sensor data from large parts of the upper deck and superstructure. Dela threw her datapad down in disgust and shut down the simulation.

Theta stared down at the empty blank screen in shock, heart racing, then slowly slumped back in his chair. He shook with adrenaline and emotion, sprinkled with more than a little disbelief at what had happened. Darker still, spreading through him was a strange creeping shame that he hadn't felt since his days on Brynton; he was weak and helpless, worse than his worst at House Selesz in many ways. The fragile patina of assuredness and the nascent self-esteem he'd begun to develop had crumbled to dust underneath Dela's cold stare. Once again he stood naked before the world and he was truly trying his best.

And he was failing.

"Did ye not read the study, lad?" Dela's voice cracked with anger and frustration as the badger turned back to him. "It's been two days now that we've wasted on these same basic scenarios, and you've killed us more often than not. What is wrong with you?"

"I just thought...it felt like it should work."

She glowered at him scornfully. "Are you addled? Are ye mad? Felt like it should work, did it aye? You can never give up the firing advantage, and to make a wide turn like that, in the face of the enemy..." Dela gesticulated wildly in Theta's peripheral vision, and he winced slightly, eyes downcast. "Did ye even read the first word of the first page of the first section of the tactics manual? What could ye have done differently?"

"Yes! Of course I read it, but I—"

Dela cut him off with an abrupt sweep of her big paw.

"No, lad, forget I asked. I don't want to hear your buts and excuses."

"Ma'am, I was—"

"I don't care what you 'was'. You know what lad...having you assigned here was clearly someone's mistake."

Big paws clutched Theta by the shoulders and hauled him up; he squeaked softly as his injuries were stretched. Oblivious to his pain, Dela dropped him onto his feet and gave him a firm shove towards the door.

"Get outta here. Go find a job where ye won't kill us all...if you can manage it. I'll still live in fear of your fla-grant incompetence somehow costing us the ship, even if you end up a janitor. Fortunately we're almost at S-21, so maybe they'll sell ye back into slavery there and save us all in the process."

Theta turned away to hide his emotion, feeling the stares of the whole department at his back. He closed his eyes and bowed his head, almost in tears.

"I apologize for wasting your time, ma'am," he mur-mured, throat tight. "I just—"

Dela growled, and he subsided. She gave him another little push. "Gracious you're a noisy thing. Out of my department. Now. Worthless, uneducated, ineducable. I have no idea how you ever got assigned to this post, but I'll have it corrected. Why are ye still standing there? Did ye not hear me? Get!"

Theta felt his ears flatten back at the scorn in her voice; his tail tucked against his rump in pure vulpine submission, a subconscious response to the threat in her tone. Snatching his flask from the desk, he turned and made his way towards the door with as much dignity as he could muster, ignoring the glances and stares.

Sneaking through the corridors with eyes blurry from holding back tears, nose dripping with those few that had escaped, he managed to make it all the way into the safety of his rack without running into anyone. He vaulted into his bunk, curling around his thin little pillow and wiping moist eyes with black paws before burying his muzzle into his bedding as he'd done so many times in his past life. Less-than-fond memories came flooding back—memories of sobbing himself to sleep after some particularly vicious treatment or other, fighting to stay as quiet as possible and hoping not to draw further attention to himself.

"Worthless," he growl-sobbed, swaying with the tides of inarticulate shame and frustration that surged up at irregular intervals. Incoherent thoughts and fears swirled through his head...memories of Knoskali's paws, of training, of death and dismemberment, of ships and torture and slaves, and of Knoskali's hips and eyes, of the many gardens of flesh and flora and fauna, of opulence and decadence and the whims and wiles of guests and knaves and slaves and all that comprised House Selesz; memories of Knoskali's sculpted chest and shoulders, and of exhibition, and of service, and dancing, and dining, and blacker things; memories of taste and smell, and permeating all else, memories of Knoskali's love, deadly and sinister, deeper than the deepest sea, hidden like a great mountain range beneath a sea of fog.

Amidst the discordant melange, a notion percolated up that stopped Theta's chaotic reflections cold and sobered him momentarily. The pirates had changed roles in his mind at some point in the recent past—No longer the dangerous enemy, they had instead become a new set of masters to serve. He now served others, and his service was at odds with what he was and who he was meant to be. He cringed at the thought, curling tighter still.

"No," he whispered softly to himself, denying the concept. It was seductive in his despair, but it was wrong. "I have only one master." Theta affirmed it to himself, raising his voice above a whisper. "And I will always be *His*, and these pirates do not serve Him. Perhaps this is

His will, and I will serve Him best by following along until He chooses to bring me back."

"Him..." Theta exhaled the breath he hadn't realized he'd held, giggling softly at the wild rush of relief which filled him—but brought only more tears.

He closed his eyes. His head spun, filled with images of black coyotes. Achieving some flavor of sickly contentment by imagining himself still under Knoskali's control and protection, he felt his soft shaking slowly calm, replaced by a pallid, unwholesome warmth in his belly and chest.

It was real enough, this world he created. It was real enough if he believed it to be; this was the reality he to which he could always escape to keep himself sane.

"I am very not sane," he whispered ever-so-quietly to himself, resting his paws over his muzzle and curling even more tightly.

"Theta?"

Theta jolted awake at the sound of his name, snapping to with a little gasp. Quickly he turned away from the opening in his bunk, wiping his eyes and muzzle to try and hide the signs of his distress. There was only so much he could do, however; after a few hurried wipes at the teary crust matting the fur around his eyes, he resigned himself to facing his friend as the mess he was.

Well, Arvinne had seen worse anyway.

He rolled out of bed, landing on the floor with an entirely un-Theta-like thump. "Arvinne, I..." he paused and blinked, staring up into the surprised face of one of the junior bridge officers. "...Oh."

"Well hi there." The young cheetah frowned down at him disapprovingly. "I'm not Arvinne, but you're Theta, right? Yeah, well I'm here with a message from Dela. She wants you to review the interception of some convoy from last week. Were you there? Well, anyway, she says to present a full and formal after-action report on the tactical performance tomorrow morning. She actually emphasized 'full and formal'. Convoy, ah..." The cheetah frowned down at his notes. "DF602. She says it's not in the system yet, but she sent you all of the raw data. She also says, to quote, 'Tell him this is his last chance to get it right, so he better make it good.' I'm not sure if I'm supposed to tell you that, or if I'm supposed to tell you that she told me to tell you."

Theta cocked his head up at the messenger, following the content if not the phrasing. "That...is that all she said?"

"No," the cheetah smirked. "She also says if you botch it, she's going to, ah, quote, 'throw you out an airlock myself'. Er, herself. Get it?"

"Thank you for the message," Theta muttered, feeling his belly knotting up once more.

"Oh, it was my pleasure, snowflake. See ya 'round." The officer tossed him a mocking salute, then turned on his heel.

Theta wilted against his rack as the messenger jaunted off, its hard frame cold even through his fur. In a way, he'd felt something akin to relief when he'd thought that his dealings with Dela and his failings in tactics might be at an end; he wasn't so certain that he wanted another go.

"Inari's breath," he muttered. "This never ends."

"Theta?" Arvinne's voice, sounding from the hatch, startled Theta to standing once more.

"Hi, Arvinne."

"Oh, you ARE here!" Arvinne sauntered up, grinning. "When I didn't hear from you, I thought you might've been working late."

"I—no." Theta grimaced. "I actually got off early."

Arvinne's grin faded slowly as his eyes adjusted to the dim light, and his eyebrows rose in surprise. "Thay? Sorry to say, but you look right awful. Is everything—"

"Things are fine." Theta cut him off a little too sharply. "Well, not...not exactly fine," he temporized, "...but they are what they are. I think, ah...we need to reschedule for dinner."

Arvinne's broad face fell even further, and he rocked back on his heels with a faint, silent nod.

Theta shook his head, grimacing as pain throbbed between his temples.

"Look, remember how I was telling you about...how things aren't really working out? Well, today...let's just say that I've been told that I have one more chance. I've been told to prepare a full analysis for the intercept of some convoy that we hit recently. I need to offer a regressive analysis of the plan, of its execution, systems and personnel efficiency...anything we could have done to further maximize profit and minimize risk and loss. Then, from that, I need to score each element and derive procedural and tactical recommendations...It's a ton of work, and it has to be presented tomorrow. I also need to build a polydimensional data plot which shows the plan of action versus the actual outcome...and that needs to be broken down into sections by element and skew. I can only guess that it's probably going to be compared against the official one to detail my unsuitability for the job."

Arvinne looked nonplussed. "Well...that sounds terrible. And damned unfair. And look, none of this makes sense, neither. Why would they put you there if you weren't gonna do well?"

"I...really, I don't know. Irrai seemed to like me. Maybe I can still go back to her. It just seems like every exercise I do for Dela hits all my weaknesses and none of my strengths... even this one. Especially this one. It's totally analysis." Theta ran his paws through his long hair, clutching it in slight exasperation. "In other words, all bookwork. Irrai said my strengths were in my intuition...yet in every simulation so far all my ideas have failed badly. Dela is very smart."

He shuddered.

"Dela is *very* smart..."

"Ah." Arvinne shifted uncomfortably, and there was an awkward silence.

"Well, look...I promise we'll do dinner tomorrow or the day after. Will that work?"

Arvinne nodded and offered his paw. Theta clutched it tight between his own, half the size.

"I won't forget, or push you off again."

"I'll hold you to it, Thay," Arvinne murmured, then shook his head and turned towards the corridor, resting a paw on the doorframe. "Best of luck with...all this. I'm sure everything will turn out fine."

"Perhaps. Goodnight, friend Arvinne."

When he was alone once more, Theta returned to his bunk, climbing up and settling in amidst blankets. Cradling his still-hot flask of verti, he pulled the thin curtain shut and turned to his terminal with a weary sigh. Folding it out from its enclosure, he logged in and began assembling the relevant reports to cross-reference. Staring at the quantity of data and pondering the enormous task at hand, he immediately felt exhausted; ruthlessly, he forced himself to start at the beginning and not succumb to distraction.

Three hours later, he was staring alertly at the display and muttering beneath his breath.

The next morning, it took him a breath to work up the courage to go into ops. As he logged in and stepped through the hatch, he was surprised to see that the only one present was the duty officer, a grey wolf named Cuny.

Tentatively he raised a paw in greeting, his ears splayed uncertainly.

"Well g'mornin, snowflake." Cuny lifted his digits in a little wave and grinned warmly, pushing away from his console and beckoning him over. "Dela will be here to collect you. Said to tell you she's on her way. Didya finish the analysis?"

Theta nodded cautiously, making his way over. "I did. It wasn't at all what I expected. I hope I did it right."

"You'll do just fine," Cuny said, lowering his voice. His eyes flicked to the door as he leaned in. "I should... ah, nevermind." A slight lift of his muzzle directed Theta's attention to the door, which was opening to admit a diagonal Dela—the only way she'd fit without touching both sides. Cuny raised his voice and backed away. "Ah, here she is, snowflake. Now get gone."

Theta nodded slightly, trying to affect a neutral expression as he turned to Dela.

"Good morning," he offered.

"We'll see about that, m'dear. Come with me." Dela gestured imperiously for Theta to follow her, then turned on her heel to squeeze right back through the doorframe.

Without a word she led him to a staff conference room, opening the door and ushering him through.

Theta looked inside and nearly froze in the doorway. Jenks, Janesson, four department heads and several staff officers were seated around the table, chatting with one another and sipping verti; as he entered, a silence fell.

He felt Dela's paw on his back, ushering him to the rostrum at the front of the briefing room. She pushed him all the way up, then thumped back to her seat and sat, looking up at him expectantly.

His mouth was dry. What was this?

After a few awkward moments, Janesson arched an eyebrow.

"I believe you have an after action analysis drawn up for our last operation. Is that right, mister Theta?"

"Ah...yes?"

"So...deliver it, ye dunk," Dela prodded, earning chuckles from the assembled.

Theta took a deep breath, then let it out and took another. He closed his eyes briefly and tried to let the tension wash away. He'd prepared this with Dela in mind, but it didn't matter; he fought to settle his nerves as he had been trained to for dancing, wishing he could summon the deadly calm he'd felt before his last fight.

He opened his eyes and straightened, squeezing the edges of the rostrum with his paws to stop them from shaking.

"So...I've performed an in-depth analysis of the interception of convoy DF602, which...ah, I'm here to present." He paused for a moment and looked down at his notes; for a few seconds, his eyes scanned over them without reading, then seized on the first paragraph.

"The intel we purchased was 99.98 percent accurate on timing data; course data was exact as per the CPCI-9226 navigation module course randomizer bug, correlated with time and position of launch. Though sixty percent above market value, the accuracy of the data offsets the increased cost; standard calculations support its purchase."

Theta took a sip of water, wiping his lips with the back of his paw.

"Now, on to the action report. *Varaunt* arrived at her planned position at zero-one thirty-two ship time, and subsequently launched ships Assault 01 through Assault 05, with Assault 06 crewed and standing ready reserve.

"The intercept event began at zero-two hours, twelve minutes, fourteen seconds, designated as zero minutes mission time, when the first target was detected on course by Assault 01's detection grid just prior to the convoy's planned course change towards the intercept location.

"The main multi-target takedown, performed jointly by Assault 03 and Assault 05, occurred at zero four minutes mission time, which was the predesignated time of deployment. Assault 04 was assigned to the main ore carrier. She poisoned the carrier's Rellin bubble, but was destroyed by the target's weapons with full loss of ship and crew."

Theta glanced across his listeners, carefully avoiding Dela entirely. Forcing himself to breathe slowly and stay calm, he set his datapad on the rostrum and assigned the strategic overview to the table's viewer, and a three-dimensional map lit up the center of the room.

"Now as I've said, zero four minutes on the mission clock was the predetermined takedown time. Assault 02 was assigned to provide fire support for the takedown vessels here." He tapped his pad, and a spot lit up on the display. "Assault 03 and 05 were not synchronized in their takedown, and there was a gap of half a second during which the two freighters and the trade ship escaped. Assault 04 was an entire two seconds late, and by the time the ore carrier's bubble was poisoned she was very, very far beyond assistance from Assault 02."

He brought up the relative positioning plot. "*Varaunt* was positioned off-axis with the intercept, and as such was unable to lend any fire support or logistical support to either engagement. Assault 06 was deployed to assist Assault 04 as soon as the ore carrier's re-entry waste heat was detected, while Assaults 03 and 05 completed the acquisition of slaves and cargo from DF602-2, −3 and −11, as well as the undesignated passenger liner *Filial Star*. With me so far?"

"Ye've given us the data on our stations, lad. Anything we don't know about the sequence or details, we can read. Move forward." Dela sounded less annoyed than usual, and Theta merely nodded cautiously.

"In summation, the ore carrier was to be taken as a prize; failure to capture it, to raid the trade ship, or to capture the cargo from the freighters who escaped, combined with the loss of Assault 04, trims the profit margin on this operation to single-digit values. Each of you will find a report at your station containing the meat of my analysis...ah, as Dela has mentioned."

"So," Janesson steepled his fingers. "We have your numerical analyses, and the sequence and report...but there's something missing from this. The most important thing I expect from my tacticians, in fact—Your opinions. Would you share them with us?"

Theta sat back, flustered. He snuck a glance at Dela, who was staring at him impassively, then peered beseechingly at Janesson. Receiving only an arch of an eyebrow, he closed his eyes and leaned forward. What he said next would surely do irreparable damage, but he'd been asked by the captain directly. He steeled himself and took a breath, opening his eyes and looking above the heads of the assembled.

"This operation was a disaster, from a tactical point of view." He bit his lip, looking down at his pad. "Strategically, it had the promise of being a huge profit center, and everything was perfectly built up for the operation, but ah..." his tongue felt heavy. "Unless I'm missing some very significant data, the execution of the entire intercept was botched. We're lucky to have achieved any profit at all."

"What? What are ye saying, lad?" Dela's brogue was thick and dangerous, and he bent like a twig under its weight.

"I'm sorry, ma'am. I...I thought I'd be presenting just to you. I didn't—"

"Enough, lad." Dela cut him off with a wave. "You think you could have done better?"

All eyes turned to Theta, who cringed, taking an involuntary step away from the podium. "I...when looking into events that have happened, it's much easier to—"

"Answer the question!" Janesson grinned toothily. "Yes or no."

Theta turned half away, looking at the floor. "Yes sir."

Janesson looked at Dela.

"Really, lad? What would ye have done different?" Dela's tone was very neutral; Theta looked around, bereft of solid footing.

"Well, ah...well, the positioning is...it's just flat-out wrong. With this, the timing is forced because of the speed differential, and tiny mistakes become huge problems very quickly. These ships are traveling at the speed of their slowest ship, in this case...and the slowest ship is the trade ship. We don't need to haul the big ships out of Rellin drive with a quartering intercept. With the timing data we had, once confirmed, we could easily trail each ship and bring them out in *Varaunt*'s local space all at once. The tactical array and fire control would stay integrated, and target ship weaponry would be neutralized before they even knew what hit them."

Forcing himself to ignore the black glares and growls from Dela, he rolled on, gaining momentum and laying out a set of plans for the operation. As he went along, his audience began to participate, asking questions here and there, and before he knew it he'd rearranged the situation plot to display his new plan of action and a tree of event management strategies. Eventually the discussion wound down and a silence fell.

"Dela?" Jenks leaned over to look at her display, frowning.

"Oh, I got it all down, I did. I've sent it."

Theta leaned forward against the rostrum, drained and peering worriedly towards Dela's display. Noticing his attention, she deactivated it and smirked at him, rocking to her feet.

"Thank you, mister Theta. Now, please return to ops—I know ye know the way."

Theta nodded. He stepped down from the rostrum and made his way out the door, staring down at his paws. The room was silent as he left, and the door was closed and locked behind him immediately after he passed through.

Theta sat in ops in stony silence, watching the celestial objects pass by in the charting tank and waiting for he knew not what. The stars out here had names like X24O and VN551, and there was little interesting on the chart. Cuny was busy and offered no conversation; Theta did not attempt any.

Suddenly he froze, staring at the tank. He zoomed out a bit and spun the display.

Why had they come *back*?

XI

Go

IN A LITTLE OFFICE ATTACHED TO *DANCER*'S BRIDGE sat Captain Jale Bercammon, surrounded by a panoramic emerald vista of Fonaci displayed seamlessly on three walls, annotated with strategic data that extended to the planet's orbital defenses, satellites, stations, communications relays and traffic zones.

An intricate mesh of space control zones and orbital object paths wove around the outer edge of the atmosphere and updated in real time, the presentation clear despite its complexity.

Jale wasn't looking at any of it. Her elbows rested on the display on her desk, and her paws were folded beneath her chin. Her eyes were closed, but her mouth moved slowly, as if she was speaking to herself under her breath.

At the sound of her doorchime, she opened her eyes and sat straight. Closing her terminals, she turned towards the door, tapping the unlock button. She waved away her tactical officer's formalities, opening her paw to chair opposite her; the lean ocelot perched there without a word, appearing to barely touch the surface.

"I have a matter of utmost importance and secrecy...a matter with which I would like to entrust you."

Naane's eyes widened in a remarkably identifiable expression of youthful innocence and curiosity. "Me? Secrecy? But why me, ma'am?"

"Because dear," Jale said, "to put it quite simply, I have a problem that needs far more tactical expertise than I possess. I have strict orders not to discuss this matter with Gnosi, but instead to pick someone I trust...and so I will need you to do work for me in secret, in addition to standing your normal watches."

"Of course, ma'am! But...me? Why me?"

Jale steepled her pawdigits and peered over them, tilting her head and making eye contact. "I trusted you once, dearie, with the lives of everyone on board and the fate of the ship. You fought for your position when challenged, yes, and you refused to back down. And you were right. Now, that may not be much reason to trust *you*, in particular—I'm sure many of this crew would do the same—but it's a fine start. I need someone I can trust."

Naane dipped her head thoughtfully, then looked up and nodded. "Alright. What do you need?"

Jale engaged the privacy seal and brought a star plot onto her display; it replaced the image on her back wall as the others faded to a neutral gray. All of known space was depicted in greens and blues in a black field, extending along the galactic plane. She spun it and zoomed in, highlighting a system on one edge with a gentle tap.

"I imagine that you may be wondering why we're still stealthed in orbit of Fonaci Prime after eleven days."

"I had been, ma'am, but I had reckoned as we were gathering intel, or waiting on it to be delivered."

"Close, dearie. Very close. We're waiting on a 'go' signal...a signal confirming a plan set in motion by Knoskali even before we'd left. I left Brynton with sealed orders, which I've now reviewed exhaustively. I need your expert touch to turn a broad plan into a very specific one."

Naane caught her breath, but Jale held up a paw to forestall the questions she saw in her eyes. "Now, just listen for a moment. This plan is quite complicated, and proper orchestration is of critical importance. Knoskali has determined that Theta is alive and well, and most likely a conscripted worker on *Varaunt*."

"Still on *Varaunt*? So...you were right, then."

"In a way, yes; I had a hunch, and did some reading between the lines. I think he meant for me to. But to the meat of things. We're to meet *Varaunt* here—" Jale tapped another section of the map, just outside of a wide, doubled red border that spanned the breadth of the chart. "—just on the border of Alpha space. This spot is where we're to, as he puts it, 'retrieve Theta.'"

"You don't need a tactics officer to negotiate for the release of a conscript." Naane tilted her head and grinned, the tip of her tongue sticking out momentarily in her excitement. "So...this isn't gonna be a diplomatic meeting, is it?"

"No, Naane. It's going to be a hit and run under full stealth." Jale's whiskers twitched. "Your next question is going to be 'why will *Varaunt* be there', am I right?"

Naane merely raised her eyebrows and nodded. "That's one of them, ma'am."

"Well, Knoskali has arranged for intelligence to be planted about a VIP movement, through an intel channel *Varaunt* supposedly will consider highly reliable. It's the bait, and we're now basically waiting to see if it gets taken... but Knoskali seems certain it will be."

"Is there a VIP?"

Jale shook her head and zoomed in on the intercept point. "No, but *Varaunt*'s stalking will keep her in one position for long enough for us to find her. When we do—and it will push our stealth to the limit—we are to plant an encrypted message from Knoskali into her comm system for Theta. Then we simply shadow them until we get a reply."

Jale sat back, biting her lower lip to hold back a grin—Naane looked as if she was about to fall out of her seat, staring at the strip of uncharted, empty space highlighted in red which would be the intercept zone.

Jale wondered what the ocelot saw in that emptiness.

"So, we get a reply. And then?"

"Then..." Jale leaned against the back of her chair and took a sip of her megvha. "Well, that's where you come in."

"Hit and run, you say?" Naane visibly squirmed. "But those ships are huge."

Jale nodded and called up the relevant diagram. "Pirate command ships have the reputation of being mobile fortresses, and *Varaunt* proves it, dear me. Here she is. Five hundred meters and change. She's a hodgepodge of several generations of technology, with weapons arrays to defend their weapons arrays, and who knows their design but them, oh yes. Now, this is where I tell you another interesting part." Fighting the urge to rush forward, Jale tapped the schematic and it updated, showing another layer of systems in perfect detail.

Naane rested both paws on the console, eyes widening. "Is this...?"

"It is. We have the particulars and design of every system from top to bottom, oh yes. Now, I haven't the slightest idea how he has this data but he does...he even claims that it's fresh. What do you think?"

The tactician took over, all but bumping her out of the way in her eagerness. Jale watched in amusement as Naane skimmed through the data, shaking her head from time to time. After nearly a minute, she exhaled softly and looked up at Jale.

"I...this is a very, very ambitious plan, Captain. It reels me back just thinking of all the things that could go bad... but when the Master's hand is in them, things do have a way of coming out right."

Naane shook her head again, flipping back and forth between the plot and the schematics of *Varaunt*. "Though this is...I mean, you have to realize that while it's nice to have schematics...when a ship is built for combat, they assume the design is known, or will be, and they build to fit, like. Sometimes engineering changes stuff just to obscure the design, but not usually. Now—hm." She paused and stared, zooming out and spinning the ship in her view. Jale could practically see the thoughts percolating through her head.

"Ah, hmm!"

Jale grinned. "Yes?"

"How long do we have?"

"Once we receive the go signal, we'll have a good seven days of travel. Seven days, dearie. The timing isn't supposed to be critical, but stealth surely is. Do you think you can work with this?"

Naane stood and locked eyes with Jale. "I'll need to study this in depth, but I think so. I think I can do it. If these are correct, *Varaunt* has extremely sensitive lateral arrays, but she's not designed for point defense. She's built to be a long range EM detector, and we can blank EM to almost nothing. Her secondary detection grid should be quite maskable, if these are to be believed—She uses old tech there with known defects...but hard to replace and usually just supplemental, for her purposes...not considered critical. If these are correct, then...yes, I think we have a chance. I can't give you a better answer than that."

Jale narrowed her eyes, rising to her feet. "I'm very much counting on you, Naane. Don't let me down...and please don't let Gnosi catch wind of any of this. I piggy-backed a message for Knoskali onto the Brynton courier as soon as we established orbit so that he'd know where to send his message. This morning, I received a reply telling me to hold position, wait, and pick a few people I could trust to help in secret."

She sighed, lifting her cup to her lips and then setting it back down un-drunk. "I also don't know why Knoskali doesn't want me to trust Gnosi, unless it was from my report back to him."

"Sometimes the Master's will isn't clear. He plays, ma'am. I'm not saying he's doing it now, but I've seen him set spies against house security in lethal games, neither side knowing. Strengthens the organization, he says."

Jale shuddered involuntarily; it seemed to start at her tailbone and creep up to her nose. "Ugh. Noted. Please use Pinky and Jewel if you need to message me. I've started to use them as couriers to the galley for bridge officers, ostensibly to keep them busy. I'm planning on extending the privilege of galley couriers throughout the ship. What do you think?"

"I think it's a good way to keep eyes and ears around, ma'am." Naane paused, and blinked, then grinned, ears swiveling forward. "And while you're at it...put them in uniform! Make it official, and we'll find a way to teach them. Ostensibly hell, ma'am—we'll find a legitimate use for them."

Jale shook her head, surprised. "I'd considered that, but...would the crew...do you think the crew would accept them? I mean, slaves?"

Naane made no reply, but her grin faded to a blank expression. She leaned forward and planted her paws on the desk, staring at Jale long enough that she began to feel uncomfortable.

"Er...Naane? Did I say something wrong?"

"You really have no idea, do you?" Naane settled and shook her head, laughing softly. "Sorry, Captain. You're...I want to come from wherever you come from. We here, all of us were slaves at some point. Most of us officers are now probate officers of the house, meaning if we do real well, we'll be allowed to apply for the privileges of freemen. House Selesz," she said proudly, "frees more slaves each year than any other house."

"Oh my." Jale shuddered again, wondering how many slaves House Selesz *took* compared to any other house. "So... everyone here is a slave? I'm not sure I'll ever understand your politics."

"No, no no..." Naane sounded aggrieved. "We're not slaves. There's only two slaves aboard. We're...well, we were slaves, but we're now probate officers. We're still in the service of the house, and we can't leave or anything, but... listen, these terms...they denote a specific legal state. Sorry, ma'am, but you should really know this. Can I explain?"

Feeling obliquely chastised, Jale quietly nodded.

"Ok...So I mean, some of this is an issue of rank. The laws of Brynton are real old, and the rules of House Selesz are old too...but generally any freeman outranks any slave, any entitled person outranks any freeman, and the Lords outrank everyone. In the service of a House, though, it's at the whim of the Lord. See, there are even slaves of House Selesz that outrank us when we're off the ship. On the ship, well...the ship itself carries a pretty high rank, and anyone who outranks the ship outranks all of her crew. You hold the rank of the ship, and nobody under your command takes orders from anyone but you. On the ship."

Naane sniffed, and waved a paw. "Now off the ship, it's more complicated. We...this'll probably sound strange to you, but we tend to establish our social order based on rank and station. That's why I'm saying that right now we find your huskies odd. Normally, they'd just be lowest of the low, taking orders and abuse and the like, if even that...beneath regard...but here, well, they're your companions, so they occupy some vague status between you and nothing. It leaves people uncomfortable, as they don't want to insult you through them...but they don't really want to associate with slaves. So I'll tell you right now, if you make them junior members of the crew I'll bet everyone here will want to take them under their wing."

"That's...let me make sure that I'm getting this right, dearie, because it sounds rather daft. Are you implying that you wouldn't befriend someone for the sole reason that they're a lower rank than you?"

"Well, kinda. It's discouraged, but not forbidden. But... really, it's just not done."

Jale snorted. "Insanity. So, if I make the huskies part of the crew, then they suddenly have a status in your world, and you could interact with them?"

"In the context of the ship, yes ma'am. Off the ship, it'd elevate their rank substantially from what they were before. I mean, they'd still be slaves, sure, but they'd be the highest ranking slaves of the HSS *Dancer*. Aboard, they'd be crew."

"Insanity. How can a society function like this? In my culture, everyone is equal, oh yes, and any 'rank' is really just respect granted based on one's abilities."

Naane smirked. "Maybe so, but it might surprise you how meritocratic our system can be. Great people rise through the system to greatness, with little to hold them back."

"And the chaff floats on top." Jale quipped, less-than-humorously. She immediately regretted it, however; Naane visibly bridled.

"You don't hold a high opinion of the Master, do you?" Naane bared her teeth slightly. "He is, I'll have you know, the greatest Lord of Brynton, the Lord who singlehandedly grew House Selesz from a twisted, intrigue-plagued minor house to the strongest on the planet. His hand spans all of known space, and he takes care of his own."

"Except the ones he pits against each other?" Jale studied Naane's face for a moment. "I'm sorry, but I'm unconvinced. I think he's a petty, evil criminal who should be put away for his crimes, or rehabilitated into the working class on some neutral planet to which his influence doesn't extend. He exists because of his system, a spoiled child who has people and spaceships for toys." Jale felt her ire rising as she spoke, much to her surprise. It felt surprisingly good.

Naane huffed, awarding her a rather scornful glare. "Child? Ma'am, Master Knoskali is nearing his half century mark. He has headed House Selesz since he came to power at thirteen. Every single provost on the interim council tried to individually bribe him for his confirmation, story goes. Once confirmed, he had them all executed. He ran all the corruption out of his house in less than a standard year. In a decade, he had all the Lords of all the major houses looking to him for advice without them even realizing that they were...within three decades, he had developed Brynton from a minor world into an economic powerhouse. Now look, I'm trained in strategy and tactics, and I feel I can objectively say that he's brilliant and cunning, and rarely loses. He's no...spoiled child." She spat the words as though they were distasteful.

Jale was taken aback, her arguments thrown into confusion. "Goodness. But—fifty years, you say? He hardly looks to have passed twenty!"

Naane nodded, her tail swishing slowly behind her. "Yes ma'am. Rumor has it that he has some sort of genetic modification that keeps him young. Doesn't matter, though... even if he didn't, I'm sure he'd pick an appearance and stick with it until he chose to age."

"Well, this is entirely too much to think about, dear. I'm sorry if I've offended you, but you must understand that from my point of view he's rather a monster."

"Oh I do understand, ma'am...and no need to apologize, nor am I offended. But he's our Master. And, if you don't mind me saying so, he's your master too, at the moment." The ocelot grinned up at her slyly. "I mean, you're not a slave, but you're *his* as surely as any of us, or Pinky, or Jewel. I don't think he means to keep you, though...not from what he told all of us. For some reason, I think that he likes you."

Jale chuckled, shaking her head bemusedly. "Well...well. And he doesn't keep the things he likes? Interesting, dearie. Thank you very much for the history lesson, but I'm still not sure what to make of it."

"Just...what we're always told, from the moment we're made part of the House, is to simply do our best to do what the Master says, and let fate carry us to where we're destined to lie. That's always guided me, for one. I'd suggest that you try it, yourself."

"That sounds nearly theistic. If I may..." Jale weighed her words carefully. "Dear, how long were you a slave?"

"I was taken at about six years old, and I was a slave until joining my first crew at fourteen."

"So young. How did it happen?"

"My parents gave me up. Couldn't pay their taxes."

"Taxes!" Jale was astonished. "You, too?"

"Yes ma'am. They—my folks—were pretty far in arrears. They had a choice, though...they were offered the option to sell me in, with the guarantee that I'd be a tech slave. Or they could have refused—and six months later me and my brothers would've be taken into the general pool."

"Taxes. Dia forgive them," Jale muttered sarcastically.

Naane cocked her head and took a breath, then hesitated. "Are you a theist, ma'am? If it's not too personal a question, I mean."

"Me? Oh, dear me no. I've met a few, in my time, mind you. No, dear...if you mean my references to Dia, well, it's cultural...We Ramesi say that we're merely appealing to the sense of good in the universe, but I think mostly it's just become a figure of speech. You should meet the Intati! If you were dropped on their planet, you'd be convinced that it was a planet full of rabid theists—all ritual and recitation and prayer—but no, they're just odd, bless them." Jale laughed at the thought.

"We've had a few on board, over the years, and they always need to know where Intaten is in relation to the ship so they can conduct their rituals accordingly. But really, they're actually just keeping their moral compass aligned, so to speak."

"Oh. Well, ma'am, I only asked because my parents were theists. It's very uncommon on Brynton, but not unheard of. One winter, when wages were low and food was expensive, they decided that putting their faith in the gods and giving to the Pantheon would somehow magically feed us. So instead of paying the minimum amount due on their tax debt, they gave all of their earnings to a church corporation."

"That seems...unwise, regardless of belief."

"Yes, well...we're all fortunate that I had the aptitude to be desirable as a tech. That's what I call the humor of the gods. I cleared my parents' tax debt, and gave them a two-year credit. Whole family was doing quite well last I heard."

Jale exhaled through her teeth and took a sip of megvha. "Point taken, dear."

Naane brushed her short brown hair out of her eyes, tucking it behind an ear; her only reply was a slight grin.

"So, back to business," Jale changed the subject quickly, "I'll make my entry in the log today confirming the huskies. Mm, should I have them report to anyone, do you think?"

"You, ma'am," Naane replied without hesitation. "You definitely want them to report directly to you. Trust me."

"Very well...I'll want your plan of attack before we leave orbit, so try and have it ready as soon as you can. From the tone of things, I doubt it'll be more than a few more days. I'll grant you access to these data right now, and you may go peruse at your leisure. Just...not too much leisure, I trust."

"Aye, ma'am."

Turning back to her terminal, Jale cleared the display and blanked the walls. She disabled the privacy lock and exchanged nods with her officer; Naane stood and left without another word.

Go

Very early morning two days later, Jale was awoken by a small shake. She sat up to find Jewel beside her bed and her cabin lights on. The husky looked as though he hadn't slept for some time.

"Miss Jale, you have a message from Naane. She needs you on the bridge now, she says."

Jale rubbed her eyes and nodded, swinging out of bed and reaching for her shipsuit.

On the bridge, she found things surprisingly normal. Most of the bridge staff were minding their stations, and a slightly strained calm prevailed. Gnosi was absent, but then Gnosi was off shift.

"What happened?"

Naane pointed at the main screen, where three targets were closing in on a position a kilometer 'below' them. "We seem to have attracted some attention somehow. Pretty sure they're trying to use gravimetry to find us, but it's not very precise. I took the liberty of bringing us to a higher orbit, and that should keep them from getting more readings off of us...but we've lost our uplinks."

Jale thumped her paw on the nearest console, walking to stand by the tactics station. She squinted at the readings from the three ships.

"Drat. Good thinking, Naane. What are they doing?"

"They're trying to ensnare our last position with a gas net, to prevent our escape. No communications traffic from them, either."

"That's ominous. We must not be inspected or detained or we're most certainly lost. Did we lose all our feeds?"

"We still have Cerebar station, but we didn't have time to update the planetary uplinks. Getting them back is going to be very difficult without returning to our orbit."

"Drat." Jale swung back to her station and dropped into her chair, swiping her console into life. She switched to the comm panel and thumbed a button. "XO to the bridge, please."

"Ma'am!" Helm interjected, voice tense. "We just started leaking EM!"

"What?" Jale gasped. She brought up her systems display, eyes wide; sure enough, a warning was displayed on starboard side sensor net. She lifted her head and pointed to her helmsman.

"Capture the leak! Capture that leak NOW. Shut it down if you can, but if that's a transmission I want it."

"We've been detected!" Naane sounded dismayed. "Defense net won't lock us, but that won't stop those interceptors from pinning us down and keeping us from escaping. We've gotta get out of here now."

"Agreed. Helm, leave orbit. Maximum speed for stealth. Head directly towards the star. Might mask us a little while longer."

"Aye, ma'am. I got that emission, too. It's in a buffer...I shut down the entire array on that side and shunted it in."

"Good enough. Thank you, Sillanen."

"Ma'am, I don't think...no, we absolutely won't be able to keep out of range at maximum stealth speed," her tactics officer muttered, eyes flicking back and forth as she jousted solutions against calculated values. Jale could see that most of the rows on her screen were red.

Not good.

"Weapons," Jale snapped. "We may have to take out those interceptors. Can you do it with one shot each? I'm going to need a shot, EM burst, jink, repeat, or we're going to be fried by their orbital net."

"Yes ma'am." The weapons officer sounded confident. "I can do it. I'll need helm override, but I'm sure I can do it."

"Approved." Jale's mouth was dry. She thumbed another entry on the comm panel for shipwide broadcast. "General quarters, general quarters. Prepare for battle."

There was a moment of silence, and Jale stared at her board, torn between two courses of action. After a moment, she lifted her head.

"Helm...Prepare an escape course with a triple course change. Get us as near to the corona of that star as she'll take on the outbound. Store your course and prepare to execute it instantly."

"Aye, ma'am."

"Tac...alternatives? We can't allow them to hold us."

Naane shook her head, ripping through the data. "Concur. No alternatives viable besides fight and hope. Our computed alternatives are nil."

"Reading lots of comm network activity. Several launches, ma'am! Lots of power signatures from outside the net. We're going to have some big ships very close, very soon." Weapons was anxious as he doubled for Tactics.

Ruthlessly, Jale suppressed the knowledge that the interceptors in pursuit of her were being operated by law-abiding citizens in the performance of their duty. She had a ship and crew that was relying on her, and she had a mission which she must not fail. She closed her eyes for a moment, then opened them to look out on her bridge.

A fine ship, with a fine crew.

"Tac?"

"Ma'am, they've got a pretty good idea of where we are. They're fanning out to triangulate us with their grav sensors, and at this range they'll pick up our trace EM very soon, then lock us down. Once the big stuff gets near, it's over, and that's tens of seconds...not minutes."

"Weapons?"

"I've got the override, and I'm ready."

"Damage control, we're going to be very visible for a moment, and it could get ugly."

"Yes ma'am. I have all my triage packages ready to go." The taciturn canid in charge of damage control was as calm as ever.

"Very good. Weapons—" she hesitated for a moment, before half-closing her eyes and baring her teeth.

"—Now."

Little seemed to change, but a series of soft pops and hums sounded from the ship around them. Jale glanced at the display. Two interceptors were dust, and the ship was jinking again...but the third was showing an energy emission that the computer didn't recognize.

Twenty seconds had passed in the blink of an eye.

Suddenly the lights on the bridge dimmed and a loud shuddering groan resonated through the hull. Alarms went off on the bridge, and emergency lighting came up.

"We've taken damage—"

"Got the third."

"Incoming!"

A series of muffled booms shook the deck.

"By the gods, I've lost—"

"Mass readings all over the place."

"Helm, get us out of here!" Jale raised her voice over the chatter. "Everything you've got. Spare nothing. Now, now. Now!"

"Aye!"

"Ma'am, damage contro—"

"Damage, stand by! Weapons, full countermeasures... Just dump everything you've got."

"Countermeasures bay two is unresponsive! Deploying the rest."

Jale just laid her head back against her headrest. They would die or they wouldn't; there could be no surrender. She felt irrationally calm, looking down at her blank display.

A haze of smoke blurred the lights around the bridge as the wounded ship began to accelerate away, as slippery as ever.

"We've got EM hotspots on the ventral hull. Very hot."

"Damage control?"

"Ma'am, we've got a few small fires in sections around the outer hull on the lowest decks. Casualties, but only a few. Primary systems are intact. If we can survive this—"

Jale's guts twisted in agony. "Vent the fires. Vent the damned sections. Vent the whole deck if you must."

Another shudder shook the ship, and the lights flickered. There was a sharp crack, and she smelled ozone. Naane cursed darkly, pounding on her display.

"Rellin drive in five seconds...two..." the helmsman's voice was very thin, the skunk clinging firmly to his console.

Jale bit her lip.

"Rellin drive! We're in. By the gods, we're in."

"Helm, we need a short spot or we'll be overtaken. Chop and change as soon as you're able. Three course changes at least, and I don't care where you take us. Don't get us more than a day from Fonaci, if you can. Damage?"

"Ma'am, that last hit...it was bad. I've got a lot of E-deck that's blind right now. The automated system has put out four fires in the machine decks, but we've lost contact with all of E-deck, and it's...been secured."

Secured.

Jale closed her eyes momentarily and took a deep breath. Such a polite euphemism for sealed and vented to space.

"Pressure? Critical systems?"

"Pressure is holding steady in all decks above E. It's too early to tell about the primaries but we've definitely taken damage to our stealth, and if I had to guess based on this pattern, the ship's hangar is destroyed along with the gig."

"Damn. Damn! That's...we'll worry about mission later. Do what you need to do. We must survive. Where is Gnosi? Dia's breath. I need him. Naane, what happened?"

Naane looked sick to her stomach. "The computer doesn't know, but I do. We were illuminated by that third interceptor. The little bastard gave up his life to mark us for the damned defense net rather than running like I'd thought. We got one grazing shot from a frigate in deceleration after that third jink. Missed us high, but left a nice hotspot for the defense net, which got two glancing shots to our belly. Very lucky."

Jale nodded solemnly.

Watching her crew do what they were trained to do, she realized that things would likely move just as smoothly were she not there at the moment. There was no sense in issuing a long stream of orders, or asking for data that she could get herself. She buried herself in her terminal, pulling up systems damage data and watching updates come across.

Half an hour of unnatural quiet passed, broken only by the calm voice of the damage control officer issuing a rapid stream of orders and coordinating with his teams. Jale could feel exhaustion beginning to set in.

"Captain?"

Jale snapped her head up, though her eyes took a second to focus. She realized she'd been drifting, and that the damage control officer had called to her several times.

"My apologies, Mellen. What do we have?"

"Ma'am, we have contaminates in the air on C-deck from the fires in aft stores. I'm marshaling casualties to triage on B-deck and shifting personnel off of C-deck. I had to close down the G-tubes, but I'm opening the port G-tube between A- and B-deck."

"Thank you, Mellen. Let's get C-deck back as soon as we can, please. We can't have that deck unmanned for long."

The damage control officer nodded, still working at his station with his methodical haste. After a quick glance around the bridge, however, Jale realized that the energy seemed to have drained from the rest of the bridge crew. Naane was slumped against her console, staring mournfully across the plot, panning back and forth between two scenes. Everyone else was more or less reclined in their station chairs with little to do. A sense of shock seemed to pervade.

She frowned to herself, then switched back to her comm panel and activated the main intercom once more. "This is the Captain. Geff to the bridge. XO to the bridge. Damage control parties, please check in at this time. All departments submit casualty lists."

"Ma'am," Mellen spoke up. "We also have a rescue from E-deck. Unconscious, but wearing emergency gear. So far I have two dead, twelve missing. Two seriously injured and a bunch of burns, bangs and bruises."

The lights pulsed as the helmsman made his first course change. Mercifully the computer showed it as undetected. A full quarter of an hour passed before the door to the bridge opened to admit Geff, who was rapidly shucking firefighting gear as he walked.

Of Gnosi, there was no sign.

"Geff, take over from Naane. She'll brief you. How are the conditions below?"

"Everything above D-deck is pretty much fine, so's I've seen. D-deck is in fairly rough shape, and we have a few pressure penetrations. I have to assume that E-deck is a total loss." The equine stepped away from the pile of gear and kicked it into a corner. "There are a lot of wounded, but only a tiny handful who are hurt too bad to work... maybe three. Your huskies are working, too. One of them is helping the surgeon. I think I saw the other with a dc party on D-deck, patching a penetration."

"Thank you, Geff. Have you seen Gnosi?"

"No, ma'am."

Jale sighed very softly. "Are we stable, Mellen?"

"As near as I can tell, ma'am. I have no idea what's happening in the blind spots all over E deck, and parts of D-deck are blind to me as well."

"Very well. Good job, and keep it up." She spoke up to get the attention of the rest of her bridge officers. "That goes for all of you. I'm going to bring in the next shift to provide some relief as soon as we're verified gas-tight and can return crew to C-deck. After that shift, we'll move to watch-and-watch to salvage and repair what we can. Keep this in mind, though, my dears—There will be no drydock or refit, nor a tremendous amount of time for repairs. I'll be talking with the engineering department soon, yes I will, but meanwhile, try to prevent damage to any further systems, unless the ship itself is in danger.

"The first order of business must be to tend to the ship, oh yes. The second order of business is navigation and maneuvering. The very next thing on that list is stealth gear, and I'm deadly serious." She collected nods from each present, then moved on. "In the meanwhile, Sillanen, Naane, I want you to pull that spurious emission into a SIGINT module and rip it apart photon by photon until you can tell me what it is."

"Aye, ma'am."

Jale rested a paw over her eyes, closing them to think.

Survival and mission were the same, though they had different terms. Without the gig, they would have to be cautious, inventive and lucky; they might even be forced to wait out *Varaunt* after transmitting Knoskali's message. Without the stealth gear, though, there was nothing. No chance.

Had she been brazen to use Fonaci as her stealth test bed? It had seemed like a good idea. Thinking about it, it still felt like the right idea. That EM leak, whether a transmission, system malfunction, or—she shuddered to think—sabotage, was a disaster that could have struck them at an even worse time.

Still, there was no escaping the fact that things were bad. The ship might still be in jeopardy—the mission was very much in jeopardy. She had lost crew.

At the very least, she was now, personally, a galactic criminal.

Somehow that didn't feel as horrifying as it should.

Captain Jale Bercammon opened her eyes, pushing the bustle of a busy bridge and the chaos of her thoughts away from her focus, a neat mental trick she'd learned over the years. There was chaos on the bridge, but it was gentle chaos. The ship was damaged, but spaceworthy; her crew was mostly intact. There would be time later to weep for the dead, and they were out of the immediate danger.

"Damage control...what is the status of our parties?"

"Disbanding, ma'am. We're keeping one DC party on ready standby in case something crops up, but otherwise...ah, I've run out of stuff to do. The rest is in Engineering's hands."

Jale nodded. "Very well. Thank you. Have you seen or heard from the XO?"

"No, ma'am."

She touched the shipwide intercom button. "Stand down from general quarters. Galley staff, second watch, report to the galley to start a full meal service."

She released the button and leaned forward, peering at her chair. Her claws had left several deep indentations in her armrests from her squeezing of them, and she surreptitiously began to smooth them out.

"Ma'am, I can confirm at this time that the emission was a partial transmission. Broad spectrum, multiple modulations...looks like wavelength division encryption. I don't think we'll be able to break it, but there's definitely data there."

Naane sounded glum.

"Thank you. Good work. Now we'll need to try and find out who sent it, if we can."

Naane leaned over to her. "Can I speak with you in private, ma'am?"

"Of course," Jale replied softly, rising and nodding to her office.

As soon as the door shut, Naane turned to Jale with a pained expression on her face. "Ma'am, do you still intend to intercept *Varaunt*?"

"I absolutely do." Jale was firm. "We must. We may have to be creative, but we *must* succeed."

Naane slumped, looking down. "I...ma'am, I'd like to be relieved of the planning."

Jale knew where this was going, but it had to play its course; she affected a confused expression, tilting her head and blinking.

"What? Whyso?"

"Ma'am, I failed. I've been thinking, and I've come up with two separate alternatives that we could've taken that might've turned out better. I...I froze, and couldn't think of them then."

"Froze, dearie? I was watching you, and you were proposing a dozen alternatives to the computer at once. It was my plan that got us into this mess, but you hold no fault whatsoever. Bless me, you can't look back, you silly thing. Now stop your moping." She grinned reassuringly, resting her paw on Naane's shoulder. "Is this the first time you've been in a ship that's been hit?"

"Well," Naane shifted. "Yes, ma'am. Most of the crew, too. Except maybe Gnosi."

"You did fine, dear. You did just fine. I will not relieve you."

"Ma'am...can I at least have Geff review my planning? And be on duty for the intercept? He's trustworthy, I swear it."

"If you trust him, I'll trust him." Jale adjusted her ship-suit, reclosing her wrist tabs. "But I'll leave you in charge, and expect you both on duty for the intercept. That leaves Krella out of the loop, the poor dear, but it can't be helped."

"I..." Naane grimaced. "Aye, ma'am."

"Now let's have you finish the forensics on that signal as best you can, and then you can get some rest. I think we all need it, at this point. I suspect I'm going to take a nap at my station for a bit."

"Aye, ma'am."

"Ma'am?"

Jale sat upright, blinking bleary eyes at the murmur in her ear. The bridge was quiet, and the stations were manned by a hybrid of two shifts; the previous shift was asleep in makeshift cots around the bridge. She turned to find a husky by her chair.

"Jewel? Good to see you're in once piece. How long was I asleep for?"

"I brought you some megvha," Jewel murmured quietly, handing her a mug. To her surprise, Jale noticed that his fur was matted with blood in places, his brand new shipsuit was torn, burned and bloody, and the tip of an ear was missing. "You were asleep for about two hours. Ma'am, there's something you should know."

Jewel looked around and leaned close, nose actually touching her ear. "Pinky shadowed Gnosi down to E-deck before general quarters."

Jale didn't move a muscle. "Yes?"

"Ma'am, Gnosi shot him."

XII

Spoils

THETA TOOK A SLOW BREATH TO CALM HIMSELF, his eyes fixed on the charting tank. A wide, low round table with stations on two sides, it would be an unremarkable piece of furniture if it didn't project above it a three-dimensional display of space around the ship. Adjustable in range between half a kilometer to all of known space, it currently was in the neutral state it was kept in during cruise, displaying the nearest systems and charted celestial bodies in a twelve hour window from edge to edge.

Normally, it displayed only systems and stars that he did not recognize, a pretty set of nothingness to divert his attention; at the moment, however, near the outer edge was a set of coordinates that he knew intimately, and he itched to find out why.

He glanced around the darkened operations room, eyes flicking from terminal to terminal. They were all secured, and he only was allowed escorted access. Stealing a quick little look up to Cuny, he found the wolf's eyes on him.

He tilted his head, but the wolf gave him only the barest little headshake in reply. Frustrated, he clenched his jaw and resumed staring at the tank.

Minutes later, a little sound and a change of pressure caught his attention, and he swiveled in his chair. Dela herself was waddling back into operations. He fixed her with a suspicious glare. Many questions sprang to his lips, but he bit them off at her knowing little smirk.

"Ah, Theta. Come over, would ye?" Dela nodded to the briefing room just to the side of operations and shifted herself that way.

He rose and followed, feeling far less affected than usual by what he'd come to think of as 'the Dela effect'. Something was up...and he wanted to know what, no matter how tenuous his footing.

"Close the door good and tight, lad." Dela arranged herself into a chair, propping her head on a paw.

Theta sat, not quite opposite her and angled slightly away. He said nothing, but locked gazes with her. Finding a glimmer of something queer in the big badger's eyes, he lifted his nose in challenge.

"Let's be straight, snowflake, and talk plain for the first time you and I, shall we?" Dela's spoke deliberately, her accent softening a bit. "First, let me say that I don't particularly have much cause to like ye. I can directly relate those ye killed with the money it'll cost me in lost take, and I don't like losing what I've worked for. Neither does Jenks, nor do any of the rest of us—we're not here for the jollies. When Janesson and that fox bitch suggested you were coming here I was not at all in favor, you better believe. Looking through your file? Even worse. Ye have no academics." She ticked off plump digits, enumerating his failings. "Ye have no background in tactics that I can tell, little knowledge of the book, and no real training whatsoever that we've been able to determine. I don't even know where ye come from. Well?"

"Well? Well what? First of all, why are we back at the intercept coordinates?" Theta asked bluntly, hoping to skip the denigration he could feel her building up to and get some straight answers. "To be frank, I think I'm being played here, and I'm not sure I like this game."

Dela rubbed her paws together languidly, looking up at the ceiling and taking her time. "Of course, all that behind us ye also have about the finest eye for tactics of anyone I've seen, and I should know lad."

Theta leaned back until his chair creaked; this was not at all the conversation he had anticipated. He held himself to the tiniest cock of his head, calming his thoughts. She looked...smug.

"What?"

"Well, now," Dela said, then sighed broadly, continuing on as if he'd said nothing. "You're quite a handful, aye. I've had to go so far as to jimmy the simulations to catch you out, and that was some hard work, let me say. All that, and you've come a ways with your academics, too. Developed a decent handle on book, and your analysis skills are good...much better than I thought they'd be. Means you try hard, too, and that's nothing with which to trifle. Ye also have an astounding capacity for visualizing, accurately holding, and properly correlating a tremendous amount of information."

Theta snapped his jaw shut in irritation, ears flicking back, then forward, then back. He shook his head, unsure whether to trust her. "Dela, I—"

"But lad—" she plowed over him "—the truth of the matter is that even if ye hadn't improved as much, I've others to do what you did this morn. Oh, we can have the computer do most of it for us, anyway. Generally it's smarter than we are, if I were to be honest. Well, for the first part, that is—directing the ship in an unknown engagement is far more a challenge for twiddly bits, on my word."

"We haven't intercepted that convoy yet, have we?"

"Ah, gems! And on top of it, snowflake, ye present the final proof for me, if any were needed, that you're not as stupid as you act. Beautiful. No," she awarded him another long sigh, shaking her head as if it pained her to tell him, "indeed, your suspicions are accurate. Assault 04 is still whole and hale, her crew blissfully unaware of their brush with certain death. We will hit them soon, however. I'm sure ye noticed where we've come, and I'm sure that if you'd looked carefully, you'll have noticed that we're staging along your proposed vector. No, lad, we hit them in but a few hours. And by the by, we'll be going with none other than your plan of attack."

Theta slowly slumped back in his chair. "But..."

"Unless, that is, ye have some last-minute revisions, hmm?"

"I— what? No, but...it was rushed, and I hadn't gotten much sleep. Very little, in fact. What did I analyze?"

"That little disaster of an engagement that ye dissected was a simulation of Lean's plan. Found most of her flaws, too, I daresay. Even pointed out a few things I didn't think of m'self, though I may disagree with you on a few points. Small ones. Nearly beneath notice, in the grand scheme. I refined slightly. Polished the edges off. For being exhausted, I'd say you did just fine. Perhaps not as well as me on my best." Dela chuckled to herself and rubbed her paws together again. She locked eyes with him once more. "Then again, I've also been doing this for three decades, so I know the odd thing or two. Don't start thinkin' you're the Gods' gift to tactics, or we may have trouble, mind."

"I don't. I wouldn't. I mean, I'm not. I won't, but why?" Theta wanted to stay annoyed, but the relief he felt threatened to overwhelm it. Annoyance seemed to him a much more dignified reaction however, so he assembled what he could, flattening his ears further and baring his teeth slightly. "I mean, what is the point of all this? All the mind games, all the hazing?"

"Simmer down, lad, and don't affect that tone. Ye aren't the manipulative sort, I think. Now ye did good this morning, snowflake, but I'd reason to doubt and so'd the rest. Me, at the first I was hoping ye'd fail as badly as I expected ye to, and wanted to get ye out of my hair quickly, and didn't hide the fact." She shook her head. "But when I first started working ye I couldn't deny I'd the wrong of it. Now we all know, and there'll be no questioning you from anyone in tactics or bridge ops on lack of faith, and, sure as breathing, none can say as I was favoring you till now. And if ye can put up with all that which I gave last week as well as ye did," Dela grinned, "you can easy enough put up with me on me worst days. Now do us both a favor, lad, and take a few hours off. Get some sleep, as ye look terrible. You'll be on duty for the mission, and that's in just a few hours."

"I...so I'm officially your apprentice now?"

Dela frowned sourly and shook her head, sending little ripples through her neckfat. "Nah lad. Lean was my apprentice, and a pain she was. Ye aren't in need of that sort of handholding. No, you're simply my tactician, and my department second, as it were. Once we've had you at it a while, I'll be expecting ye to even stand as my surrogate when I'm off shift. Now, you're low seniority, so don't ye think to try to rank anyone at all—not that I think ye would—but if you prove yourself today and a few more times after, I think ye will find your troubles mostly behind you. This crew respects people who make them money and prevent loss, and in that we make the point of the spear. Besides which, anyone disagrees with ye, just come to me and we'll see what's what."

Theta stood. "I don't know if I want to work tactics for three decades, but I'll certainly give you and the ship my best." He shifted, started to say something, then stopped. After a moment, almost reluctantly, he made eye contact with her, holding it until she leaned back incrementally. "Just one thing. No more lying to me. I'm tired of it."

Dela snorted, squinting up at him.

"Lad, lad, I'll make no promise of that," she growled. "If I did such, I might find myself unable to live up to it without neglecting other obligations of duty."

Theta hadn't expected that reaction. He blinked and exhaled, thinking it through. "I...suppose I can see that. If that's how it is, though, you should never expect my full trust."

A cool silence fell, and Dela regarded him—pityingly?—for a moment before speaking.

"Theta, my dear, I would never dream of expecting or demanding any such thing from ye. Keep in mind where you are; there are many here I trust partially, many I mostly trust, quite a few I trust not at all, and only one," She thumbed her chest firmly, "that I trust completely. I'd recommend the same to you. I don't know where ye come from, but clearly it was a trusting place. You'd be wise to keep your own council, make your own decisions, and take great care in who ye befriend. Especially you. We are not all friends here, even when it may seem so. We're every one of us loyal to one thing, and we're here for one thing, and one alone. We're loyal to leaving this ship with a lot of money, and mark me: we'll keep those out of our way who won't help us achieve that goal, no mistake."

Theta felt a little chill run down his spine at Dela's words, but he could see the truth in them. As if she'd changed before his eyes, he looked at her and saw not a taskmaster but a business partner; it was a radical but immediate shift, and it left him dizzy. It struck him that his years of slavery had instilled a strange sort of social obedience, and a need for dependence. He *needed* to be owned and loyal. The realization that he was now supposed to be a creature out for his own gain, his own benefit, and his own future was shocking. It shook him to the core. Everything he was rejected it as thoroughly as he'd rejected being slave to the ship.

A cavalcade of thoughts and conflicting ideologies ran through his head.

What am I? Whose am I?

Why am I here? I can't accept this. I can NOT *accept this.*

He stared off into space, frozen.

I am. I will be. But what will I be?

Dela was watching him stonily, one eyebrow raised. Theta suddenly realized that he'd been wrapped up in his thoughts, and felt an embarrassed flush start under his fur; his ears and nose grew hot. He could see the doubt in her face growing by the moment.

"Ma'am, if you don't mind…I'm definitely going to take you up on that rest. I was—" he caught himself and shook his head. "Nevermind. I just need to get some sleep. I assume I'll be paged when I'm needed?"

Dela nodded slowly, then waved him away. He could feel her eyes on him as he left the conference room.

He went straight to his bunk, feeling very self-conscious. As he walked, he analyzed everything he'd said to people, everything he'd felt and done. He didn't feel over-trusting; he thought himself naturally a good judge of character, and he'd been trained in analyzing behavior. But Dela's comments often left their mark deep within him, and this time was no exception.

So deep was his doubt that he avoided eye contact with crew passing in the hallway, didn't respond to greetings, and didn't even lift his head until he climbed into his bunk. He pulled the privacy curtain shut and stretched his length in his covers, expecting and hoping to quickly achieve the silent oblivion of sleep. Try though he might, however, it eluded him; though his eyes burned and his body was inert, the endless parade of thoughts and emotions continued and sleep hung just out of reach, as if he was too tired to find it.

Minutes passed, and he rolled over, pulling his blankets over his head. His injuries ached and burned, and no matter how he oriented himself he was unable to find physical comfort. He spent half an hour sweating into his bedclothes, rolling around in circles in increasing distress, tortured by the pain in his body and waking dreams of finding who he was meant to be. When his teeth began to itch, however, a sure precursor to another of his headaches, he gave up entirely.

"This is ridiculous," he growled, sitting up and kicking his covers off. With an irascible sigh, he rolled out of bed and rubbed his eyes.

Exhausted though he was, he padded to the head. The computer wouldn't dispense another analgesic strip yet, and he punished it with a soft blow, grinding his teeth. After rinsing and drying his face and paws, he decided to go find more verti.

"Hiiii, darling." Vaese intercepted him before he even made it into the galley proper. "Lovely to see you again. Arvy's not here, but I can take care of you just as well. Better, even!"

"Thanks, Vaese. How've you been?" Theta strove for politeness, though his head was already throbbing.

Vaese rested his paw on Theta's shoulder. "Oh, I'm just fine, just fine. Living the dream, you know. Sooo, what all can I get you, hmm?"

Theta tried not to flinch, though he felt his hackles rise at the deer's touch. He did his best to control his reaction and smile affably in reply, but Vaese pulled back slightly, his happy grin fading.

"Sorry. It's been a crazy...ah...I started to say a crazy few days, but really it's just been crazy for as long as I can recall. Maybe it's not the world, but me," Theta sighed, rubbing his head again. He could feel the ache spreading to the space between his eyes. "Anyway, I just came down to get some verti. I'm exhausted, but I can't sleep. I have to...ah, I have to work in a few hours here, and I just need something to pick me up a bit."

"Are you feeling alright, mm? You look awful, and worse than just tired."

"I...also get headaches. Pretty rough ones."

"Let me try something, hmm? I have something that might work better than verti. We don't generally serve it, but we carry it around to mix in with the verti when something's going on and the boys don't have time to get any rest."

Theta's ears perked, and he coughed softly into his paw, eyes on Vaese. "I'd be obliged for any help you could give this fox, sir."

"Be right back!" Vaese flashed a grin and swung into the galley; Theta didn't follow, but slumped against the bulkhead with a little sigh, half-closing his eyes against the light.

A short time later the deer reemerged with a little flask. Though it was sealed, Theta caught and recognized its scent immediately.

"That," he stated matter-of-factly, "is most certainly megvha."

"Oh! You know it, darling?"

"You're a lifesaver, Vaese. You have no idea...Arvinne didn't think you had any of this when I came down this... ah...yesterday, or whenever it was."

"It's controlled. Addictive, you know. Anyway, Arvinne doesn't have access to those stores yet, 'cause he hasn't needed them."

Theta's paws clutched at it and he held it to his muzzle, tilting it up to suckle some of the thick beverage. He'd had the best megvha in the galaxy at Knoskali's side, and had developed quite a taste for it.

He could tell easily that this wasn't great megvha, nor even particularly good megvha.

It was, however, so incredibly welcome that it was the best thing he'd tasted in his life, and he slurped it eagerly.

"Addict?" Vaese leaned close, quiet and concerned.

Theta leaned back against the wall, feeling the coating warmth course down his oesophagus. Even though the chemical properties of the beverage were minutes away, he already felt better.

The fragrance filled his awareness.

"Nooo," he sighed after a moment, eyes nearly closed. "Believe it or not, I haven't had any for..." he paused and blinked. "Quite a long time. So it's not dependence, but just desire."

The deer frowned down at him. "I'm not sure that distinction means so much, darling, if it drives behavior."

Theta laughed and shook his head. "Well, it does to me. I have plenty of things wrong with me, but chemical addiction isn't yet among them. Thank you, Vaese."

"My pleasure, dear Theta." The cook edged back towards the galley and, Theta presumed, his duties. "Come again soon? We can all share a mealtime, you, Arvy, and us."

Theta nodded. "That sounds rather nice. Soon!"

With a half-bow and a little wave to the retreating Vaese, he turned on his heel and left. Sleep was beyond his reach, but that didn't mean he couldn't go review his mission plan.

Theta wiped the sweat off of his tactics station's wide display with a little rag while he fine-tuned the ship's scan rate with his other paw. The bevy of fat targets on his screen wasn't a computer simulation, nor were the assault ships deployed to them, nor the ground troops engaged in boarding battles within. His plan had brought the convoy out of Rellin and gotten the troops aboard, just as smooth as anything. Though right at the limits of *Varaunt*'s takedown and orchestration capabilities, so far the plan had gone without a hitch; for his part, he had nothing else to do at the moment unless something went wrong. Tense but calm, he contented himself with watching reports come across one by one.

Irrai, working at her station across the room from him, was the one on the hot seat for this phase of the operation. He could picture her dispatching orders from behind her soundproof partition, moving units and executing her own plan of action.

Curious, he brought up Irrai's command stream in a subview; to his surprise, she was mostly idle, sending occasional requests for status but otherwise just monitoring her subordinates now that her own battle plans were set in motion. He approved—Irrai was good at this.

Efficient.

Watching the various points on the target ships be taken in parallel as the ground soldiers and conscripts earned their keep, he couldn't help be impressed by the speed and accuracy. He'd originally expressed a slight discomfort with the narrow window allocated for this phase, but watching the teams work it became obvious that even that thirty minutes had a substantial margin for error. Dela's knowing smirk made much more sense now.

These were professionals.

He blinked. One new report in particular stood out to him, though it took him a second for the 'why' to percolate into his fatigued mind. When it did, it was all that he could do to restrain a laugh. He raised his head to tell the room.

"I'm happy to report that the prize is under our command."

There was a round of happy chatter, though it quickly died back down as eyes returned to mission parameters. Theta watched the assault ships check off one by one on Irrai's terminal and then his own; in well less than half an hour, he was staring at a clean board and every assault ship was either enroute to *Varaunt* or in range and requesting docking permission. He shook his head in near disbelief and sat back in his chair, broad grin splitting his muzzle, surprised by how good he felt.

"Well, lad, I'd say ye right nailed that one. Any loose ends?" Dela leaned over his shoulder to look at his screen.

"I'd have to say—" Theta paused to double-check himself. "I'll have to say no, ma'am. Not from what I can see."

"Good. I concur. Well handled, lad, well done." She raised her voice. "Let the log read that as of 20:42 ship time, mission DF602 is complete. The prize and her skeleton crew are preparing to enter Rellin drive enroute to S2, and all assaults are docked or in the process of docking."

A hearty round of cheering swept around operations, and the partition that sectioned off the 'ground' area slid open.

Theta turned to Irrai and flashed her a shy smile; she returned it with enthusiasm, shooting him a toothy grin and a gesture of approval from across the room.

"Bridge," Dela held down the intercom button. "Tactics reports completion of operation DF602 at 20:42 ship time."

"Good job, Tacs." Janesson's voice was larger than life, audio only. "Everything go well?"

"Yes sir," Dela sounded more chipper than Theta had ever heard her. "We have a great haul, sir. Computer is giving me some very high efficiency numbers. I think you'll be happy."

"Very well. Thank you; we've boarded our assaults, and we're preparing to follow our prize. Bridge out."

"Alright." Dela looked across the dark room, straightening. "Alright! Good job each and all of ye. Irrai, I love ye, lass. Stroke of genius to hit that junction on the ore carrier when ye saw it. Theta, top notch work, lad. Cuny, you're a wiz on that ECCM net as always." She beamed. "Everyone is now officially on leave until we hit S2, except for those of ye on duty shifts. Go get some sleep, and enjoy the time off. I'll do the analysis for this myself."

After a few more moments of mutual congratulations, people began to close up their terminals and stand. Some stayed to chat with their teammates, some began to file out of ops. Dela motioned for Theta to stay, and he shuffled up beside her.

"I'll get ye set up on a duty shift, and get your access grants up tomorrow." She thumped him on the back softly, grinning. "It's going to be a four hour per day shift before we get to S2, unless something pops up. After S2, I'll put ye on regular eight hour shift rotations. You'll need to meet with Jenks to talk about share-out for your ongoing duties, sign your contract and such. However, I'll have ye know lad... I made right sure ye got a full crewmate share for that last mission and no argument about it from anyone."

Theta restrained his negative reaction with great difficulty, nodding. Dela was clearly pleased with what she'd been able to do for him, and clearly thought he would be. He rose, faking a small grin. "Thank you. It was very kind of you to work that in. Now, I never did sleep. Probably should try to get some...unless there's anything else?"

"No lad, that'll do. And again, well done."

To Theta's surprise, Irrai was waiting for him in the corridor. She pounced him as soon as he was through the hatch, resting her paws on his shoulders and all but spinning him around.

"I told you! I told you that's where you belonged. You did great."

"And to think, I never got to use that helm." Theta grinned. "Or go fight a boarding battle without armor. But I do seem to enjoy it...it's intuitive to me." From what he could tell, nobody had exposed the secret of his background and training, and Dela's advice quelled his desire to tell Irrai. He grinned again, as winningly as he could muster. "And you...you do pretty well yourself, I'd say."

"It's what I do." The red fox said simply, then frowned down at him. "Say, I was wondering, snowflake..." She hesitated for a moment, seeming suddenly a bit shy.

After a slightly awkward pause, Theta tilted his head encouragingly. "...Yes?"

"Nevermind," she said, turning away. She glanced back, sidelong. "Aw, to heck with it. I...do you like girls? A bunch of us were wondering, but I...confess I was...um, personally hoping that you might."

"Oh my." Theta wanted to sit down. He tried his flask of megvha, but it was empty; sucking out the last few drops, he wiped his muzzle with the back of his paw before looking back at the red fox. She was very pretty, and she looked hopeful.

"Irrai...*like* has nothing to do with it. Of course I—" he paused, suddenly worried that he might be misreading her. "But, ah, what did you mean, specifically?"

"Well..." She looked down at her feet, as if she regretted saying anything. "I...find you attractive. Very attractive. And I even like you, too."

Theta turned away slightly, looking at his feet. He didn't want to hurt or embarrass her. "Well, I *like* every-one equally, but...I'm...I've been rebuilt just a bit. I'm, ah... modified. I wouldn't be of any use."

Irrai looked confused. She opened her mouth as if wanting to ask for details, but then just shook her head. "Oh. Well," she brightened. "I'm sure we could find some-thing. No?"

Theta shook his head, genuinely sad. "I'm sorry, Irrai. I find you very attractive as well, but my..." he shook his head. "I belong to another."

Irrai slumped for a moment—but only for a moment— then perked back up. "Well...friends, then?"

"Please! That would please me greatly." Relief washed over him.

"With benefits?" She eyed him slyly, and he couldn't help but laugh.

"We'll have to see," he said, then chuckled. "For now, though...friends, at least. And thank you."

She peered at him, thrown a bit. "For?"

"For believing in me. It meant a lot. It still does."

Irrai took his paw and clasped it firmly. "I believe in you because you're worth believing in, even if you don't believe it yourself."

Touched, Theta hung his head and licked his lips, squeezing her paw in reply. "I think you're excessively generous, but thank you."

When *Varaunt* and her prize arrived at slave base S2, leave was granted to the entire crew on a shift-by-shift basis. A slave base might not be much for entertainment, but it was a change of pace, and most of the crew jumped at the chance.

Theta declined, opting instead to spend his time with Arvinne, Irrai, and Vaese and Merrol when they were aboard. After a few days he even began to feel decidedly more confident in social settings, bluffing and faking his way through various social situations with some degree of aptitude, managing well as long as too much attention wasn't directed his way. Cooled by Dela's advice, however, he chose to redirect personal questions and downplay everything they knew about him, though Vaese and Merrol had seemed to be much less restrained.

He'd learned that they had both been slaves from birth, set to work in the kitchens of a mining outpost at a very young age. Sent out together on a transport run, they had come to *Varaunt* when their ship had been hit by the pirates. Janesson had a penchant for freeing slaves and enslaving their masters in the process of taking a ship, Merrol had confided; the pair had been brought on as free galley crew less than a week after. Theta had laughed at the appropriate times, nodded at appropriate times, and otherwise been quite a receptive audience. Indeed, he'd actually found himself quite enjoying hearing someone else's story, and was actually disappointed when it was over. Reflecting on it for a while afterwards, he realized that his own memories of life before slavery were almost a complete void. It hadn't occurred to him that it was unusual, but now it seemed that he should remember more. The concept bothered him a bit, but there was little he could find, and trying to retrieve older memories only gave him a headache.

On the sixth day, just as estimates as to the disposition of their latest haul began to reach the crew, leave was canceled across the board and the ship was made ready to depart, reprovisioned, repaired, and upgraded in places. A sense of merriment pervaded, and though a few hands expressed unhappiness at having to depart so soon, there was an overall air of eagerness and adventure that had taken hold.

The morning of the seventh day, the computer woke Theta early with a message: he was to report to the bridge conference room in twenty minutes. Assembling himself in a hurry, he hoofed his way over without even grabbing anything to drink, assuming that it was time to talk to Jenks.

To his surprise, however, he found himself walking with a few others into a filling room.

Looking around, he found Dela, who was pointing to the seat beside her. As he pulled out his chair and settled in, he was surprised to note that the terminal had his name on it. A warm feeling spread within him at this small mark of acceptance.

A few minutes later, Janesson himself strode in and people quieted. He walked straight up to the front of the room and settled his datapad into its holder, then grinned at the faces looking up at him.

"Good morning, my friends. As you all probably know, this's been a great month. So far, it's been a great year. If we ended the year with only one more haul as good as our last, we could mark it as a record year, and we're only a third of the way through. Now, from the same source that brought us that last convoy and the passenger ship two months ago, we have some new intel. This one was a very expensive tip, but if it pays off it's potentially very lucrative for very little work. We have a VIP movement out here along the border of Alpha space. The intercept point is a mere four days from here, and the estimated value of this VIP is very, very high. Jenks and I have decided that this intelligence is worth pursuing. Dela?"

Dela groaned under her breath, but rocked to her feet. She waddled up to the rostrum—displacing the captain, who stepped to the side in deference—and glared out at those present. "This is to be a very simple takedown. Our target is already enroute from Hope to a planet named Zyktona." She plotted a line between the two systems on the star chart. "Our intelligence shows him not to be flying an evasive path for this tiny segment here, strictly due to his proximity to Alpha space, so we will deploy our assault craft here," she indicated a point on the line, zooming in to show the details of the intercept coordinates. "Here, and here. We will be right here," another point, "and we'll meet him when we've forced him out of Rellin drive. His ship is quite modern, aye, but equipped strictly for personal transport. It's got no weaponry and very limited countermeasures. In short, if he's there he's there, and we've got him. If he's not he's not. We're going to lie in wait a little longer than we need to, just to be certain we don't miss him. If he shows his face, we'll intercept him, poison his bubble, knock out his engines and say hi."

"Risk factors?" The engineering chief spoke up, his voice a gravelly growl.

"A few, mostly concerning ambush, which is why we'll be deploying listening buoys and a sensor net to augment our early warning systems. Other questions?"

"Yes. Who is this VIP?" the same chief asked, rubbing his chin.

"A diplomat from a major faction. The intel doesn't specify which." Janesson filled in, then smirked. "It's assumed that he'll tell us himself."

There was a round of slightly sinister chuckles at that.

Theta stared uneasily at the plot. He took a breath, started to speak, then bit his lip. Dela noticed and glanced at him, but there was question—not censure—in her eyes. He shook his head minutely and kept quiet.

"Now, we have a few things to do, but at this time I'm ready to signal all departments to make ready to depart." Janesson taptaptapped at his datapad. "Do I have any last minute questions or concerns before we launch into this? If he doesn't come or we miss him, we'll have wasted no more than a week. I think we can spare it."

A silence fell.

"Alright. You all know what needs to be done. Let's spin this thing up." The captain stood, flashing a predatory grin to the room. "Dismissed."

There was a rush as everyone stood and headed for the door. Dela came over to Theta and nudged him, bending down. "Something to say?"

"Eh," he leaned back in his chair, stroking his chin. "I'm new at this, so don't mind me. I think I'm just naturally more suspicious...probably due to inexperience. It's just that I can't help but think that we're risking drawing some serious heat down on us for this sort of game."

"Oh that we are, lad, make no mistake. We're not, however, in the business of avoiding risk."

Theta shook his head. "No, no, nor should we be. It just..." He stood, watching the last few file out of the little room. Dela gestured for him to follow, and he walked with her to the door. "I don't know. I do wonder if someone might be setting us up for a fall."

Dela eyed him for a long moment. "And what might ye base that on, lad?"

He grimaced and looked away, with another little head-shake; he hadn't quite been able to pin that down himself. "Good question. Mostly why I held my tongue." He sighed, glancing back up to her. "Ehh. Like I said, don't mind me. Maybe just...keep it in the back of your mind, in case something else comes up?"

"Aye, I will. I've a thing for hunches, even the unfounded ones. Shall we head over to the sim tank and see what we might find for vulnerabilities in our little plan?"

"That would seem wise."

Dela grinned and thumped him on the back. "Aye, it would. I changed my mind, though, as I'm rather hungry. Care for some breakfast first? No good trying to think on an empty stomach."

He smiled a little smile, patting his own rather empty belly. "Mm, that would seem wiser."

XIII

Organism

*D*ANCER WAS NOWHERE, adrift and silent in a vast sea of nothing; lying low in deep space, well away from any shipping lanes, in a pool of her own gas and vapor—an injured predator, nursing her wounds. Her ventral hull was awash with little sparks, personnel flitting here and there in the process of shifting hull plating, removing damaged metal for resynthesis, running cables and conduit and performing more specialized work.

Deep within, in the back of a small, greasy conference room on C-deck near the main drive hall, a somewhat disheveled Jale stared down at her console, counting her thoughts in a rare lull. Freed momentarily from dealing directly with the state of the ship, a matter now entirely in the hands of her capable engineering department, her thoughts had turned to softer things and she found herself once more reviewing the final casualty list.

Four of her crew were already dead, and one more might join the ranks within the hour. One was missing, presumably spaced. Two had injuries that would require an advanced medical facility to repair. Quite a number sported 'minor' broken bones, lacerations, bruises and the like, and plenty of burns to go around.

The numbers from the casualty report now had faces. Jale had known each of them, some better than others.

She shook her head and set her jaw, steeling herself against the rush of emotions that she'd unwittingly invoked. It was not yet time. Hers was a warship, on a mission. The mission itself could be the only priority; to fail it was to fail them all.

Even most of the injured held on, working doggedly where there was any work they could do.

Jale swept away the casualty list with a flick of her paw and stuffed her feelings back into the recesses she'd developed to keep such things.

The pane that took its place contained the ship's consolidated damage report from just after the attack. She scanned over it again without thought, her eyes moving across the fields without reading them, a slightly more active form of staring off into space.

At least they were alive.

For now.

"Ma'am?"

She straightened at the soft voice, but her head swam with fatigue and it took her a moment to focus weary eyes.

"Goodness. Yes, XO?"

Naane blinked, then knelt beside her chair with a little snort. "Not sure I'll get used to being called that. Makes me want to look over my shoulder. I came with news, but it looks like you need rest more."

Jale forced her eyes further open and shook her head. "Thanks, but not yet dear. I'll rest when we're back in Rellin drive, I've decided, and no sooner. While I'm on the subject, I've also decided to say damn the go signal—we have the coordinates. Let us go there. Poking around for a signal could waste precious time."

Naane nodded and wiped her brow, leaning against the side of the desk.

"It's a gamble, though," Jale found herself speaking again, gazing at a wall, the weight of her thoughts carrying an inertia all their own. "If the coordinates shift, if *Varaunt* finds out about our little game, if, if. So many ifs. For that matter, even if all goes just according to plan, it's still quite a risk. At this point, I just hope Nathaniel can get us some stealth capacity back by the time we get there. I don't look forward to what happens otherwise." She frowned down at her brevet executive officer, noting for the first time the signs of strain and fatigue in Naane's young face. "And as for resting...you're one to talk."

"Yeah. Well there's a lot of work to be done, as you know. Just nudging. Ah, the news I came with, though. Was talking to the engineering second, and he gave me the rundown. From what he said, we've done as much as we can for D-deck, and we're almost at a stopping point on E. At this point we're just waiting on a few more pieces to come back out of the machine shop. We hit that diminishing phase—what did you call it?"

"Diminishing returns?" Jale covered an unstoppable yawn, her eyes watering. "How's our stealth capacity, weapons and ECM?"

"He didn't say anything about that. Need to ask the chief for those, but he's up to his ears right now and I can't even get near him."

Jale grimaced, then straightened. "Whether it's ears, nose, or the whole creature, I need to know our combat status more than anything else. You tried to ask?"

Naane nodded again.

With a little groan, Jale pushed herself a little stiffly to her feet, then stretched. She raised a paw to smooth her facefur back, feeling more than a little unkempt.

"Perhaps a little more assertive next time, hm? You are the XO, you realize. Well, no matter. Let's go see what we can find out from the chief together, shall we dear?"

Naane stood as well, swaying on her feet.

"I'm sorry, ma'am."

Nearly every part of Jale ached with fatigue, but she quickly secured her belt and jacket and brushed past the ocelot, stepping out into the drive gallery.

"Ah, ma'am?" Naane turned and trotted behind, holding out her datapad. "There's something else—"

Jale paused and turned back, lifting her nose in inquiry.

"I took some time to review the security logs and cross-check the records. I just wanted to tell you...I can confirm Jewel's story. What he's saying is true."

"I never doubted Jewel's story, Naane. Is that all?"

"Ah." Naane stopped walking, brow furrowed. "But... then...why do you have them confined?"

Jale sighed. "To maintain my sanity, dear, among other reasons."

Naane didn't appear any less confused by this clarification, but Jale felt too weary to explain. With a shake of her head, she turned and resumed her rapid stride aft, gesturing for Naane to follow.

Engineering was remarkably dismantled; conduit and cables criss-crossed the floor, patching power and data busses, descending through makeshift through-decks and climbing bulkheads like creeping vines. Wall panels and deck plates were removed wholesale, revealing the skeletal interweaving of the structure, filled to bursting with discrete interconnects, processing clusters, piping and all manner of gadgetry beyond Jale's comprehension.

In main inductance control, she found a tall brown rat working furiously at the center of an immense amount of activity. No sooner had she'd set foot into the room, however, than motion and noise ground to a halt as engineers, technicians and deputized off-duty crew came to attention.

"As you were, carry on! There is no time for that," Jale snapped, slightly cross. As people resumed the course of their activities with wary glances her way, she leaned close to the rat, resting a paw on his shoulder. "Sorry to interrupt your work, Chief, but I needed some answers."

"Ma'am?" Nathaniel looked plainly worried, his whiskers a-twitch.

"I'm sorry to just drop in like this," Jale lowered her voice, aware of an already-growing semicircle of people needing the chief's attention, "but I really must know the status of our stealth and ECM. We can almost sacrifice the rest, but we need to get underway as soon as we are able— the mission is at stake."

"Ah. Ma'am, ah..." The engineer paused for a moment, fumbling through datapads in a satchel on his waist. He pulled one free and handed it to her sight-unseen. She took it, frowning at its display. "Ah, we're good as we're gonna get, far as our stealth systems go. I've known that's your top priority, ma'am. We've enough in place to get stealth back, at rest. Biggest problem is, ah, we've got minimal drive ducting now."

Jale felt her stomach clench. "And what does that mean for me, practically speaking?"

"Ah, well, can stealth at rest fairly clean, but we can't maneuver much under stealth without giving off trace detectables. I'm sorry, ma'am." He seemed almost afraid. "We tried everything we could to gasket those nozzles, but this is the best we all could do."

Jale closed her eyes and took a breath, more than a little relieved. She could almost feel herself unclenching. "But we'll be stealthed during our run-down from Rellin, yes?"

"Oh yes yes, *yes* ma'am. Only maneuvering's where we'll have problems. Ah, we've also got one ventral ECM bay back in—add that to the dorsal bays and we've a bit of ECM capability back. Rellin, fine. Engines, fine. Maneuvering is, well, mostly fine. She'll run less nimble. Sluggish. You'll mostly feel it on bow thrust and translation, but bow up will be duller.

We, ah, put a limit on thruster acceleration, too. Keeps us from shearing our makeshift lower plating. Overridable."

"I...hm." Jale rubbed her paws together thoughtfully, considering her options. "That—let us just say that that's more to work with than I expected to have and leave it at that. Good job, mister Nathaniel, quite good, and nearly half a day under my deadline. Still, I should like to get underway as soon as possible. What do you advise, sir?"

The chief engineer looked more relieved than pleased by the approbation. "We're close to done with external repairs. Two technicians out repairing the ventral array, but that's the last of the major outboard. Little else we can do without, ah, significantly advanced facilities."

"Will we be ready within the hour?"

"Ah, oh yes. Within the fifteen minutes, I think."

Jale wiped her slightly-too-long hair back with a moist paw and nodded. "And how are D- and E- decks?"

"D-deck's manned again. Aft third of E-deck is pressurized and stable, but, ah...I'd call it accessible at best. Very dangerous place to be right now, even if you can breathe down there. I've got teams on rotation to fix it up, regardless. Not in Rellin, though."

"And the power issues?"

"Yes ma'am. Lost one of our main power busses when we were hit. Ah, it was severed—the buss, I mean—but the hit also induced a massive current flow, blew out two of our buss ties. Ah, we were lucky to make it into drive with that damage. The initiators were receiving unbalanced power, but backups and skeletal conductance created enough of a path to create the cavity. But, ah... only just barely. Still not sure if that was design or happenstance." He paused, leaning close to her. "Or perhaps the ship was taking care of us. But the buss, we've patched it! We reclaimed plenty of conductor, and we have both ties back, and a shunt around the buss break."

Jale's head spun. "Goodness. Sounds like we're quite lucky, indeed. She's a good ship, aye?"

"She's a right bitch," the engineer laughed, "but does take care of her own. And she sure saved us. She's not a good ship—she's a great ship."

Significantly happier, but conscious of the increasing number of staff waiting for the chief's time, Jale nodded sharply, thumping him softly on the shoulder. "Good job. Excellent work; if you need anything whatsoever, please do let me know. Remember, just as soon as we're clear to go, I want to hear from you. I'll be on the bridge."

Nathaniel returned her nod, then immediately turned his attention back to his staff, who all started talking at once. Jale moved out of the line of fire and tugged Naane over.

"I want you to get to the bridge. Please get everyone ready so that we can get underway just as soon as Nathaniel gives us the all-clear. You know where we're going, so update helm. I'll hold a staff briefing once we're in Rellin drive."

"Aye, ma'am!"

Jale shooed her off, then turned back to gather her things from her temporary command station, fatigue momentarily in check.

Despite sending Naane before her, Jale startled everyone when she swept onto the bridge, striding quickly through the door and making for her station. A ring of faces turned to her as her officers paused in their preparations, and she took advantage of the momentary silence.

"Well, now, for better or worse this is what we've been waiting for. I'd like all departments to begin standing down from repair stations where we haven't already." She spoke briskly, meeting each set of eyes in turn. "I want to get a ready signal from all department heads. If anything is amiss, bring it straight to me—We have little time for troubleshooting. Are we clear?" Seeing only nods, she nodded back.

"Good. Let's get it done."

As the bustle resumed around her, Jale settled into her chair and looked down at the deck. Despite her drive to action, she showed more confidence than she felt. As her thoughts had turned to the future from the immediate needs of her ship, she'd become more certain than ever that she needed help to find a way to get under *Varaunt*'s guard with their current damage. She'd played things close so far, at Knoskali's advice, but the time for that was over; her senior staff, at least, must know as to what the mission entailed if she wished them to be able to function effectively.

She stared off, eyes unfocused. No matter what angle she examined it from, she arrived at the conclusion that alone, she was over her head. Naane had shown herself to be effective, but was inexperienced and had no cross-check; furthermore, as second in command she'd have many new responsibilities outside of the domain of tactical planning. Krella, Jale's chief tactician, had been shocked to have Naane snatched out of his group. Though he hadn't said anything directly, she knew he had been more than a little put-off by being left in the dark and never consulted. She hoped that she hadn't irrevocably alienated him.

Jale shook her head, wishing for the hundredth time that she knew what Gnosi had thought would happen on this mission. Clearly things had not gone according to his plan.

"Navigation is all set, ma'am." Naane said, then stepped around to settle into the chair beside Jale, tapping to authenticate her own console. "I think we'll be ready to go as soon as engineering reports in. Everyone else is ready to go."

Jale didn't look up, but rested her head on her paw and rubbed her burning eyes. "Good. Very good. I've decided that I intend to fully brief the senior staff on our mission once we're in established on course."

"Ma'am?" Naane dropped her voice, affecting a casual air. "Did you rule out additional threats?"

"Not exactly." Jale slid her paw down and discretely engaged the aural baffle around the command station. The sudden anechoic effect was suffocating. "I have no idea what Gnosi was doing, but at this point I must work under the assumption that he was acting alone. We simply don't have the time, between the two of us, to keep hunting spies, running the ship, and planning the mission."

"Agreed. Is there any way I can help?"

"Yes, as a matter of fact. I'm going to engage Krella and his department, but as second in command you are on point. You will lead the discussion—I shall need you to come up with some way to make all this work with what we have, and keep the others in line."

"Very...well, ma'am."

"I'd also like to leave personnel in your capable paws until the completion of the mission. You have the rotation, and the assignments, and I'm counting on you to get the right people in place."

"Aye ma'am." Naane said. "I was thinking about it, and I'd recommend just cycling to third watch as soon as we're in Rellin drive. That'll put us near the right schedule, especially if we immediately send everyone else to their racks."

"Good, good." Jale leaned back in her chair with a long, soft sigh. "Frankly, I want little more than to collapse into my quarters as soon as we're enroute. This has been quite a long span of being awake."

"It has, for me too."

Jale frowned and glanced up to her exec. "For most all of us, I think. I wonder—" she paused. "Do you think... Am I making the right call? To go straight to the intercept, without a confirming signal?"

"Yes, ma'am." Naane's reply was instant. "My opinion, absolutely. Was worried you'd insist on bouncing around to try and find his message. Far better to make up the time there, I agree completely."

Jale nodded, relieved. "Very well. That eases my mind some, thank you. Now, if you could prepare that shift change, that would be wonderful. Once I'm on the other side of sleep, I'm going to hold that briefing."

"Yes ma'am."

Resting her head back on her paw, Jale pulled up her tactical notes and disengaged the baffle. Normal sounds returned with a surprisingly loud roar, and she glanced about to see if anyone was looking her way. Finding all attention elsewhere, she turned back to her notes, then frowned. She had hoped to put together a coherent outline for the meeting, but she couldn't even focus on the words. She squeezed her eyelids shut, resting them for a moment. Her vision was quite blurry, and her eyes burned terribly.

It felt wonderful to close them.

"...Ma'am? Oh."

"What?" Jale came to alertness, feeling her heart beating rapidly. She felt as though hours had passed. Her head spun for a moment, and she shook it, then blinked; her eyes took a long few seconds to uncross and focus on the rat standing in front of her chair.

"Nathaniel? Goodness me. Fell asleep, did I? What are you doing up here?"

"You were totally out." Amusement twinkled in the rat's eyes. "I, ah, wanted to give you my ready status in person. We're completely secured from repair stations. Ah...We've salvaged waste gas, run head count and checked in all our vac gear. Everything checks out good."

Jale glanced around the bridge, squinting slightly. She found Naane looking back at her from beside the helm station.

"Do we have ready from all stations, XO?"

"We do, ma'am."

"Engines?"

"Engine reaction is at nominal." Helm's voice was steady and calm.

"Marvelous." Jale grinned, giddy with exhaustion. "Helm—"

"Ah, ma'am? Wait. One moment, meant to tell you." Nathaniel touched her shoulder, looking apologetic.

"Standby, helm." She sat straighter, tilting her head up to peer at her chief engineer and trying to control her irritation. "What is it, sir?"

"I'm sorry, but I was saying in engineering...we have minimal inertial dissipation for our ventral hull. It should hold, oh, even at peak acceleration, but, ah...It'd be better to use the minimum shift acceleration curve I programmed."

Jale stared at him, feeling quite stupid. "We've...the what?"

"Min shift. It's, ah...it's a...program acceleration curve. He'll know. I mean, helm will know. It's an option on, ah... yes, you see. I mean, he'll see it."

She nodded a beleaguered little nod; whatever it took to get them enroute was fine by her. "Very well, as you say. Helm," she raised her voice. "Let's go. Rellin drive on our new course, with Nathaniel's minimum shift acceleration curve, if you know what that is."

"Aye, ma'am." The helmsman sounded pleased. "Course set, curve selected, engines engaged. Acceleration underway."

Nathaniel wandered over to an unused terminal, settling himself comfortably and pulling up overlays of the ship's systems and repairs. Having nothing quite so distracting to look at, herself, Jale merely watched the ship's status on the main screen and fidgeted.

The ship crawled forward, barely seeming to accelerate at all. She frowned at the velocity display.

"How long until we're in Rellin drive, helm?"

"After the linear phase is an exponential phase," the helmsman muttered, almost to himself. "Ah...oh, beh. It shows me right here. Sorry, ma'am. I've never done this before. Twenty two minutes, twelve seconds to Rellin drive, it says."

Jale held back an entirely unprofessional groan—she was so exhausted that she felt physically uncomfortable, but there was nothing right to do but wait. Steeling herself and sitting up in her chair, she tried to focus on writing notes for her staff briefing, mostly to prevent her eyes from again closing of their own accord.

After a few minutes, she glanced back at the speed. To her irritation, it was barely faster than before.

"Are you sure we won't leave parts of us behind if we need an emergency acceleration, chief? I could get out and walk faster."

"Fairly certain, ma'am. Ah, this should be a one-time thing. I'm measuring the shearing forces. They're well within limits, well within. If nothing breaks, I can certify us operationally ready at 90% of maximum acceleration, with a 10% margin."

Jale nodded to him and leaned back in her chair, trying to rein in her crabbiness and stay awake.

By the time the ship had finished the agonizingly slow linear phase and hit the exponential curve, she'd nodded off half a dozen times for less than a second and was having great difficulty keeping her eyes open. The moment the helmsman finally announced that they had entered Rellin drive, she wasted no time.

"Third watch on standby, XO?"

"Yes ma'am."

"Change the watch at this time, please. I'm going straight to my quarters."

Naane thumbed up the intercom and announced the change of watch, then turned to Jale and grinned. "Sleep well. Captain. I'm off too, just as soon as the change of watch is complete."

Jale barely managed a grunt in reply, turning away immediately and shuffling doorward.

Dancer's brig was a small but dedicated affair on B-deck above the drive gallery, tucked away against the hull at the end of its own short little corridor. Jale, feeling much better after a full sleep and a busy morning, strode up and paused before its thick steel door, exchanging nods with the duty medic she'd asked to meet her there.

"Alright, open it up."

The short wolf stepped around the clean, prepared gurney that he'd brought and pressed his paw against the access panel. Once he'd authenticated himself and pressed the unlock, the door slid open and Jale stepped through; its programming snapped it shut on her heels.

Two sleeping forms lay together on the thinly-padded flat surface that ringed the room, and she couldn't help but grin down at them.

"Lazy bones," she chuckled softly. "Wake up!"

There was a stir, and one of the pair scrambled up to stand abruptly, alert but not quite awake. Blinking the sleep from his eyes, he shook his head dazedly before leaning down to help the other to achieve sitting position.

"And how are we, this morning, my dearies?"

Pinky grinned up at her as Jewel checked his bandages. "They've been taking good care of us. I—ahh." He winced in pain as Jewel brushed over a particularly painful spot. His ears wilted slightly, and he looked away. "Has...he been found?"

Jale frowned, crouching down to bench level. "No. We've concluded that he must have been lost when E-deck blew."

The husky looked away. "Oh. I—"

Jale held up a paw, serious. "Now hold on, dear. I only got fragments of the story from Naane." She reached out and turned Pinky's chin toward her with a finger, holding eye contact and trying not glance at his mangled arm. "I'm very glad to see you two alive and well, but I very much would like for you to tell me what happened. Please, start at the beginning. If you get too tired, you can rest, but I must know, and I must hear it from the pair of you."

"Well," Jewel started, settling on the bench beside his brother. "We were both on our way from the galley that morning, after the early wakeup, and-"

"No dear," Jale interrupted, resting a paw on Jewel's knee. "The beginning. Tell me about Gnosi, tell me about Knoskali. I have time now." She smiled to soften her implied censure. "My senior staff is busy buzzing over all the data I've just dumped on them, so for now I'm yours. But I want it all, and now please." Dropping into a firmer tone of voice, she fixed them in turn with a searching stare "I don't like intrigue on my ship, and I don't care who gives the orders."

Jewel huddled fractionally closer to Pinky, who sat up straighter.

"I understand." Pinky leaned forward. "Jewel and I, we have some history with Gnosi. Before the war, you know, as I said before. He is...was...capable of a funny sort of mean. I, ah—" Pinky paused, looking down at Jewel. "Can you accept that without me going into details? I promise it's not important to what you want to know."

Jale nodded softly.

"You might've guessed that Jewel was trained to be a personal chef, but they also trained us both in covert security, though we weren't supposed to say anything about it. Cross-training for the both of us, it increased our value since we could be bodyguards as well as servants. Nothing fancy or all that special, mind. Not like—" Pinky stopped abruptly, all but snapping his jaw shut; Jale blinked, and made a mental note. "But anyway, just before you came to Brynton, we had a very...difficult customer. He had some complaints, and was moved to a different set of servants.

We were brought all the way up to the slavemaster, and it didn't go well."

"Not well...?"

Jewel bit his lower lip; both huskies nodded.

"Not well," Pinky continued. "We were to be split up and reassigned to Orders of the House far worse than hospitality. We might not be alive today, except that on our way to main processing a courier intercepted our guard. We were turned back around and marched to an annex, where we were met by Lord Knoskali himself. He told us we'd serve you, said you were to be our ex...pat, uh...exter—"

"Expiation," Jewel supplied. "That's what he said. The majordomo said it means something like forgiveness."

Jale steepled her fingers, resting her chin on her paws and grimacing softly at the running theme. "Not quite exactly that, but close enough as to not matter. Please, dear, continue."

"Well, see, he sat us down for a good quarter of an hour and lectured us on our duties to you. But he said we were to feel you out and report back to him. Anyway, when you actually arrived, he sent one message to us through the majordomo. 'Nevermind spying. Keep Miss Bercammon happy...and safe.' He emphasized the 'safe' part."

"Goodness me, safe? I felt no danger; why should I need protection within Knoskali's house? I thought he had things in good order?"

Pinky shrugged. "He really does, and didn't explain. I kinda thought he might send us out with you somewhere on the planet, but obviously not. I don't know if he knew what he wanted with you yet then. But that's not most of it. See, before he turned Gnosi loose, he took us aside, and very carefully instructed us to watch him, and not to let him dominate or betray you. Said to us then that we should remember what he did. Like, meaning what he did to us before. Didn't know what he meant about the dominating and betraying part, since we didn't know we'd go out with you."

"We're glad we did, though," Jewel murmured earnestly. "Even still."

"So," Pinky glanced at Jewel. "We haven't had any new orders since, so we just kept watch on him. Mostly he wasn't doing anything interesting, and he never seemed to notice us. But when we got in orbit he started acting funny—started sneaking off a lot down to E-deck more and more. We tried, but we never figured out what he was doing down there."

"And why," Jale tried to keep her frustration from coloring her tone, "why did you not bring this to me? Why did you not tell me any of this? It could have possibly saved us much."

Pinky hung his head, ears flat. Jewel draped his arm across his brother's shoulders and cinched close.

"Honestly, ma'am, we didn't know what to do. Knoskali had said to keep it all quiet, not to bother you." Jewel's voice was hushed and worried. "We thought about telling anyway, especially after you asked Pinky about him, but we didn't know if maybe it was another test."

"I'm truly sorry, ma'am. We were very proud to be made crew, and we're both real sorry to disappoint you. I—"

Jale waved her paw for silence. "Hush, hush. Forget my question, just please continue, for I must know—What happened that morning?"

"Well, he went down to E-deck again, and I followed him. Except this time I was a little closer, trying to see if I could see what he was doing."

Jale felt her breath quicken. "Yes? And what *was* he doing?"

"Well, I couldn't see much. He had a piece of equipment hooked into a terminal. Small, the size of a medium power cell." Pinky grimaced. "Guess I tripped some kinda proximity alarm, though. Next thing I know, he's turned around and got an energy pistol on me. I was gonna try and play it off, but then he says something like...something nasty about us and you, and then he kinda straightened and just shot me. I jumped when he stiffened up, and he missed a little I guess. Got my arm and side, but it honestly didn't hurt much. Didn't feel real, like it was happening to somebody else and I was just watching. I fell behind a bulkhead and tried to run away. I don't remember much after that except that I got real dizzy after my first few steps, and there seemed to be a lot of blood, and then I was on the deck." Pinky seemed cowed. "I thought I was going to die. I guess that's when Jewel came in."

Jale nodded, squinting slightly. "Do you remember exactly what he said?"

"Yes, mostly ma'am, but he was just being foul. I was surprised by how he reacted, but that wasn't anything compared to when he shot me."

"So," she turned to Jewel, "you came in to find Pinky lying on the deck?"

"Yes, Miss Jale. He was kinda folded over his arm on the floor, and Gnosi was aiming at him. I don't know why, reflex, I guess, but I just drew and shot."

"Just like that? Where did you get the sidearm?"

"It was just part of our kit." Jewel seemed surprised by the question. "I carry mine shoulder whenever I'm outside of the House proper."

Jale nodded at this, rubbing her chin. "I see. And then?"

"Well, see, at that point Gnosi kinda just collapsed. Fell against the bulkhead and got propped up, but he didn't drop his pistol. I shot him again, but he didn't really move. As I was dragging Pinky away, I was so scared that he was going to shoot us...just scared." A little quaver caught in Jewel's voice. "I didn't even look back. I got us halfway into the G-tube when the deck decompressed. No warning or anything. I n-nearly lost him before the pressure hatches went, and there was fire everywhere, and so much heat. I just barely got him inside the G-tube, and then we both passed out."

For a long moment, there was silence. It stretched on as Jale considered. She had no reason to doubt the huskies' story; as a lie, it wouldn't have been terribly compelling, and Naane's account of the security archives had been pretty much the same: Gnosi shooting Pinky without any apparent provocation, stepping around a bulkhead, lifting his weapon, and being shot by someone just out of view. From what she'd said, Gnosi had visited the deck on a number of occasions while in orbit, but 'vanished' from the records each time while down there. With his clearance and knowledge, creating a hole for himself would have been trivial.

Jale shook her head and regarded the pair of huskies waiting silently, leaned against one another and looking down at the deck.

"Well, I do believe you. Even though we haven't yet managed to locate the body, we are missing mass well in excess of his, and we lost a lot of deck in that section. Security footage is unclear, but we think it likely he went out when the deck depressurized. Along with whatever equipment he was using and the knowledge of whatever it was he was attempting, I might add," she grumbled. "But I can see no reason to keep you locked in here any longer.

'Now listen—I'm not going to commend you for this, but neither shall I scold you, at least not publicly. Your hearts were in the right place, oh yes, but your actions... though I suppose it's really not fair of me to judge. These are confusing times for all of us, oh yes. Still, I expect the two of you are as safe as any of the rest of us. No more sneaking around on my ship without asking me, though, do you understand? We have repaired some of our damage and we're back underway, but things are quite a mess still. Quite a mess."

"What do you want us to do, ma'am?"

"I have made Naane my exec, and she's in charge of personnel. I'd like you," she nodded to Jewel, "to talk to her and see where she can use you. I do have one set of orders first, though. I'm heading to my office, where I shall wait expectantly for a cup of megvha."

Jewel brightened and beamed at her. "Yes, ma'am!"

She turned to Pinky, whose right side was a mass of bandages. "As for you..."

"Oh I can work, ma'am," Pinky spoke quickly. "I can—"

"No. I heard that you helped out on the lower decks, even dazed and terribly injured. I know you want to help, and I understand well, but the medic told me that you need to stay down or you'll likely lose what's left of your arm. Didn't she talk to you about this at all?" Jale frowned, hearing Jewel's sharp intake of breath.

"She...no." She could see tears in Pinky's eyes, and felt her throat clench in response.

She rested a paw on the husky's good shoulder.

"There is nothing they can do for your injury here. They are trying to slow the damage and degradation and keep your arm stabilized until they can get you to a facility to repair it. They want to move you to sickbay and keep you abed, and that is exactly what they shall do."

"Oh." Pinky smiled up at her, but it didn't reach his eyes. "Well, ok. Is there anything I can do from in bed, then?"

Jale drummed her clawtips on her chin, trying to restrain an emotional response entirely unsuited to her station. Once she had her voice under control, she nodded slightly. "Perhaps there is. Once they've moved you into a bed, I'll be sure to send Naane down to talk with you. For now I must hand you over to the medic and be off. Be well."

She turned away preemptively, smile frozen on her face, and tapped the request panel on the door. When it slid open, she hurried through without another word, brushing past the startled medic and making her way towards the G-tube.

"Miss Jale?" Jewel sounded worried, padding along behind. "Miss Jale?"

She closed her eyes and took a deep breath, blotted her eyes with the back of her paw, then turned. "What is it, dear?"

"You said he might lose his arm? His whole arm? They can't fix it?"

"From what Ososkne said, no. They need to get him into a large medical facility where they can install synthetic structures and essentially build a new arm and hand for him. The more of him can be saved, the less artificial...componentry will need to be put in." Jale blinked more moistness from her eyes. "But he told me that the artificial parts will actually work better than the scarred organic tissue, oh yes he did, and that skin and fur can be regrown atop them in a few short weeks. Don't you worry, Jewel. He'll regain most of the use of his arm in time. Even if we must replace the whole thing, nobody ever need know from looking at him as it'll be his own skin and fur atop. And he is alive, and that is by far the most important thing."

"But...what if we're out here for a long time?"

Jale grimaced. "As I said, it is possible they may have to remove the arm entirely. As gruesome as that sounds, though, it is certainly the faster route. They can build a temporary prosthesis that will allow him quite decent use. Ososkne gave me the option." Jale rolled her eyes. "Asked what to do as if it was my choice. I told him to do whatever he could to save the arm, of course, and that I didn't care if he wasn't able to work for the rest of the trip."

"Oh." Jewel blinked. "I promise, he'd rather have an artificial arm than a crippled up one. Just ask him."

"This...we'll discuss this later. I'll never understand you people." Jale felt her head spinning with emotion, and closed her eyes. After a few breaths, she felt calmer, and a little foolish. "I think...perhaps I need to clear my head, and possibly clear my head of my own values that do not apply. In my culture, and in the religion that I don't intentionally follow, if you die incomplete, you will lack the parts you've lost in the life after. There are a bunch of silly things like that, and nobody believes any of it in this day and age, but perhaps we're all shaped by it nonetheless. I find it particularly horrendous to replace organic parts with synthetic ones."

"In our culture," Jewel smiled slightly, expressive eyes a little unfocused as if looking far away, "when you die, you cease to exist. Do you believe that?"

"I don't know, dear. I truly don't know. I am certainly not a theist, but even I have trouble believing that lives spring into being and vanish just like that. At the very least, one lives on through the indelible mark one leaves on the past and the future. No, it is a problem too big for me, frankly, and inapplicable to my life." Jale stood. For some reason, she suddenly felt better. "You may tell your brother what I've said, or ask Ososkne do it. If he chooses...well, I shall not stand in the way, whatever he decides. But not immediately, oh no."

"I'll tell him tonight, ma'am."

Jale ruffled Jewel's hair. "Megvha now, more talk later."

"Yes, Miss Jale."

Late evening ship time, eight days later, an increasingly anxious Jale convened her senior staff in the biggest conference room. She watched over them as they laid out the various final plans and contingencies and backups without her saying a word. What to do if *Varaunt* was there and had sensor nets up, down, or was maneuvering, what if *Varaunt* wasn't there, how to dispatch Knoskali's message to Theta, who would be on ciphertech duty for the breakout, all the various recovery contingencies. All were laid out to nods around.

In slightly less than six hours, the ship would begin to collapse its Rellin bubble and decelerate beneath cavitation velocity, silently sliding back into normal space, eyes and ears open for her prey. Each department knew what to expect, and everyone knew what they were doing. An eager gestalt pervaded the discussion as her crew flashed through diagrams, systems, simulations and data analysis, moving through patterns of thought born of training and ingenuity in combination.

Despite the competence of her staff, Jale's level of unease increased with every passing minute. With no knowledge of what would await them, she could easily imagine emerging to a very hostile welcome.

Or, as seemed more likely, nothing at all.

It seemed an incredible long shot to her now that there would be anything there, odds nearly impossible to imagine. No confirmation, no final timeframe, no knowledge of whether *Varaunt* had taken the bait, no reason to suspect *Varaunt* hadn't shifted their intercept plans, absolutely nothing at all suggested to Jale that they would find anything but empty space.

She frowned the conference room chronometer as the discussion died to the last few little items. People were reclined in their chairs, staring across the table at one another.

"Is there anything else? Anything at all?"

A ring of faces, young faces, confident faces stared back at her.

"Very well. I am going to go take a nap, and I expect everyone to check in by zero-three-hundred. If anyone has any questions that the duty officer can't answer, bring them to me. For now, you're all dismissed."

When all had left save Naane and herself, Jale turned to her exec, swallowing her fears and forcing a smile. "They're a wonderful crew, XO. I'm truly lucky to have ever had such as them under me."

Naane nodded firmly. "Oh they are...and they have a great captain."

Jale snorted, her momentary happiness draining from her as if a plug had been pulled. "Oh, Naane, this crew deserves a real captain, not the chief steward of a passenger liner. I—"

"Ma'am," Naane snapped, suddenly seeming irritated. "I don't mean any disrespect, but knock it off. I've only seen your self doubt limit you, and the only poor decisions you've made were when you were feeling that way. I haven't seen it for a while, and this is the last time I want to see it resurface. I don't care what you think, you're a real captain, as real as any other. Less technical than some, perhaps, but good at command—you have a ship, and your crew respects you. You've held up under pressure, you've kept everybody on their toes, and you've kept us moving and coordinated when we otherwise might not have been. I don't care if you're just acting a role, you're acting it right. We need *that* you now, not the doubtful you."

Jale was taken aback. She was so surprised that she sat down into her chair in meek silence.

"Sorry for my outburst, ma'am." Naane murmured, though she didn't seem terribly contrite. "But at some point, you've got to realize that you're good at this. You don't seem to be getting it, so I thought I should tell you."

"I'm not sure what to say, Naane. Thank you, I think?"

Naane grinned impudently. "You're welcome, but it's true. Now get to bed and nap for your three hours." She smirked. "And stop your moping."

"Yes, ma'am," Jale murmured demurely.

When she got back to her quarters, she measured out a three-hour nightcap, then rolled into bed without even removing her shipsuit.

"Time?" Jale rubbed her muzzle, reaching out automatically to take the proffered megvha as she settled into her station a few short hours later.

"Time is minus fifteen minutes, twelve seconds," the helmsman responded automatically. "All systems nominal, all stations report ready for combat exit under stealth."

"Thank you, Sillanen. Krella?"

"Glad you remember my name." The panther at the tactics station shot her a little teasing smirk. "But as far as the ship's tactical readiness, we're definitely ready to have some fun, if anything's there."

Jale nodded. She'd come to like Krella; more aloof to rank than most of her officers, he was comfortable to work with, and she'd found that he, Geff and Naane functioned quite well as a trio. Watching them together over the past week, she had been struck by the grace and humor he put into the tasks at hand just as much as the ingenuity he displayed in a pinch.

She certainly had plenty to learn from him.

As the clock ticked off the minutes, little more was said for there was little more to say. Even as the bubble collapsed and they began their deceleration run there was just a sense of heightened attention across the bridge.

Jale's display registered nothing. As the ship decelerated, and the ship's passive detection systems gained sensitivity, blankness dominated. She sighed. All the work that had gone into this was probably for naught.

"Nothing?" She murmured to Naane.

"Oh, I wouldn't say that. You know they may not be here yet, and even if they are they're probably damped down tight. It'll take a while for our computers to correlate the interference in background radiation patterns."

"Not that long," Krella laughed. "Our target is right there in front of you, less than a thousand kilometers away. Can't you see them?"

Jale and Naane glanced at each other, then stood nearly simultaneously, leaning over to look at Krella's display.

"I still don't see it," Naane muttered. "There's nothing there."

"Why Naane, I'm disappointed." He prodded her in the back with a claw, then dragged it along a column of data tucked away beside the main display. "What do you call this?"

"Ah...baseline radiation? Oh! Oh, you're right. That's not random." Naane leaned closer. Suddenly the computer began to highlight a trail, adding a target onto the main display and flashing a warning.

"Helm, we have our target; please initiate phase one." Jale ordered. She tagged the target, associating it in the computer with the data they had on *Varaunt*, then turned back to Krella and lowered her voice.

"You beat the computer to that?" Jale asked Krella in an undertone, slightly awed. "How? I always thought the tactical computers were ridiculously fast."

"Oh they are. They're fast, and very smart...but not at all clever. That's obviously *Varaunt*, and she's deployed her listening net just as we expect. The computer hasn't had enough time to figure that out from the data it can interpret. The tactical comp also can't tell you that her take-down vessels are out, but I can. Even you, Captain," he said, smirking in mock condescension, "could probably beat it to the punch here...you just don't realize it. That net might be deployed to look for us, or to scan for any number of other things, but we know that it's not. It's looking for the shockwaves of their target's entry into local space."

Jale frowned and nodded. "You are also watching for any signs that *Varaunt* may have detected us, are you not?"

"Oh, should I be doing that?" Krella's eyes widened, and he placed a paw over his chest. "I would never have thought of such a thing."

Despite herself, Jale grinned and rolled her eyes. "Fine, fine. I get your message. Forgive me, I'm just antsy."

"It's alright Captain," Naane muttered, glaring at Krella. "We're getting there. The payload is ready and I have a report here from our lead ciphertech. He says that they're already passively piggybacked on *Varaunt*'s system and busy working out their encryption. Intel is good, he says. Estimates five minutes until he can upload the message."

"We won't be in position by then, but good. Very good. Any surprises? From anybody?" Jale felt a little stab of worry. She didn't dare to think it could be this easy.

There was silence.

With a little shrug, she sat back and sipped her megvha, watching as *Dancer* eased slowly around, arcing gracefully up behind *Varaunt* to seek the theoretical protection of her baffles. Every little correction was a cause for worry, as was the energy expended in their slow deceleration. Theoretically, she had a certain small margin to work with, and helm was staying just below the threshold, but engineering estimates were not infallible and a little bad luck could sink them.

Nothing to be done about it now, though. She had contingency plans in place, and a very alert crew.

A pleasantly boring hour later, *Dancer* settled in absurdly close to *Varaunt*'s massive stern and fired off the last of her deceleration, coming to a silent little halt less than her own length from the other ship.

"Very well. So far, it almost seems as though we're in good shape. Naane, signal the ciphertechs. We're ready to engage phase two." Jale sat forward in her chair, settling in for a long wait.

"Tech signals they're in, and the payload is deployed."

"Excellent, Naane. Most excellent. Now we simply wait and hope. "

"Picking up ripples. Looks like one of the takedown ships is back." Krella murmured. "If they bring them all back, it could be a sign that they're preparing to leave within a few hours."

Jale nodded. She was tapping out a quick log update when she heard Krella suck in a little breath. "Wait—"

"Krella?"

The panther stood and jabbed at his screen, turning wide, angry eyes back to Jale as if demanding explanation.

"What is that? I thought you said—"

"Ma'am, I have...comm traffic!" Naane sounded shocked.

Jale felt a shock of alarm shoot through her. She stood. "For us? Let's hear it."

XIV

Contretemps

THETA GAZED IMPASSIVELY down at the main display, munching a neré bar.

A large fleet battle was developing in the center.

Again.

They always seemed to do this; every new ship went from their shipyards straight into the melee at the systems in the center of the map, right up the middle, fighting for center control as if it mattered. He kept them occupied, feinting with his own handful of ships, nibbling along the fringes of their flanks and ducking back, hiding his numbers while marshaling a dreadnought in behind them while his spy ships slid through the ranks of his enemies to their shipyards, subtly damaging their production in ways unlikely to be detectible.

His gathering facilities fed raw materials into his rapidly growing industrial base, which churned out three ships for each one of his opponents'. His carefully-placed interceptors nabbed couriers carrying requests for a treaty from one nation to another. His science vessels, disguised as couriers, carried black ops troops to land on the homeworlds of his enemies.

Theta was only half paying attention to the game; most of his time was spent watching his real fleet—*Varaunt's* assault ships, hanging stationary in nothingness along their target's arrival corridor. He tapped out a quick out-of-game message to ops, then almost reluctantly turned his attention back to his play.

Once he'd figured out the interface, he'd been shocked to discover how bad his friends were; even Irrai, with the second biggest empire and half-decent intel gathering, was too tied up in the center battle to notice his machinations. He snorted to himself as his long-range intel reported that she was just beginning to send scouts toward the outlier systems he'd taken long before. A few taps, and his forces attacked her capital, a heavy cruiser began sweeping through her undefended shipyards, and a handful of interceptors slipped out of hiding to strafe her commercial shipping. In the melee, he snuck a ship over to take out her scout ship and she never noticed.

He restrained a small sigh as Irrai began withdrawing her entire fleet from across the map to protect her home front. Sensing an advantage that didn't exist, Vaese greedily poured resources into harrying her withdrawal.

Theta's obscenely massive shipyards were now producing ten to one.

He attacked the center. He brought an assault carrier forward and began launching interceptors and jammers to pick off the fringes of Irrai's fleet in transit. His troops attacked capitals and strategic bases. His main fleet, split into two, loomed large on the wings of the board, out of sight but within striking distance. He sent two more dreadnoughts into the center to distract them and clean up the mess, and destroyed another scout that hit his detection net. A muffled curse from Arvinne across the table brought the whisper of a predatory smile to his lips; in response, he launched his main thrust, assigning battle orders to his fleets, splitting them off to divide and conquer what would be left of his opponents.

Any moment now.

"Theta to operations. Theta, report to ops." The intercom's strident tone almost masked Dela's rolling voice.

He stood, tapping a control to dispatch orders to his virtual fleet. His ships turned aside to attack his outposts and each other. After that, they would attack his homeworlds, and then they would self-destruct.

"Well, it looks like I've gotta run." He shook his head ruefully, deadpan. "I didn't have much, anyway."

Vaese snorted and looked up fleetingly. "It's alright, darling. It does take some time to get good at this game, but you're doing fine, just fine. You did great in the center, even though your attack was so late. You'll get the hang of it, I'm sure. Need to learn to commit for center control earlier."

"You shouldn't have gone for dreadnoughts so early in the game. Next time, we'll give you a economy bonus to help you get started," Irrai murmured, wiping her brow. "I'm surprised you're not better, though." She shot him a dark little glance; he raised his eyebrows in innocent surprise.

"Well, strategy and tactics are fairly different, you know," he murmured noncommittally. He raised his paw in a little wave, then turned away before his amusement could exceed his restraint and break onto his face.

He bounced out with his head held high, muzzle split in a teeth-cooling grin.

He actually had friends. He'd never thought of himself as friend material.

Up he went, up many decks, and a few more, then forward. *Varaunt* was not a small ship, and even being "close" was relative. When he scanned himself into Ops, he found the room darkened, lighting indicating readiness.

"Well, lad?"

"Sorry. I was losing another game of Abyssus, and I needed an excuse to get out before it got too ugly. You know how it is."

Dela guffawed, thumping him on the back. "Now was Irrai, ah, winning by that much?"

Theta grinned slyly, settling into his station. "Oh yes, she was the worst of the lot. The others were winning by much more."

"Aye, I'll bet. A bunch of winners, that." She chuckled, clearly amusing herself greatly. "Well now, since you're here, I might as well be updating ye. We've our sensor nets deployed and our assaults out, here, here, here and here. I'm a mite worried about 02's proximity to Alpha space, but Coxly is in command. I've not seen mistakes from her."

"Surely the Fedos won't hit her if she merely nicks their space." Theta took another sip of his verti, thin and sweet. "But even still, she has a six kilometer buffer...and she's the outside edge of the funnel, so even that seems unlikely."

"I trust nothing about the Fedykeralli, lad. I've heard that the buggers stay strictly within Alpha, aye, but I'm reluctant to risk it...I've half of our additional scanners and sensors pointing that way. I've heard told tales of ships that study them by sitting meters from their border and watching, but mind—now and again, one vanishes."

Theta looked over the deployment and shrugged. "So we watch and wait. It all looks good to me. The net is deployed and active?"

"Aye, lad. Window gives us a day or so, but ye know how those can be. We're smack in the middle right now, so statistically he should pop in soon. I don't have faith in the intel, or statistics, and I'm feeling pretty vulnerable sitting here."

"Any birdies?"

"Few ripples, a wash, and a high energy rock," Dela laughed. "A slight elevation in energized particles abaft consistent with our launch activities, a few burbles of long-range particles interacting with the net, and the rumbling of my stomach."

Theta nodded and smiled, twirling his mug. "Well, I can resolve one of those, now that I'm here. If you want to take a break, I'd be happy to cover."

"Oh lad, much though I appreciate the offer, never fear: food is on the way. You don't think I'd leave all this," Dela indicated her expansive form, "to chance now, do ye?"

Theta opened his mouth to respond, but couldn't figure out what would be an appropriate response. Fortunately for him, something caught his eye and he closed it again, pointing beyond Dela to the main display.

"More ripples, lad? Oh ho, no no!" Dela leapt to a console, moving with surprising agility for her size. She thumbed the interphone button even as Theta swung around into a vacant station.

"Bridge, Ops." Dela's voice was thick and eager. "Bogey!"

"Roger, Ops. We see it too. Takedown in progress."

"Ma'am," Theta snapped, all business. "Mass readings in spec, structure sound, no significant weaponry, no scuttles. It's our VIP, no doubt."

Dela nodded. "Glad you're here. You have the grapples, I'll take countermeasures."

Theta reassigned his controls and began to activate the grapple emitters, warming them up slowly by keeping the target from turning or accelerating, letting its inertia carry it right to the waiting arms of *Varaunt*. He blinked and shook his head as a message notification blinked on his console. Encrypted? He'd have to check later. He looked up as Cuny, looking disheveled with his shipsuit half zipped, dashed through the door and angled for the station beside Dela.

"Ahead of you, Cuny. Take over from me on ECCM. Theta? Are we broadcasting, lad?"

"Yes ma'am," Theta said, teeth bared, tonguetip slightly out the side of his muzzle as he concentrated. "I—We're broadcasting. He's painted. Holds are out, and his engines are capped." He took a breath, speaking as fast as he could. "The Assaults will have surround when they come out, which should be fairly quick. Ah... now, here they come. Right on top of us in thirty seconds."

"Operations, this is Janesson. Do not let our little friend here budge an inch. We're giving him the standard friendly greeting to try and extract him undamaged."

"Aye, sir," Dela replied. A few more taps, and she sat back and grinned. "He's trussed up like a *folla*, and he's nowhere to go."

Cuny shook his head. "Ma'am, this little bugger doesn't want to stay. Ship's not armed, but it has as much ECM as anything I've seen. He's trying to wriggle free even now, and he's bloody almost got it. Must be packed full of get-away gear."

Without conscious thought, Theta tapped a few buttons and redirected energy from the grapple array, manually targeting a dozen emitters. The target began to slide forward. Before Dela could say anything, however, there was a spike of EM and it stopped dead.

"Brilliant, Cuny. What did ye do?"

"I...not sure, ma'am."

There was a moment of pause; Theta said nothing. He knew exactly what had happened. He also knew that he shouldn't have done it without asking, but he was reluctant to speak up. Let Cuny take any praise; he'd happily take the blame should any come due. He'd discovered that he liked the feeling of being hidden magic that bound things together, silently improving the system.

"Ops, bridge. Our target says you took out his engine controls? Good job. He's surrendered. I want full localized mass readings to make sure that ship isn't dangerous, and then I want you to grapple him into bay 4. Keep the Assaults out, just in case."

"Aye, sir. We've started on the mass readings, and we're pulling him in just now."

"Ma'am," Theta raised his voice to Dela. "You have grapple control."

"Thanks, lad, I have the controls."

"You have the controls," he repeated automatically. Switching viewports, he watched each angle in turn as *Varaunt* ate the sleek little ship that she held her grasp. As the doors slid shut, he permitted himself a little companionable grin to Dela and Cuny, who returned it.

It felt better than he ever thought it would.

A chime at the door announced the arrival of Dela's lunch, and she moved nearly as quickly as before to get to the door. Before sliding it open, she turned back to the two of them.

"Prepare your reports," Dela said, then yawned. "And while you're doing that, boys, whip one up for me too. Rank hath its privileges, after all, and I choose to eat at a table for this once."

Grumbling good-naturedly, Theta dug in at once, rattling off a blow-by-blow and copying chunks of his station's log. Half an hour later, done with both reports, he was bored once more, sipping his drink and watching the video feed of the painstakingly cautious surrender in bay 4; his secret hope that the VIP might be a tall black coyote was dashed when it turned out to be a young red fox wearing a black shipsuit with silver insignia.

The VIP was being escorted out of the bay under polite (but sincere) guard when Dela finally returned.

"Cuny?" Dela frowned over to the wolf's screen. "Do you see that? What is that?"

Theta perked his ears and zoomed in on his own display. Four new small ripples had been detected in the time since the takedown, but Cuny didn't seem concerned.

"These? I've been tracking them. They're just ripples and echo, ma'am," Cuny chuckled. "Aftershocks from the Rellin disruption, you know how it is. See how they line up along this vector? Nothing to them."

Dela seemed dubious. "Recall the detection frames. I'd like a peek at the data on those."

A reminder flashed on Theta's screen, informing him that the message from earlier was marked urgent. As he had a few moments free, he leaned back and pulled it up. It was probably another letter from Irrai; he couldn't help but grin at the thought. She wouldn't take no for an answer, no matter how many times he said it, but she was never rude.

The message decrypted against his key, and his eyes scanned the first few words, then stuck.

My dear Mishy,

Theta froze solid, staring at those three words, stiff as steel and barely breathing. After half a moment, he exhaled and instantly swiped his terminal closed, wiping its cache. He spent another long moment staring at his blank screen while Dela and Cuny rambled on outside of his awareness. As soon as he recovered a bit of his wit, he stood. Little tremors ran from his nose to his tail.

"Excuse me," he whispered hoarsely, then made for the exit. He didn't even turn around to see the curious little wave Dela gave him as slipped out the door in a daze.

Privacy. He needed privacy.

"Well now, where do you think he's off to?" Cuny broke the silence a moment after the door closed behind Theta. "That was a little strange, even for him."

Dela shook her head. "Aye, but he's a strange fox, Cuny m'boy. I do so wonder about him and his background at times. The captain knows, aye, and Janesson...but neither will speak."

"I want to like him but...he's come up awfully quick to his current job, wouldn't you think? I don't...well, I don't know him. It feels strange that we've given him the keys to the castle."

"Janesson insisted, ye realize. Jenks, now, he doesn't trust him, either. I've yet to make up my mind on the score. Between us, old friend, Theta flat scares me at times. He's a ruthless streak, and behind those eyes he holds much back, I'm sure of it."

Cuny shook his head. "I don't really understand. Is the captain crazy?"

"Oh no. Janesson isn't crazy—he knows a good thing when he sees it, lad. I'm experienced, aye, and a bit cagey, but Theta's pure genius, and between the two of us we're rather potent I must say. Still, even so I'm still a mite surprised at Janesson's faith."

"You're watching him close, then?"

"Oh aye. Closer than he realizes, I think. Still, even for that...he's a good lad somewhere in there, I know it in my bones, even if I don't trust him. Still scares me. Now me, though, I'll tell you—I suspect I know what's bothering him presently, though." Dela looked around, then leaned closer to the wolf. "Me, I think it's that Irrai lass. Scuttlebutt has it she's after our little fox, and ye know how she can be," she laughed.

Suddenly her eyes widened, and her laugh caught in her throat, turning into an inarticulate, choked gasp.

An alarm sounded, and her panel lit up.

"Cu-ny!"

Dela fumbled for the bridge interphone button with shaking paws that kept missing their target.

They both stared at the display and froze.

"By the gods."

"Ma'am…" Naane sounded uncertain. "The transmission isn't for us. It's from *Varaunt*—they have another ship, and they're ordering it to stand down. I don't understand."

"Jale?" Krella's voice was soft, and a little cool. "I thought you said there was no VIP. You did say there was no VIP, did you not? I didn't mishear, right?"

"I've no answer for you at the moment, Krella. Like a trapped insect," Jale whispered, staring at the display. "Would you look at that."

"The make of the target ship is Alaran, but I've never seen a model like it." Naane broke in. "I think it may get away." She sounded cheery, for some reason. "Looks like *Varaunt* is trying to hold it with brute force, but it's got…hm."

"Yes?" Jale turned to her as she trailed off. "It's got what?"

"Nevermind." Naane seemed sheepish. "I thought it had a chance, but it looks like *Varaunt* just took out its engines."

"Oh." Jale leaned back in her chair. "They are experts at what they do, after all. Listen, nothing changes. No contingencies have been triggered, no. We lie low here and wait for a signal from Theta. If they start recovering to leave, we implement our plan for that. It also occurs to me that they won't have much harder a time locking us down if they detect us."

"On the bright side," Krella chimed in merrily, "for us, they'll probably just use the mass weapon banks and save us the struggle. Let's not be seen, shall we?"

"I do hope." Jale murmured.

She tapped up a request to the galley for food to be brought, then drained the last of her megvha and set the cup aside. She didn't know what to think. Could this be a random ship that *Varaunt* had caught?

"Absolutely not," she whispered to herself. "This is part of his game."

What is *Knoskali's game? Is it even his game anymore?*

She brought a fist down on the arm of her chair, ever-so-lightly.

"Ma'am?" Krella sounded hesitant. "It may be nothing. It's most likely nothing, but I just picked up a ripple. I can't find anything out passively, and it looks like an aftershock."

"Alright?" Jale tilted her head. "Clearly you don't think so."

"No ma'am, I don't." Krella frowned, panning around, then blinked. "Oh look at that, there's another. No chance. The instruments think it is, but if they detected our ship coming in, that's exactly what they'd label it."

Jale's eyes widened. "Alright, I've heard enough. Helm, I want you to very, very slowly open range on that ship. I don't know what's about to happen, but I know better than to be at its center, Theta or no Theta."

"Aye, ma'am."

"Good choice, Captain," Krella murmured. "I am deeply concerned. I just registered another ripple. Same vector."

Food arrived, and was mostly ignored; Jewel brought it, and stayed at Jale's request. Time ached forward with nothing happening aside from Krella cataloguing more ripples and one strange effect he couldn't identify. After the last one, he stood up and rested his hand on his head.

"By the twin gods, what addlebrained nit do they have running tactics on that ship? Why haven't they accelerated their recovery?" He seemed distressed for their sake. "This is...none of this could be more obvious."

Jale was not unmoved, but more concerned with the immediate. She flipped through her console data, wondering what she would think if she herself were on watch aboard Varaunt. She shook her head.

Had she noticed, she would have trusted the computer.

She took a few spare moments to pass around some rather succulent meatrolls that she suspected Jewel had a hand in; even in a crisis they were far too good to waste. Megvha was poured, and people settled in, alertness undiminished by the creature comforts.

"I'm open to suggestions, Krella," Jale admitted after a while. "My thought—"

"There's activity over the border!" Naane blinked. "Ma'am, I'm reading...There's...energy discharges in Alpha space. Massive discharges!"

"What? What sort of energy discharges?"

"I—" Naane froze.

"Gods." Krella groaned.

Jale turned to him, lips pressed together in frustration. "Yes, Krella? What is...it?"

Her irritation left her at his expression.

"I'll...put it on the main display."

Jale turned back to look, and felt the energy drain from her. She slumped in her chair and watched, awed and helpless. After a moment, she shook her head, straightened, and stood. She was still the captain, and her ship was still a ship.

"The game has changed, boys and girls. All stop, maximum stealth, power to a minimum, and no station-keeping. We drift and hope."

She sipped her megvha and rested a paw on Jewel's shoulder.

Aboard *Varaunt*, in a dark, empty berth, white fur was dimly lit by dim red text; hungry eyes were locked forward.

> *My dearest Mishy,*
> *I write this in a curious state for me: a complete lack of knowledge. My plans are opaque and distant, and my hand can protect none of those who work for me. I know only where you may be, and where I hope to find you, and if the stars have aligned and*

you have received this message, then more has gone right than I would have dared dream.

When we commingled, you were drawn into a web far deeper and more deadly than you could possibly have imagined, and I allowed it of my own ignorance and pride. I became so very taken with you that it blinded even me to the consequences, and I was soon confronted with an attack for which I had no defense.

You did not start the war on Brynton, but most certainly you finished it—The lord who demanded your death is dead, and with his dying breath he begged for your forgiveness. From the throats of his and theirs I wrested equal pleas before I ground his name to mud, House and home, hearth and soul. Lord Harrol is Lord of the void into which he watched everything he ever loved pass before him.

And yet revenge is no apology, for the error was, and shall always be, mine. I picked the loveliest flower and groomed it as my own, as if a thing I might possess and keep, forgetting that I am naught but my keeper's keeper.

You are my dancer, but you do not belong in my world; as Myshel, you may never return or we both will surely be destroyed. Your death was the foundation of my revenge, and though I rescinded one in secret, the other is forever.

Now for my confession: I had plans for you when I sent you away, and to this end I notified Varaunt of your existence. From what I hear, my original message did not survive its transition intact, and I nearly betrayed you to your end. You may remember my dear cousin Gnosi; I know not yet whether it was incompetence or malevolence, but I will know. If I find the latter, his life is yours.

I send him to you.

Yet by some wonder you weren't lost, and you arrived aboard and alive and sound.

This pleases me beyond words.

I know not if my prior message reached you, but as it falls that means nothing now. This is the moment, ripe and full and magical. I have given you one gift, locked and tamed, and this message is the key:

Kotoraski morota gera elechen das rolk.

Isn't it lovely? Do you feel the power in this thing? My love, your death, our triumph and resolve, the power of form growing within. Say it aloud, whisper it, sing it, embrace it within yourself and cry it to the heavens.

Quietly.

I have for you, my dear, one last request, one last duty I would have of you.

Upon the ship Varaunt, *there is or will soon be a prisoner. A red fox, taken alone from a single ship traveling in deep space. If he is on the ship, I have but one simple thing to ask:*

Kill him.

This is the task I have set you upon; you are the knife, a tool in my hand, and a weapon of war for the last time. Once this task is complete, I give you the second and final gift. You should find near your ship another ship. Dispatch a message with this encoding, and your rescue will be arranged.

Once your mark is cold and gone, and once you are safe and whole, you may keep the ship and its crew to find your fate. Go wherever you will.

Or return to my open arms.

Yours through infinity's breadth,

~Knoskali

Theta wept openly, his world spinning around him. The void from whence he'd escaped before swept up around him. He sobbed into his pillow, body shaking.

He wept for the nascent wisp of a life that had begun to take root. He wept for the trust that had been granted to him, and the faith shown by this new family. He wept for his future.

He knew that he wept for the dead.

"Kotoraski morota gera elechen das rolk."

It rolled from him in a voice unlike his own, an accent foreign but familiar, a whisper that was an ice cold breath of air. His sobbing stopped slowly, tapering off into a gentle rocking around his pillow.

A minute passed.

"Kotoraski morota gera elechen das rolk."

The words took on a sing-song character, their 'R's rolled and rich, the vowels languishing in his mouth as if too big for it. He sat up and took in his surroundings, realizing his hyperawareness had returned, that single-minded alert clarity that had so eluded his efforts to achieve. Drying his eyes and wiping his nose, he rolled from his bunk. The air currents around him, all the details of the texture of the floor, he felt. The scents in the room, the sounds of people moving, talking, walking. He heard them all.

"Kotoraski morota gera elechen das rolk," he murmured; the words fell dead and flat, and at last he knew their meaning. A rousing one-ness swept through him. In absolute silence, he slid to the nearest main terminal.

He was Theta.

He was Myshel.

He was something else, something that he'd never known before.

Alert and alone, he was aware that, above all else, he was now something new, something defined. He was Knoskali's hand, reaching into the abyss to pluck forth his enemies.

The attenuated connection he'd felt slipping away, his sense of purpose, of identity, his very sense of being returned with full force.

The computer yielded to his credentials. The prisoner was being stored in deck 6, section C. He opened his locker and slid out the knife he kept, the memento of his most recent near-death experience, and tucked it into his shipsuit.

His movements were silent, always outside of the detector arcs, leaving no trace as he slowly made his way towards the G-tube down.

"Theta!" A familiar, happy voice stopped him in his tracks. He froze and spun to find Irrai reaching out to embrace him.

His reaction was immediate and unrestrained.

The look of shock and confusion on her face as she sank to the deck struck him sick, and he held back the trained killing blow. A strident little groan of loss trickled from his lips as he lowered her unconscious form, but it only drove him forward. There was no turning back now.

Sucking in his breath and looking around, he dragged her over to a communications locker and slid her in. He cupped her cheek and planted a little kiss on her black lips, tears running down to drip from his nose onto her face.

"I'm sorry you believed in me, Irrai. This is who I am, the monster you never met." His throat was tight with emotion, and he tore himself away, pushing the door of the little locker shut and diving down the G-tube headfirst.

"Damn them, anyhow. They're pirates, aren't they? They started this whole mess, didn't they? This is no more than they deserve."

He didn't believe it. He didn't believe anything. Only the void called him now—only Knoskali.

Nothing exists but you, my Lord.

Nothing felt right.

Deck six, section C.

One of the guards outside the door gave him a friendly greeting as he approached, and he recognized Prell. Sick to his stomach, he smiled in reply. Neither of the pair expected his lightning-quick attack, and the confusion on their faces echoed Irrai's and shook him to the core. Neither had even thought to fight him or run before they lay stretched on the deck, inert.

Of course they're confused. Why would a shipmate do this to them? They trusted me.

Theta sobbed a raw sob, digging through Prell's pockets until he found the quickkey for the cell. He swiped it across the pad and stuffed it into his pocket. The door opened and he looked down at the two guards, fighting the urge to rearrange them in more comfortable positions.

It'll all be ok. Knoskali will make it ok, when I am back in his arms. This is just a passing nightmare; these people mean nothing, they are of a world that is not ours.

I will watch it burn.

As he stepped inside, tears threatening to blind him, he entirely missed the lanky black shadow that slid into the hallway behind him and sprinted to the door in near silence, arriving just after it closed and locked.

He turned to find the red fox calmly regarding him, eyebrow arched quizzically.

From his shipsuit, he produced his knife.

"Ops, bridge, what the hell are we seeing?"

"Dela?" Cuny's voice was very small.

"We're done," Dela replied softly. "We're up and done."

"Ops, this is the captain. Respond!" The intercom seemed louder than normal, echoing into the dampened silence that was ops.

Dela sat back into her chair so firmly that it cracked; words failed. The comm board lit up, and she tapped it, sending it to the bridge and the local speaker both.

"Free fleet *Varaunt*," the signal was crystal clear, power level leaving nothing to imagination. "We are Dazi. Stand down at once and offer no resistance or you will be destroyed."

Dozens of massive warships, the smallest of which out-massed and outgunned *Varaunt*, hung silently in space all around her, and more were hopscotching in by the moment. Patrols of smaller ships hung in tight formation, tracing coordinated paths within their ranks. Debris, the remnants of the Fedo ships that had massed on the border to stop the fleet, were casually avoided or destroyed as they floated through.

"This is *Varaunt*, actual speaking." Janesson's voice was remarkably calm. "We are open to negotiation."

"Ops, dammit," Janesson was on the interphone the moment he released the ship to ship comm, dripping with all the emotions he'd restrained. "I need options. Tell me what I can do. Give me something!"

Dela looked at Cuny, then turned to the charting tank, spinning the situation in vacuum.

She tapped the comm button.

"Bridge, ops, ah." She let it go, pausing for a moment, then ground her thumb against it once more. "I'm sorry, sir. I've nothing to give ye. Boxed, blocked and held. Our VIP is now our hostage, and our only bargain piece. Put more guards on him, and try diplomacy, or fight and die."

A snarl clearly worked its way through the interphone before the captain released.

"But I thought the Dazi were extinct," Cuny whispered.

XV

Occlusion

THETA CIRCLED AWAY FROM THE DOOR, taking a deep breath to center himself. He blinked the tears from his eyes, suddenly calm. His focus had narrowed to this one moment of his life, and everything present and past was in shadow. Emotion was shut out completely, as was reflection and thought; this was the domain of training and instinct. Destiny. The sum of his own life.

The black clad fox he faced seemed oblivious to this; leaning against the opposite wall of the small unadorned cell, his arms folded across his chest, he awarded Theta a bored gaze.

"Oh dear, an assassin." His voice was calm and mocking. "I might have guessed. A little small for a trained killer, aren't we short stuff?" He tilted his head nonchalantly.

Theta seized the instant, springing to the side then lunging forward, closing the gap. His paw shot forward to grab the red fox's shoulder and he brought the knife across with the other, aiming for the spot under the ribs just as he was trained—but the thrust never found its target. His blade met only air, and found himself sprawling towards the floor, legs momentarily entangled. Rolling fluidly into a crouch, he spun back around to find the other fox facing him from the center of the room, looking slightly surprised. The red fox's smirk was gone—the forearm of his shipsuit was cut through from elbow to wrist, and fur leaked out, stained with blood from a shallow cut. He sniffed the air, eyes unfocused for a moment, then narrowed them slightly at Theta.

"Pretty quick. Intriguing. Not much for talking, though, hm? Too—"

Theta dipped, dodged, and came up under the fox's guard.

Pain shot through his knife arm as it was redirected to the wall with force and his own blade cut deep across his palm. He felt a paw on the back of his head, and his nose and face met the same wall very hard. Smooth as silk, quicker than thought, a paw wrapped around his throat and another held his muzzle tightly shut, an unrelenting weight forcing him downward.

"—Bad," the fox whispered into his ear. Every motion seemed to tighten the vice around his neck, no matter how he struggled, and he quickly began to feel lightheaded. Thought began to return, unbidden. Something had gone horribly wrong. Little grunts and choked little gasps escaped him as he sank towards the floor and confusion began to creep in. Digging deep within himself, he tapped his well of resolve and lunged for his knife, carrying his opponent with him.

He scrambled with his good paw, and his clawtips even touched the steel handle briefly, but before he could pull the weapon into his grasp he felt a shift atop and a black-clad leg came around to drive his arm against the wall. Something gave with a little pop, and he went numb from shoulder to pawpads. Though the fox's grip on him had loosened momentarily, he was unable to take advantage of it and was slowly and steadily pressed flat against the deck.

Lithe paws, strong as iron, tingled against Theta in a way he'd never felt; the other's strange scent, alien and tantalizing and at the same time extremely familiar, made him itch in the back of his head. Combined with the pain and concussion, the disorientation from his injuries and the lack of blood reaching his brain, it made him feel warm and tingly. In a way it was soothing, as if easing him into death with a soft whisper.

Theta could feel destiny slipping away as weakness spread through him and the world took on a surreal haze.

"Well, my little assassin," his erstwhile victim spoke calmly with no signs of exertion, lips lightly touching Theta's ear, "as you see, it's one thing to know, quite another to do."

Theta's scattered thoughts were interrupted as the door was forced open with a scrape. He rolled rapidly dimming eyes up to see a tall black canid slide into the room, a pair of glimmering knives out. Momentary hope spread within him, but even through watering eyes and fading vision he could tell very quickly that it was not Knoskali that stood before him but a trim black jackal nightmare.

"Pull her head back," he heard an urgent hiss from the blurry form.

"No, Onari." The fox's voice was soft and warm behind his head, grip never slacking. "I want this one—he has no business being here...can't you smell it? The room is full of it. Stick him and we go."

Theta was given little time to consider his complete failure, and less to consider the red fox's words. He felt a searing pain in his side, and a different sort of warmth, much less comforting, spread almost immediately through his torso. The pressure on the arteries of his neck slowly eased as the fox released his throat. He tried once more to twist free but had no strength to do so; a fox knee pressed casually but authoritatively into his back in response, and the jackal placed a booted foot on his neck, holding it to the floor with far more pressure than necessary.

His paws were quickly wrapped in a tight binding material, restricting his motion (though they also stopped his bleeding); his muzzle followed, leaving him able to breathe but naught else. A strip went around his waist and shoulders, holding both his arms secure. Though the pain was overwhelming, he could do nothing but whimper mutedly—all the strength was gone from him, and his body felt like lead.

"Glad you could make it," he heard the fox comment to the jackal, quiet and distant as if a world away. "What's the plan?"

The jackal's reply was lost to him; everything began to feel soft and gooey, and then he knew no more.

"Battle stations. All hands to their posts. Battle stations. Battle stations." The refrain echoed through the empty corridors of *Varaunt*'s lowest decks, unheeded by the six black-clad forms slinking aft as a unit. The last two in the line carried a small, inert form between them as they made their way to a hole in the double-walled outer hull. The body was passed through and taken by the first; the next four dove in one at a time, transitioning from the ship's artificial gravity to zero-G with practiced poise.

The sixth form, taller than the rest, stepped quickly inside and grabbed a section of inner hull, swinging it back into place and flash-welding it with a quick pass of the same tool that had sliced it out in the first place. The outer hull came next, and then the armored figure made a little stylized mark on its surface before kicking off to follow his comrades. As he passed through a steel ring at the far end of the tube behind them, it irised shut and the tube quickly retracted.

Jale was on her third mug of Megvha, but it was no longer providing her quite the sense of alertness as before. Jewel had given it to her only hesitantly, and only when she demanded it.

She sipped the liquid, feeling her stomach roil slightly in protest. It could mind its own business—she needed to be sharp; many lives depended on her actions.

There had been no reply from Theta.

"Huh." Krella broke the long waiting silence and sat up with a little snort.

"Yes?" Jale straightened.

"I'm showing a hotspot on *Varaunt*'s hull."

Jale's leaned forward, startled. "What? Is it weapons fire?"

"No..." Krella said slowly, rubbing his chin. After a few seconds, he brightened, clapping his paws together merrily.

"Ooh, I bet I know what it is!" His voice was nearly sing-song. "Let me just check my little theory."

Jale stood and paced, clasping her paws behind her back. Time dragged on slowly, and her annoyance grew.

"Any day now, mister Krella."

"Just one more moment, ma'am."

"At least tell us what your theory is, dear."

"Hah, yep. I'm right. Of course I'm right, I'm always right. You want my theory, here it is: I have good reason to think that the prisoner *Varaunt* took in that cute little ship just got rescued, covertly."

Jale froze. "Oh. I was afraid that that might happen. That could be rather bad."

Krella's grin slipped a bit. "Bad? Why bad?"

"Because," Naane jumped in, speaking as if lecturing a stupid child, "without the hostage, they could simply destroy *Varaunt*."

Krella looked surprised by her suggestion.

"Oh. Would they do that? I suppose they could do that. Do we know anything about these...ah..."

"Dazi," Naane filled in.

"Dazi." Krella repeated with a little moue, whiskers twitching. "I've never heard of them. They sure have some nice tech, for someone I've never heard of."

Jale squinted, clenching her jaw, suddenly and significantly irritated with his mannerisms. "They sound very familiar, but I can't say why. I...hm. Listen, can we risk injecting another message for Theta? We simply must get him off. If we can find some way to do that, we may be able to sneak away from this little party, or drift somewhere safe and wait it out, oh yes. Naane, I want you and the tactics department to combine heads and get me some sort of miracle if you please."

"Aye ma'am," Naane said. "If we can, we will. I think we can inject another. What do you want us to say?"

"Send it to Theta, encrypt it against his key, obviously. Tell him that he must escape the ship himself. If he and Arvinne can get off the ship undetected, even in vac suits, we can pick them up and go. Stress that *Varaunt* is in a fairly ugly situation and must be abandoned as soon as possible, as he may not know."

"Alright." Naane nodded. "I've sent it to the ciphertechs. I know you know, ma'am, but don't forget that he might not even be on *Varaunt* at this point. Our information is old, after all."

Jale glared at her. "Oh I know, yes. If I get us all killed here and Theta isn't even around, well, I don't know what I'll do."

"Ah, ma'am?" Helm chirped. "I think we have another problem."

Jale bit her tongue on her first waspish response; she was getting tired of hearing that, but it did no good to shoot the messenger. "Yes? What, Sillanen?"

"Debris. This fleet came in through Alpha space, and they popped a bunch of Fedos right at the border. But look—we've got a big chunk of that debris that intersects our drift line. Used to be a ship, but now it's an expanding shrapnel field."

"I see it." Krella's voice was hushed. "Yes, ma'am—If that hits us, we're suddenly going to be very conspicuous. We should avoid it if we can."

"Helm?"

"We can't do it within our amended stealth envelope, ma'am. Not by a fair bit." The helmsman tapped his panel. "We have six minutes to alter our trajectory, and every second we wait will take more power."

"Damn it all." Jale brought her paw down on her armrest. "Krella?"

"Do it. Moderate risk, but less risk than letting the debris hit. I looked it over, and we'd probably take a bit of damage as well as being blindingly obvious for anyone who's watching."

"Helm, go."

"Aye, ma'am."

"Krella, you must let me know instantly if there's any sign of trouble."

"Of course."

Jale hunkered down in her chair.

Captain Janesson, pacing the expansive bridge of *Varaunt*, could feel the jaws of a great trap clamped around his leg.

His world had come down to a set of equally unpalatable choices, and he cast desperately for a way out.

"Captain?" his comms officer called to him from halfway across the bridge. "The Dazi flagship is calling again. They say that they want to speak with you to discuss terms and verify the safety and condition of their ambassador."

Janesson could feel his hackles rising in anger and frustration. He had never been pinned like this, and he had no knowledge of his foe. They displayed overwhelming force, but were they experienced in battle? Were they trustworthy? Would they negotiate? Was this a trap laid intentionally to catch Varaunt?

If so, what did they want?

If not, how were they even here?

"Tell them that we're willing to trade their VIP for safe passage away," he growled. "Tell them that he's alive and unharmed, and has been well treated as befits his station, but that if they try to make a move we'll kill him."

The comms officer nodded.

Janesson felt like throwing something. He'd never been so completely powerless.

He turned and gestured to one of the bridge runners. "You! Get down to operations and tell me what's going on down there. Tell them I want Theta and Dela to give me something to work with. Anything at all. Tell them that if they don't, we're all dead. Go!"

"Yes sir," the runner said, then nodded sharply and jogged off.

"You realize that if we kill him, they'll turn us into dust." Jenks rumbled, for his ears only. "He may be the only thing keeping us alive at the moment."

"I damn well know it," Janesson barked, not bothering to speak softly. "I don't even intend to kill him—there's no profit in it, and I'm sure they know that. But Dela is right, damn her. Unless she and that fox can work up some miracle for me, we'll have to hand him over and pray, and I don't know these Dazi at all, or what they're like. At least nothing went wrong during the takedown. I shudder to think—"

"Sir!" a signalman waved to him. "I have an urgent message from deck six, sir."

Janesson's stomach sank to his knees. "Deck six?" He glanced at Jenks, then turned to the speaker. "What is the message, signalman?"

"Sir, the security officers we sent to reinforce the prisoner's guard sent a reply back. The guards were unconscious, maybe dead, they said. The prisoner's gone. Said that the lock's busted, and there's a trail of blood leading out."

Janesson strode up and clutched at the collar of the signalman's shipsuit, pulling him forward. Throwing Jenks' paw from his shoulder, he pressed his nose right up to the chubby raccoon's and stared straight into his eyes. "Are you lying to me?"

The raccoon was frozen in fear at his intensity. He opened his mouth to speak, but it took him a few moments to find his voice. "Nosir, NOsir."

Janesson fought to control himself; eventually he took a deep breath and released the hapless signalman, crouching down and clutching his head.

"I'm...sorry," he murmured, staring down at the deck. "Jenks—"

"I'll start a sweep of the security tapes," Jenks growled, glancing worriedly down at him. "Signalman, have the medical team analyze the blood. Tell them it's time-critical. I'll need a forensics sweep, too."

Janesson turned hollow eyes up to Jenks. "Either he's dead, or he's escaped. If he's dead, we're probably dead too. If he's escaped..."

"Captain?" The signalman sounded hesitant.

"Yes...Rossi?" Janesson tried to soften his tone.

"Captain," the comms officer raised her voice from across the bridge, cutting in. "Coxly sends a message—if we give the word, the Assaults will try to blockade fire and help us escape. Says all the other captains are with her."

Janesson closed his eyes, nodding softly. "That would be a terrible price, but it's an option at least. Might work.

Better than anything I've gotten from my own tactics department—Please signal back that we may accept. Have these Dazi acknowledged our terms?"

"Yes sir. Acknowledgement only."

"Thank you." He touched Rossi's shoulder lightly. "What was your message, signalman?"

"Sir, it's an emergency message...deck twenty, section D. No, two of them now. First is that Crewman Irrai was attacked, sir. And—"

"On this deck?" Janesson was aghast. "Call down to security and get them to send more personnel up here right away. Have them deploy everyone they've got to secure against boarders. If they have coverts moving through..."

"Captain," Jenks cut in, resting a paw on his arm. "Just found we're blind below deck eight. Security systems are blanked. We're definitely in trouble."

Janesson snarled and seethed and swore, and even Jenks shifted away from him.

"Sir!" The signalman dared Janesson's wrath once more. "I have three messages for you now. Two came in at once."

"Tell me," the captain growled through clenched teeth.

"First message is from ops: 'We're short on miracles, sir,' she says. 'Theta's missing. Advise against any aggressive action and stand down the assaults.' That's it. Second one is from medical staff. They say some of the blood is from..." He paused. "Huh. From crewman Theta, they say, but that there's other blood as well, from the prisoner. Last one is from Irrai. Ah, she's on the way, says—"

"It was Theta, Captain!" Irrai stumbled onto the bridge, supported by a security officer. She looked up at Janesson, eyes unfocusing. "The little bastard, going for the tube down. Whoops, hold on—"

Irrai fell forward before anyone could grab her, nearly landing flat on her face. The security officer knelt by her unresponsive form, calling for medical staff. Janesson waved for the signalman to dispatch for a medic, then sunk into the nearest chair and closed his eyes, resting his face in both large paws. He felt himself break a little inside; with that one little piece of the puzzle, the rest had quickly fallen into place. Suddenly everything made perfect sense to him.

"Captain?" Jenks prodded.

Janesson was beyond options; after a moment, he looked up to find the eyes of the bridge upon him. He straightened, suddenly calm. For him, there was one answer.

"Jenks...you have command. You were right many times over, and I am a fool. He's played us like a child's strategy game."

"Theta?" Jenks asked, genuinely surprised.

"No, no, no. Well, yes. But no. Lord Knoskali, of Brynton."

Jenks looked momentarily sick. "Captain, I—"

Janesson growled. "No. I'm sure of it. He set us up with this, I'm sure. He set us up with the last intel, too, I bet, where somehow little Theta managed to come up with an almost perfect performance. The tipoff about the passenger liner was the first piece, I'm sure. Oh, his little puppet has led us all a merry dance, as well. Showing just enough doubt, confessing just enough of his past to win my trust, even directly addressing my concerns in such a way that they seemed impossible." Janesson spat bitterly. "I was so willing to believe, so eager to help him that I was blinded to your advice. Leave it to Knoskali to create such a masterwork of manipulation and deceit as Theta."

"Captain," Jenks shook his head. He looked as though he wanted to say something, but then looked away. "Captain, that's a terrible thought, and I do understand your feelings, especially given...but don't do this to us now. We need you. We don't know—"

"Don't you see?" Janesson plead, almost desperate for the vilification he felt was his due, "I trusted that little sneak, and I've been wrong about everything I've done since he came aboard. This was a hit. This was a very cleverly orchestrated hit, and now it's time for the evidence to be cleaned up. Namely, us. I've led my entire ship and crew to their death!"

"Well, now lead us out of ruin, or save us from it. We've been too lucky, too often. Forgotten that death is an occupational hazard in this line of work." Jenks growled, grabbing him by the shoulders and shaking him hard. "But you are Captain. I will not assume your command—we need you now. This is when you must show your mettle."

"You'll follow my orders?" Janesson asked, peering up at his quartermaster.

"Always, Captain."

"Very well, then you'll have them. Comms," Janesson spoke up, voice gruff. "Get me their fleet commander."

"Yes, sir. What should I relay, sir?"

"Tell him that I wish to confer to...to negotiate the terms of our complete surrender."

Many faces turned his way.

Faces he dearly hoped would be alive tomorrow.

"Oh dear," Krella stated.

"Oh dear?" Jale repeated irascibly. "Oh dear what *now*, Krella?"

"The movement on the escort vessels that I told you about after our last jink? Well they've shifted into a formation for a type of detection."

"Echo scatter?" Naane spun her display. "Are they...? Yes, they are. Blast! Captain, they're setting up for surround. Means that they probably saw something during one of our jinks earlier, and want to find out what."

"Damn it all," Jale swore again, raising a shaking paw to rest on her nauseous belly. "Options, now."

"Rellin drive," Naane said, though she sounded unhappy with the idea. "We get out of here, and come back further away."

Krella rubbed his chin. "If we leave, we'll never come back undetected. A fleet is a mass of linked detectors, all comparing notes. We're as close as we'll get."

"Well," Naane spoke softly. "We might be able to sneak in right against *Varaunt* and hope it disguises us."

"No. There is too much active energy converging on *Varaunt*. On one of the Dazi ships, though..." Krella's eyes flickered as he looked at his display. Suddenly he cocked his head. "Hum, I'm showing more transient ripples. Very different orientation..."

"Comms traffic, ma'am!" Naane spoke up. "Broadcast. Modulation is captured."

Jale's belly had suddenly begun to ache severely. She clutched at it. "Just put it on, Naane."

"Huh! It's a packet. Hey, it's a packet encrypted for *us*! And...hey, the content is encrypted for your eyes only."

Krella jumped to his feet. "That's a message drop, ma'am! And there he goes, transit ripple out. It may be what we're waiting for!"

Jale's console told her that she had a new message available. She shook her head and logged out, rising.

Her stomach hurt more by the minute, and she could barely stand straight.

"I shall read it in my office."

The Dazi shuttle loomed in the hangar bay, hissing noisily as it pressure-matched with *Varaunt*. Sleek and broad and silver, it sported a logo on the aft section that resembled a twisted, three-spoked wheel.

Janesson fastened the collar of his formal coat, a uniform item he'd never worn outside of fitting, then turned back to the small group of senior officers there to see him off.

"What I want while I'm away?" He shook his head. "I'm surprised you even ask. What I want is plain. Find that little *niiza*, find the body of the ambassador, and if shooting starts, take our Assaults up on their offer and get the ship or what's left of it into Rellin drive. We agreed to surrender, in principal, so if they start shooting it's reasonable to assume that they won't stop. Jenks, you have command."

"Until you return," Jenks insisted firmly, awarding him a little meaningful glare.

Janesson nodded, smiling an empty smile in reply and turning towards the shuttle. Given the news he came with, he was certain that this would be a one-way trip; he'd prepared his documents to formally transfer command to Jenks once he'd departed. Having quartermaster and captain be one and the same was considered poor form, but that wasn't something he'd have to worry about himself.

With a little clunk, the shuttle's boarding ramp extended and its hatch slid open. A pair of unarmed canid soldiers in dress uniform stepped down to flank it.

Without so much as a backwards glance, Janesson picked up his case and stepped forward, moving quickly up the ramp and in. A third soldier half-bowed as he entered the main cabin, taking his bag and gesturing for him to sit.

The trip to the Dazi flagship was very smooth, precise, and fast. Janesson first watched *Varaunt* recede from view, fighting down strong emotions. *Varaunt* was a big ship, a beautiful ship, and she had been his home for much of his life; leaving her embrace to presumably die on some cold, alien deck twisted something deep inside him. Leaving her, and her crew—a crew that had depended on him to keep them safe and bring them profit—at the mercy of a hostile force that he had failed to deflect wrenched him further.

As the shuttle turned and *Varaunt* faded from view, he turned forward to look towards his destination, but immediately reeled back from the window as the mass of the Dazi ship seemed to dominate the space just beyond where he'd been focused. The shuttle was heading for one of the biggest three ships, and he was awed anew by its size. A slightly flattened ovoid, hugely massive, it nevertheless projected *sleek*; strakes started at midline and widened aft, making it appear as though atmospheric transition was a design characteristic—unusual for a deep-space vessel. Weapons batteries were numerous, but nowhere did they break the lines of the ship; her aft ventral hull was pockmarked with hundreds of little doors that puzzled Janesson for a while...until he realized that they were fighter launch bays. Everything about the ship conveyed an aura of immense power, as if it were a ship designed to make worlds tremble.

As they neared, sweeping under the midpoint of the giant starboard strake, a door slid open near the keel of the ship. At first it looked impossibly small to him, but as the shuttle approached the darkened bay it became clear that the size of the ship had thrown him yet again. As the blackness of the bay engulfed the shuttle, its lights came up and he shifted his attention back to the cabin. Suddenly all the emotions he had felt, and the wonder of the Dazi ship, melted back into a cold reality, and fear gripped him once more.

When pressure matching was complete, the door opened once more to reveal the inside of a tube leading into a very well-lit area. The guards escorted him calmly out into the largest hangar bay he'd ever seen, and he squinted against the lighting to take in its details; four identical shuttle berths rested aft of the one he'd left, and forward of it was a wide bay for marshaling and moving cargo and personnel. Hundreds of armed and armored troops and technicians sat idly in ordered array, waiting for he knew not what; the familiar smell of oil and ozone was dominant.

His guards led him forward to where four other soldiers, also unarmed, flanked a cheetah in dark green.

"Captain Janesson? I am Commander Gaul of the Dazi; I bid you welcome to *Derash*, flagship of this little fleet. I regret that you aren't able to visit under better circumstances, but I welcome you aboard nevertheless. Please, come this way."

Mutely Janesson trudged along behind the lanky cheetah as he made his way towards the center of the ship. To his surprise, he was led into a small room with a control panel on the wall; Gaul tapped at it, and everyone paused. A moment later, the door opened and everyone exited once more.

"Was that decontamination?" Janesson found himself unable to restrain his curiosity. "Some sort of scan?"

Gaul turned to him and smiled softly. "That? Oh no. That's just a transport. The ship has a network of G-tubes, and the transports are simply containers inside that network. They go where we tell them. Saves swimming and walking, though we do of course still have personnel G-tubes for emergency use. The transport put us right here, however, and that much more quickly. After you, Captain."

Gaul gestured to a large unmarked door, then swiped his paw and ushered Janesson forward. Inside, three forms regarded him from behind a large table set upon a dais. A single chair sat at the natural focus of the U-shaped platform, and Janesson settled himself into it, leaning forward and resting his elbows on his knees. Gaul sat across from him, and the door shut.

"Captain Janesson, please allow me to introduce commanders Rennik and Rant." the two green clad canids nodded in turn. "They are my counterparts from *Gresec* and *Venom*. Also, this is Jilles." He seemed a bit less certain when introducing her. An older female red fox, clad in black, she glowered down at Janesson.

"What is your business? Why did you intercept him?" The fox snapped, straight to the point. "Explain yourself."

Janesson dipped his head humbly; this was more the treatment he'd expected. "Ma'am, we paid for intelligence on a ransomable VIP at our last stop. Among the items I brought from my ship is a datapad with all the details of our transaction, our plans, and our records of the intercept. I turned it over to your security before leaving the shuttle; it contains everything, including statements from my bridge officers."

"I don't need to review your data when I have you right here. We prefer to avoid confrontations like this, but that particular envoy is not to be a pawn in some economic game. We require you to tell us everything about this intelligence; I don't trust you, and I won't begin to do so until you've given me what I need and I've cross-checked it."

"Ma'am," Janesson paused for a moment, dreading what he had to say next. "There's more. I am a fool, and I have come to offer myself for my crew. I believe that an assassin, working amongst us, has killed your ambassador."

There was surprisingly little reaction; he held his jaw tightly shut to keep himself from babbling into the silence that followed. After a moment, Jilles leaned forward.

"This assassin, what do you know of him?"

"The name he gave us is Theta. He's a short white fox, with purple hair—the north Oailim physiotype, perfect match, though he has a few modifications you should be aware of. All his records, medical, service and otherwise we've included on the datapad. We believe that he was sent by Knoskali, lord of a major house of Brynton."

At this, there was considerably more stir.

"Knoskali. That is a name I know," Jilles murmured with a shake of her head. She straightened, blinking. "Yes, that fits."

The door slid open and another red fox entered. Janesson half rose, eyes widening in disbelief.

"Ambassador?"

"Hello again, Captain." The fox he'd thought dead nodded politely to him, then stepped up onto the dais and clasped paws with Jilles; after a brief greeting, he turned back to Janesson, leaning across the corner of the table. "Thanks for your hospitality; sorry I had to leave abruptly, but we had some things to work out. I'm sure you'll agree it's better for me to be over here, after all. As I told your people, my name is Rema, but you can call me whatever you like. Ambassador is a cute one...I like it. You can consider me your ambassador to the Dazi, if you like, and I'll do my best to help."

"Ambassador," Janesson was immensely relieved, if perplexed. "We all thought you were dead. We found your blood..."

"Yeah, about that. Sorry to usurp your authority, Gaul, but Jilles and I have some things to say to our guest in private. I trust you'll support any arrangement we come to?"

It was not a question, Janesson realized.

"Of course, sir. Gentlemen?" Gaul gestured to his co-commanders, who stood.

"Sorry, boys...and thanks again." Rema grinned.

Janesson peered at Rema searchingly as the fox exchanged nods with each of the commanders filing out. Short, he was typical of his species with red fur and black ears, but he had the sharp gaze and the hyper-alertness he'd come to associate with Theta. A pair of shiny stripes diagonally across his muzzle appeared to be freshly tended cuts, but otherwise he seemed to be in good shape and good spirits. As the door slid shut, Rema and Jilles both turned to regard Janesson.

"Alright. Now that the three of us have a bit of privacy, let's chat. Madam?" Rema swung around and sat on the table, nodding to Jilles.

"He says that it's Knoskali's doing," she growled. "Do we trust that?"

"I sure do. No doubt, in fact. What disturbs me is how he got his intel, and how it took us so long to find out about this."

"Heads will roll, I promise you that." Jilles seethed. "This is a gross failure. I—"

"Hold on a moment. They did catch back up to you in time to get you here, didn't they?" Rema laughed. "I'd say they probably did fairly well. Not all leaks are leaks, after all, and no system is perfect. You know that—even me! I was probably a bit too glib about my travel plans when I left Hope, and I certainly hope you don't plan to roll *my* head. Well, we'll have to deal with Knoskali at some point, you know. I've been waiting for this to come for quite some time, but it caught me by surprise even so. So, Captain?"

"Ah, yes?" Janesson tilted his head.

"You and your crew were unaware of the attempt on my life."

"Yes, we were. We just—"

"Your goal was to simply ransom me for money."

"Yes, sir." Janesson played abject. "We thought it would be quick profit."

"Your assassin—"

"Theta," Jilles filled in.

"Your assassin Theta was not operating with your authority?"

"Absolutely not," Janesson breathed. "We wanted to sell you, not kill you. I...know this Knoskali. I was once a slave of his, and I believe he intended for Theta to kill you, then for your fleet to destroy us all."

"Not impossible, but incredibly unlikely. Captain, let me just say that I believe you, but that things are more complicated than you may imagine. I'm sure you've come to ask for your ship's release. Let me try to ease your mind a bit:

We're not looking for revenge, and we don't intend to harm your crew. Of course, whether we allow you to continue as a crew is another matter...one that we want to settle very carefully. But not here in dead space."

"What do you mean?" Janesson growled, thinking that more than a little ominous.

"I intend to continue on to my destination. I expect that you'll come with us." The fox leveled his eyes on Janesson, studying his face. "We've detected an increasing level of interest in this little pocket of space, including a few random EM patterns that we suspect to be a stealthed ship near your own."

Janesson sucked in a little surprised breath, ears perked.

"And there's more," Rema said, leaning forward. "A moment ago, we heard a clear arrival ripple followed by an encrypted data broadcast and departure ripples. Our flag tactics department identified it as a stealthed warship, and though the imaging window was brief, they've identified it as one of several possible ships known to us in the service of our enemies. Know anything?"

Janesson shook his head, surprised. "I know nothing of this. Our ship received no transmissions while I was aboard except from you. My operations department said nothing. You think there could be more going on here?"

"I'm certain of it, and I don't want to hang around and find out what someone else is plotting. If you say you don't know, I'll take your word for it." Rema glanced down at his desk. "Well, your word...along with the results from this somatic scan that I've had going this whole time, but don't mind that. I'm going to detain most of your crew and install my own prize crew aboard your ship, but only for the journey. I'm sure you can see that I don't want or need it as an asset... but I do want to get under the friendly guns of Zyktona's defense and detection net. So are you alright with this so far?"

"Do I have any choice?" Janesson asked softly, standing to stare straight at the fox, eye level despite the foot-high dais.

Rema grinned happily to him in reply, resting his chin on his paws. "Oh definitely not. Not unless you want to fight us, of course, but I'd prefer you didn't, if only for your sake. And it would be. Now once we make it to Zyktona, I'm going to do something that's a specialty of mine—I'm going to get everyone but the grunts in one little room, and we're going to have a nice long talk. Those are my terms for this stage of the game and I won't negotiate. I will offer you a guarantee, though: On my personal authority, none of your people will be harmed...so long as everyone plays along. I don't intend to 'bring you to justice', or anything silly like that, but this location is compromised and I'm not gonna stay here, fleet or no fleet. Obviously you can see that you're also in danger, and not just from us. If we wanted to destroy you, we would have done it by now. If we wanted to take your ship, we could easily have done so covertly and killed you all. However, the Dazi waited on me, and now I'm waiting on you."

Janesson nodded, studying Rema's face. "I realize I have no option but to trust you, but can you tell me why I should believe that you'll leave us unharmed?"

"First and foremost, curiosity and professional interest. Me, I want to gather as much intel as possible from you and your crew so I can get an idea of how this played out. Useful info can be found in the strangest places. Second, we've had...useful dealings in the past with your 'Free Fleet', and I'd rather stay friends with your cohorts. Third and last," Rema paused, then grinned slyly down at him. "Catch and release is just more fun."

Janesson snorted suspiciously at hearing one of his favorite lines repeated back to him. Nevertheless, he nodded and straightened.

"I accept your terms. What do you need me to do?"

XVI

Purity

THE MONOCHROME VISUAL NOISE spinning in Theta's head resolved itself with a snap into a small, blurry room. His eyes were open, and suddenly his brain switched on, identifying objects, naming things, processing senses and wondering how it got where it was.

"Good morning," a cheery voice sang, responding to his return to awareness. "I trust you had a nice sleep?"

Theta looked around, but his blurry eyes couldn't find the speaker. He tried to respond, but found his muzzle sealed shut. Instinctively, he tried to reach around to clear it but his paws were restrained.

"I'll take that as a yes. What do you see around you?"

Theta's eyes had cleared, but he saw nothing. The walls were dark grey, and there was light, though he couldn't discern its source. Suddenly memories rushed back; he remembered his defeat, and his stomach fell. He blinked a few times, and then tears began to run down his muzzle. It felt like waking up from a nightmare only to realize that it had been real. Irrai's face, falling away, lingered with him for a long moment, no longer a thought he could dismiss to focus on the mission. His ears flattened back and his heart sped up, breath coming more rapidly. Little daydreams of

Knoskali seemed a lifetime away, a child's fantasy, a halcyon of myth and legend built into a simple cult of attraction.

He'd thought before that he'd lost everything, but that did not compare to his emptiness now. Now he stared, bereft of form and of function, into the face of nothingness from behind empty eyes. From the void he'd come and to it he felt ready to return.

"Lovely, isn't it? So you betrayed who trusted you. For him?"

Images of Knoskali rose unbidden to the forefront of his mind, the Lord ascendant, resplendent in the black robes of his house, green eyes shining brightly. Memories of Terial, the *other*, urging him to greater feats of lethality.

Memories of...

Theta jolted, eyes widening. He was being scanned.

No!

Pain dribbled through his nerves as he clamped down on the intrusion, neuron by neuron. Sweat beaded across the bridge of his muzzle, running down across his fur, and his eyes rolled back. He held his mental discipline until at last the pressure against his mind eased.

An indeterminate amount of time passed, broken only by his breaths; he began counting, focusing all his effort on the duration of each inhalation, precisely matching the length to the length of his exhalations, blocking out all other thought and all further probing.

"So it is Knoskali then." The voice sounded suddenly more normal, though still quite cheerful. "He trained you well, but not nearly well enough. Why, I wonder?"

Breathe in. One, two, three, four, five.

Hold. One, two, three, four, five.

Breathe out. One, two, three, four, five.

"Yes, you're very cleverly blocking me. I doubt pain would work, and I'm certain that coercion is out of the question, if you can abandon friends so quickly at the whim of your master." The voice was chiding. "Of course, I do have drugs that will destroy your ability to resist, but brute force is never nearly as much fun."

...Two, three, four, five...

"Still, I wonder—why would you serve that creature? He sent you to commit an infamous crime and die on his behalf, but you're still loyal?"

It was his right!...Agh. Three, four...

"Very interesting, very interesting." A very long pause. "You love him. Do you truly know the evil which you serve?"

Not evil! Nobody ever understands. Nobody knows but me.

Images flashed unbidden through his head, images of Knoskali's rare tender moments. He writhed, straining his muscles to provide pain for him to focus on, but the thoughts and memories spilled forth. In desperation, he finally exhaled and held his breath, clinging to the immediate urgent need to inhale. After a few moments, his body began to starve for oxygen and his head spun. And yet even still the thoughts poured out.

He began to shake and tremble, but he couldn't break the thrall. Memories, knowledge, thoughts of *before*. Surprised, he took a ragged breath; images rose to the surface, places and faces he hadn't known since before awareness dawned on the *Freeta*.

He'd never been able to remember *before*.

He remembered his den group, and the time long before. Memories of his home on Oailim, of comfortably cold winters and warm, sweaty summers, of rich soil tilled and tended by little paws, and the smell of land warmed by sun, of grains and flowers and heather. Memories of playing in the snow, of trying to blend with a patch of snowflowers while his brethren searched for him in the flat light. He subsided into a near trance state, watching his early life drift by as if viewing it from afar—growing up on a farm and tending the crops, and his many brothers and sisters and all the matrons and patrons of his den, the kind and the nasty, the lazybones and the strong-backs. Memories of long days of harvest and planting in the fresh, clean air, an agrarian existence for which he'd willingly neglected study.

Glazed eyes blinked, unseeing, as a new face entered the picture.

Carson.

He remembered meeting Carson totally by chance on a den outing to the nearby town. He'd been unprepared for the giddy mutual attraction that had swept him off his feet at sixteen, surprising them both. The secret meetings, the little gifts, the talk about the future. The tickets to Carson's new job and new life on Brynton, and the dreams and excitement that they'd shared at the prospects of their new life together.

He bared his teeth.

Brynton.

He remembered Brynton, and how he'd hated it from the moment he arrived. Hated Brynton and Fenna City, and Carson's horrible job, and Carson's horrible friend-cum-recruiter Renn who he never trusted. He remembered the unbreathable air, ground travel in sealed vehicles, cities built on the ruins of cities, built on the ruined ecology of a ruined planet. He remembered the careless, horrible parties Renn dragged them to, full of careless, horrible people with no expectations, no dreams, and no future.

His pulse quickened, and he could feel himself trembling with anticipation as he remembered how he'd met Knoskali in a little restaurant. At the time, it had seemed completely random chance.

A cold shock gripped him.

For the first time, he remembered his capture, drugged and stolen away. The memories all came back, memories that had been crushed beneath the weight of eventuality. He remembered his first death—the death of Myshel of

Oailim under the firm hand of Knoskali, and his rebirth as the Lord's own creation.

The rest spilled forward like atmosphere through a blown hatch, and no force in the universe could have slowed the memories that poured forth, unhindered by Theta. Years of memories, in little broken scenes, were reconstructed from fragments and figments into his life's story; reconstructed from the details and patterns in his head by a bank of computers somewhere on the other side of the wall, it featured people and events relegated to the darkest reaches of his subconscious. Imagery and memories of the tender moments, of those not so tender; of every manner of torment and training and service.

As his memories rushed forward towards his final dance, they slowed to real time once more, and slowly he sank into himself, unable to stay aloof despite his urgent desire to avoid reliving it.

He stood atop a broad, long table, surrounded by the Brynti elite, the Lords and scions of the major houses resplendant in gilt robes of rank. The remains of an extravagant dinner had long since been cleared away and the stage was set for his performance. The smells of the room, the tastes in his mouth, the sounds in the background, everything was as it was then, and he remembered it with perfect clarity.

Even the feel of the slate beneath his hindpaws was familiar as he spun, exquisitely slowly, pivoting on his toes, then slowly began to walk along the table's length. The faces around the periphery were a blur to him as he looked outward, head high. A slow beat softly accompanied his steps, and he began to move with it, across, then down, then lift... Every step, every motion was precise as he spun, yet he still managed to slowly become lost in the throb and rhythm. A stringed instrument spoke up in counterpoint, a new partner with whom he danced counterpoise.

Slowly he began to pick up speed. Step and step, and more instruments joined, following him and he them. Leap and spin, closing his eyes, opening his eyes, sliding to his knees to mime touching some lord to whom he'd been trained to favor. Every breath was as it was, every motion perfect. The music, the pace increased over ten minutes, twenty minutes, frenetic and driving, until his paws were pounding the table with every triplet, sweat flinging from his nose and paws, blood from a cut on his lip artistically spattering his muzzlefur. He was so completely immersed in the moment that he could taste the blood and sweat, feel the breath racing through his body, sense every motion flowing into the next. The flow of the music spun him and sped him through each step and twirl, until at last with a chaotic, polyrhythmic crescendo he and the music and the beat and the air in the room and the feeling and drive..

.. Elegantly ...

... Collapsed to leave him bowed on the table, one paw across his chest, the other atop his muzzle.

He panted with exertion, unsure whether it was he who breathed or his remembered self, barely conscious even of the fact that he wasn't truly there again. The little part of him that retained its sense of self willed his memories forward desperately, wishing more than anything to skip what came next, but he had no control. Just as it had happened before, it happened again.

The scene played out before him; the same feelings that had coursed through him then coursed through him now, accompanied by a sense of dread that was all current-Theta's. Unlike his younger counterpart, he knew what was coming...but knowing how it would end only made it worse.

Knoskali stood to address the room, breaking a tense silence.

"In all the years of our charter, we have had rules about our hospitality. You, my guests, have witnessed the common ones filled tonight. A gathering of the faction heads has a certain protocol to it." Knoskali's voice was carefully neutral as it rolled from his great form.

"Well, there are other rules. Old rules. Rules that are still in effect. One of those rules, Lord Harrol has invoked."

There were murmurs about, but attention remained fixed on Knoskali. Beneath the surface, Theta knew, the black coyote was seething.

"Harrol, I give you one last chance to withdraw your request. If you follow through with it, I promise that there will be consequences."

Lord Harrol stood and smirked, tossing his jeweled goblet onto the table.

"Knoskali, your arrogance and insults come with consequences themselves," he mocked. "This is one. I request *Elechen*."

The black coyote closed his eyes and trembled; Theta had then been shocked to notice moistness in the corners of his eyes, though he now knew why.

His trembling was not from fear.

Knoskali wept for me.

The coyote opened his eyes, then bent and whispered something to the slavemaster, who looked stunned. The slavemaster glanced at Theta, then glanced around almost wildly for a moment before dashing off.

"*Elechen*, then. Are you, my guests, familiar with it?" Knoskali's honeyed voice was strained, masking great tension.

Only questioning glances returned to the head of the table.

"No, please, no..." Theta whispered, but he couldn't even hear himself. He was locked away, a prisoner in his own memories and as helpless to stop their progress as he had been to stop the events then unfolding.

Time jumped forward a bit, then slowed back down abruptly, as if someone were playing his memories, paws on the controls.

"Lord Harrol," Knoskali was saying, voice flat and harsh, "I will honor your request for *Elechen*. My dancer will die for custom."

The terror that sank into Theta's stomach was as real as it had been then. He couldn't move his limbs, frozen in terror.

"However, know that at this moment we are at war with House Elara. You are our prisoner. You and the assembled will watch the process of *Elechen*. Guards!"

Harrol shook in rage as he was surrounded. "War! You cannot declare war on Elara! This is unacceptable!"

"No, Harrol," Knoskali smiled mirthlessly. "It is *customary*. If you'd studied the charter you supposedly follow, or if you had read deeper into the old laws, or in fact if you'd done anything other than try to find a part of our custom with which you could hurt me, you would have realized that."

Harrol's eyes widened. "I..." he swallowed nervously. "Fine, I withdraw! I redact! Damn you, Knoskali."

A sigh of relief swept around the table.

Knoskali leaned forward across the table, over Theta.

"No, Harrol. Have the courage of your convictions. We have declared our mutual intent. I will see your house razed, your people annihilated, to a man. I will see your family raped and slaughtered, your children sold into slavery. I will devour your firstborn myself, and destroy everything your family has ever been. No, Harrol," Knoskali seethed, "You may no longer withdraw, for the damage is done. To go otherwise would go against *custom*."

Absolute silence gripped the room—Knoskali's breathing was all Theta could hear.

"My Lord Knoskali," Lord Breth appealed, "We've endured a century of peace, and we have the greatest profits in the known systems."

"I offered an opportunity to put aside spite, and I warned of the consequences. My offer was rejected. I do not offer again. Master at Arms, Harrol will be seated."

Harrol's eyes were wide as he was forced down into his seat.

Jorl placed a trembling paw on the table in entreaty. "Lord Knoskali," he breathed. "May we retire while this takes place? My heart..."

"...Jorl, do you feel for my dancer?"

"Yes, Lord Knoskali," he bowed, closing his eyes.

"It is the tiniest fraction of what I feel, if that. I will remain, as must you. Myshel," he barked, turning to Theta. For a moment, his anger modulated to something softer, if no less steely.

"Myshel, this is the end of us. I will not ask you to forgive me, for what I do is unforgivable."

Knoskali climbed onto the table once more, lord of war and death, with intent. He reached a paw down and guided Theta to his feet with surprising gentleness. A rope dangled overhead—the rope that had haunted Theta's nightmares since he'd awoken on the *Freeta*. Thick and braided, its end was fashioned into a simple loop.

He stared at it.

The coyote knelt before him.

"Mishy," he murmured, loud enough for the assembled to hear. "I love you. I never thought I would fall in love with anyone, least of all a simple slave, but I did. A dancer was what I saw in you, and a dancer you will remain in my heart forever, and I'll never take another."

Theta opened his mouth, then closed it. There was nothing to say. Panic had raced through him as realization dawned, and his had knees wobbled; Knoskali kept him standing, just as he had then. He wouldn't let him fall or waver. Drawing the rope down, he slid the loop around Theta's neck and drew it tight; Theta rose to his tiptoes with a grimace as the cord tightened beneath his jaw.

"No other will kill my beloved dancer," Knoskali rumbled, and pulled up on the rope.

A strange sound reached his ears, and Theta realized that he was screaming. Abruptly he came out of his memories, screaming muffledly in the little room, restrained and writhing. After a few more moments of frantic blind struggling, he wound down, slumping nervelessly. Before he knew it, he slid back into the oblivion of his mind as images marched ruthlessly onward, barely conscious of his second rebirth, as Theta, and all that had transpired. His recall resumed its pace, carrying him to Rema's cell aboard *Varaunt*, and to his fall.

To Theta it could have been a lifetime lived again. As his thoughts arrived at the present and settled into the familiar blackness he'd experienced just before waking, the entirety of his awareness faded back to the simple, stark reality of where he was.

Theta stared at the wall in silence, his body covered in sweat which dripped to the floor and formed, unseen, a ring around his anchored feet. His head was fuzzy and his mind ached, and he could still feel the grip of the rope around his neck. The mental probing had ceased completely, its absence palpable, and the voice was silent; he couldn't move an inch in any direction, leaving him nothing to do but sag against his restraints and contemplate the strange and tragic journey that had been his existence.

> *Dear Captain,*
> *I trust this letter finds you well. Your last message quite amused me, I must admit, as did Gnosi's little addendum—I would have delighted in seeing you dress him down so thoroughly. I have new intelligence, and so I have left a new message for Theta which you'll find happily tucked away in this little packet. Please dispatch this one and discard*

the old. You'll be interested to know that my last information has Theta quite comfortably ensconced aboard Varaunt *with some degree of autonomy, so rescue should be somewhat more straightforward. You may proceed to your destination at your leisure. One last thing: Please consider my earlier recommendation not to trust Gnosi completely rescinded.*

Well, mostly.

Good hunting!

-K

Glowering at the display, Jale swallowed against the bitter, cool taste in her mouth that made her oesophagus numb and dry. The message would have arrived on the courier ship from Brynton to Fonaci on the day they'd been forced to leave.

She'd missed it by hours, not days.

She shook her head ruefully. There was nothing to be done about it now. For good or ill, whether a slip of timing or sabotage, Gnosi's actions had forced her out of range. Two more messages remained in the message packet from the stealthed courier's message drop; as she reached to move to the next, she realized that her paws were shaking softly against its smooth surface. Whatever was wrong with her was getting much worse quickly. Fighting a creeping revulsion at her body's betrayal, she forced her attention back to the screen.

My dear Captain,

I'm certain that there is some good reason that the Fonaci authorities found the body of my cousin floating in space for the universe to see, but I'd really love to hear it from you. It is possible that my previous message was unclear, but by 'rescinded' I did mean that you shouldn't dispatch Gnosi from an airlock. Then again, given what the Fonaci have been reporting, I do realize it may have had an accidental component. Except for the part about him being shot, I would suspect it wholly so.

I look forward to your explanation.

Well, no matter. I have several cousins I have yet to kill, but only one Theta. Still, my concern grows steadily for the success of the mission. The favor of a response is requested. Required, even. I have reattached the revised message for Theta, in the event that the first message went astray. Consider this your 'go' signal, if you haven't already gone.

-K

Jale sat up straighter, grinding her teeth instinctively at the burning pain in her gut. She sipped some water and advanced. The next message, however, straightened her completely in her chair.

Captain Bercammon,

The situation is dire. I have dispatched an ally to what I hope is your location. They will render assistance if they are able. If you are alive, it is imperative that you send this third and final message to Theta. Send it in the clear if you must, but you must rescue Theta from Varaunt immediately and at any cost.

I repeat: AT ANY COST.

Do not fail.

-K

A frisson of fear ran through her at the gravity of the words and their shift of tone. Jale stared at the last line for a few moments before dismissing the message and closing her eyes. In truth, she'd begun to feel as though this was the beginning of the end of everything, and all she wanted was a bit of time to be herself, whoever that was, before fate caught up with her.

The panel beneath her paw buzzed with a signal from Naane requesting voice communication; instead of answering it, she closed down her terminal and rose, wiping her numb lips with the back of a paw before striding through the door.

"Ma'am!" Her XO stood and waved her over as soon as she set foot on the bridge. "Ma'am, you better see this. Ciphertechs came through...they say that they've broken the ship's low-security key. They've been monitoring comms and they think Theta's in some kind of trouble. They—ah, *Varaunt*'s crew, that is—they're trying to find him. I haven't read in depth yet, but—"

"Have we any response from Theta yet?" Jale snapped, striding over.

"No." Naane looked surprised by her interruption. "Not yet, but—"

"We've got a real problem." Jale leaned close to Naane, who leaned back obligingly, and lowered her voice. "I screened the messages I just read, and I've passed them to you. You must read them, dear. Now, please, while I look at these."

Naane looked a little shaken, but nodded. Jale gestured for the ocelot to take her console, then leaned over to see what the ciphertechs had intercepted. She'd barely made it halfway through the first, a message talking about search priorities, when her concentration was broken by Krella silently gesticulating at his console.

"Krella?"

"Eh!" Krella snapped, agitated. "I'm showing a significant mobilization from the three big ships. Fighters, I think, or heavy interceptors. They seem to be...yes, they are. Converging on *Varaunt*."

Overwhelmed, Jale sank into Naane's seat and whispered a little prayer to Dia. No sooner had she lain back, however, than a wave of dizziness overcame her. She sat up abruptly; fighting down nausea, she swung her console to the side and clutched at her belly. After a few breaths to calm her agitated middle, she lifted her head to affix Krella with what she hoped was a properly interrogatory glance and not a sick leer. "Are the escorts still moving into position for echo scatter detection? What is our estimated time until they're in position? In minutes, please."

"Detection in...wait." Krella made a face at his panel, running his fingers through his dark hair. "I've never felt more behind a situation. They've changed formation again while the other ships have been launching! They're...It looks as though they're beginning to move away from the capital ships. The big subcapitals are moving, too, but I can't identify a pattern in there. I don't...I just don't know what they're doing."

Nauseous but momentarily stable, Jale dragged her console part-way back and studied its representation of the positions of the ships around her. Figures began changing as the vanguard began to accelerate and the computer's tactical projections began to develop leader lines and probability arcs.

"Now they're—"

"I can see it all for myself, Krella. They're leaving, but where are they going?"

"Zyktona, ma'am." Naane replied for him. "I ran the extrap. Computer estimates they're aligned above Zyktona's arrival corridor with zero ambiguity, and they're accelerating for Rellin drive. And the ships closing on *Varaunt* are combat shuttles, not interceptors. Sorry, Krella, but she's opening her hatches and broadcasting approaches. I think *Varaunt* is being boarded, and accepting it. I bet she's surrendered."

Krella raised his paws. "Let's count these off. We can finally be sure that Theta's on board *Varaunt*. That's good.

However, he's in trouble somewhere, and hasn't responded to our messages. That's bad. We've sent him messages to do whatever it takes to get off the ship, which is good, but we have no idea if he's seen them, which is bad. Now the hostile fleet has abandoned its attempts to detect us, which is good...but they also appear to be boarding *Varaunt*, which is bad. Unless the ciphertechs can come up with a miracle, I'm out of ideas."

"Ideas are your whole job, Krella. Come up with three good ones for me within the next five minutes or get off my bridge." Jale surprised even herself with her waspishness. "Meanwhile, XO—please ask the ciphertechs to try and find the status of Arvinne. Perhaps we can use him as a contact on the inside."

"Aye, ma'am. Did you find anything in those communiques from Varaunt?"

Jale shook her head. "Not yet, but I've not finished them yet. Get on those ciphertechs."

She pulled the intercepted messages back up, narrowing her focus to scrutinize them. When she'd read them all, she felt more ill than ever. Her head spun again when she looked up, but this time her disorientation lasted only moments. Resting her elbows on her knees, she wiped the drool from her lips and closed her eyes for a moment to calm her nerves. When she opened them again, she found Naane and Krella regarding her; she gave them a weary shrug and a 'what can you do' grin.

"It would seem as though they don't know where Theta is, either. Helm," She spoke up, "Plot a Rellin entry vector to get us to Zyktona above the vanguard's projected entry."

"Aye, ma'am."

Jale turned back to Krella and Naane, lowering her voice. "Our problems are compounding: Like us, the crew of the *Varaunt* would very much like to find Theta, but like us, they cannot. They want him because they suspect that he's killed their VIP."

There was a surprised pause, broken when Krella brought his paw down on his console with a muted thud and an appreciative curse. "There. There! That's the missing piece. Oh you devious, clever bastard," he waxed admiring. "Do you see it, Captain?"

Jale's reply was interrupted by the arrival of Ososkne, who came through the bridge door with Jewel hiding guiltily behind his elbow. He strode quickly up to her, his normally jolly face lined with worry.

"Theta?"

"Yes? What?" Theta sat up, eyes blurry. Dizzily, he tried to wipe them, but found himself unable; though he tried to move his limbs, they didn't respond.

"Calm. You won't be able to move much, so don't hurt yourself trying. If you put yourself into a parasympathetic feedback loop, we'll have to put you back under."

Recalling where he was, Theta cast about, blinking up at a tall, blurry shape that loomed over him. He tried to glare, but found himself wavering.

"Calm. Calm yourself and accept your position. I am Anast, and I have been in charge of your interrogation to this point. You had blocked memories, and I recovered many of them. We suspect that they were blocked to you as well. Is that correct?"

"Yeah," Theta murmured, looking downward. He didn't feel particularly cooperative, but neither did he much care. He was empty, like a vacuum in the shape of a fox; used by everyone, abandoned by everyone, forced to turn against the few people who had given him a chance, love now seemed to him as much of a misty delusion as absolute theism. The dredging of his memories had left his thoughts in a chaotic depression, and he wanted little more to do with life or anyone in it.

Raising his head once more for lack of anything better to do, he found his vision steadily improving; looking around, he found himself sitting in a floating chair, suspended in a small room. A nondescript grey wolf in a black shipsuit sat on a molded bench beside the single door, regarding him with a professional disinterest.

"Your sight has cleared?"

"Mostly, yes. Are you done with me?"

A moment passed before Anast answered, as if he were silently laughing to himself. "Done with you? An odd concept. No, we're not done with you. If we were, you'd never have woken. You had quite a few memories that we recovered, but some that we could not. Our technology is good, but not perfect; there remain gaps in the picture, and we require answers of you. Once we have all of the information we can extract, you will then most likely be put to death."

Theta nodded very slightly. "I expected so."

"Wise, for someone of your profession. There are several who wish to meet you and ask questions. You are in a chair that I will move around, but you have a collar with a neural block. You are also anchored securely to the chair. Don't try to escape; there is nothing you can do for yourself at this point, and there is more dignity in accepting that."

The tiniest flame of rebellion spawned in Theta's heart, but was snuffed out in an instant by a wash of unemotion. He nodded again, closing his eyes momentarily.

Anast stood, striding to the door. Theta's chair followed like a shadow as he made his way through several decks and across a broad corridor to a large door marked with yellow and black chevrons.

At Anast's touch, the door opened to reveal a darkened room, two decks high and twice as wide. As his chair hauled him through behind his captor, Theta caught a whiff of a scent that caused him to reel. He was overpoweringly reminded of Knoskali, but there were other smells...more subtle. Smells that he associated with wind and trees and caves, and a host of sensations/memories/colors/shapes.

Images of a familiar but unfamiliar world danced before his eyes, and his pulse quickened in response. He hadn't seen any of these memories yesterday.

The dream?

His eyes widened as a dark shape, not illusory, resolved itself from the gloom into a huge approaching quadruped with a long nose and large green eyes. It had no fur, merely glossy mottled black scales that spanned its length. Its proportions and shape vaguely reminded Theta of Oailim's reptilian species, but its movements and the sharpness of its eyes did not.

Theta stared at the creature unabashedly; though clearly alien, he found it somehow familiar. Compelling. Comfortable.

He *trusted* it.

It paused, nose a meter from the floating chair, regarding him curiously, nostrils flared as it sampled his scent.

"This one, yes." The creature's jaws split to reveal big, sharp teeth in a pink mouth. "It smells...strange, but I know its line." Theta was startled by its fluent speech—Its accent and vocal pitch was similar to Anast's, but its timbre much deeper. It tilted its huge head, moving slightly closer and regarding him with an intensity that made him suddenly less comfortable.

"Yes...yes, I do know its line. I would speak with the other hybrid at once."

"As you wish. I do not know if he has yet returned from the *Derash*, but I shall find out."

Anast bowed his head and turned to a nearby terminal. The alien regarded Theta for a long moment, its eyes piercing. "It listens, but does not speak to me," it murmured thoughtfully. "I must taste its blood."

Jale grimaced up at Ososkne.

"Captain? I came to update you, but you look as though you could use my attention."

"Indeed. I do need a moment with you, Medic, but it must wait. XO, please stand down the off-watch. I want to move to watch-and-watch, or we'll have nobody fit for it in ten more hours."

"Aye, ma'am. Sorry, ma'am. I meant to do that hours ago."

"It's fine, dear. I just realized the ship's schedule is askew, myself. Few of our scenarios projected this sort of delay. Now, we also certainly need to relieve the bridge, and send for galley service."

"Yes ma'am."

Ososkne slid up beside Jale. "Captain, ship's business is your business, but her captain's health is mine. What's wrong?"

"It's my stomach, Medic. Hurts rather badly. I'm nauseous, dizzy, and cramping—It's almost incapacitating. Whole host of symptoms. I'm worried about poison, though it seems a little slow-acting for that."

Ososkne looked her over, then, to her surprise, leaned forward and sniffed at her breath.

"Uh-huh." The otter regarded her as one might regard a misbehaving child. He dropped his voice to an undertone. "Poison, indeed. Just how much megvha have you been drinking, Captain?"

Jale frowned suspiciously, cradling her cup. "Well now, this is only my fourth, and I doubt—"

"Ma'am, Jewel said he warned you."

"Well yes, but I've—"

"Here, let me take that." Ososkne pulled it from her grasp with quick, firm paws. Jale felt a surge of anger, but moderated her response to a hard stare.

"Ma'am," Naane murmured quietly, as if embarrassed to interrupt. "The little ships have entered Rellin drive."

"How many cups per day?" The medic dragged her attention back by waving her mug. His voice was low, but his implication was clear.

Feeling boxed in, Jale merely glared at him. "I really don't know, Medic. I mean, every day is different, of course. I simply can't imagine it's related, though...I—"

Ososkne shook his head, leaning close. "Your servant here is concerned about you," he murmur-whispered. "You should listen to him. You're showing what look to me like signs of megvha addiction, which is quite common but can be very damaging. Musteliforms like yourself are especially susceptible."

"We are? Nobody seemed that concerned on Brynton." Jale grimaced. "Dear, listen...I desperately need the focus right now. I simply cannot afford to be foggy-headed, but I just feel like my insides have been pickled. Wouldn't you need to run tests and the like to be sure? Right now isn't the best time."

Ososkne shook his head solemnly. "I'm as sure as I need to be, from what your servant told me and your current state. I brought a sublingual that will help prevent further damage, but if you keep drinking that stuff you'll override the effect. It has a low threshold for harm, which is the chief reason it's controlled in many places."

"I need it right now, however. The next few hours are life and death for all of us." Jale spoke louder than she meant to, but she didn't have time to waste with Ososkne. "Can you give me something else to keep me going?"

"Take this," Ososkne took her shaking paw, placing a small packet into it. "Take two. Take two more in an hour. I'll send your servant up with a strong stimulant that will keep you very alert for nine hours or so, after which you will crash very hard. Make sure you're done thinking before then. And no more meghva until I've cleared it, or you'll find yourself unable to command."

"The subcaps are moving too, Captain," Krella touched her elbow. "They're spreading out to prepare for Rellin drive, if I had to guess. Can't jump ships that big too close together. Shuttle traffic is picking up between *Varaunt* and the capital ships, too. I'm tracking each one individually, and I'm counting returns."

"Have you gotten mass readings?" Jale peered over.

"Either they're jamming our mass readings, or they're nearly equivalent."

"Two main theories, ma'am." Naane spoke up. "They're probably either bringing enough soldiers to search and depopulate the ship, or they're putting aboard a skeleton crew and taking prisoners. If they're putting aboard a skeleton crew, I bet the whole package is going to Zyktona as well."

"Do we chance it?" Jale asked through her teeth. "We either go there early and find a place to watch, and hope they didn't see us leave, or we follow them after and hope they don't see us arrive. Early or late?"

"Early," Naane said with certainty.

"Late," Krella spoke at the same time. The two frowned at each other momentarily, then turned back to Jale to argue their cases simultaneously. She stove them off with raised paws, grinding her teeth.

"See what I have to deal with, Medic? Urgh, I feel awful."

"Of course you do, ma'am. Just take your sublinguals, and no more megvha for a while. I mean it. If that's all, I must return. We're in the middle of removing your other servant's arm to save what we can."

Jale pushed away concern—too much was at stake in the now to worry about the future. She stood, fighting down her another wave of nausea.

"Go. Take good care of him, Ososkne." She swung around to look at her tactician. "Krella, give me your objections quickly and succinctly."

"We risk detection on the way out." Krella completely ignored the medic's departure, locking eyes with Jale. "The data I have suggest a near equal probability of success, but there's always a chance Theta will make his move if we leave early. Your idea of using Arvinne might pan out. Also, we have no way of being certain where Theta is, or if the ship he's on will go to Zyktona, or if he'll be caught and executed. Basically, missing critical data."

Jale nodded, smacking her lips against the medicinal taste that was growing in her mouth. "Very well. Naane?"

"Our data and intel on that system is limited and old. If we're forced to maneuver, we may find ourselves real obvious. Not listed as having any planetaries, though. It's...a surprising choice for a destination. Extremely low population, very low technology. Anyway, getting there early might help us scout. It's not guaranteed that Theta will be on *Varaunt*, or that he'll go to Zyktona, or that he'll be alive, but probability suggests that he will, and we can see they're setting up to get out of here."

Jale nodded again. "I think we'll go as soon as we see signs that the warships are moving. Have those ciphertechs found Arvinne?"

"Haven't heard a thing. I'll get on them again."

"Very good. Once you have, I'd like a word with you in private."

"Aye, ma'am."

Theta watched the alien's jaws part and gently—almost tenderly—slide around his arm and slowly clamp down. A nervous Anast hovered behind him, but he felt no pain as the alien's teeth pierced his flesh; everything below his throat was completely insensate. For a long moment the alien simply held fixed, its eyes closed, body motionless save the rise and fall of its great ribs. Theta stared down at it dispassionately, watching a crimson stain spread through his white fur around its closed muzzle.

Suddenly the alien tensed. Its eyes flew wide, pupils narrow, and it began to breathe faster, hot fetid breath washing through Theta's fur. The near eye fixed on his face, and its lips peeled back to display half a meter of vicious teeth, red with his blood. A gurgle built in its throat, and then the alien screamed, jerking back with a wild shudder, spattering the wall with crimson in the process. It writhed with anger, gnashing its teeth and hissing in rage.

"The gift...its gift...our gift! It was not given willingly." The creature's voice had thinned to nearly a snarl. "I have them. I have the memories, long and far though they have traveled to rejoin us. Remove this thing from my habitat and dispose of it!"

"Ah, of course. As you wish!" Anast bowed quickly, seeming unprepared for this reaction. The wolf's paws shook slightly as he worked to align some sort of medical device with the wound on Theta's arm. "Now...just allow me a moment to stop the bleeding. You've torn his brachial artery."

"If it dies, it will be none too soon. In fact, given your actions I believe I will do this service myself to be sure of it." The alien swung its neck forward and opened its jaws; its hot breath washed over the immobilized Theta, who stared helplessly up into a wide mouth filled with teeth, fear stealing his breath.

Anast stepped back, paws up, eyes wide.

"Gytriest! Stop." A familiar voice rang over Theta's shoulder, commanding and powerful.

The alien and Anast both turned, though Theta could only peer up at broad blood-stained teeth.

"Friend Rema, this one has stolen our essence. It is contaminated with *alinki*. It tried to kill you. I wish to end its existence. Is that not right? Is that not MY right?"

"Friend Gytriest," Rema stepped forward, softly resting a paw on the alien's long snout, "we are not done with it yet. It is the creation of an enemy, and it has not been acting of its own free will. The essence and the *alinki* were forced on it, as was its attempt on my life. Ending its existence is my right alone."

The alien identified as Gytriest drew back, sucking in a breath. "You...I see through you. I can see what you intend—you will not take this as a pet. I will not allow it! Do not require me to involve the council. It is evil!"

Lost and bewildered, Theta turned his head slightly to find the newcomer regarding him. The shock of meeting the eyes of the one he'd tried to kill shook him deeply He wrenched his gaze away and closed his eyes.

"Evil? Are you evil, Theta?" Rema's voice was soft.

"I must be." The words sprang unbidden to Theta's lips. "But I never meant to be."

He felt Rema's paw under his chin, lifting his head softly, and opened his eyes.

"If I let you go right now, placed a knife into your hand, and turned my back...would you try to kill me?"

"Yes," Theta murmured voicelessly. "Absolutely. It's not p-personal, but.." Suddenly overwhelmed by cognitive dissonance, Theta cringed back and bit his lip.

Not personal...just business.

".. But nothing is more personal than death, is it?" he whispered softly.

"I witness its words—this thing is already ruined. Killing it would be mercy." The alien said softly, voice persuasive. "It has nothing left to its existence, and can only pose danger."

"Do you want to die, young Theta?" Rema seemed to ignore Gytriest's comment entirely, eyes locked on Theta's. His voice was soft and calm, and Theta's breath caught.

"I..." Theta closed his eyes, partially to escape, partially to reach for the void inside him. It lay just beneath the surface, everpresent, and took no effort to tap. "I can't change this course I'm on. The alien is right."

"Alien?" Gytriest broke in almost petulantly, seemingly affronted. "Truly you are no blood kin of mine."

"Not now," Rema snapped to Gytriest, voice sharper than Theta had yet heard it. "This isn't simple, my friend. Theta, look at me."

Theta raised his head, opening his eyes. It was hard to look up to Rema's gaze, but he did. The fox moved close to him and lowered his voice to a soft murmur.

"You are not the first person to try to kill me, you know. You are not the first person to be shaped by your master and sent on a mission like this, either. You are not the first anything, but you are the sum of your life's story...and you are unique. I must go back to the bridge to oversee our departure, but I want you to survive at least as long as it takes me to get back."

"Why?" Theta asked simply.

"Because I don't want you dead before you understand the reason. Doesn't seem right." Rema spoke quickly, voice regaining its edgy quality. "Anast, take this one back and toss him in. Just...keep him there no matter who asks to see him. Unless it's me, of course. Friend Gytriest, please calm yourself." Rema turned and made a placating gesture to the agitated alien, who seemed to want no part of it. "Fresh memories sting the most, but memories without stories are words without song, right?"

"That is not your rede to repeat to me!" Gytriest growled, looming over the three. Theta found his chair spinning away as Anast quickly and quietly led him towards the door.

Swiveling his ears back, he could hear the alien's breathing mingle with Rema's soft, soothing words. As the door slid shut behind them, he let out his own lungful of air with a little sigh.

Anast paused once his chair was outside the door, turning back to peer at him with a strange look on his face.

"Well that was unique."

Some sort of black humor overtook Theta, and he snorted. "If the alien kills him now, can I take credit?"

The stare Anast leveled on him was chilling, and he immediately regretted his attempt at levity. The wolf turned and resumed his motion, and Theta held his tongue the rest of the way back to his little cell. Inside, Anast pushed him in roughly, aligning him to face the corner, then locked down his chair and left without a word.

Naane slid into the bridge office a step behind Jale, who engaged the privacy lock.

Jale could see the signs of exhaustion and worry creasing her XO's face. She already looked older by a decade. Standing up straight, Jale put on her best captain face, grateful at the reduction in discomfort. What she had to say would be difficult enough to sell standing tall, impossible if she were still hunched over. She raked Naane with a slightly challenging look.

"Dear, you must stop deferring! This is not a knock on your ability, but you're not thinking, and if you are you're not speaking. You're not acting autonomously, and I expect much more of you in that regard, both as my XO and as Naane. I want you to be coming to me with ideas, not waiting for mine. I plan to have the same talk with Krella, but the pair of you are acting like junior officers when you most certainly are not. Drive those ciphertechs to whatever end you see fit. Get out of the second in command chair and sit on near-side tactics, and give me real alternatives before I know that I need them. I have a great deal of faith in you, but I need you both to be the brilliant tacticians you are."

Naane looked a bit shaken. "Aye, ma'am. Sorry, ma'am. It's just...I've never done this before."

"Adapt," Jale snapped mercilessly.

"Aye, ma'am."

"I'm deadly serious," Jale was stern, and she kept her voice sharp. "Do you understand me?"

"Aye, ma'am!" Naane stood more stiffly to attention.

Jale let that hover in the air for a moment, then relaxed a bit, settling in. "Now, I didn't bring you in here to yell at you, dear. I'm sorry, but it's just a bad time for indecision and...well, what almost seems like apathy. I need fire from the two of you. Ah, me. The prime reason I called you here was that I have a job for Geff and that engineering second of yours. I'd like you to oversee it, though I need you to stay at my right hand."

"Ma'am?"

Jale leaned against her desk, shifting up onto its top and crossing her ankles. "This is a big one, in some ways. I need Geff to come up with a contingency plan..." The words came hard, but she plowed on. "I need a plan for putting the crew off. If things go sour, or if they've already gone sour, I mean to give the crew the best chance of survival I can and take *Dancer* off to draw away Knoskali's pursuit. The ship may require a minimum crew to run for any length of time, and so I'll eventually need volunteers...but not yet."

"Ma'am?" Naane's face was slack. "Do you think...I mean...he really means to kill us if we fail?"

Jale closed her eyes and leaned forward, resting her chin on her folded paws. "Oh I most certainly believe so."

"Then he will, regardless of what you do." Naane sounded certain. "He doesn't fail."

"But my dear, consider a little thing: if we fail, he *has* failed. Now take your personal opinions and superstitions and push them aside; Knoskali is a very powerful individual, yes, but he is no god. He has an incredible intelligence department, but it's not infallible. You read those messages. You try and tell me that they were written by someone in complete control of a situation. Go on, tell me! I defy you to tell me that." Jale kicked herself from her desk and paced her small office. "And then, failing that, I would not care if he were a god, oh no. Your orders are to come up with a plan that will work to keep as many alive for as long as possible, and that is that. Do you understand? Even if it means full surrender."

"Yes, ma'am."

"Now I know his reputation, Naane, but I also know that you are quite good at what you do. You can't outreach him, no; you can't overpower him, and you most certainly can't out-strategize him. What do you have? Cunning and guile. Cunning and guile. Nothing is off-limits. Give this plan your second best."

"Aye, ah...Second best, ma'am?"

Jale smirked softly. "Yes. That's whyfor I wish you to involve Geff for the heavy lifting. I still want your mind turned mostly to the problem at hand. If we can find Theta, we don't need to worry. This is about survival, got it?"

"Yes, ma'am."

"Good." Jale clasped her paws behind her back, inclining her head towards the door. "Get Geff started on that contingency. Get to the tactics station and be creative. Drive the ciphertechs relentlessly. Use your initiative. Make me proud. Dismissed!"

Jale held her mask of confidence as she watched Naane leave. As the doors slid shut, she sank into her chair, face settling into its normal lines of private worry.

XVII

Coterie

"THERE THEY GO. They are definitely going! All of them."

Jale sat up with a start, dropping the remains of a protein bar onto her terminal and shifting her attention to the main display. Though wide awake, she felt sluggish and her vision was notably fuzzy; it took effort for her to focus on the velocity indicators. She frowned, unable to determine anything from them that would lead to Krella's conclusion.

"I'm afraid I don't quite see it yet, mister Krella, but if you're absolutely sure then please do initiate acceleration right now."

"I am absolutely sure. Let's go!"

"Aye, sir," the helmsman began working quickly at his controls. "Curve?"

"Normal curve," Jale interjected quickly. "Tac, disconnect all links and shut down radiometric interpolation. Weapons, please be ready on the ECM should things go awry." She thumbed the ship's intercom. "General quarters, general quarters. All hands to their stations."

Naane tapped her on the shoulders. "Cipher just sent me a message. They say it just came in for you from Arvinne."

Jale started to speak, but found that her voice caught. She swallowed in surprise, trying to suppress the unexpected relief that washed over her. Nobody was out of the woods yet.

But he's alive.

She closed her mouth and nodded back to her XO. "Very well. For now, we must focus on the task at hand."

"We are, ma'am." Naane quirked her eyebrow. "All departments report ready, and all of our acceleration numbers are nominal. Detectable particles are on the high side, but there's enough background noise from the other departures that we're ok. Don't have much to say, but I thought I should let you know."

Jale cringed softly. "Oh I wasn't criticizing, dear. That was more for me than for you."

Naane nodded. "Sorry, ma'am. Long day."

Jale smiled. That had become a running joke. She rubbed her eyes with a paw, blinking blearily.

"Right. Helm?"

"We're at thirty percent and increasing right on curve, ma'am. Plating sensors are all green."

"Very good." Jale subsided, settling back into her chair and watching the tactical projection as the large ships began to accelerate, far behind them.

The run up to Rellin drive went with perfect efficiency. As they neared entry velocity, Jale was amused to note that the indicators on the main display had finally decided that the movement of the fleet as preparatory to acceleration. How Krella had been able to tell so early Jale had no idea, but she silently praised his abilities.

Varaunt, clearly under escort by the larger vessels, had shifted its identity broadcast to match those of the fleet.

"Threshold velocity, ma'am. Rellin engaged...And we're in."

The red "stale" flag popped up on Jale's screen as the ship entered drive and contact data was lost.

She pushed the console away.

"Good work, Helm. Most excellent. I think that's our best time to drive yet. Tac, assuming they travel in formation, what is their time in drive?"

"Their shortest LOA is longer than ours. Computer estimates we'll arrive slightly after them, about plus thirty."

Jale nodded, clasping her paws together. "That's a hair later than I'd like, but it will quite possibly work to our advantage. Our time enroute is thirty hours?"

"About twenty-nine and a half, Captain."

"Very well. I shall rest for a little while. Obviously you shouldn't hesitate to call me if something comes up between now and then. You have the bridge, XO."

"Aye, ma'am."

Once off the bridge, Jale jogged immediately to her quarters, kicking off her boots and sliding out of her ship-suit once she was in the door. Jewel was asleep in his little alcove, but she snuck quietly past him into her sleeping section and closed the divider. Turning to her terminal, she pulled up Arvinne's message.

> *(Captain!?) Jelly,*
> *I'm just flummoxed to hear from you. Things are a bit messy at the moment, but I've met some of these Dazi and they're most of them real nice to us. Haven't seen Theta today at all, sorry to say. Bet he'd want to add his own message. Congratulations on being made captain! I'm in a nice cushy cook job here. You'd be proud.*
> *Proud of you!*
> *Your friend,*
> *-Arvinne*

A warm glow spread within Jale as she read his message; though she had no idea why, his words both touched and reassured her. She closed the terminal and lay back in her bed.

Arvinne was alive. Perhaps everything would turn out right after all.

Jale knelt beside Pinky's bed in the little infirmary late the next day. He was sleeping restlessly, shifting and moving often; a very soft whirring and clicking from beneath the sheets told Jale that his replacement arm had been fitted and was operating as fitfully as the rest of him.

She sniffed softly, looking around the darkened, red-lit room. Between Pinky and the other two 'residents', all of the permanent beds were taken. However, the row of cots that had tripled the capacity of the little room was now absent, she noted happily, as its former inhabitants had all recovered sufficiently to return to their own bunks.

And Arvinne was alive and well.

His message, short though it had been, had raised her mood. Even in through the mental fuzziness, that shaky, achy withdrawal state that she had previously ascribed to gross fatigue, his simple, merry words had kept a smile on her lips and a little lilt in her step. In absolute defiance of logic, it was a seed of hope, a catalyst that had fragmented the hopelessness she hadn't realized she'd felt. After a ten hour sleep, she'd woken up feeling physically horrible but emotionally wonderful.

Driving her tactics staff hard for half a shift, she'd been surprised to note that they responded to her newfound enthusiasm in kind. Despite the bleak situation, morale among her senior staff was higher than it had been for quite some time, and by the time she'd taken her leave to visit Pinky, the entire tactics department was working energetically on the full contingency tree.

She smiled to herself.

Perhaps, if they were just lucky enough...

"Miss Jale!" Pinky sat up quickly, causing Jale to jump. She wasn't sure what had woken him, but suddenly awake he was, sitting up straight in his bed and looking as if he was trying to figure out the best way to stand.

"Pinky!" Jale whispered stridently, leaning down to rest a paw on his chest. "Lie back down, dear. Your arm..."

"...Is fine." Pinky flashed his teeth in a little grin, then raised it for her to inspect, voice lowered to a hushed murmur. "My arm is just fine—I've already been released, ma'am, as far as the books are concerned. I'm just here in case Jelith goes back into respiratory arrest. They're growing him a new set of lungs now, they say."

"Oh. Yes. Hum, yes, I'd heard about that." Jale was distracted by the fact that Pinky's arm looked basically normal, and that was not at all what she'd been expecting. Its articulation didn't seem quite as smooth as he demonstrated the motions of his digits, but even so, it mostly just looked like a normal arm and hand, stiff from disuse. Having lost the course of her thoughts, she merely shook her head. "I... goodness. I'd expected something much less...ah, complete. So they've released you already, have they?"

"Yes ma'am. They say it's as good as it's going to get. Fully integrated, is what they said."

"And you've full use of it?"

"Yes ma'am!" Pinky spoke a little too loudly, then winced. Glancing at his roommates, both dead to the world in drug-induced sleep, he lowered his muzzle and his voice.

"Yes ma'am. Mostly. It's still adapting to me, and some things I try to do are a little jerky, but it's actually stronger and quicker than my old arm." He grinned up at her, looking a bit sly. "Almost makes me want to have the other one done to match."

Despite the obvious intent of humor, Jale was unable to dampen a full-body expression of revulsion. She found herself turning slightly away and shaking her head.

"I'm just kidding, ma'am." Pinky was suddenly serious, ears flattening back a bit. "It's—"

"No, it's fine." Jale spoke too quickly, grinning slightly. She knew that her expressions were probably an odd jumble, and tried to get herself back under control. "I'm afraid—ahhh!"

Between one word and the next, Jale's stomach flopped. She clutched at her belly in a moment of extreme disorientation before she realized that the ship's gravity had gone out.

"Oh, that is *not* good." She reached a hand out to Pinky, who was clutching to his bedframe. His paw crushed hers slightly as he dragged her back down towards the deck, but she managed no more than a little grunt as she found herself a handhold.

"Captain to the bridge!" Naane's voice rang through the public address, rapid but calm. "All hands, set condition one—General quarters! Ship is now rigging for zero gravity and stealth. You have ten seconds to clear away from the stanchion bars before I deploy them."

The lights flickered.

Jale cursed a vile curse. It had never seemed quite appropriate before. She dragged herself to the terminal on the wall, swiping her paw and thumbing the intercom.

"Bridge, this is the captain," she growled. "What the hell is going on?"

For a long moment, there was silence; before Jale could close down the terminal and slither out the door on her way to the bridge, however, Naane's voice crackled back over the circuit.

"Ma'am, just get up here. Stanchion bars are coming out now, so use them to drag yourself up here as fast as you can. It—"

The transmission cut off with a little pop.

"Pinky, you're coming with me."

"Jelith—"

"—Will have to fend for himself. This is Ososkne's station, so there should be two people to take over for you in less than a minute. Come!"

Jale kicked herself off, sliding expertly through the door. Turning to look behind her, she found the husky clinging to his bed for dear life.

"Pinky?"

"I—ma'am..."

"Pinky, come this way. There will be handholds along the corridor, but I want you on the bridge."

"I don't know how," he all but whimpered. "I feel sick."

It took Jale a moment to realize that Pinky hadn't been a spacer, and that meant that he hadn't spent the hundreds of hours performing the emergency drills—many without artificial gravity—that most ship's crew were intimately familiar with. She shook her head at her thoughtlessness.

"Right. Sorry, dear. You stay."

She turned and half swam down to the stanchion rail which was extended from the walls of the corridor. Hand-over-hand, she worked her way to the G-tube and up to the bridge.

The door was on lockdown, but opened to her paw-swipe. She kicked towards her chair, dodging a slightly tumbling helmsman, struggling to fight off the nearly overwhelming sensation that the ship was on its side. When she got her bearings, she noticed that to her shock the ship had exited Rellin drive and had slowed below two-thirds of threshold velocity. The bridge was eerily silent.

"Naane! Report."

"Well, you must be the captain." A steely satin voice brought Jale immediately to alertness. She pulled herself into her chair and fastened the thigh straps, still fighting the sensation that she was leaned over. Glaring up to the bridge's main display, she saw an unfamiliar canid face supported by a very trim uniform.

"You have the advantage of me, I fear." Jale fixed her gaze grimly on his collar tabs.

"That is my job," the canid snapped humorlessly. "You will stand down your stealth systems instantly or we will destroy you."

Jale glanced briefly at Naane, who returned a wide-eyed nod. Her stomach clenched.

"Very well. Helm, secure from stealth mode."

"Aye, ma'am."

For a long moment she and her adversary simply stared at one another. Jale maintained a careful neutrality, trying to think of what lines she could play if pressed.

He spoke first.

"Very good. Now depower your engines, Captain. We will cease jamming your internal systems once your vessel is dead in space. You will immediately begin preparations to receive our boarding party and to transfer command. You are being detained as a hostile force; if you fail to comply with our instructions, or if you offer any resistance, we will destroy you. Acknowledge."

"Acknowledged," Jale's throat was tight. She snuck another glance at her panel, finding *Dancer* slowing between five other ships, caught tightly. The display indicated hot weapons, and she felt a little creep crawl up her back. "We will comply."

With a curt nod, the canid immediately cut the channel.

Around the bridge, there was a stunned silence.

"What is the name of your ship?"

Jale sighed, leaning back in the same squeaky chair. Predictably, it squeaked. She'd lost track of the number of times she'd been asked that question since being brought aboard the Dazi frigate what seemed like days before, and her normally deep reserve of patience was wearing thin. Somehow they seemed to have an inexhaustible supply of interrogators and a tiny pool of questions, though they had otherwise treated her with respect. She closed her eyes and rested her paws behind her head, tired and bored.

"Once again, dear, the name of my ship is '*Dancer*'. Pocket cruiser, in the service of House Selesz of Brynton. My name, and I tell you again only since you seem to forget all this regardless of how often I repeat it, is Jale Bercammon of Ramesan, unlimited tonnage master."

The short cervid across the desk from her tapped her fingers on its flat surface; Jale cracked her eyes to find her staring at her.

"Captain Bercammon, please constrain your responses to simple answers of the questions I ask."

"Oh now why would I do that, dear? I'm bored stiff."

To her surprise, the deer seemed to be fighting back a grin. "Fair. Captain, what do you know of the Circle of Calus?"

"Ah, bless me...that's a completely new question! Are you sure you didn't mean to ask me about where I come from...again? Well, as for your Circle of Calus, I've never heard of it."

"Them. It's a them." her questioner snorted. "What of the Caylum?"

"Haven't heard of those, either, I'm sorry to say," Jale shook her head.

"Have you ever heard the name Rema?"

Jale shook her head, though her ears pricked a little.

"Galendron?"

"No."

"What about Myshel?"

Jale drew a little breath, sitting straighter. A moment of consideration passed before she nodded solemnly.

"Well now, there's a question. That is indeed a name that I recognize, an alias for the fox named Theta that I've spoken about before."

The deer simply nodded at this. "Of course. And Knoskali?"

"You know I know him. As I've explained on many occasions, he funded this ship, and provided this crew, oh yes. Our mission was to find and rescue Theta."

"Rescue?"

That apparently was rather a confusing point for their captors, whom Jale assumed were associated with the mysterious Dazi. She wondered why they seemed to have such trouble with the concept.

"Yes. I've spent what feels like hours telling and retelling the whole story. Shall I start again?"

"Not this time, Captain. That won't be necessary. Back to names. Do you know Terial?"

"No. I've never heard of anyone by that name."

"As you've said before. Would you tell us if you had?"

"In this case, yes," Jale said with what she hoped was an honest-looking nod. While she had so far needed to hide nothing, the extra scrutiny had her second-guessing what should be normal reactions. This time, she went unquestioned.

"Very well, Captain. And you did not know of an assassination plot against Rema?"

"I did not," Jale dropped her voice to an inviting, inquisitive little murmur. "Please, tell me more."

The deer pushed back from the table and stood, smoothly shrugging her jacket back onto her broad shoulders. She gazed down at Jale, expression blank.

"That's all I have to ask you tonight. Rest assured that we do feel you're cooperating, and your cooperation is appreciated. Please don't take our repetition or requests for clarification on certain points to indicate otherwise."

"Of course not," Jale murmured politely. "I understand that you're doing your job. Could you perhaps tell me what that job is?"

The deer raised her eyebrows.

"Good night, Captain."

The hard-looking young soldier assigned as Jale's escort, assistant and guard stood. Jale stood, too.

"My cabin?"

"If you like, Captain. During your conversation, I received a message I was to relay. We've arrived at Zyktona, and our commander has signaled to request a short, informal meeting with you on the surface. Five hours from now, about 04:00 ship time. You don't need my advice, I'm sure, but if you were to ask me I'd suggest you be frank and open with him. He's very smart, but has a reputation for being very fair."

Surprised by the small hyena's departure from taciturnity, she allowed herself to be led out of the little room before clearing her throat.

"I see. Now, if I asked again what this...interdiction was about, I assume I would still be greeted with the same tight-lipped silence as all the other times?"

"You would from me, Captain."

"Wait," Jale stopped, and he did too. "Not to nibble on the edges of how much you want to divulge, but could you perhaps tell me the extent of our situation? Obviously there's nothing in my power to do about it, but I would like to ensure that the sovereignty of my flag is intact."

"That much I can tell you, Captain. We have committed no intrusions upon your sovereignty. Your vessel is merely detained and under escort." He paused, hesitated, then shook his head. "Well, actually, we did take your wounded into our care, with the permission of your surgeon. He was doing an exemplary job, I'm told, given his tools, but our facilities are...mm, significantly more advanced."

Something niggled in Jale's memory about admissibility of testimony of personnel lawfully aboard an interdicting vessel. Space law was a very weak point for her, having been considered the least of her worries, but she was suddenly alert.

"I see. My surgeon may have authorized the transfer, but let me please be clear: I will have no interrogations under the guise of help unless you wish to contest our flag."

The guard fixed her with an annoyed stare. "Captain, I know how you Brynti can be, but we're not like that. We have no interest in games of subterfuge. If we pursue action against your sovereignty, which we may legally do if we determine you're a belligerent entity, you can take it from me that we'll just flat out tell you. There will be nothing subtle about it."

"You seem to know an awful lot for a guard, dear," Jale poked softly. "Is this your normal duty?"

"This isn't the ship's normal function, so no. Not intending to be rude, but as to my job I have nothing further I can tell you." He nodded down the corridor. "If you would please, Captain?"

With a little resigned sigh, Jale gestured for him to lead on; he brought her back to the little cabin to which she was confined and unlocked the door.

"Goodnight, Captain." He nodded amiably enough, holding the door for her. She dipped her head in reply, then stepped inside. The door was locked behind her and she exhaled a tired little sigh. As she went to settle into her bed, however, she was surprised to notice that the room's little terminal was unlocked, illuminating the wall. She hadn't been granted access before.

Something was displayed on its screen.

Jale leaned forward to look, with a little puzzled frown.

❖

"Get up."

Theta opened his eyes, and immediately closed them again against a splitting headache that seemed to suck the breath from his body with its intensity.

"Ut," he groaned. He felt hot all over, and he could immediately feel himself beginning to sweat.

"Come on, get up." The voice cajoled softly. It seemed warm and amused.

"Hrf," he muttered. Even that single noise caused his head to throb. It felt as though it were being crushed, splitting down the middle. "hrf..."

"Their absence will have left him with a massive hormonal imbalance." A weasely little voice penetrated his awareness. "I can give him an adrenaline shot and an analgesic if you need him up."

"Yeah, I do. He's been asleep long enough."

After a moment, a cool sensation spread through Theta's back and down to his belly and, though his nose began to run noticeably, the pain began to immediately recede. After a few minutes, he took the chance of opening his eyes slightly, blinking them against the light.

What he saw seemed grossly unusual.

The face near his own looked familiar, but he couldn't figure out why. There was far, far too much light and heat, and purple hues formed a disjointed bokeh behind a set of blurry figures dressed in black. He was seated, but the world spun slowly around.

Nausea gripped him hard, and he fell sideways from what he was seated on, landing on his knees and paws. He vomited softly into what felt suspiciously like dirt against his pawpads. Helpless, he emptied his stomach of bile before collapsing weakly to his side, shaking softly.

"I'm afraid, my little Theta, that we're not really that merciful. Can you see?"

He tried to open his eyes again, but the world was just as disjointed as before, and nausea reclaimed him nearly instantly. He rolled onto his back, away from his mess.

"I was afraid of that," the weaselly one moaned. "I thought we had purged their influence on his optic nerve, but I fear he may now be blind. Or his brains could be scrambled eggs."

"Theta?" The warm voice from earlier was suddenly serious and sad. "Can you hear me? Just nod if you can."

Theta growled, lifting a paw to cover his eyes. "I can see. Very dizzy. Where am I?"

"What's the last thing that you remember?" The voice sounded relieved.

Theta paused, frozen in time.

Memory?

Memory failed. Nothing came back. Suddenly a feeling of overpowering loss gripped him, and he found himself sobbing uncontrollably, still nauseous. He curled around his paws, stomach clenched.

"Oh come on," a different voice chimed in, annoyed. It was waspy but melodic. Velveteen. It, too, sounded familiar to Theta's ears. "Are we ever going to get past the melodrama and into some sort of judgement? Rema—"

"Judgement is mine, Onari. Mine alone, I'll have you note, for purposes of flag and commission. Theta," warm paws touched his shoulders, flattening white fur warmed by a strange heat, intrinsically familiar but from memories beyond recall. "What's the matter with you?"

"I—" Theta shook, tears pouring down his nose. Something was missing. Something black, a part of him that did not answer. "I can't remember anything at all."

"Doctor!" Rema sounded perturbed. "I specifically said—"

"No, no, no, no, no!" The thin-voiced one protested. "It's fine. I just checked him over, and he's merely adapting to the loss of genetic replication."

"But the gift remains, right?"

"YES, yes, yes Commander. It is largely dormant, as we promised Gytriest. The Elech will be satisfied, although encoding will continue. Your Theta is currently experiencing a cortico-thalamic feedback cycle as a result of the loss of his genetic memory. Once that is broken, he will undergo a period of inhibited axon function through the entire region. Nominal activity will resume only after the Warmann cycle. I explained that this was a possibility."

Theta wanted to cover his ears. His brain desperately tried to correlate and define, but no data was returned—it was an almost physical discomfort. He felt a firm hand touch his head, squeeze an ear, touch his nose...but he kept his eyes firmly shut, reminded of the consequence of opening them.

"You said it was a remote possibility. Remote. You put other things in that category, too, like permanent loss of memory."

"You are impossible." The doctor's voice quavered. "I'm going to put him back under for two more hours to get him through his window. If he has troubles after then, then and only then should we worry."

"Fine, fine. Do that, if it's safe. Make sure he's awake by eighteen-thirty, and make sure you're done meddling. And he better have his memory back. I'll want you to leave me alone with him for a bit before our little party."

"What? Alone?" Onari snapped. "What, so he can have another chance at you? Rema, I—"

"Was not asked, fair Onari. Don't worry. I handled him easily when he was armed and at his prime. I definitely don't fear him now. I want to have a chance to just talk, without all the posturing."

"So what about the captain of the covert ship? She's scheduled—"

"I'll still make my appointment with her. C'mon, you know me. Besides, it's not like she's going anywhere. I'll bump up my meeting with Janesson, and then have her sent down. We can send the fleet home as soon as I'm done, though. You can relay that to the...admiralty." Theta could hear a laugh in his voice. "Oh, and send my thanks along, as well."

"Yes, master," Onari was acerb and sarcastic. "Do you have any other orders for me?"

"Sure! Get preparations underway for our little summit tomorrow. Get my PsyOps staff ready to come land-side for this one, but we should probably release the fleet. We'll keep *Ghekke* and *Coil* on high station, of course. Send them out and bring them back, just in case we have any more fleas. And..." he paused. "You know, prime the net, if you would — Not sure why, but I'm feeling a bit edgy. Inform our boys and activate it as soon as they jump out."

"Should we be talking around *this*?" Onari's tone was increasingly acid. "Are we certain he won't remember this little conversation?"

"He will most certainly not." The doctor's voice was close to Theta's ear, and he could feel something cool pressing against his side. "As I explained to you, the Warmann cycle—"

"I'm sure, I'm sure—I remember." Rema interrupted, brushing off a technical dissertation he seemed determined to avoid. "Eighteen-thirty, Doctor. He and I have business."

Theta felt a little tremor pass through his body, and a nothingness began to spread to his limbs.

"If you go and get yourself killed," Onari hissed, "I...I—"

"Will die alone and heartbroken after a life of celibacy and theological study, I know. I won't. Now shoo."

Janesson gazed idly across the large warehouse space. Nearly a thousand people milled about aimlessly, a huge rabble with no cohesive structure or intent.

He'd never seen all his personnel in one place before.

Somehow, he reflected, the ship gave structure to its crew just as it was brought to life by them. Without the ship, his reasonably efficient, well-organized crew was disorganized, disoriented and lost.

He'd been idly mulling over such concepts in silence since their arrival several hours ago. Unloaded batch by batch onto the ramp of a desolate shuttleport, high on a lonely plateu above a wide expanse of sea, they had been outside on the purple-hued planet for less than an hour before being collectively herded under guard into a giant, empty warehouse space.

To his people, he had little to talk about—there was little to be said. Occasionally, confused or worried faces would turn his way looking for answers, but he had none to give. Defeat was an unfamiliar state. People seemed generally uncomfortable around him, as if unsure what to say; at every turn, however, Jenks sat by him in stony silence, a public affirmation of his faith.

He didn't feel he deserved it. Even if he hadn't *betrayed* his people by surrendering, he had certainly *failed* them by trusting Theta. Even the thought of that treacherous creature made him sick with anger.

"Captain Janesson? Quartermaster Jenks?" A smooth voice broke in at his elbow, startling him from his funk. He glanced up to find a sweaty, blue-clad opossum with dark goggles on his forehead and a comset in his ear.

He set his snack bar aside, rising from his chair.

"Yes?"

"Commander Rema would like a word with the pair of you."

He snorted and locked eyes with a weary-looking Jenks, then turned back. "*Commander* Rema, is it? Yeah, that makes more sense." He sighed. "Well, we're obviously at his disposal."

"Of course." A little smugness leaked into the opossum's tone. He fished around in a little haversack, then drew out two sets of goggles identical to his own. "Right this way. You'll want these."

The officer led them past the crew of *Varaunt*, past the heavily armed guards at the exit, and out across the tarmac. The air stank of unfettered floral bloom; masses of water vapor built in the sky, forming into towering grey mountains that floated ominously through the atmosphere building dangerous levels of energy, threatening to dissipate it randomly through whatever was in its way. The heat was far above shipboard nominal, and the humidity levels were barely survivable, and yet every surface was contaminated with uncontained life. Even the direct impact of radiation from a nearby star bathing the tarmac was insufficient to sterilize it; organic matter persisted, even broke through the thick concrete in places.

Janesson shuddered, wiping the sweat from the bridge of his muzzle, careful to keep his eyes covered.

Planets were truly the stuff of nightmares.

As they walked on towards the cluster of buildings that made up the commercial terminal, crossing nearly the entire shuttleport, Janesson took slight comfort in noting that it was not he alone who was uncomfortable. Sweat soaked through the back of the Dazi's blue shipsuit, and he seemed to be slowly wilting in the heat; as soon as he reached the door he'd been angling towards, he yanked it open and ushered them inside the darkened, cooled interior. After a brief pause for eyes to adjust, Janesson and Jenks were chivvied into a small meeting room and bid to wait, the door quickly closed behind them.

"Well," Jenks muttered, "it's a nice planet, but I hope we don't stay here."

"What would you have had me do?" Janesson growled, voice cracking. He turned on his quartermaster, taking a step closer. "If we had fought, we would have died, and there's no profit in that. Everybody bought in on the idea that got us into this situation to begin with, including you. I will absolutely take responsibility to my crew, but what do you want from me?"

Jenks stared at him for a long moment, broad muzzle hanging open slightly. "Not what I meant! You haven't done anything wrong. I didn't mean to—"

"I got suckered by that little...that little *niiza*."

"Captain..." Jenks seemed uncharacteristically uncomfortable. "There's something I should tell you."

"Gentlemen?" The soft, amused voice came from a head protruding through the open door. "If I'm not interrupting."

"No, come in." Janesson lowered his voice and sank into a chair, slightly embarrassed.

"Gentlemen." Rema entered, gesturing for them to be seated. A tall black jackal with blood-red hair and silver piercings along the outside of his ears flowed in behind him, lean and lithe. While Rema flopped nonchalantly into one of the padded chairs across from the pirates, his sinuous companion leaned back against the wall and said nothing.

"Well, I've got most of the story pieced together now, I think, and I'm comfortable talking. First, to hopefully calm your nerves, I want to just make it clear again that your whole crew will be spared. Even better, I will let your ship go, and put 'em back on it. As you probably expect, there are a few caveats." He trailed off, looking expectantly at Janesson.

"Go on?" Janesson perked his ears.

"First, recruitment. Namely you. Your familiarity with certain operations, however old and wan it may be, will prove...ah, valuable to my interests. I'll leave it at that. You have a great deal of local knowledge that I want. This isn't an unpaid position, and it's not an ultimatum. You can say no."

"But you'd rather I didn't." Janesson scowled, resting his paws on the table. "You want to strike back at Knoskali?"

Rema shrugged noncommittally. "Interesting idea. What if I did?"

"Then I could help."

"I'm sure you could," the fox murmured. "Quartermaster Jenks, I assume that you'd retain command of *Varaunt*?"

"Tully is more than capable," Jenks answered slowly, almost reluctantly. "I have local knowledge of Brynton as well. And some detailed knowledge of the House Selesz intelligence arm."

Janesson glanced sidelong at Jenks, with whom he'd spent almost every moment of countless years. Rema seemed equally caught off-guard, if only for a moment; his companion shifted, stiffening slightly.

"Jenks? What do you mean?" Janesson's mouth was dry; conjecture had beaten him to the point.

"I was going to tell you. I should have told you earlier. Years earlier. I was the contact on *Varaunt* for their intelligence department until about half a year ago. My...partner... we became estranged." Jenks stared down at the table, his deep voice soft but monotone.

Rema looked fascinated, black ears perked. He gestured for the quartermaster to continue.

Janesson just ground his teeth, feeling anger build within him.

"We had a daughter and a son. Took them both onboard a transport to Fonaci when she found out I was a pirate. I didn't know until I took shore leave three standard months later. I had several messages. First from her, very short. The second from a law bureau on Fonaci. Third a menacing request for arrears taxes on Brynton. The fourth, a death certificate for my wife and son, 'lawfully terminated fleeing authority' on Brynton. Don't know how they ended up there. Never will."

He paused, and the silence was absolute. After a moment, he hung his head and closed his eyes. "Daughter was alive, but listed only as 'seized'. Tried for months to find out what that meant, never got a response. Got a message half a year later, after I'd given up hope. From someone named Terial within the House Selesz intelligence department. Daughter's life for intel—I'm sure you can fill in the rest. Promised I wouldn't have to betray my crew, and I never did. He wanted reports, steered us to targets. Sometimes very nice ones, so I didn't feel too bad. When Alixa...My daughter...when she died," his words came out in a rush, "Terial sent me a personal message the same day. There had been an accident, he was sorry for my loss, and my services were no longer required. Nearly punched through the terminal."

"I remember that. At the time—"

"Nevermind what I said. I lied. I lied a lot back then. Captain, I know..."

Janesson turned half away, then turned back. Jenks wasn't really looking at him.

"You could have told me at least."

"I'm sorry. Couldn't risk her life."

"Theta? Was he another convenient target we were steered to by Knoskali?"

"No." Jenks looked at the table. "At least, if he was it wasn't my doing."

"Gentlemen," Rema broke in, voice calm, "I'm sorry to be rude, but at the moment my time is finite. The nature of your affairs is not my concern, and as for us, we'll happily take you both, pending somatic scan. I'm almost afraid to bring up the next issue now, but...I was going to ask you," he nodded to Jenks, "to do for me exactly what you were apparently doing for Knoskali's house."

"Have Dela do it," Janesson muttered. "She's as mercenary as they come. She'll have no compunction about such dealings. Jenks...I honestly don't blame you."

"You should, Captain." The hyena's jaw muscles worked visibly under his fur as he clenched his teeth together. "I took oath to the crew..."

"I won't." Janesson rested a paw on his shoulder. "Blood is the first loyalty, and if what you say is true, you didn't truly betray the crew, and you didn't betray me."

There was a long pause, and the silence stretched on.

Rema stood, seeming a bit embarrassed. "Well. I'll track down your Dela and have a word with her. For now, you may return to your crew. Don't say anything yet, please—I don't want to give anyone the wrong idea. Got it? Good. Onari, have Bri take them back. I'll be here with the captain."

The jackal nodded silently.

Towering above the shuttleport, the great clouds had grown far into the planet's stratosphere, stretching many miles above the surface; a cooling zephyr washed across the tarmac accompanied by a rumble of thunder, ushering the few transient Dazi towards shelter with the threat of rain. Across the broken paving, the trespassing tendrils of plantlife that had forced their way to the surface rustled softly in the breeze, before being trodden into the ground by an oblivious boot. Their fragile structure broken, the life crushed from them, their lifetime struggle to survive against all odds came suddenly and irrevocably to an end.

Jale didn't notice the swath of destruction she left in her wake as she was escorted from the shuttle pod to the terminal building—her mind was on other things. Her own lifetime and her own future hung in the balance, and she was on dangerous ground. Thoughts raced through her head, many repeated, and her restlessness betrayed the weight of her conscience; her sense of right and wrong, which she'd intended to guide her actions, suddenly seemed amorphous and conflicted, and she found herself without the protections of any objective morality.

The message that had awaited her in her cabin the night before had been a lifeline that she had clung to with all her might, and she had quickly made her secretive reply without even pausing to consider the ramifications. Denied moral guidance and flailing in an information vacuum, she had taken the path walked often over thousands of years—she had fallen back on her duty.

Pieces were now in motion that could not be stopped.

Just before she and her guard reached the door of the little terminal, it opened to emit a white wolf and a burly hyena, escorted by a wolf in a black shipsuit. The white wolf paused as he passed, staring at her; glancing back at him, she was surprised to recognize the leader of the band of pirates that had sacked the *Freeta*. Both parties were urged to continue forward, and she stepped into the terminal with only one more quick peek over her shoulder. She was brought into a small, dim room where a friendly looking red fox in a simple black shipsuit waited behind a desk. He awarded her a little reassuring smile and indicated that she should be seated. As she was settling into her chair, a black shadow walked around her in near silence. Circling the desk, the black jackal took up a casually alert position against the wall beside the fox, folding his arms across his chest. A moment later, to her surprise, Naane was escorted through and seated beside her.

She turned to her XO with a wintry little smile, quickly studying her face for any sign of distress. "Good to see you, XO. How is the ship and crew?"

Naane glanced quickly up to the fox, then back to her as if afraid to speak out of turn. "Fine so far, ma'am. They brought me down here a few hours ago."

"Good, good. Thank you." Jale turned back to the fox. He looked indeterminately young, and she wasn't entirely sure he wasn't some junior officer standing in. Something about the way he carried himself made her doubt it; she lifted her chin in challenge. "You. I assume that you're the commander?"

"My name is Rema," he replied, folding his arms on the table and leaning forward. "Apparently, I was your little assassin's target."

Jale damped her emotions as much as she could, locking eyes with him. "I realize that it doesn't likely signify, but we did not know that at the time, oh no. When I left Brynton, I had two goals: Rescue Theta and Arvinne, and keep my crew safe."

"You transmitted his orders."

"Double encrypted, of course. That's not just plausible deniability, you realize."

"Right down to it, hm? I am not quite ready to concede that point." He leaned back. "You claim that you're working under the orders of Knoskali himself, and that you're under a death sentence if you fail. Is that right?"

"Well, that's certainly one way to put it."

Rema nodded to her. "Well, that all logically checks out, and my intelligence and PsyOps personnel have been working overtime. We mostly believe you. What if I were to offer you and your crew amnesty in my service? I can practically guarantee your protection, if you'd consent to being split up, and we're always recruiting, for the right calibre of misfits."

Jale stiffened just a little, breath quickening. She hadn't considered that possibility, and she was momentarily shaken from the mental course she'd set.

She forced her emotion deep—his words were likely just a test. It was too late now, regardless. She was committed. Painting what she hoped would look like a thoughtful frown, she shook her head slowly.

"Hmm. That does actually make sense, in a way, but it's more complicated than that, of course. It's not solely the threat of retaliation, really." She felt as though she were picking her way through an asteroid field; in her peripheral vision, she could see Naane squirm. "I...suppose that's more just an incentive."

Rema was completely unreadable as he gazed at her. "Well, then. You claim to have nothing whatsoever to hide. No secrets you're afraid to divulge, no lies that you've told me."

"That is correct," Jale said warily. "To the best of my knowledge."

"So a simple somatic scan, just to prove that you're not hiding anything...that would be ok, right? I have the equipment right outside."

Jale fought down her shock of fear, replacing it with synthetic anger. She stood, bringing a paw down on the desk. "Now that...sir, that will not do. That is a gross violation of our sovereignty," she improvised. "And doubly, a gross violation of my rights."

"It was an offer to help clear up this little...misunderstanding." Rema seemed a bit hurt. "It wasn't a threat. Still, I wasn't aware that Brynton guaranteed its citizens any sort of rights," the fox retorted coyly, glancing sidelong at her. "A world that has little provision for galactic law hasn't earned a lot of diplomacy in return."

"In reality, I am not a citizen of Brynton but of Ramesan," Jale tried to shift the conversation, thinking hard. That wasn't quite right and she knew it, but she needed time.

"Ah Ramesan. Yes, the accent...that could be. Fascinating government, theirs." The fox tapped his claws on the little table, then stood and began to pace, brow furrowed slightly. "Really fascinating. Not quite fascinating enough to extend their protection to the actions of a citizen acting as captain on a foreign-flagged ship, but still fascinating."

He rested his paws on his hips, then turned back to Jale with a strange expression. "Actually, onto a different subject, equally fascinating: you know the little assassin. His memories of you are strange but there. He remembers you clearly. He doesn't remember you as a captain but as a low ranking officer attending to passengers, so I'm a little confused as to how you fit in, and why you're here. I have your interrogation records, but they're all about your ship and your mission. Your XO here I have a full dossier on, pulled from our intelligence network." He inclined his head to Naane—who nodded back—then clasped his paws behind him, tail flicking seemingly autonomously. "You, however...Ramesan. That'll take me a bit to get data. Either you're being very clever, or this is more broad than I'd realized. Indulge me—Who are you, Jale Bercammon?"

"I was the chief steward of the OCS *Freeta*, Ramesan flag. I myself am from Ramesan's Palagian nation. Catti City and province. I was, until my...involuntary recruitment by Knoskali's thugs, an employee of OCS Lines for all of my adult life." She could feel Naane looking at her in surprise, but kept her focus on Rema; she could feel the weight of the minutes slipping by, and every one counted. She pinned the fox with what she hoped to be a challenging little stare.

"Now, however, I am the captain of the *Dancer*, and responsible for two hundred twenty six crew, oh yes. As such, there is a reason I have had very little to say about me. What I'd like to know, dear, is who you are, why—ah, what legal basis is that for which we are being detained, and what you plan to do. And just for my own information, since my crew isn't entirely sure—how did you know we were there, and how did you catch us?"

"Me first, Captain. One simple question—did you or anyone on your ship know that Theta was sent to kill me?"

"No." Jale shook her head. "Not until our ciphertechs got into *Varaunt*'s comm system. Of course, Gnosi might have known...but we'll never know now."

"Gnosi." He tapped his temple thoughtfully. "Ah, yes...your former exec. How again did he become your... ah, former exec?"

"We were in orbit of Fonaci, when we believe he began transmitting a signal that was being detected." Jale nearly stumbled over her words when she realized who Gnosi had been talking to, but she managed to catch it in stride and turn her breath into a pregnant pause. "Which, as you might guess, was bad. One of my crew happened to be near that deck at the time, and Gnosi shot him. Another of my crew shot him in reply, and shortly thereafter that entire deck was lost as we took a hit from one of Fonaci's orbital cannons. He was lost to space."

Rema acknowledged that with a blink and a nod. "I'm satisfied. So, to the answers I owe you. First, the legal basis is very simple. The Dazi are a sovereign nation, and you are apparently part of a plot on my life. We are entitled to detain. We also may convene a hearing to determine what crimes were committed and by whom. Now, you've advanced some pretty dubious arguments about interspace law, so I'm going to be rude and assume you don't really know what you're talking about. I can simplify our situation to a very simple set of facts: We're detaining you because we're bigger and we have bigger guns, and they're trained on you because you make us nervous. That's our legal basis, and if you don't like it you may appeal to some council somewhere...when and if we decide to release you. And that brings me straight to my second point: you're hiding something from me, Captain Jale."

"So why haven't you scanned us as we sit here?" Jale growled slightly, a bit terrified of his perceptiveness but refusing to allow herself to be baited. Seconds mattered. "I thought you had bigger guns."

Rema shrugged nonchalantly. "We do, but that's an awfully big gun to swat an insect. I scanned Theta, and I scanned the captain of the other vessel, but they'd both committed overt acts against me. Do you intend to?"

"Not that I know of," Jale chuffed at the shot across the bow. Narrowing her eyes in a calculated display of irritation, she half-rose and planted her paws on the table, looming over Rema. Out of the corner of her eye, she saw the jackal take a step away from the wall, but she kept her eyes locked on the fox. "Alright, dear. Is there a purpose to this meeting? Or do you intend to dance around the point with cute expressions and veiled threats until I die of old age? I'm sorry. I forgot, you don't threaten—softly spoken warnings is surely what I meant to say."

The fox looked genuinely taken aback. His companionable grin faded a bit, and he sat more upright. "Sorry. I was hoping to have more of a casual, friendly conversation among potential allies...but I suppose that's not meant to be. Business it is. I'm holding your ship in part responsible for your assassin's actions until you can prove otherwise to me in some tangible way. We can get through this with a quick somatic scan, or we can stand you up over the next day or so and examine your statements and data to decide how to proceed. An attempt on my life is a hostile act between your government and mine, and depending on your level of involvement I may intern you and your crew here indefinitely until our diplomatic affairs are resolved. As to your last question, our detection methods are proprietary, and our technology is secret. Is that more to your liking?"

"Yes." Jale stood, drawing herself to her full height. "My own formal response is quite simple. My ship and crew arrived at the rendezvous in full stealth to rescue Theta. We certainly were not sent out to assassinate anyone, although had those been our orders we likely would have complied. I will not allow you to scan the memories of my crew under any circumstances, and I will consider it a hostile act."

Rema glanced thoughtfully at Naane, then leveled his eyes back on Jale. "Onari, would you please escort officer Naane to her apartment?"

Silently the jackal stood, inclining his head toward the door. Naane rose and followed him out without a word. A moment later, Rema slid the door shut and turned back to Jale.

"I realized that including her might have been a poor choice when the discussion drifted. Listen, I'm going to assume your story is true for the purposes of this talk. Your ship and crew are operating under the threat of death?"

"It's not quite that simple," Jale snapped softly. She wasn't sure if it was manipulation or charisma, but she found herself uncomfortably compelled to trust Rema, and that made her very mindful of her words. The thought of putting her faith in him and his fleet was almost hypnotic, and she shook herself. Too late.

Any second now.

She looked down at the fox, who tilted his head curiously. "Your offer is not unappreciated, but we have our duty. You see, sir, mostly it's not simple because the threat is there only if we fail to rescue Theta."

"But you've already failed. So if that's all true, why not seek our protection?" Suddenly he straightened, snapping to alertness. Jale cringed slightly at the intensity of his sudden stare, watching realization dawn very quickly. "Unless..."

In one fluid motion, Rema started for and reached the terminal just as a dull thud shook the building. Instantly he produced an energy pistol from somewhere and rested it on the flat surface, his paws dancing as fast as light across the input side.

Jale could feel the blood throbbing in her veins, heart thrumming at a rapid pace. She shifted slightly towards the door, but found herself immediately staring down the business end of the fox's weapon. A little shake of the head and a twitch of the barrel and she subsided meekly into the far corner.

There was another thud, and the door to the little office burst in, followed by an off-balance soldier and then two more, less off-balance, weapons silently leveled on Rema. He took a step back, paws raised. Jale saw his eyes shift a few times as if weighing his chances, but another pair of soldiers piled in behind the first set and he dropped his weapon to the floor.

"Let's go, Captain!" Battle armor muffled the voice of the first canid who'd entered, but his intent was clear as he grabbed her by the paws and pulled her behind him. "This Rema?" He nodded to the fox, weapon leveled.

She locked eyes with Rema for a brief moment, then pushed the emitter assembly of the soldier's rifle down with a paw, unsure of why she did so. "No. Rema just left with Naane, but we don't have time to hunt him down. He's only a secondary priority, anyway. Restraints on this one and leave him, then let's move. Good to see you."

The soldier cursed unhappily and lowered his weapon. As two of the others pushed forward and reached for their mag restraints, Jale gestured urgently for the rest to secure the exit. More thuds resounded through the relatively thin walls.

When the fox was secure, she strode with the soldiers, erect and defiant amidst their low-crouching forms as they made their way down one of the exterior halls.

At the last junction before the exit, she leaned forward to tap the point soldier on the shoulder to get his attention. "Have we found Theta?"

"Yes ma'am." He glanced back over his shoulder at her, the vector matrix projected on his visor shimmering for a brief moment before he turned his head back and waved a paw forward.

Two burly grey felines, brothers by their look, swung forward and kicked open the exit door, spilling out into the heat with weapons ready. Quickly the rest followed through into the bright purple-hued light and showery rain of a late Zyktona afternoon, Jale dead center of the squad. A mere ten meters away, a black and red drop shuttle sat in a badly-slagged circle on the ramp, its loading doors spread wide. A veil of steam rose from around it as precipitation evaporated on contact.

They ran for it, meeting no resistance. From another direction, a different team of six emerged around the corner of the building. The last two of their number stopped to lay down suppressing fire; the quiet hum of their energy weapons was offset by a loud pop as an electroflash grenade took them down. Between the front two, a small, slender, nearly naked white figure was dragged along, black hindpaws making slow, vaguely walking-like motions as they scuffed across the blacktop.

"Theta," Jale whispered, eyes wide.

Everyone reached the drop shuttle nearly simultaneously and piled in, leaving the fallen. Jale clenched her jaw tightly and didn't look back. It had been agreed, and everyone knew the risks.

The two felines strapped Theta and Jale in side-by-side, the ship already moving beneath them as they prepared for a full power climb. The one who was buckling the inert fox into place seemed to have trouble fitting the straps to his small form. He began frantically pawing for his harness as he lunged for his seat, but was too slow to get himself in place. Ten sets of eyes watched helplessly as he slid through, dangling by his neck and arm from his harness, strangling under rapidly increasing acceleration. His brother, one rack over, desperately tried to reach him but couldn't. For a long moment, he just stared. Then, despite the shouted warnings of the mission commander, he unstrapped himself from his reduced-G couch and hauled himself along the deck, wheezing, until he reached the dangling form. In an amazing feat of strength, he dragged himself up the bulkhead and freed his brother from the harness with his combat knife.

Jale looked away as they both collapsed together into the acceleration couch with tremendous force.

The risks, the risks.

She lifted her head again, with some effort, to check over the white fox. Blood dripped from Theta's nose and mouth in accelerated little drips, and his eyes were glazed over. His head hung limply under the force of acceleration, shortened purple hair plastered down around his face. His elegant little muzzle was tucked down against his fluffy chest...but she could see his shoulders slowly rising and falling with his breathing.

"I hope you're worth it," she growled in the back of her throat, staring at him. "This has gone so very far, and for what? For you. I do so hope you're worth it."

After a few minutes, the bone-crushing acceleration began to ebb, and eventually it cut entirely, traded for strange twisting forces as the ship began to maneuver in zero-G.

The mission commander looked up to her and grimaced, then struggled out of his seat to check on the inert felines.

Jale dragged down a battered console on a hydraulic arm, desperate to know what was happening.

The drop shuttle was making for an empty patch of space labeled '*Quillion*', very near an empty spot of space called '*Dancer*'. There were no other ships in system, and no indication of any response from the planet.

Seventeen minutes remained until they docked with *Quillion*, and she could be on her own ship within the hour.

"With just a little bit of luck," Jale whispered to herself, then felt a pang of bitterness. "And only Arvinne, Naane, and those three soldiers and who knows who else to grease the wheels."

XVIII

Endings

THETA FELT AS IF HE WERE IN A DREAM WORLD. Dizzy, aphasic and weak, he did not trust his perceptions, nor did he trust himself to speak. The face that examined him appeared to be the nice chief steward from the liner on which he'd awoken, except in House Selesz colors, and in command, and that made no sense. He let his eyes drift unfocused, ears ringing.

In his mind, he replayed the events from hours before. The doctor had been wrong—his recollection of them was crystal clear. All of his life's memories had returned between one blink and the next after he'd awoken. Memories clearer than his senses, and clearer than the emotions and the sense of destiny which had guided him for so long.

Love or not, he was nothing but a broken tool, and he had failed the single job he had been built to do. A sharp bitterness had supplanted his sense of loss; there was no recovery from his situation, but he simply didn't care anymore. He felt used, manipulated, lied to and wronged. Nothing made sense to him anymore, least of all himself. Whatever life he had left, he intended to live for himself... whoever that turned out to be. It was a rebellious thought, defiant and disobedient.

He felt little duty to anyone or anything else.

Activity and a change in the ambient noise aroused him, and he looked up once more, eyes reluctantly coming to focus. The shuttle was deboarding, and Jale was trying to unbuckle him from his seat. After a few false starts, he managed to find the harness release and stand up on his own.

Jale lifted his paw in her own, tugging him towards the door. He caught a blurry glance of soldiers gathered around something, and a lot of blood on the deck, and turned away to peer up at his escort. She seemed grim and determined, and he began to reevaluate the reality of his perceptions as he stumbled along behind her.

"Welcome aboard *Quillion*, Captain. It is good to finally meet you," a male voice reached his ears from above as the light surrounded them. Jale paused before him; he looked up, but winced away, eyes overwhelmed by the stark light of the hangar deck—everything bloomed into a blurry white mass that made his head throb, and he snapped his eyes shut, looking towards his feet.

"Captain Hanscom?" Jale's tone was guarded.

"Who else? Hm, so that's the one? All this trouble for that? If it wasn't the Master, sometimes I'd wonder." Hanscom chuckled blackly, as if making a private joke, and Theta felt his ears grow hot.

"Captain." Jale, Theta judged, was entirely unamused by the other's banter. "While I'm glad to be aboard, and would love to ask questions about your mission and how you've been tracking us, immediate business first please. How is my ship?"

"Intact, free, and right beside us. Your Dazi are being held under guard and your ship is prepared and awaiting your return. You even have fresh orders from the Master. As for your questions, I wasn't sure if my note to you was sufficient—apparently not." Experimentally, Theta opened his eyes a crack. As they adapted, he opened them a little further to find that they were standing beside the shuttle in a little hangar bay. Captain Hanscom—some sort of weasel very similar in height and appearance to Jale—was nose to nose with her, regarding her with a fatuous smile.

"We were dispatched as your backup just after you were underway," Hanscom said, clutching his paws before him. "Had regular communication with your XO from your first stop until a few days before you were scheduled to leave Fonaci. Really, I thought you certainly were lost or on the run once we stopped hearing from you. The Master sent us on ahead anyway, guessing at where you'd be. He told me to get his messages to you, if you were alive, and lend our aid if we could.

"The Master had far more faith in you than I did. That point, at least, is yours," he laughed. "When we saw what was there at the rendezvous, we knew there was nothing we could do, and came here to wait. You came out of Rellin under guard, and so we snuck a message to your tactics officer, then to you on that Dazi ship. I'm surprised our little drop worked so well, but here we are."

Theta shuddered as he began to realize what was happening. He looked up at Jale, whose face was contorted into a small scowl, more severe than Theta had seen her.

"Captain," Jale lowered her voice, words clipped. "Might I remind you that we are still in a combat situation? Let's keep this brief."

Theta nodded in agreement.

Hanscom arched an eyebrow, awarding Jale a calculating stare. His smile turned slightly condescending. "Not to worry. That armada only stayed long enough to drop off the pirates and their ship. The last two jumped out hours ago, and we're seeing very little activity from the planet's surface in response. And no orbitals. No, the real shame is that you missed the opportunity to hunt down that Rema, but it's not safe to go back. That is very unfortunate—you will have to answer for that failure, I'm afraid...though most of the blame falls on Theta. He might have been spared if our people had succeeded."

"*Coil*," Theta grunted, voice harsh. His pulse had begun to speed up. This rescue would fail. It was unfortunately-timed and overconfident, and Rema had read it as if with some sixth sense.

"What, dear?" Jale knelt, eye to eye with him.

"*Coil* not out." His frustration built—he knew what he wanted to say, but the words came out wrong, just as they had on the surface. "Back from out, it is, and shomething near... near primed! Onari—"

Hanscom seemed annoyed; he cut Theta off with a gesture and shook his head to Jale. "Regrettable. Gibberish, just like you said. Well, I'm going to have this little failure of an assassin placed in sleep storage for the journey home, so maybe the intel department's medical staff can sort him out before they...mm...interrogate him. Putting him to sleep could also keep this damage from getting worse, and save what's left of the information he carries."

"So Theta goes back with you?" Jale eyed Hanscom, rising back to his level. Theta perked his ears at an odd tone in her voice, and a stiffness in her posture.

"Oh of course. We're going straight home once you're back on your ship, but I've been told that you have new orders, for your eyes only."

"And you have orders to bring Theta back?"

"Not directly, but it's implied, of course. Besides," Hanscom looked smug, "he's my prize. It was my crew who retrieved him. You only managed to make a mess—so if you're thinking of taking credit...don't. There's none for you here."

Jale frowned for a long moment, then arched her eyebrows and shrugged. It seemed to Theta that she became calmer, almost cheerful.

"Very well. That certainly makes my decisions easier, Captain. Now certainly I don't care about credit for the mission, oh no, but it might have saved lives to know you were there, you realize...and we would certainly not have lost so many prisoners on the surface. It would have made far less of a mess. Another mistake by your Master, perhaps? They seem to be adding up heavily for this little mission, I can't help but notice."

Hanscom drew back, seemingly surprised by her statement.

"If our Master fails," he growled after a moment, glancing pointedly down at Theta and then back to Jale, "it's only because his people have failed him."

"Ooh, that's a rather good catchphrase for a tyrant," Jale laughed, so entirely unlike the almost mousy steward of a passenger liner that Theta remembered her that he wondered again if she was the same person.

After a moment of tense awkwardness, she grinned and shrugged again, nodding to the irked-looking Hanscom and drumming her claws on her belt. "Sorry, Captain. Forgive me my strange sense of humor? I do think...yes. Fair enough. Take this," she pushed Theta forward by the shoulders, "and be ready to go. I don't feel as safe as you do, oh no. Oh! Before I forget...in your message, you claimed as to have replacement equipment and personnel for my losses if I needed, yes? Our gig was badly damaged, and we had to reclaim it as scrap mass. Might I request the loan of a single drop shuttle to give us back inter-ship and orbital capacity? I could send a pilot to pick it up, and my brevet XO to select a few crew, if you could spare them."

"That'll work." Hanscom's mood had settled, and his expression had returned to its previous smug superiority. "We're going straight home, so take what you need—just make it quick. Number three there is our hot standby, fueled and crewed, so you might as well take it back to your ship and use it for the next run too. You may have the crew, as well. All I need is this." Hanscom pulled Theta roughly over to him by the scruff of the neck. Though the fox felt Jale's paws linger on his shoulders for a moment, a cold chill ran down his spine as soon as she released him.

Symbolic.

The Master would not be kind, Theta was certain. In all likelihood, he would never even be allowed to see Knoskali again. Terial, perhaps, but there would be no pleasantries this time. He snorted bitterly. There would be no time or opportunity for living for himself, and no free will left to him. He wished he'd never been rescued; he wished, in fact, that he'd been left entirely alone...left to his new life aboard *Varaunt*. Left to his original life on Oailim, or Brynton, or even just left to die the first time, before he'd become a pawn in a Master's game.

He lowered his head, then lifted it again to smile mirthlessly to Jale. She glanced down at him, eyebrow raised, then took a step back and nodded to Hanscom.

"Very well. I'll see to my ship and send back a few officers to do some...ah, selective recruiting." She nodded to his belt unit. "Can I forward along a message before I go?"

Hanscom frowned and nodded, tapping the little box at his hip.

It beeped.

"Jale to *Dancer*. Coming aboard from *Quillion*. Make all preparations to get underway immediately. Krella to resume trunk alpha, branch twelve, and prepare plan omega."

The unit beeped again, and Hanscom glanced at it. "Enqueued. What does that last part mean?"

"We were working a rather complex tactical problem when I left. Somewhat of an exercise in contingencies. I'd like them to complete it before I return, if they haven't already." Jale snorted. "Well, Captain, my thanks once again for coming to our rescue. It is good to know that the Master protects his own."

"It is my job, and my ship's mission, to protect the Master's hand as he works his business on the fringes," Hanscom said with a smirk and a little bow. "Though usually we do it invisibly to all. Goodbye, Captain. I hope for your sake that you never have to see us again, and that your future missions meet with more success."

Jale nodded. She awarded Hanscom a half-bow, then turned and strode off; Hanscom turned, too, closing his paw on Theta's scruff and dragging him along. Looking back over his shoulder, Theta watched Jale approach one of the shuttles and gesture for the crew to get it started. How was she involved in this? Had she been one of the Master's spies from the beginning?

Always more intrigue.

He looked away as he was jerked forward, staggering along behind the Captain, held fast by his firm paw. His coordination was returning quite rapidly, he noticed, and his mental fog was beginning to clear.

The brig was close to the hangar deck, and yet by the time they were there Theta was walking almost normally. Hanscom gently shoved him into one of the three cells without a word and closed the door behind him.

"In again," Theta said to himself, slightly pleased that it came out right. He sighed, watching the captain walk out of sight and then looking around. The walls were transparent and there was no furniture.

Even the toilet was a simple hole in a recess in the floor.

Curling up on the dingy deck, he closed his eyes; he felt mentally exhausted but at rest, as if he'd just completed a hundred miles of walking to reach his final resting place. A small smile brushed his lips.

A metaphor for his life, perhaps.

He stretched, then rolled onto his side. The smooth flooring was hard and the cell quite cold; the air was stale and smelled of sweat and other things, but he truly didn't care. He'd spent so much time confined that it almost felt more natural than having the run of a ship and clean sheets. Somehow it was peaceful to settle into the Master's care once more; regardless of the outcome, he had no decisions left to make, no knowledge to protect, and nothing to do now but breathe.

Jale settled herself into the cargo area of the drop shuttle with a cool nod to the flight crew. She sat alone, silent and stoic, as they prepped the shuttle for launch.

Inside, she was in turmoil.

"You will ensure Myshel is not brought back to me, no matter how much I may wish it..."

"...you are at all times working for Theta, and Theta alone."

She sat in silence, not even bothering to use the mobile terminal as the drop shuttle powered up and departed *Quillion*'s hangar bay. *Dancer*, keeping station beside her, would be a two minute trip.

Knoskali's quote drove her on, and stilled her desire to contact Krella to abort. Once more, she was committed and conflicted. Of course, even if Krella had understood, it was unlikely that he would have enough time to prepare.

Even if he did, he might choose not to obey.

She could do nothing but wait.

The drop shuttle maneuvered. Once, twice...she heard the blowers begin to hiss, and watched the status light over the door.

She took a deep breath, breathing *Dancer*'s air again. It even smelled familiar.

Home.

Her paw slid down to the release at her right hip.

The status light changed to amber, then to green, and the door hissed open.

She pressed the release, ready to spring to her feet.

Nothing happened.

Controlling her disappointment, she unfastened her harness and stood, taking a step to the exit. Before she could swing out, however, armed soldiers poured in, weapons raised. As they saw her, a few nodded; the squad continued forward. Surprised yells came from the unsecured flight deck, and she tried to bite down a spontaneous grin. It felt good to be on the offensive, however briefly. She steeled herself against a sense of guilt and strode to the exit, sticking her head out to find Krella himself looking anxiously up at her.

"Captain!"

"Krella." Jale beamed. She'd never been so proud of someone in her life. "You got it. You actually got it, dear."

"Alpha 12...our inside-out attack. But *Quillion*...? I thought for sure you'd yell at me that I had it wrong when you came out, but I could think of no other way to take it. And...did you actually mean to prepare for the omega plan? Now? If it wasn't your voice, I would not have believed."

"I am as serious and as immediate as death, Krella." Jale drew herself up grimly, smile vanishing. "Get him and get back. Move unseen. We all live or die in this moment, and we'll worry about the omega contingency later."

"Aye, ma'am." Krella's acknowledgement was crisp and offered no hint of doubt or dissent. He saluted and swung aboard even as the baffled flight crew was hauled out under guard. Jale ignored the pair's confused, entreating glances as they were dragged past her on the way to the brig.

"Get back fast, Krella. We'll keep the drive warmed for you!" she raised her voice over the hiss of the closing door, then turned to sprint for the bridge.

Back at her station, Jale immediately set to work running systems checks, preparing her departments, and scrambling her crew. Her terminal flashed at her incessantly, insisting that she view a message relayed to her from Knoskali.

She ignored it for a while, then silenced it. Whatever he had to say, she was committed to this course of action and there could be no retreat.

Barely breathing, she watched her tactical readout as the drop shuttle slid into *Quillion*'s open hangar bay. With only light armor, her squad had no remote telemetry or video feed, so as they filed quickly out of the shuttle, they ceased to exist to her. All she could see in her field of view were her two armed pilots standing by to guard the vessel.

Any moment, the comm officer would tell her that Hanscom was calling, and *Quillion* would go on lockdown, trapping her crew inside. She had no plan if this failed, and no idea what she would do.

Her countdown timer was synchronized with the mission clock; at three minutes—four seconds ahead of schedule—the first of her crew swung back into her view and the flight crew leapt back to their stations. In the middle of the small squad was a slightly-less-dazed-looking Theta walking under his own power. Before she could even contemplate the upcoming moment of truth, it had happened: the shuttle had sealed its doors, received departure clearance, and had cleared the other ship's hull.

"Helm," Jale's voice sounded brittle to her own ears, and she cleared her throat. "I know you are ready and alert, but I want you ready to accelerate the instant the order leaves my mouth, dear. As soon as that ship is within our inertials, I need acceleration to escape velocity, emergency curve. We'll rip the ship apart if need be, and just hope that what survives holds air."

"Aye, ma'am."

"Ma'am!" Geff leaned over from the tactics station and tapped her shoulder with a broad hand. "I have a new contact in system! Now two contacts! They're Dazi! Right here in the decel lane, just came out of Rellin drive, and they're going to end up in a compatible orbit."

"Blast it," Jale growled, then paused, biting off the order that had sprung to her lips. This could buy time. "Geff— Contact *Quillion* and point out the new contacts. Ask for advice. They'll have seen them, of course, but perhaps we can keep them distracted from what's going on in their lower decks. Times, Tac?"

"Shuttle will be aboard in one minute thirty. The Dazi ships will be in firing range in under fifteen minutes. Rellin drive...it will be very tight, ma'am. Technically, we have to be nearly perfect to escape, if the Dazi ships or *Quillion* takes action."

"Make it happen, Geff. I have faith."

Geff straightened and nodded. "Aye, ma'am. *Quillion* has replied. They say that the shuttle is detectible, suggest we accelerate as soon as we have it aboard. They are accelerating and preparing for drive, themselves."

"Good, good," Jale murmured. "I do hope that they don't think to check their lower decks before we're gone. It sounds like they don't know yet, but I bet they're at least suspicious of our fast, silent turnaround when we were supposed to have specialists picking new crew."

"Ma'am! *Quillion*'s weapons just went hot." Geff sounded suddenly frantic, and Jale's heart caught in her throat. "The shuttle..."

"Helm! Spin us around the shuttle's position. Ah, move us towards the shuttle and...I'm trying to use our size to block *Quillion*'s line of fire, just make it work." Jale's hands clenched her console so firmly that her knuckles hurt.

"Aye, ma'am!"

"Ma'am, *Quillion*'s signaling!"

"Stall them for now. Make something up, but I do not want to talk until our shuttle is safe. Weapons, be ready.

Keep targets on *Quillion* and keep countermeasures ready. It may come to a fight."

"*Quillion* outguns and outmasses us significantly, ma'am." The weapons officer eyed her reluctantly.

"I know she does, weps. No choice. Geff?"

"We have the angle. Shuttle aboard in fifteen seconds."

The lights on the bridge dimmed slightly. Jale stared at her terminal window, but for a moment she couldn't parse it. She shook her head, trying to force herself to read.

"Warning shot, ma'am. Damaged the patched plating on our ventral hull."

"Roll us dorsal on, and make sure the shuttle takes telemetry so that we can recover it. *Quillion* doesn't have the armament of a planetary, and we can take a few hits from her up top."

"Ma'am! Broadcast signal from the lead vessel coming in system. They—"

"Shuttle's aboard, ma'am!"

"Go, Helm!" Jale snapped, her voice cutting through the chatter. "Get Krella and Theta up here, Geff. And...prepare to implement omega. Put me through to *Quillion*. Just voice."

"Aye, ma'am."

After a moment, and an angry crackle, Hanscom's furious voice rang shrilly across *Dancer*'s bridge.

"What have you done?"

"Captain Hanscom, my original instructions were to free Theta." Jale's mouth was dry, and her heart raced. "Knoskali did not wish him returned, and that is why he chose me to lead this mission. Now keep going—get out of here, Captain, and we'll do the same."

"Absolutely not. I will have your head for this. You are a trait—"

Jale pulled up the switcher and cut the communication herself.

"Ma'am!" Helm's voice was anguished.

"Yes? What is it?"

"Ma'am...I don't know. Come look at this."

Krella raced onto the bridge, a stumbling Theta firmly in tow, just as Jale stepped around her console to leap to the helm station. She pushed him out of the way, ignoring his questions to focus on the helmsman's display.

"Captain, we're losing velocity. The more energy we apply, the more energy is required." For the first time Jale had heard, Sillanen sounded afraid. "I—ma'am, we cannot possibly achieve cavitation. It's obvious...they must have hidden orbital defenses."

Jale nodded calmly, resting her paw on his shoulder. "I see. Can we use the emergency reactant drive?"

Sillanen tapped at his panel, jaw clenched. After a moment he smacked his paw down on its surface and pushed the console away. "No ma'am, it's clearly ship's motion that's being constrained, not just our system drive. We can maneuver but we cannot accelerate. *Quillion* is pursuing at the same velocity, and she has more power to spare."

"Understood. It's alright, Sillanen. You've done your best. Krella," she turned to find her tactics chief settled at the XO's station. "We're out of options. No questions—implement plan omega."

"Aye, ma'am." The panther seemed to sink into his chair, but began working immediately.

"Planet and ships," Jale added with a little sigh, returning to her chair. "Helm, drop all stealth. Secure from stealth mode, and bring up position, navigation and recognition lights."

"Say again?" Sillanen had pulled his console back in at her voice, but just stared at her in disbelief when she'd finished.

The lights dimmed again, and there was a small snap. Out of the corner of her eye, Jale saw Theta push up beside Geff and stare hard down at his panel.

"That was a light hit, ma'am. Slight damage to dorsal hull. *Quillion's* trying to take out our engines." Geff murmured, with an annoyed glance at Theta. "She's committing full power, but whatever it is that's slowing us down seems to have attenuated a bunch of it. Compo can't say."

Jale rubbed her temples and nodded. "Understood. Follow my instructions, helm. We're done. Keep the drive power up just in case, and weapons...dump whatever countermeasures you need to keep us alive."

Krella was scanning his console. "Ma'am, I sent the omega message. They've replied, asking for voice confirmation. They've given me channel and encryption details."

"Put me on it."

The panther nodded, tapped a few times, then gestured to her with an open palm.

"Dazi forces," Jale raised her voice, though she didn't really need to. "This is *Dancer*, Jale commanding. As per our last transmission, we offer our full surrender, on the condition of your amnesty and asylum as offered by commander Rema."

There was silence. After a moment, Jale closed her eyes and sat back in her chair. She could feel the eyes of the bridge upon her.

"This is *Ghekke*." The signal was strangely modulated, as if interfered with. "We are not in contact with Rema. Stand on—maintain course and speed, and your request will be considered."

"*Ghekke*, this is urgent. We are currently under fire by a ship of our flag, and seeking your protection," Jale's voice cracked on the last word. "We require assistance."

"Countermeasures expended, ma'am." Her weapons officer sounded frustrated. "Shall I return fire? I can't promise it will help."

Another hit glanced off their port dorsal hull, and Jale could see at once that they'd taken significant armor damage in that section. Theta was waving to her, but she looked past him, locking eyes with Geff.

"What do we do?"

"At least twelve minutes before the Dazi ships will be effective. Even with the attenuation of their weapons, I don't see...I can't. Krel?" Geff looked desperate.

Krella looked equally strained, glancing up at Jale then back at his panel. He shook his head, paws splayed impotently across his panel.

"Control." Theta's spoke into the silence. His voice was light but harsh, and he slid between Geff and his panel. "Give me all. Please," he entreated.

"Get away from there," Geff rumbled, dragging an irritated-looking Theta from the console. Before anyone could say anything or interfere, Geff's boots were in the air and the deck shook as he landed flat on his back, a surprised look on his face. Theta was back at the console the next moment. He pointedly deployed the manual maneuvering controls, staring insistently at Jale.

Jale glanced around the bridge, but found no suggestions.

"Fine. Transfer all control to the tactical station. Geff, let him be." Jale lowered her voice. "And...If any of you are theistic, now might be a good time to ask for help."

"No need," Theta snapped, and then jinked the ship so hard that the stability systems blinked off for a moment.

Jale tugged a staggering Krella to her, putting her lips to his ear in the guise of supporting him. "Just stay with him and try to make sure he doesn't kill us all," she murmured. "I'm not sure I trust his sanity."

Krella made a face and dragged himself back into his chair.

"*Dancer*, this is *Ghekke*. We cannot legally open fire at this time. We have attempted to warn your adversary off, but that's all we can do unless your request is granted." The female voice sounded apologetic. "If you can survive long enough, we will attempt to physically intercede."

Jale placed a hand over her chest and awarded a silent bow to the unseen ships inbound just as two more hard jinks shook the bridge.

A strange noise resonated in the hull; Jale glanced down at her display and was shocked at their proximity to *Quillion*. She grabbed for her armrests and froze, but there was no impact; the other ship was making an emergency maneuver, down and away. Little humms and tremors through the deck signaled *Dancer*'s own weapons firing.

Another hard turn drew a strangulated little noise from Krella, who stared at his display, equally transfixed. *Dancer* was sweeping down across *Quillion*'s aft quarter, nearly touching, under nearly full acceleration and at the absolute maximum maneuvering power limits.

One tap at these relative speeds, Jale knew, and both ships would most likely be lost.

She resisted the temptation to close her eyes, though she noticed Sillanon's were squeezed tight. Weapons hummed again, and hotspots painted *Quillion*'s aft armor and drive section as *Dancer* slid across.

Back on the underside, more weapons fire. *Quillion*'s own weapons were blanketed by her hull.

"Weapons! Need your help," Theta barked, high voice clear. "Can't...can't f-fly and fire."

"What are you trying to do?" The wolf at the weapons station peered down at his panel. Of all the personnel on the bridge, he alone seemed unfazed by their maneuvers.

"Distract. Hit we–weapons, maneuvering drive," the fox spoke as if it were a struggle. "I—"

The bridge audio system beeped, and Theta snapped his jaw shut. Rema's voice came across, clear, powerful and precise. "Hang on a little longer, Captain! Your request is granted. We'll talk terms later, but stay alive for ten more seconds."

Caught by surprise, Jale tore her eyes away from the wildly fluctuating power graphs to stare at Krella.

"Well, send an acknowledgement dear! What happens in ten seconds?"

Krella stared right back at her, but had no answer. He looked down and tapped a reply.

"Move away from the other ship, Captain. Quickly." Rema's voice was soft but urgent.

The lights dimmed and the stability system went out again briefly as Theta complied. Once more within *Quillion*'s firing arc, *Dancer* began taking damage to her ventral hull, losing makeshift ventral plating wholesale. Jale thumbed her panel and spoke urgently. "Evacuate E and D decks! No personnel on E and D."

Suddenly realization dawned on Jale, and she stood, thumb still holding down the intercom key. "No," she whispered, eyes wide. "No!" She shouted. "Don't destroy them!"

A stream of alerts flashed on her panel, and she fell back in her chair, clutching her head. A shocked silence gripped the bridge, and the computer began throwing up datatags on the main display at a rapid pace, cataloging the debris field that had been *Quillion*. The camouflaged orbital defense net now stood out in computer-mapped hotspots of the weapons discharge.

"Oh, by the gods." Krella groaned.

"Move in close. Seconds matter." Jale's voice was hoarse, heart beating in her throat. "Helm, take back control. Get someone in the new shuttle. We'll launch if there's anything to rescue. Krella...coordinate the search."

Her flat, humorless voice fell into the hush, and she felt compelled to continue. "I'll announce it to the crew later, but since you are all witness to it you now know that this is likely the end of our mission and of our allegiance to House Selesz. I don't know what the future holds, but I ask that you bear with me a little longer."

"He warned us, Captain." Krella said softly. "He told us that this mission might take us entirely outside of his service, when he briefed us on it, and he told us that it was within his conation. Captain...the computer detects no survivable sections and no...ah, intact biomass. That was a tremendous amount of weapons energy."

Jale hung her head in the ensuing silence. *Quillion* had been two thirds larger than *Dancer*, and had carried a significantly larger crew.

This was loss of life on a scale she had never witnessed.

She felt ill; Hanscom had brought his ship in-system with the sole purpose of helping her.

"Excuse me. I'm going to go negotiate with the Dazi. Route the link to my quarters," she murmured. Taking a deep breath, she turned and left the bridge, not looking back. She managed to make it inside her cabin before she began to cry. Weeks of contained stress and bottled-up emotions were released at once, and she clutched her pillow to her chest. Somehow, despite all of the close calls and loss of life, the threat of imminent destruction and the constant fear, nothing had brought reality home to her as firmly as the destruction of *Quillion*, a ship she'd stood on an hour before. The faces of the crew were much like those of her own, and now every one of them was dead, their atoms committed forever to the soulless, endless void of space.

After a few minutes, she became aware of a warmth pressing against her. She opened her eyes to find Pinky and Jewel snuggled up on either side, silent and supportive. A faint, quavering smile broke across her muzzle, and she felt her heart lighten. Wiping her tears away with the back of a paw, she hugged each in turn. "Why hello there, my dearies. It does me good to see the two of you alive and well."

"Are you ok, Miss Jale?" Pinky's voice was soft and concerned.

"I...you know, yes, I suppose I am. It could be over, did you know? It may now be truly over." She felt relief wash through her, as if it had been waiting for her words. "I mean, if the Dazi prove true to their word...and if Knoskali is satisfied and true to his."

"Who are the Dazi, ma'am?" Jewel tilted his head.

"None of us are sure, and nobody here knows much about them. It took a bit of digging, but I did manage to dredge up a few facts. We have lost many records from the time before the progressive period, but from what we can see a race named 'Dazi' from a planet called Daz operated the trade routes at the very beginning of our colonization. Historians claim that their planet and civilization was destroyed by a war started in 822 year, and the collapse of their trade system in 826 year was the very event that began the period of isolation."

"Oh. And these are the same Dazi?" Jewel tilted his head the other way, and Jale couldn't resist the temptation to ruffle his hair.

"I haven't the slightest, dear—that is all I could manage to find. I shall make a point to ask them, if you like...should they prove friendly."

"If it's over," Pinky seemed troubled, reaching a paw up to blot fresh tears from Jale's cheek, "why are you crying?"

Jale sighed softly, closing her eyes and rocking back to lean against the bulkhead at the head of her bed. "The cost was very high, you see. A ship named *Quillion*, in Knoskali's service, was sent to help us, and I was forced to betray them. Ach, No." She shook her head. "Weasel words. I betrayed them—I chose to betray them—because I made a mistake and hadn't the quick wit to make up for it. They were destroyed," she snapped, the sting of remorse for the loss of the *Quillion* returning with its bitter draught. "I had the opportunity to call them off before any of this began, but I thought they were a gift from Dia—figuratively speaking."

"Why did you turn against them?" Pinky took her paw, holding it gently.

"Because of what Knoskali said, and what he almost said but didn't quite. He wanted Theta free, or some part of him did. I still believe that to this very moment. I think...I honestly believe that he didn't have the will to free Theta himself. Perhaps it went against his conscience, or perhaps he was too emotionally involved in the issue? Truly, I cannot guess. And had Hanscom taken Theta back, I think Knoskali would have kept him. He couldn't have done otherwise. I had to take Theta from his ship if I was to free him."

"Why did you destroy them?"

"Oh! I didn't directly, Pinky. They wanted to stop us from leaving, to take Theta back. We requested assistance from the Dazi. But they...they intervened far more harshly than I had expected or desired."

"I think you did the best you could, given what you knew. I'm sure of it," Pinky stated flatly, squeezing her paw in his.

A chime on her console announced reminded her of the secure channel to the Dazi, and she sighed, blotting her eyes once more with the back of a paw before rising to her feet.

"Well. I suppose I've kept them waiting long enough, haven't I?"

The black of a moonless Zyktona pre-dawn inked the world in shadow around a small pool of light. A little pavilion stood at its center, its sides open to the cool night air. In the center stood a wide table, its surface wrought of dark stone; around it were gathered four silent forms who regarded one another in the veil of a calm, appraising silence.

On one side of the table sat a tall, lithe jackal with midnight black fur, and a short, compact red fox; across from them, an even shorter white fox looked off into the shadows and a reasonably tall ferret sipped her drink with a patient air about her.

The red fox stood, and three pairs of eyes turned to follow him as he began to slowly pace.

"Well now, here we are at last. This is where I expected to end up when I left Hope, but not how I expected to get here. Still, we're all here, and that's good, even if I do keep wanting to look over my shoulder for another drop. I was born in space, so you'd think I'd feel more comfortable with my back to a bulkhead when danger threatened. Still, for some reason I can't begin to fathom, I'm one of the few spacers I've met who feels more comfortable with my paws in the dirt." Rema's voice was light, but held the attention of the group. He raised his glass to his lips and then set it down untasted.

"Personally, I say it's you. You captains and crews out there lurking in the dark, ready to spring on victims at the will of some tyrant or another, or for a little money, or for who-knows-what. All the beauty and vastness of space, and we come to the same little sections to fight over them. We mark our territories, and have our silly little wars over the least of things. I come out here to plant my paws in the dirt for a while and this whole mess drops in my lap, starting with a little assassin who wanted to take my life and nearly ending with a rescue squad that easily could have.

"Now I have hundreds of vaporized Brynti littering my orbit, a thousand pirates and a couple hundred living Brynti on my soil, two empty ships in orbit, and I'm having to spend my time and resources to untangle this mess. I'd half a mind to blow you both up and walk away." He shook his head, looking more disapproving than Theta had seen him yet.

Jale tipped her head in a dignified nod. "I'm surprised that you didn't."

"It would have saved me a lot of work," Rema scowled, seeming almost petulant. "But I can't un-kill, and a ship full of people represents the near end of a timeline that goes back to the ancients and beyond. Every thought, every breath, every uniqueness represented within your genetic diversity is a story eons in the making, and to end them capriciously to save a little effort on my part does not befit my intent or office." The fox's gold eyes narrowed, and for a moment Theta caught a glimmer of immense depth behind them that betrayed the fox's apparent youthfulness.

He exhaled very slowly, shocked. He managed to only allow a slight tremor to pass through him, which nobody seemed to notice. For an instant he had been reminded very much of Knoskali, and in that instant he realized that there was something far deeper at play. He sat back and held his tongue, listening with every sense he possessed.

"So why," Jale sounded aggrieved, "if the stories of each individual are so important to you, did you destroy *Quillion*?"

"I offered them the chance to stand down," Rema shrugged. "They declined."

A gust of wind ruffled through; both Jale and Onari twitched uneasily at the moving air. Jale took her drink and sat back from the table to sip it, looking thoughtful; Rema settled back into his chair, leaning across the table to her.

"It was very clever to slide the 'amnesty' word in there at any rate, Captain." Rema broke the silence, with a flicker of a glance toward Theta. "I spent a few precious seconds considering its ramifications before I assented, and now that I've spent a good while wracking my brain and my legal datastores, I've finally just about figured out how to make it work. Here's what it looks like: You and your crew and your little ship have been legally annexed. Not taken prisoner, not detained, but annexed as a defecting body. On paper, you now could be considered Dazi citizens anywhere in the known universe, I think."

Jale nodded somberly.

"I bent a few laws for that, you know. Based on your condition of working under threat of death, I managed to 'prove' that you were slaves. I know how much your type object to that, so...we'll keep that quiet." The fox shook his head, humor momentary. "But the simple fact is, as inclusive as our culture is, you don't belong to it. You're not of us, and you carry different values. So what do we do with you?"

"First," Jale spoke up, "don't judge us all for Brynton's follies. My crew is composed of individuals, many with quite disparate backgrounds, so please let us decide our fates individually. We know very little about your culture. If Theta is free, as amnesty implies, then some may even wish to return to Brynton."

"Theta..." Rema sighed. "Amnesty for your ship and crew, and asylum for those who wish to remain? Yes and yes, done and done. I won't let you return to Brynton with your ship, and I won't let you leave whole, as a force, ship or no. I bet you can figure out why. But Theta...you are a problem. I don't mean you harm, but I cannot allow your release. Not yet."

Theta nodded, remarkably clear-headed; his improvement had continued rapidly, and he now felt better than he had in quite some time. For the first time in his life since coming into Knoskali's dominion, he felt unencumbered, and for the first time he truly understood why so many would fight so hard to remain free. He stood slowly to address Rema; out of the corner of his eye, he saw Onari shift warily.

He spread his paws, palms up.

"Set me free. I'll send a message to Knoskali, truthfully announcing it. Once that is complete, I will voluntarily surrender to you and you may dispose of me as you wish. He will accept that, I can promise."

He eased back into his chair and lowered his paws, staring down at the table.

A thoughtful silence reigned.

"That is a decision made under duress," Jale spoke softly after a moment, her voice low and earnest, though reluctant. "I cannot allow it."

Rema inclined his head to Jale after a moment. "You're not prisoners, nor is he. We won't hurt him, and we'll absolutely give him his freedom eventually, but he's got to be 'ours' for a while. No more interrogations. No more probes. Not before he surrenders to us, and not after."

"And if he announces his freedom and then chooses not to voluntarily surrender?"

"If Theta gives me his word," Rema arched an eyebrow, "then that is a risk I will take. And if he chooses to break his word, then that becomes my problem."

"If Rema gives me his word," Theta met the red fox's eye, still resonating from the moment of familiarity, "Then I give mine."

"Done?" Rema held eye contact.

Theta closed his eyes, breaking the spell but not his resolve.

Come what may.

"Done."

Epilogue

A WARM WIND WHIPPED across the plateu in the face of the coming evening, lifting the dust from the wide slab that formed the shuttleport. One lonely transport shuttle was parked on the ramp, glimmering beneath the purple sky, its engines turning slowly, whispering soft metallic whispers to all in range.

Beside it stood Captain Jale Bercammon, brushing the dust from the sleeves of her uniform jacket and gazing down at the last connection to her old life.

"You're certain this is what you want, Arvinne? What ever shall I tell your family?"

Arvinne looked up from packing his belongings into a cargo pod, his usual broad grin wider than ever. "Why, tell them the truth, of course. Just between us, my family...we have history, if you take my meaning. Dating back to the period of isolation. All you'd need to say is that I've taken up the 'family trade', just in space an' all. Or maybe I'll be telling them myself. I'm not a prisoner, you know."

"No, of course you're not. But...a galley cook?"

"A galley cook with one full share, same as the rest of the crew save for Captain Dela. A ship is only as strong as her kitchen, you know."

Jale snorted a single laugh, then shook her head down at the snow leopard. "That's my line, you little thief."

"Pirate, ma'am," he bowed.

Jale shook her head, rubbing her chin. She tilted her head, angling her ears away from the increasingly noisy engines of the transport behind Arvinne. "And you, dear... one of the nicest people I've ever known...you have no problem with the ethics of this life?"

"Naw. Dela, she's gone ahead and promised us all a target spread from the pockets that need lightening. Said she has some contacts that should put us on the right track. Well," Arvinne extended a paw, "Sorry, but we're coming up on time here real quick, an' I've got the baking tonight, so I can't miss this transport. I think we'll be able to keep in touch through the Dazi."

Jale took the proffered paw, then tugged Arvinne into a tight embrace. "As if you were getting away that easily, you rogue," she laughed softly.

After a moment, they parted.

"Good hunting, Arvinne."

"You, too, Jelly."

Jale nodded and turned away, a small, confident smile on her face. She, too, had much to do.

"Alright. Round two. Theta, this is Gytriest. Gytriest, this is Theta. You will be nice to him this time." Rema continued the process of peeling off gloves and armor suit, resting them beside his helmet in the heat-crisped grass.

A thousand miles of forested hills surrounded the little round valley, stretching in all directions around its lone little meadow. Lurking at the treeline, a large reptilian form stood beside the two-seat atmospheric transport vehicle parked just at the tip of the late-evening shadows that stretched across the meadow, cast by the last light of the primary star through the purple atmosphere. Stars shimmered through the mist, and a cool breeze carried a billion distinct scents straight to Theta's senses.

None of the scents were nearly as strong or as potent to memory as the scent of the alien who stood before him, who had promised his death when last they met.

"I agreed to this when I called for this meeting. Do you doubt me, friend Rema?" Gytriest shifted sideways, and Theta ignored the instinct to flinch away.

"Your temper outpaces your will at times, my friend," Rema chided gently, stepping closer. "But you know I'd never doubt your intent."

"I can forgive. I have seen this one's story. It was subtle. It was not deeply encoded. It was more of a whisper of thought. I dreamed on it, I sang it, I considered it deeply, and I allowed myself to flow with it." The alien's scent again assailed Theta as the breeze died, powerfully familiar. He took an involuntary step forward, attracted to it at some subliminal level. "I have forgiven him, for he shares no fault I can find save his misguided attack on you, friend Rema. That, you have forgiven, and that is enough."

"Theta, you are not our prisoner." Rema turned to him, resting a paw on his shoulder. "But there are many things you have to learn before you can choose your path. I brought you here to meet Gytriest to learn this one, and it is the most important to us—you're no longer of pure-blood north-Oaili arctic fox morphology. Knoskali, for some reason we cannot know, hybridized your genetics with those of the Elechen. He has done the same for himself. We know that from your memories of him. Subtle, yes, but the mark was clear. I suspect you know what I mean."

"What are the Elechen?" Theta found his voice, cocking his head up to Rema. He felt surprisingly un-surprised.

"I am Elechen," Gytriest rumbled, and then settled to his haunches, raising his foreclaws "We are a peaceful race, long forgotten by all the children of man save our friends the Dazi. We owe our lives to them. Our stories are told by blood, and the greatest of them ring out clearly to us."

Theta considered this for a moment. "By blood...Is that why you...tasted me?"

Rema smiled, leaning back against his little transport and flexing his paws. "Let me explain, in my crude way. The Elechen were the original occupants of the world we call Brynton, a world where their race was nearly destroyed. They speak a very poetic version of our language, and they have an additional type of memory—genetic memory. Memories are encoded directly into the genetic structure. They have the ability to share them with each other by sharing blood, although memories of memories only encode small 'whispers' without resonance. So big memories...stories, dreams and songs...those things resonate more widely and become part of a massive shared culture dating back to the beginnings of their race. They remember their history without telling. They share their wisdom with each other...and with us."

Theta felt dazed.

"Us? You're also a hybrid?"

"Yep. Like Knoskali. The difference between us, though, is that my 'gift' was given by the Elech, while his was taken from a captive. The Brynti never seemed to understand the Elechen beyond the basis of their original symbiotic relationship, so we never considered that they would discover the true depth of the race."

"Your progenitor is legend, friend Theta." Gytriest nosed Theta's shoulder softly, voice gentle. "He was lost fighting the children of man, and we thought his voice forever silenced. You unify the stories of our last, darkest days, and I am eager to share with my kin. I forgive you for receiving his gift unoffered, for you were as unwilling and unaware as he; I ask your permission to share, as your memories are inseparable and will be passed along."

Theta looked up at Rema, then back to Gytriest. "Of course you may. I no longer hold any secrets." He managed to keep his tone neutral. "Are your kin...here?"

Gytriest laughed softly, lifting his head to gaze into the crepuscular sky. "No, mostly not here. My kin travel with the Dazi and Caylum. Some do live here. Some permanently on ships, some on Liberty. Some inhabit the skies of Dazi-settled planets. I live often on *Ghekke*, often here, often ground that I find. One day, we may choose another home...one day, but we have not yet found such a place."

Theta's ears flattened. "And...who or what are the children of man?"

"They call ancients 'man', Theta. We, all of us, are the children of the ancients to them. There is some origin that is beyond even their memory, or not so important. Speaking for the Dazi, the Elechen are our equals...but we hide their existence. Gytriest is on the council of the Caylum, which I myself serve. I have lots to teach you about the Dazi and of the Elechen...if you want to learn." Rema knelt slightly, until he and Theta were eye-to-eye.

"But why?" Theta frowned lightly, blinking into the golden eyes of the other fox, bright despite the failing light. "Why waste time on me?"

"It's not simply because of what you are, if that's what you're wondering. It's also not because of who you are. It's because of what you can be, and the potential that you have yet to grow into." Rema softly touched his nose with a paw. "And because I'm intrigued by you, and likely will try to recruit you for your skills, which match certain missions of mine very well."

Gytriest made a strange gurgling noise, but Theta was lost in his own thoughts. "I...am willing to cast my future to the wind, but as I warned Janesson, I'll warn you—I do not wish to ever fight Knoskali. I will always love him."

Rema nodded, placing a hand on the Elech's neck to still any reaction, but none came. Moments later he lifted Theta's chin slightly, meeting his eye.

"I do understand, Theta. There are pits of the spirit that we can't pull away from to save our life, and sometimes we want nothing more for our lives than to dive in to meet our fate."

Theta nodded, captured by—almost enraptured by—the accuracy of his words and the feelings they conjured. "Yeah...that's...exactly it."

"It is good to stretch the wings." Gytriest interrupted softly. He sat back and fanned his illustratively, sending ripples through the grass. "You stretch his wings, friend Rema, and I shall stretch mine. I will rest with you here for the month, and then we may see where fate leaves us."

"How long has *Ghekke* been out for? Barring enders?" Rema peered up at the large creature.

"Eight standard months."

"Too long, old friend. Shore leave for all, once our new friends have left, and we'll all go together."

"They will like that." Gytriest moved his head close to Theta, looking into his eyes and stealing his attention from Rema. "I bid you welcome, Friend Theta. We will teach, if you will listen. I wish to welcome you home, even if you do not recognize it yet."

"I...thank you."

Theta raised a paw entreatingly. Gytriest touched his nose very softly to it, then fixed his eyes on Rema, then took a step back and leapt into the sky, wings bearing him aloft with great pumps. After climbing nearly straight up into the starlit sky, he dove down across the two foxes, the wake from his wings buffeting them and tossing Theta's hair back from his face.

"I..." Theta felt a longing to join him, his whole body trembling with desire to leap into the night breeze. He raised a paw, following the Elech as he glided out of sight behind the treeline; there was magic in the moment, amorphous and flowing, and Theta felt saturated with it.

"You feel it too."

Theta looked up to find Rema's gaze resting on him knowingly. He nodded very slightly.

"I knew you would, just as I know it was you maneuvering *Dancer*. I saw it in your eyes when you attacked me the first time, but then, fortunately for me, your mind was unclear. *Alherié*, the Elech call it in their tongue. Joy in flight, grace in motion, it's always something in or from something else, but its meaning is flexible. Some few feel it who are not of the Elech, but almost all of us who are find it inescapable. Grace in the dance, in the kill. Joy in the moment. It all fits."

"Yes," Theta whispered softly.

"Walk with me and learn."

Taking Theta's hand, Rema led him towards a break in the trees, to a thin path lit only by starlight.

"Helm."

"Standing by, ma'am."

Jale kicked up her feet and leaned back.

"Tactics, are we clear to leave orbit?"

"Aye, ma'am. I've received our routing outbound and passed it to Sil." Naane's cheery voice no longer held the worry and weight it had borne as XO. Though she had been offered the position, she had declined; Krella had accepted a position aboard *Coil*, and Naane had asked to take his spot.

"Very good. XO, if you'll do the honors?"

The Dazi canine in at the exec's station nodded to Jale, reassigning the main display to the Rellin entry parameters. "Helm, please engage acceleration, minimum shift curve. Prepare for Rellin entry on our set course as soon as we reach velocity."

"Aye, ma'am."

A little groan in the deck reflected the onset of acceleration through the damaged plating, and Jale bit her lip softly, glancing up at Nathaniel. He caught her eye and smiled reassuringly, then turned back to his numbers. Fortunately for the ship, her entire engineering staff had remained unchanged. Some had indicated that they might choose to depart when they arrived at Liberty, the Dazi's secret station-world, and many had offered to stay around for the refit, but all had agreed to remain until they arrived.

With nothing to do but wait, Jale took the liberty of glancing around her bridge. There were a few new faces, and a few faces at different stations, but overall the crew was her crew, and she felt comfortable with them. A little grin split her face, and she stood.

"Very well. You have it, XO."

"Aye, ma'am."

Jale stepped down and strode to the bridge exit, then wended her way aft to the galley.

"Ma'am?" The head cook stared at her as she entered the galley, then snapped to attention. She laughed, waving him off. "No, it's alright. We're mid rotation, are we not?"

"Ah...yes, ma'am. We're ah...preparing a small service for the wardroom, but otherwise we're about to rotate off for a break. Shall I bring 'em back?"

"Oh no, certainly not dear. I merely wish to borrow the facilities for a moment."

"...Ma'am?"

"It's alright, Lancen," she beamed at him. "I know I have been remiss in coming down here, but you've all done such a fantastic job these past few weeks that I haven't needed to. I just need a few minutes to make something special."

"Of course, ma'am. If, ah...if you need any help..."

Jale smirked to herself, nosing around and finding that everything was in obvious places. "Oh no, it's quite alright dearie."

Pulling down cookwear and rummaging through the foodstore, she ignored the sidelong glances cast by the galley crew. She was sure their thoughts ranged between curiosity and horror to have someone uninitiated working in their sacred, organized space.

After a while, having completed what she came for and left things in better shape than she found them, she left carrying a large tray, the stares of half the on-shift department following her into the corridor.

The forward storeroom, now converted into a stateroom, had a thick pressure door with no bell. Grumbling at the oversight, and too encumbered to press the call button on a terminal, Jale contented herself with kicking the door until it rang.

After a moment it swung open, and she had a pair of huskies trying to relieve her of what she carried.

"No, no, no...close the door behind me and then go sit down like good passengers, will you? This time I'm serving you myself, and I'll have no contradiction, oh bless me no." She swung inside, brushing by the pair, and began setting the table for three. She knocked away helping paws and shielded things with her body until at last the two gave up and sat, gazing sheepishly up at her.

"There, all done. You are my passengers, and my guests," Jale smirked, standing and indicating the feast before them.

"And even though I haven't set a meal service in quite some time, I have now. You're going to eat it, oh yes, and you're even to pretend you like it. And I don't wish to hear 'Yes or no, miss anything'. Am I clear?"

"Perfectly, Miss Jale." Jewel said, watching her seat herself and slide up to the table.

"So I hear that the two of you have reached your decision."

"We didn't have much choice, Miss Jale."

Jale smiled down at them. "No, you didn't. You're willing to accept too little, just to continue to be demure. It almost seems a habit, oh yes. Stay low, stay out of trouble. You don't need to be that anymore—you should be safe from now on. In that vein, however, I must ask...do you object to your future plans? Is there anything you would rather do?"

"Oh no, Miss Jale. Thank you so very much...definitely no," Pinky's eyes were wide. "I still can't believe we'll actually have the opportunity for an education. I never thought we'd survive this long, much less..." He shook his head.

"If Rema's to be believed, and I have no reason to doubt him, given what I've seen of the Dazi, the school on Liberty is supposed to be extremely flexible. Whatever you choose, be it art or engineering, science or warfare, the training facilities will adapt to you and help you find your way to the peak of your interest. From what they say, Liberty is absolutely immense. Nearly the size of a small moon, they say, with some sections dating back to the ancients."

"They told us the same, Miss Jale." Jewel said. "Are you going to be there long?"

"Long enough to see the two of you settled," Jale nodded. "We're due a full refit, including some new technology that should help us with our new mission. Improvements to stealth, even, or so they say. We'll be taking on new crew, as we're offloading nearly sixty. All that will take quite some time, no doubt about it."

"What will they have you doing?" Pinky glanced at the food before him, clearly torn between talking and eating.

"I can't tell you much," Jale laughed. "But I can say that it will largely involve information gathering for the Dazi. Now please, eat while it's hot!"

Jewel took a bite of his food without further prompting, and then pricked his ears up, focusing on it as if noticing it for the first time. "Oh..." He took another bite; Pinky, too, sampled his, then smacked his lips, blinking up at her.

"Did you bring aboard new cooks from the Dazi? This is amazing."

Jale just grinned.

Red clouds raced over a stark urban skyline, lit by continual electrostatic discharge. Each flash ignited and activated a different set of toxic chemicals within the melange of dielectric, casting various shades of red against the darkening overcast and dancing shadows across the buildings thrust deep into the poisoned sky.

At the very top of a massive tower, the tallest and broadest of them all, the light show lit a room with a wide panoramic view. Terminals lined the walls and surfaces, all displaying detailed data, graphs and information from all aspects of a tremendous multifaceted economic and military intelligence gathering and espionage organization.

The sole occupant, a huge black coyote in a simple shipsuit, sat before a single terminal, in the same chair that he'd passed nearly the entire week in tense silence, sending away any and all who sought him. For weeks he'd declined in his social attendance, becoming more reclusive as time had passed.

It was, of course, his right, and his house chugged along with not a soul thinking the less of him for it. And yet even those in his closest council, those who saw more of him than any other, could scarcely understand the strange energy, the near desperation that had drawn nearer the surface with the passing of time.

Tonight, however, something new was in the air. There was a solid tension to his silent form, a predatory focus on the console in front of him. The display had been reduced to a single view, focused on a single message that sat unopened on his terminal. One message where many should be—one message that he, at the peak of his power; he, who feared nothing; he, to whom the rest of the universe was naught but a plaything feared to open.

He had examined its header data for almost an hour—its origin mark, its transit path. He had authenticated them, cross-checked them, and verified the encapsulating encryption, but he had been unable to summon the will to read the message itself.

Hours he had spent in silence, paws resting on the terminal, reluctant to make the one tap that was required to view the message text.

At last, drawing on every last drop of his will, he moved his paw to the center of the terminal and opened it.

> *Master,*
> *It was the end of us.*
> *I will always love you.*
> *I am free.*
> *Theta.*

Great green eyes widened, and searched the display frantically for more, then searched the words for deeper meaning. Finding none, he pushed back from the terminal, shaking. The desire to throw something, to forcefully rearrange furniture, to bellow...he suppressed.

Swallowed.

Only a slight tremula and a slow blink of his eyes betrayed his underlying emotion as he slowly sank back in his chair, the tension held in his taut muscles releasing bit by bit. The little tremor found its way to his breath, and a strange, barely familiar sensation pricked his eyes and challenged the firmament of his jawline.

Slowly, as elegantly as befit his position and stature, he laid his head on the table, hiding his face in his great paws.

"Forever, my love," he whispered to himself, and then grew silent and still. After a moment, small, soft sounds leaked from his composed form.

Knoskali wept.

The opossum fixed Geren with a long, unfathomable stare, then turned back to his terminal.

"Ramesan? For one?"

"Yes," Geren sighed, thinking of his last trip and how much more promise life had held then. "Yes. Yes, it's just me from now on."

"Ah, me. Well, next available liner will be a little over one hundred twenty-three thousand more than what you've got on this here chip."

Geren's breath froze for half a moment, then he stepped forward, tilting his head. "Wait, wait—istaks?"

"Istaks. That's what we use here, is istaks."

Geren rattled his claws firmly on the counter in a staccato beat, looking at the back of the agent's terminal as if he could see through it. "No, look, I just want the lowest fare, not premier. Even lounge seating is fine."

"Kid, that's already basic class." The ticket agent turned his terminal toward Geren, pointing out the fare line with its complicated code and associated price.

"Uh . . ." Geren glanced back over his shoulder at the glum line of workers behind him, noticing for the first time that most held red relocation loan chits. He gulped down a tiny thread of panic, resting a paw on his churning belly. "Ok. Ok, look . . . just . . . find me the cheapest within a week. Two weeks, even."

"Well, now, that does bring it down a bit. We're looking at . . . hm . . . one hundred five thousand istaks. So this here card is short by about eighty thou. Got a relocation card for me?"

"That's . . . a hundred and five? That's crazy!" Geren rested a paw on his head, aghast. "This chit has gotta be at least a year's pay! How much is an istak worth?"

"Oh, let me think, here. I'd say . . . 'bout one istak. You know, plus or minus."

Geren snapped his jaw shut and glowered.

"Welp, kiddie," the opossum seemed almost gleeful, lips pulling back in a nasty sneer to reveal stained teeth. "Looks as though you ain't goin' to Ramesan any time soon, now, doesn't it? What, you think twenty thousand istaks is a lot? Enough for a pumped up factory worker at Cerion, I s'pose, living on your factory credit. You're not just some dirt-bag local, after all. Well you're right, twenty thou is a lot to us locals . . . not so's you can do much with it . . . but it still ain't enough to get you to Ramesan."

"But I—I just went to Hope last year, and for two of us it was only nine thousand!" Geren could feel the eyes of the others on him, as if they finally had started listening to the conversation, and felt himself flush beneath his fur.

"You may not have noticed, up in your cozy factory, but out here in the real Fonaci, we're ruined. Thanks to you people. You got local currency, but our currency ain't worth anything to the rest of the universe anymore."

"I . . . but . . ." Geren felt dizzy, short of breath.

"Guess what? You're a local now." The ticket agent smirked down at him, then turned the terminal back around, pushing his glasses back up. "Let me help you out, one local to another. There is one world that you can get to with your money, and that's Brynton. Want me to book you a ticket, sir?"

... An excerpt from *Dreams of Refugium*
Book Two in the Draconyma Cycle

www.ingramcontent.com/pod-product-compliance
Lightning Source LLC
Chambersburg PA
CBHW031053260626
47172CB00001B/52